...ARNETT'S NOVELS

WILD

"Marvelous . . . a tale of pure romance. Filled with the wonder and real enchantment of love, *Wild* is a very rare and special novel. Jill Barnett knows how to touch readers' hearts with joy showered with laughter and sprinkled with poignancy. Perhaps her most radiant book to date, *Wild* is as unique and delightful as anything you'll read this season."

—*Romantic Times*

" 'Classic Barnett': a wonderfully sassy, intelligent heroine who tames the wickedly arrogant hero who thinks he will win their lustfully wild, sensual battles . . . Serious romance readers must save a special place on their keeper shelf for this remarkable Medieval trilogy that includes *Wonderful, Wild,* and *Wicked.*"

—CompuServe Romance Reviews

WONDERFUL

"A sizzling romance filled with passion and a love that brings tears to the eyes. *Wonderful* has a sexy hero, a spirited heroine, sensuality, and a fast-moving plot."

—*Rendezvous*

"A *Wonderful* reading experience. . . . A humorous, fun-to-read medieval romance due to its varied, eccentric, and exciting characters."

—Amazon.com

"*Wonderful* will find a way to curl up in your heart and stay there, keeping you warm and wonderful. Jill Barnett brings a unique joy to writing that is infectious and makes her books shine like a priceless gem."

—*Romantic Times*

"Positively stellar! This book is not only funny, it's caring and compassionate . . . and magical!"

—*Heartland Critiques*

BEWITCHING

"Jill Barnett has a sophisticated sense of humor and is an author not to be missed!"

—Meagan McKinney, author of *Till Dawn Tames the Night*

JUST A KISS AWAY

"Absolutely wonderful and totally endearing 'love and laughter' romance. . . . Just keep *Just a Kiss Away* nearby whenever you need a 'pick-me-up' read."

—*Romantic Times*

SURRENDER A DREAM

"A lighthearted, often amusing struggle of wills. . . . Their tug-of-war battles created a love story that kept me emotionally involved until the very end."

—*Rendezvous*

"Five Gold Stars! This is one delightfully funny read with witty, witty dialogue."

—*Heartland Critiques*

THE HEART'S HAVEN

"This delightful book is a winner that will warm your heart. Superb characterization, a fast-moving plot and gifted words—a reader's heaven!"

—*Affaire de Coeur*

Books by Jill Barnett

Wicked

Wild

Wonderful

Carried Away

Imagine

Bewitching

Dreaming

The Heart's Haven

Just a Kiss Away

Surrender a Dream

Published by POCKET BOOKS

JILL BARNETT

WICKED

POCKET BOOKS
New York London Toronto Sydney Tokyo Singapore

This book is a work of fiction. Names, characters, places and incidents are products of the author's imagination or are used fictitiously. Any resemblance to actual events or locales or persons, living or dead, is entirely coincidental.

An *Original* Publication of POCKET BOOKS

POCKET BOOKS, a division of Simon & Schuster, Inc.
1230 Avenue of the Americas, New York, NY 10020

ISBN: 0-671-03412-X

First Pocket Books printing September 1999

10 9 8 7 6 5 4 3 2 1

POCKET and colophon are registered trademarks of Simon & Schuster, Inc.

Front cover illustration by Lisa Falkenstern
Tip-in illustration by Steven Assel

Printed in the U.S.A.

To the mistakes we made,
To the fools we were,
To young love.

Wickedness is a myth invented by good people to account for the curious attractiveness of others.
—*Oscar Wilde*

BOOK

ONE

She sat in a tower room. Alone. Perhaps forgotten with the hubbub going on inside the castle. Her hand rested on a heavily carved table where a clock sat, a whimsical water clock that counted minutes and hours in single, clear drops of water. 'Twas an odd-looking contraption with a metal and glass globe and birds that flapped their wings when enough water dropped to form an hour. She had bought it many years past in a moment of fancy at a small May fair, where it had been quite the spectacle.

On that warm spring day when the farmers and villagers of Kent had gathered around a hawker's brightly striped booth, Sofia had stood nearby, watching and listening while he showed them all how time was truly passing right before their very eyes.

Count the water drops! See the courses of time!

Like the rest of the crowd she had been drawn in, had stepped even closer, amazed that someone had actually trapped time inside that globe. She left the May fair that day with the wondrous water clock hugged tightly to her chest and her purse empty.

Perhaps it was her wishful thinking or youthful ignorance, but owning that clock made her believe she had gained some sliver of power over time, and thereby, over her own future.

But when winter came that year, one day the water inside the clock froze as if time itself was suddenly standing still. Day after day, hour after hour passed in spite of the frozen clock, until Sofia saw the plain truth: she never did have the secret of passing time tucked safely away inside her chamber.

Now she needed no clock to see time pass. In the mornings when she awoke and looked into the polished glass, she saw the changes time had made on her face—the small lines above her lips and on her neck and brow, the creases in the corners of her eyes. Her face had changed as much as her life. Like single drops from a water clock, time passed by in seemingly minute increments.

When she was young and so anxious to grow up, she had rushed headlong into life. She had lived her feckless youth in the same manner as one of the castle goats, stubborn, blinded to reason by the need to butt anything that by chance or by purpose got in her way. But now she realized that for all of her headstrong determination, for all of her need to race toward the future, none of it had made time move one single drop faster.

Time, death, life, they were all on her mind this day. Because it was on special days, days that marked your life, when you always dreamt backwards.

She rose from her chair near the window, then crossed her chamber in the tower, over the flat, painted floor tiles where amber sunlight coming through the leaded-paned windows formed a scattering of diamond patterns. She opened the heavily carved doors of a cabinet and took out a birchwood box, a gift from a merchant who wanted favor with the lady wife of the earl of Gloucester.

Inside the box were two manuscripts. One was made up of thick pages of old paper so soft that they almost felt like cloth. Those pages were bound together with covers cast of solid silver inlaid with copper from the hills of Castile, Queen Eleanor's childhood homeland. The covers were secured with a small lock shaped like a swan with its head tucked sleepily under its wing.

The other manuscript was plain; it had no expensive silver covers, no finely crafted locks that kept the contents from prying eyes. Its covers were made from a soft brown leather and tied together with rough laces of rawhide.

Sofia took out the ornate manuscript. A moment later, with the twist of a small iron key on a chain around her neck, the silver cover was unlocked. She turned back the heavy metal plate and the rich, exotic odor of cinnamon and anise rose from inside, the same familiar scent that had always shadowed Eleanor into or out of a room.

It had been so long since she looked at these books, for it was no easy thing to see yourself from someone else's eyes.

She picked up the book and moved to a seat nearby, a beechwood bench with a tapestry pillow that had a tourney scene depicted in the small, colorful stitches Queen Eleanor had tried and dismally failed to teach her.

She set the book in her lap and again flipped open the covers, skimming through a few pages until she found a page marked with a pressed rose. At the top of the page, gilt letters formed her name, ornately inscribed and pigmented with color the shade of the rich wine Eleanor had loved. Then Sofia began to read.

Sofia

Since the age of four, Lady Howard has been ward to My Husband, Edward Plantagenet, her cousin, who is the King of England. Sofia was a lovely child, cherubic and striking, but willful and full of mischief. As each year passed, she grew lovelier, and more stubborn.

By the age of two and ten, one glimpse of her fair

face would cause grown men to stop and stare open-mouthed, for her black hair had grown thick and long, her skin was like snow in the meadows. But it was her eyes, those light purple eyes, that make you look at her and think there could be nothing lovelier. She is tall in stature, so all are aware that she is in a room as surely as if she were the King Himself.

Brave lords and knights who have caught only mere glimpses of Sofia's profile in My Carriage claim they must have her to wive. As the King's Ward, she comes heavily dowered, which combined with her exquisite beauty makes her a prize of the Land.

Until those same foolish men meet her.

Many times over recent years, the sound of Edward's bellowing has echoed off the castle walls. "She has burned my brain with her foolery and now no hair will grow from my head that is not white!" Once my Edward called in Italian physicians to examine Him. He claimed that His Brain was boiling and the next hairs on His Head would grow in the color of the flames of Hell. This was after a spurned betrothal between Lord Geoffrey Woodville and Sofia. She was four and ten at the time of the match, which was considered by all to be a splendid one.

Sofia considered nothing about the match splendid. When the bright-haired young lord came to seriously court Sofia, she rubbed pork fat in her hair so it hung in dirty shanks. She scoured her face with what she later confided to me were willow leaves to make her skin turn sallow and a greenish color, then she wore a gown of a murky saffron yellow that seemed to blend with the putrid tint on her skin. Watching her entrance into the Great Hall was most amusing, for she made her footsteps slow and shuffling, like the mad old hag who begs for buckets of gold at the castle gates.

Upon first meeting Lady Sofia, I remember that Lord

*Geoffrey asked if the girl was not in truth very ill.
Whenever Edward was looking elsewhere, she would
cross her eyes and stick food in her ears and nose. Lord
Geoffrey Woodville and his entourage left in a rush before Matins and under cover of night, for he did not
want to displease the King. But word came back that
even for royal favor and blood bond, he vowed he
would not marry and breed sons with the castle idiot.*

*There have been others, sons of all the noble families
in Court, even a Castilian prince. Sofia has continued
to refuse her suitors . . . all of them, until Edward
threatened to force her hand. I have been able to keep
him from doing so. But there have been no more offers
so the only thing to plague Sofia is boredom, something
she can never tolerate for long. Just this morn, the day
of the Miracle Plays, she said to me that she almost
wished for another suitor if only to keep time from
moving ever so slowly.*

*I have prayed, beseeching God in Heaven to please,
please send someone, the right someone, for my willful
Sofia.*

Sofia closed the book and she was overcome by that
old feeling you get when you remember something from
long ago. Amused. Embarrassed. A little sad. All at the
same time.

She knew she was still the same woman written about
on those pages. She still had the same black hair, the
same purple eyes, that same wide mouth from which
spouted those unexpected comments that kept her husband from growing complacent and thinking he knew
her all too well.

She was the same inside, but she had mellowed from
life and love.

How odd it was that now when people met her and her
husband for the first time, they saw the tender way he

would look at her, and she at him, their gentle manner, how they were unafraid now to show the world that they loved each other. Those same observers often said, "Ah! Your marriage was a love match! Love at first sight, no doubt."

Then her husband usually glanced at her, amusement in his clear blue eyes. His answer was always the same: "Love at first sight? 'Twas more like war at first sight."

While all laughed at his wit, he would give her a teasing wink. But he did not know that those strangers spoke the truth. Even now, all these years later, whenever she looked at him her breath still caught in her throat just like it did on the very day that Eleanor wrote those words, the day that she was in Queen's prayers, for that was the first time Sofia ever truly saw Sir Tobin de Clare.

CHAPTER

1

All Fools' Day,
Leeds Castle in Kent, England

It was the time of year for the Miracle Plays, which was good, because she needed a miracle to break the boredom of her feeble existence. She moved listlessly across the battlements. The sun was unusually hot that spring day, even hotter than the King's temper.

Edward was her guardian, and guard her he did, particularly since he had somehow discovered her plan to ride in the squire races that were scheduled for after the play. Since the day before, she'd had little freedom. She had been forbidden to go near the stables and banished to her chamber for the whole evening while the King raged on about her faults.

She exhaled a huge sigh, then crossed her arms in frustration and continued to pace the stone wall. She might as well have had her ankles chained together and been locked in the bottom of the donjon. Or . . . fed only bread and water like the German and Welsh captives the King kept for ransom.

She reached the end of the battlements and spun around swiftly. Her braids came loose from their tight knots above her ears and she impatiently slapped them out of her face, then paced back in the opposite direction.

Women were supposed to be content only sitting in

the stands watching, while they waved their silly silken favors. A woman was supposed to wait until some knight chose to honor her with his attention.

Sofia hated to wait for anything. She truly believed that if one stood around and waited for something special to happen, it never did.

After her mother's death from desperately trying to bear a son and heir, Sofia waited for her father to come home. He was all she had left; she was all he had left. She was not yet four at the time, but she could remember it clearly, almost as if twelve years had not passed. She remembered the way she stood at the creneled walls, then at the arrow slits in the tower. Her ankles had rubbed together and been bruised after standing on her tiptoes for so long. Her neck had ached from the strain of stretching her chin high enough to be able to watch the horizon, to search the green hills for the first glimpse of her father's pennant waving over the crest of the hill.

She waited all those long and lonely hours for him to come home.

He never did.

Word finally came to Torwick Castle that he was too distraught to come home to a puny daughter when death had so cruelly taken his newborn son. His heir. And his wife.

So while she was frightened and lonely and waiting futilely for him to come home to her, he rode farther north, farther away from her.

A fortnight later he was mortally wounded in the siege at Rochester. He lived for only a few days, long enough to send messages to Edward, then Crown Prince.

But not long enough to send words of any kind to his only child. No good-bye. No deathbed wish. Nothing. Sometimes Sofia wondered if he had even remembered that she existed.

She learned early, and in the cruelest of ways, the true

value of a woman. She also learned that sitting around and waiting was much more painful, more futile, than seeking out what she wanted. She could stomach failure. She could not, however, watch the world and all she wished for pass her by.

She stood still, frustrated and tense, because there was so little she could truly do. She turned and propped her elbows on the wall that was so far above the rest of the world. She rested her chin on her damp palms and gazed heavenward as if there were magical answers waiting for her there.

But there were no answers. Only a sky so brilliant blue it hurt your eyes to look at it and a few puffy clouds that moved as slowly as the hours of the day, almost as slowly as her long and boring existence.

After a moment she pulled the silver ribbons from her hair and tucked them into the bodice of her blue silk gown, then she began to unweave her braids because it gave her something to do with her hands other than to tap impatiently on the stone. Soon her hair was loose and fell heavily down past her shoulders and over her back. It was free. Free. The way she was not.

She looked down below her because there was nothing else to do. Immediately she spotted the King and Queen taking their seats in an awning-covered dais near the stage erected for the Miracle Plays.

One could not miss the King because he was so very tall. His golden hair caught the sun and shone so brightly sometimes it made people think he was some kind of god. But Sofia knew he was not a god.

The people called him Longshanks; she called him merciless.

His whole purpose on this earth seemed to be nothing more than to make her life truly miserable. She watched the Queen sit there serenely because the poor sweet woman had no idea she was wed to an ogre of the worst kind.

She loved Queen Eleanor, who was kind and did not raise her voice at Sofia even when she was not pleased with something she had done. Certainly it was not poor, dear Eleanor's fault that she was married to a tyrant with a will as strong as a castle wall and a head that was probably just as thick. Marriages were made for reasons of politics. Her cousin was fortunate that Eleanor was so good and kind she could not see his vile faults.

Sofia glared at the King and hoped his scalp burned from it. Her pride was aching and her memory echoed with his angry words from the night before, when Edward had scolded her in front of his guests.

You, Sofia, are bound to drive me mad with your foolishness. What you need is a husband to teach you humility and obedience!

In recent years she had heard that speech too many times to count. 'Twould be like trying to count the grains of salt in a cellar or the number of angels that could dance on the head of pin.

As if a husband could make her obey him. She was no slave. She was Sofia, and someday they would all know she was worthy of being called more than just a *woman*.

Later, when she'd had her ear pressed to their chamber door, she heard him lamenting to the Queen:

Eleanor, Sofia's antics are a disgrace. Tell me why in God's name she cannot spend her days stitching tapestries or at some other female entertainment.

As if sitting around listening to women's chatter while she was poking a needle into a piece of cloth was entertaining.

When Edward had suddenly opened the door and she had rather inconveniently fallen inside, caught once again eavesdropping, she'd asked him if sewing were so entertaining, then why did she never see men doing it? Edward's neck had turned the color of blood before he bellowed that sewing was not men's work. For just a breath of a moment, she had actually thought his liver might go up in flames.

But the truth was she had not really cared that he was angry. Life was terribly unjust and someone had to change it. Men could ride across the hillsides freely. Women were supposed to plant their hind ends on plodding mules or in pillion chairs where you wobbled precariously atop a mount that was about as close to dead as a horse could possibly be.

Why, a whole lifetime could pass you by before you even got where you were going.

She, Sofia Howard, did not ride on ancient mules or ride pillion. She had learned to ride astride at age six, when her guardian was off to London to deal with his newly established Parliament, a body of men who would make laws for all the land and probably despotically decree over their wine goblets that women were to have the ugliest of duties like stitchery and meal planning and laundry.

By the time Edward had returned from telling all of London and the rest of the world what they should do, she could already outride his squires. Thankfully, Queen Eleanor stepped in on her behalf and Sofia was allowed to ride as long as she was escorted by one of her keepers—a man-at-arms.

Always a man.

Why were there not such things as women-at-arms? Everyone thought men were strong and courageous and honorable. The Church and most men claimed that women were weak creatures.

It did not seem fair that all women must suffer because once, too long ago for it to truly matter, Eve handed Adam one small apple.

What Sofia wanted to know was, if women were so weak, why did strong, brilliant, and honorable Adam, *the man,* eat that apple?

As far as she was concerned, Eve was only feeding her man. Was that not a woman's duty?

When Sofia said as much to the Archbishop of Canterbury, she was accused of blaspheming and had to spend a fortnight at a nunnery outside of Avon, where she was to pray with vigor for a pious heart, a sweet mind, and a quiet tongue.

Instead she vastly entertained the novices when she made wax candles in the shape of the Archbishop and Mother Superior in *flagrante delicto*.

But this was not a nunnery. She was still pacing along the upper wall of Leeds. She stopped near the edge of the western steps and braced her hands on a low crenel, peering through the square opening and looking off into the distant west, far on the horizon where she was certain all of her dreams lay waiting for her.

Aye, she thought. Out there somewhere was the life she was supposed to live, while she languished at Leeds under the tyrannical rule of her cousin, the cruel, cruel King of England, who made her behave like a lady just to torture her.

What she did not understand was why she felt so different inside. Different from everyone else. Did the rest of the world not see these things that drove her moods?

Once, not so long ago, when she was perhaps three and ten, she had lit twenty candles, knelt on the cold stones in the chapel, and asked God why.

Why God? Why does my heart feel like it is going to fly right from my chest? Why does my blood turn hot and cold when I'm angry and sad? Sometimes, when I want something very badly or when things move slower than honey in winter, I feel like there is a whole hive of bees just buzzing through me, trying desperately to get out.

God had not answered her. She knew God did not talk to people. She had not expected a huge voice from heaven to boom overhead and tell her what was wrong with her, but she had secretly hoped for a sign, or a change.

Neither had happened.

She looked down at the scene below, her eyes on her cousin Edward.

She raised her chin and closed her eyes, taking a deep breath. She wanted to ride across the hills as fast as a charging army. She wanted to practice archery, to hit a target dead center. She wanted to learn swordplay. She wanted to walk outside the castle walls freely and unescorted. She wanted to wear braies and chausses so her legs would have the freedom of movement that a man had.

Now that, Your Majesty, would be true entertainment!

A moment later a raucous cheer drifted upward from below as if everyone agreed with her thoughts. She looked down over the edge of the parapet, scanned the lists outside the castle where the crowds had grown thick, almost cattle-like. They were milling in a huge herd toward the stage where jugglers and acrobats wore their clothes backwards in honor of All Fools' Day, performed magic while musicians played jaunty tunes, then caught copper pennies in their broad-brimmed hats.

Another excited cheer filled the air. She stood high and away from the rest of the castle, her back straight as an elm, her palms flat against the stone wall. The music grew louder and the crowd in the lists laughed and sang. She craned her head slightly so she could better see.

Now people were dancing on the grass to viols and hurdy-gurdies near the stage platform.

She loved to dance, even if it meant she had to hold the damp hands of some young courtier just so she could spin 'round and 'round and 'round, as fast as she could, until her head swam and she felt as if she were a bird, flying, until her breath came fast as the tunes the musicians played.

She spotted Edith, her friend, as well as Princess

Eleanor, her young cousin. Eleanor was four and ten and was the eldest of Edward's five daughters and would soon be married to a foreign prince. Everyone was down there amid the day's amusements—everyone but the men guarding the battlements.

And her.

One more swift glance down and she lost her need to teach the world a lesson by completely ignoring it.

Sofia gripped the skirt of her silk gown and took the stairs in hurried steps, then moved outside the castle gates, over the moat and into the glade, her long black hair floating out behind her like the curling ribbons of a Maypole.

Brightly colored tents of scarlet and green spotted the field behind the stage where the actors would perform their play based on the religious miracles of Christ or the saints and prophets.

She walked along, munching on an apple she'd plucked from a basket. No sooner had she swallowed a bite than her heart suddenly picked up speed and her skin began to tingle as if touched by an icy wind. She spun around swiftly, the apple poised at her lips.

Her gaze lit on him the moment she turned, a tall and richly clothed knight with a strong build and an unreadable face. She cocked her head and frowned. Odd, how she had felt his presence before she ever saw him.

She glanced back.

He stood a head above the milling crowd, his features partially hidden by the wavering shadows cast from a royal pennant that flew overhead. His arms were crossed so she could not read the design on his blue tabard.

She stepped up and onto a shallow wooden bucket someone had dropped nearby, pressing her ankles together and rising on her tiptoes just a bit so she could better see his face.

And see him she did!

The apple fell from her suddenly limp hand and plopped on the ground, forgotten.

The breeze died suddenly, as if the midday sun had just upped and melted it away. The pennant hung still, its angled tip like a sign from God, an arrow that pointed directly to the knight's dark head.

In the sudden brightness, his face showed clearly: strong, so deeply angular that the dark, icy shadows on his cheeks and creased brow looked as if even the sun itself was not bright enough to melt them.

Beneath a dark slash of thick brows, his gaze wandered lazily over the crowd. He looked bored, expectant, knowing, as if he had seen this all before and found it not to his refined taste. He wore his arrogance the same way warriors wore their colors, proudly and prominently, a challenge for anyone and everyone to dare not notice.

Sofia found this fascinating, having spent so much time watching grown men grovel at her feet and praise her fine features as if they had no pride at all.

She had truly thought most men were a sorry lot. Until she had looked upon this man. He was not sorry in any way. In fact, she would wager her dowry that the word "sorry" never crossed his lips.

No. He surely would not grovel at her feet. Or anyone else's feet from the look of him.

His gaze flitted around the crowd, ran over her and past her, then stopped, and he turned back for another look.

For the first time in her life she was grateful for the fine features that made men stare at her. She could feel this knight's eyes on her, watching her closely, intently, for the longest time. The day grew even warmer as she stood there. The sun seemed to shine with more intensity. Her blood sped under her skin as if it were in the greatest hurry.

Then the oddest thing happened. Sofia suddenly wanted to disappear into the crowd. 'Twas unlike her, for she prided herself on the fact that she could face anyone's stare with an icy coolness, without feeling any fear, even the King himself when he was furious with her.

But now, when this man looked at her, the skin on her arms prickled with gooseflesh and her lips grew dry from the quick breaths she took. Something inside of her belly crawled 'round and 'round and made her head feel light as if she had been dancing in circles for hours.

He was different; his look was different. For one thing he was young for a knight, perhaps eight and ten, but better than that was his expression. 'Twas not awe at her beauty that made him stare at her, for she knew that kind of look all too well.

No, it was as if he were trying to see inside her mind, right through to that place where she let no one in, that place where dwelt her hopes and secrets, her dreams and her fears, those thoughts no one knew but her.

Some part of her wanted to turn away so he could not see too much, but she knew if she did so then he would win this contest of cool looks. She would appear weak if she looked away first, and too, there was the fact that she truly wanted to keep looking at him in spite of what he made her feel. He was a handsome devil for all his cool and superior look.

He was also the first man who could make her feel something other than disgust in too many months to count. *He* would not grovel at her feet as other men had.

Men would seldom look at her face for very long; it seemed to have some odd ability to render the most confident and strongest of men into babbling idiots and bowing fools, their expressions rapt and rather like that of pilgrims who traveled the countryside for a glimpse of a miracle and had, to their surprise, suddenly found one.

Knights and lords and warriors looked at her and the

next thing she knew they were at her feet, kissing her hem or other such foolishness. She could now spot most courtiers merely by the backs of their heads, since that was all she usually saw of them.

Her sheer stubbornness aided her well, for she refused to look away from this handsome man who made her burn inside. She played a coy game and smiled, a small smile, one she knew could and had sent men panting after her. A come-hither-you-fool kind of smile, but before she could gauge his reaction, someone called her name from behind her and made her blink. Still, she did not turn away.

Not first. She would not be the first to break this spell. 'Twas a challenge between them, one she would win. So she kept looking at him, smiling that barest of smiles.

He cocked his head slightly. Curious, or perhaps giving her something more than a mere challenge.

The stage players began to sing a loud and bawdy song, typical of the Miracle Plays, and the crowd around her cheered, then shifted suddenly, moving forward to catch pennies the actors were throwing from the stage. She was jostled and jabbed and lost her balance. But when her feet hit solid ground, she was still craning her neck to keep up the staring game with the wonderfully intriguing knight.

She used her elbows to try to move back where she could see, jabbing at the crush of bodies swallowing her. But it did no good. She could not see him even when she jumped up and down; there was nothing before her but a mass of bobbing heads.

The song ended and the Miracle Players took their numerous bows. The crowd cheered and applauded and called out to them to do more skits.

God in heaven above . . . no more, she prayed, still wedging her way through the crowd.

'Twas the first prayer God had answered in months.

Suddenly those actors turned and skipped off the stage like leaping lords, the ones warbled about by minstrels during the Twelve Nights of Christmas. The crowd calmed down, then finally moved back and broke up, heading for the amusements of the jugglers and booths. Finally, she could see across the lists.

But by then, the knight was gone.

CHAPTER
2

"Sofia!"

She turned around at the familiar sound of her friend's frantic voice.

"Wait!" Lady Edith ran so quickly to catch up with her that her golden chaplet slipped down into her eyes and the thin veil that covered the back of her hair came unpinned and drifted behind her and onto the ground.

Bright red curls fell into her friend's eyes. Edith stopped suddenly as if blinded by those bouncing curls, patting her head for a moment, then she frowned, turned and looked down as a group of wild lads trampled over her thin and proper veil. She picked up the small, square swatch of saffron-colored silk, then shook it out, chewing on her lower lip in a moment of indecision.

Even from a short distance Sofia could see the footprints; it was ruined.

Edith looked up at her, caught her gaze, then shrugged and tossed the veil over her shoulder as if it were a chicken bone. With both hands, she grabbed the gold chaplet that crowned her head in such a cockeyed manner and shoved it back down over her flaming hair and brow as she scurried to catch up to Sofia. Her breath was swift and short when she came alongside.

"You missed the dancing, Sofia!"

"There will be more dancing after supper." Sofia looked left, then right. Where was he?

"Where are you off to in such a hurry?"

"I am in no hurry." Sofia slowed her steps to a saunter, but she still could not keep from watching the crowd for a glimpse of a sky-blue tabard.

"I thought you were going to stay in the tower all day to annoy the King."

"I changed my mind. I decided I could be more annoying down here among the throngs."

Lady Edith frowned at her, then followed her searching gaze. "Who *are* you looking for?"

"Looking for?" Sofia whipped her head back around and gave her as innocent a look as she could muster. "Me?" She paused. "Why, you of course!"

She linked her arm with Edith's, forced herself to look straight ahead and smiled brightly when she added, "See this huge crush of people here today? I was afraid I would never find you. There was so little room I could not even get near the booth where they sold honeyed figs and dates." Sofia paused. "Can you imagine?

"I am famished!" she went on. " 'Tis hard work to call down dire curses upon Edward's golden and hard head." She looked away from Edith's stern face and added fiercely, "Now do not look at me so, he deserved those curses!"

"I do not know if I should be envious of your sheer courage or happy I am not so foolhardy."

"That is because Edward does not make your life miserable. You are fortunate to have a brother who cares about you."

"The King cares greatly about you, Sofia."

"Aye. It amuses him to destroy my life." Sofia kept watching the crowd for the man. When she saw nothing, she tugged on Edith's arm. "Come along. The races will be starting soon. We shall go first to the date seller's booth. I will pay." She grinned and patted the small silk purse that hung from her belt. "I still have all my coins from Candlemas, the ones Edward gave me to be silent during the wrestling match between his man and Lord Giles."

Edith groaned. "I still cannot believe that you actually called the King's champion puny, a man who had no more strength than the fleas on the kitchen hounds. Sofia, the man is huge."

"A veritable giant." Sofia was still smiling. "With an ego just as big as his ham-sized hands."

Edith shivered and muttered, "I have not the courage to do such foolhardy things."

" 'Tis not foolhardy, but necessary, Edith. And I shall continue to speak for myself whenever I feel I must."

Edith shook her head, her expression a mix of awe and envy. " 'Twas a foolish thing to test the King so."

"Not too foolish, for I left the Great Hall that night with five coins tucked inside my shoe. Two golden marks from Edward and three pieces of silver from my wager with Sir Lowell."

Edith stopped so suddenly it was almost as if she had hit a wall. "You placed a wager?"

"Aye. On the opponent."

Edith quickly made the sign of the cross.

"Why should I not place a wager?"

"But it is a sin."

"That did not stop Bishop Culbert and Father John from betting," Sofia added in a wry tone. "Just because we, you and I, happened to have had the vile misfortune to be born women should not mean we cannot have the same amusements as do men."

"Of course we cannot. We are not men. We do not have their strength and power—"

"If you say their sharpness of mind, I will leave you here and now."

"Well, even I would not go that far, but Sofia, you go on as you have been and you are asking for something terrible to happen. Truly. The King will not let you keep pushing him. He cannot like it. Even Eleanor will not be able to speak for you if you keep this up. What if he gets truly frustrated with you and marries you off to someone awful like . . . like . . ." She lowered her voice and whispered with horror, "Like Lord Alfred?"

Alfred De Bain was a lecherous man of five and forty, with hands the size of oxen and small, beady, brown eyes that promised cruelty. He had one and twenty children and had buried seven wives, and none of his offspring ever made it to the ripe old age of fifteen.

"If Edward tried to fob me off on someone horrid, I would stab myself in the heart, damn my soul forever, and then spend eternity haunting him."

"You should never jest about taking your own life. 'Tis a mortal sin."

"Who is jesting?"

At that, Edith was quiet.

Too quiet for Sofia. Edith was her true friend and her sudden silence bothered Sofia in a way she was not comfortable with. A little nagging voice of doubt flickered through her mind. "Edward knows I would do something horrid. Have I not been able to outwit every man Edward has tried to thrust upon me?"

Edith gave Sofia an odd look and said softly, "I think that someday you will meet a man who is quicker witted than you. Someone who will not run from your schemes and jibes."

"Good, then at least I will not be plagued by boredom." But she did not say what she was feeling, that she knew the truth: that men left you.

"Perhaps you should have wed Lord Geoffrey," Edith was saying. "He is very wealthy."

"Lord Geoffrey is dull as toast. He is not someone I

could ever love, Edith." Her voice trailed off and she
looked at her friend and confessed, "With every suitor, I
would try to imagine being in his arms. Being kissed and
held. But I could never imagine being with any man
without wanting to think of something, *anything* else."

"But you keep claiming that you will make your own
destiny. Could you not make it as easily with someone
who wants only you, someone like Lord Geoffrey?"

She shook her head. "If I ever wed—and I am not saying I shall—I want excitement in my marriage."

Edith stared at her as if she had grown another head.

"What is wrong with that? My life is quiet enough
now. I could never abide it if my marriage were just as
dull. I would rather become a nun." She paused, then
added, more to herself than to her friend, "Except Edward says they will not take me as a novice in any convent in the country."

Edith covered her mouth with a hand and tried to stifle
a giggle.

"Just what has you so amused?"

"What you said." Edith kept laughing.

"I do not find it one bit amusing that I should want
some excitement in my life."

Edith kept laughing.

Sofia frowned at her, then planted her hands on her
hips, tapped her foot and awaited an answer while Edith
was in fits of silly laughter.

"First of all you cannot become a nun," Edith said,
swallowing her laughter. "The Church could not take it.
And you must know the King would never let your huge
dowry go to the Church. And finally and most impor-
tantly, no marriage of yours would ever be dull. Not with
you, Sofie. It wouldn't dare!"

"You sound like Eleanor," Sofia said with disgust.

"Good." Edith looked delighted. "That is a fine thing.
I would love to be exactly like the Queen."

Not Sofia. She would never want to be like the Queen, having to be wed to such a monster. "The man I marry willingly will have to be a knight. Brave and true." She cast her face toward the sky and a face came to mind so swiftly it almost took her breath away. "A man with hair as black as sin and shoulders as broad as the drawbridge. He must be tall. Assured. Strong." Her chin still high, she looked back at her friend. "I would accept no less than a great warrior."

"Men of war have hard hearts. Some of the women say that those men carry their battles into the bedchamber. Many beat their wives."

Sofia searched the crowd, still looking for that black hair, those same broad shoulders and assured expression, adding blithely, "If my husband beat me, I'd cut out his heart and feed it to the castle pigs."

Edith tapped her on the shoulder, frowning. "Are you certain you are not looking for someone?"

"Edith." Sofia stopped. "Tell me this. Who would I be looking for? You are here." Sofia nodded at her, then plopped her palm on her own chest and shrugged her shoulders. "I am here. There is no one else who interests me." She waved a hand through the air with more drama than the actor who had played Saint Peter. "Come, now. There is the booth. See?" Sofia pointed toward a palm tree–emblazoned banner that was flying above the heads of the crowd. She grabbed Edith's hand and pulled her along.

The seller's booth was small, merely a tent with poles and a table. But it was richly draped in fine Turkish fabric of scarlet with saffron-gold threads and was hung with silver bells that rang whenever someone walked past and happened to brush against the tent braces.

Under a swagged green awning that thankfully gave her a moment of shade from the pounding sun, a hawker with dark skin and brows sold honeyed figs and dates along with small casks of savory palm and olive oils brought in by caravan from the East.

"Milady!" The date seller gave Sofia a quick nod, after his gaze had spied the plump purse hanging from her girdle. With a sweeping bow, he gestured to his goods. "Look before you. See here. Fruits so sweet just the taste of them brings you closer to heaven."

Before her were trays of plump, sticky brown fruits. Succulent. Tempting. Her mouth grew damp, as if it couldn't wait for a taste.

The date seller was no fool and must have gauged her reaction for he added, "Sheer pleasures for milady's tongue."

"Give the lady half a peck's worth!"

A large silver coin flipped past Sofia's left ear and was snapped from the air by the quick hand of the date seller.

"All of England knows the tongue of Lady Sofia Howard needs *something* to sweeten it!" Male laughter echoed from behind her.

Edith mumbled something Sofia did not hear and stepped back. But Sofia did not need to hear her friend's words. She knew Richard Warwick's obnoxious voice. 'Twas like listening to sword blade scraping sword blade.

He was the son of Baron John Warwick and had been her nemesis ever since they were small, when he used to pinch her during Mass, put frogs from the moat down her back, and steal the shoes she had slipped off during High Mass. There were times when she had to walk from the chapel with her knees bent so Edward or Eleanor would not see that her bare toes were showing. Every time she heard Richard's voice she could almost feel the sharp pebbles of the bailey cutting into the soles of her feet.

She had refused a betrothal offer from him two years past, not only because she could never love him, could never, ever imagine herself in his arms, but also because he was still a most annoying person. She would gladly place a wager that it was he who ferreted out her plans to ride in the races and spilt the news to the King.

Sofia did not turn around. Very sweetly she said, "Give him back his coin, date seller. I need no man to buy my sweets for me." She pulled one of Edward's gold bribery pieces from her purse and held it up.

There was a gasp, for gold was worth ten times Warwick's puny silver coin and a woman seldom had her own money. It was the man who paid for purchases, who held the coin, and who was thought to retain his manhood and brave spirit by controlling the strings of the household purse.

Then she turned to face Richard Warwick. He was the same old Dickon; he had that same pale hair that would thin with time. His eyes were dark brown, but they turned almost black whenever he looked at her. She never knew what it meant when he looked at her like that, but she knew she did not like it.

Otherwise, Richard Warwick was impressive, for he had grown tall, his build was strong, and his face was handsome. Sofia always felt that he was like an egg that had been left in the nest for too long: perfectly normal to look at, but completely rotten and stinking when you cracked it open.

Warwick's eyes narrowed at her the way they always did, and turned that dark color that unsettled her. She would not let him know his look affected her. She raised her chin and shook her head before she turned her back on him and said to the date seller, "I shall have three of those and five of those." She pointed at the trays of dates and figs. "What will you have, Edith?"

Edith sidled closer to Sofia as if she could hide from the hard and annoyed look Warwick was casting at both of them.

Sofia decided then that he was like most men. If they could not control a woman with their words, their power, or their wit (although in Dickon Warwick's case the term wit was surely a loosely descriptive one), then they would try to break her spirit by the strength of their glower.

Richard Warwick's face said he did not like the turn of things. He swaggered the few steps over to Sofia's side, then announced in his big, braying voice, "Pray, tell us, my lady. How did you come by gold coin?" He paused meaningfully, then scanned his audience. "It does make one wonder."

There was a soft murmur coming from the people who had stopped and were watching this interesting banter between lord and lady. That murmur drew a satisfied smile from Richard Warwick and sly grins from his companions, a group of young nobles and recently dubbed knights: Sirs Thomas Montgomery and Robert de Lacy, along with Alexander Mortimer and William Pembroke. They all gave Sofia the same knowing male looks.

She chose to pretend they did not exist.

But a moment later someone pinched her bottom, hard. Very hard.

Sofia flinched because it hurt and because she could not stop herself, but then she turned and glared up at Warwick, who was looking so nonchalant she would have known it was him even if she did not recognize the cruel pinch of those fingers.

He was an ass, utterly contemptible, so of course he then said, "Perhaps the lady received her gold by selling something."

She gave him a square look. "What are you implying, Dickon?"

He shrugged as if it were nothing. He cast a quick glance around him at the faces that were watching.

"Say it!" she demanded.

He lifted his hands in front of him as if he were surrendering to her and his brow creased in feigned innocence. "Nothing, except that a woman has little to sell," he paused again, "but her . . . favors."

He had just called her a whore in public. She wanted to slap him so badly her palms itched. She willed herself not to react.

By sheer will and pride, she turned back to the date seller, gave him a smile, and pointed with casual ease to a row of plump honeyed figs displayed on a salver. "Three of those, please."

While the man slid the sweets into a dried fig leaf and tied it snugly, she turned slowly, rested her hands on the edge of the display top as she leaned back against it, an easy stance that took almost every drop of willpower she had.

She looked directly at Warwick. "This *lady* is not for sale." Then she averted her eyes, glancing downward as she swiped at some imaginary dust on her silk gown. After a moment of silence she added, "I believe you and Lord John discovered that fact last year."

Two more swipes of her hand and she looked up, giving him her brightest smile.

He said nothing.

"Did you not make five, no eight . . ." She tapped a finger against her pursed lips. Then she nodded. "Aye, that is the number. Eight offers?"

His friends laughed then. At him.

"That is true, Warwick." Thomas Montgomery slapped him on the shoulder. "She would not have you any more than she would agree to take any one of us to wed. Even on your knees!"

Warwick turned bright red. His neck was almost purple. From the corner of her eye she saw his hand slip downward, toward her bottom.

She swiftly side-stepped in front of Edith and almost stumbled, but she managed to grab onto the tent pole. The bells hanging from it tingled into the warm, dry air as if they were warning of what was to come.

"Ouch!" Edith jumped almost a foot. Her hand flattened on her backside and she rubbed it as she turned around. For a bewildered moment she frowned up at Warwick. "You pinched me."

Warwick stammered something inane.

"You pinched me!"

"Wait, Lady Edith—" He held his hands out in front of him.

"Do not try to deny it. Whatever you are about, Richard Warwick, I suggest you cease. I surely shall tell my brother of this."

Edith's brother, Henry, Lord Peveril, was a burly man of some thirty years, incredibly wealthy and a renowned warrior, and the master of three of the strongest castles in the Midlands, and another one as far north as Newcastle. His vast wealth and reputation gave him men-at-arms that numbered in the hundreds. He was the King's man through and through, honest but fearsome, and he adored his sweet, meek younger sister. Everyone in the land knew that he would not hesitate to challenge anyone who he thought had offended her.

"My apologies, Lady Edith." Richard bowed deeply from his waist, sweeping his hand before him in a grand gesture that was about as insincere as possible. A moment later the group of rowdy young men began to walk silently away, but not before Warwick glanced back over his shoulder and gave Sofia a narrow-eyed look that should have cooked her.

She grinned and gave him a small wave of her fingers, which made his jaw tighten as he spun back around and continued walking, his back as rigid as a battering ram.

She turned to her friend.

Edith eyed her for a moment, then said, "That pinch, the one that still burns my bottom, was meant for you."

"Aye." Sofia tried not to smile. She truly did. She did not like it that her friend was pinched. However, the world was a hard place and one did have to look out for oneself.

Edith must have read Sofia's thoughts, or something in her own expression gave her away, because she began to laugh.

"You are wicked, Sofia. So very wicked. You will even let your dear friend endure your punishments."

"That is not so, Edith." Sofia did grin then. "I just move more swiftly than you."

"Aye, you did this time. But next time I shall watch where I stand whenever Richard Warwick is nearby."

"Can you imagine being wed to him?" Sofia shivered. "Lud! I swear he must be part lobster."

"His face turned as scarlet as a lobster when I said I would tell Henry." Edith looked at her, bit her lip, and grinned.

Sofia thought of Dickon's face.

A moment later Sofia was laughing too. "I know you. You will not tell your brother."

"Aye, tempting as it is, he would skin Warwick alive. But the threat of Henry's displeasure certainly has its advantages."

"Aye. There are times when I wish I had a brother to watch out for me."

Edith gave her a wry look. "Another man for you to either drive mad or wrap around your smallest finger?"

"Me?"

"Aye . . . you."

Sofia just laughed again and slipped her arm around Edith's tiny waist. "Come now, choose your sweets. The whole day is wasting away."

Edith turned back to look over the sweetmeats and

Sofia stood there, tapping her foot to pass the time and trying to be as patient as she could. Finally, so much time had passed she felt ancient. "Edith. I can feel my skin wrinkling from age. Choose your sweets. Please."

"I will. I will." But Edith still stood there just chewing on her lip.

Sofia could take it no longer. "Here. I will help you decide. Date seller—" She pointed to a fig and started to speak, but Edith stopped her.

"No, no! I have decided. Truly."

Finally!

"At least I think I have."

Sofia mentally groaned. "What is there to decide? Figs or dates. Which will it be?"

" 'Tis not so simple. There are honey-covered ones . . . And here are some that are dusted in Cyprus sugar. See there? These on this tray have cinnamon. These have cardamom and nutmeg. And look at these. The date seller says they have almonds in the their centers."

The man nodded. "Only the best almonds from north of Rome. But these, my lady, are very special for they are soaked in wine and many eastern spices, then rolled in crushed filberts from France."

"Take one of each, Edith. Please."

"I could not. That would be gluttony and then I would have to spend all morning tomorrow in prayer. I only need another moment. True almonds," Edith said with a sense of awe. " 'Tis almost as if the precious nuts were grown inside of them like a miracle."

"The only miracle will be when you finally decide," Sofia muttered, then shook her head and turned back toward the crowd again, her hand on her hip, and wondered why the rest of the world could not think and act as she did. 'Twould make her life so much simpler.

She decided then and there that her knight had completely disappeared. It was almost as if he did not truly exist. After a moment or two she began to ask herself if perhaps she imagined him.

Then a flash of blue came 'round a corner. His dark head showed above the crowd on the opposite side of the green.

'Twas him. Lud! Could he not have walked this way?

She turned back to Edith and tugged on her sleeve. "Edith!"

"I have chosen. See there. He is wrapping them up for me."

"Good!" Sofia spun around. "Come along, then." She snatched Edith's hand and started to drag her back through the crowd.

"Wait! Your coins! And my sweets!" Edith snatched her hand from Sofia's and scampered back to the booth. She grabbed her packages and the coins from the date seller, then rushed back to Sofia, who was determined to find the knight this time. She pulled Edith along with her. She was not going to lose sight of him. She would not.

Edith squeezed her hand to keep up and Sofia heard her making excuses and begging everyone's pardon as Sofia half-ran, half-elbowed a path through the crowd.

"What *is* your hurry?"

Sofia looked in both directions. "The races are starting."

"But the races are that way!" Edith tried to point toward the lists.

"Not this race," Sofia muttered as they reached the spot where she had seen the knight. She stopped, looked this way and that.

Gone again. The man must be made of smoke.

Edith had her hand over her chest and she was trying to catch her breath. "There is nothing here. No races. See? I told you we were going the wrong way."

"Stay here." Sofia hopped up on a fieldstone wall as if she were a stable lad instead of a noblewoman. There she stood, wobbling at first, so she stuck out her arms from her sides to keep her balance.

"What are you about? Get down from there! 'Tis not safe." Edith walked along with her, peering up with an expression of concern.

A few stones cracked under Sofia's feet and she heard Edith take a sharp breath.

"I am fine." Sofia moved along the wall with all the bravado of the rope walkers who performed at the May fairs. "Look! See?" She took a couple of quick steps just to prove to Edith that she was in complete control.

But Edith did not see because she had her hands over her eyes and she was hunched over as if Sofia had actually fallen.

No confidence there, Sofia thought, then eyed the way of the wall; it grew high, then even higher still to the north. Now if she could just move up to the highest part, where the wall met an archway that opened onto the lists, then she could see almost as well as from the castle walls.

She moved more carefully toward the highest section of the wall, taking smaller steps because the wall was steep and old, there from a century before and not puttied together as well as the newer castle walls. In fact, it was so old that it was made only of flat stones layered with a little mud and stacked atop each other.

"You have been lying to me." Edith was looking at her with a scowl.

Sofia looked back to the wall before her and took the steady steps of a rope walker, her tongue out of the corner of her mouth, her arms out and stiff as she concentrated on her balance. "Just what is it I have been lying to you about?"

"Only a fool would believe you are not searching

for someone. I should leave you. Right this moment. 'Twould serve you right."

Sofia caught the hurt in her friend's voice and she stopped and looked down. "Fine then. I shall tell you in a moment. I need to go a wee bit farther . . ."

"Tell me what?"

"Not yet. I've no wish to break my neck." Sofia just had two more easy steps and if she concentrated she could reach the top, where the stones looked flat enough to hold her without crumbling. Once more she looked across the crowd; she almost lost her balance.

"Watch yourself, Sofia. Those stones are loose. Nothing could be important enough to risk falling. Please. Come down."

"But it is important!" Sofia lowered her voice and whispered, "I am looking for a man."

Edith's eyes grew big as beef platters. "I knew it was something!" Edith tried to snap her fingers but they were sticky from the honeyed figs. She frowned down at them, then looked up. "Who is he?"

"I do not know him. Perhaps you will. Help me search for him."

"How can I search for him? I do not even know what he looks like."

"He is tall and wearing blue. Sky blue. He has black hair, the color of a raven, and a face so angular and beautiful that just looking at it, Edith, can make you forget to breathe." She placed her hands on the higher section of wall and put her foot on a small ledge, ready to lift herself up. "If I can just get a little bit higher, then surely I shall be able to see if he is nearby . . ." Still gripping the stone, she cast a quick glance down.

Behind Edith, and looking squarely at her, stood that wonderfully handsome knight.

CHAPTER

3

Close up, he was even sweeter on the eyes, this man of her dreams whose intense looks made her blood boil and her head light.

He was looking at her now, even though he spoke to Edith. "Lady Edith. Your friend seems to have lost something."

Aye, I've lost my heart.

"She has not lost some*thing,* but some*one.*" Edith pulled a fig from her bag and added casually, "She is looking for a man." Edith bit into the fig. "A handsome man."

The knight laughed, a deep rumbling sound.

If she could have stuffed the whole bag of figs, or better the whole tray of them, the whole booth of them into Edith's big mouth, she gladly would have. Instead, she looked away for just a moment, only as long as it took to take the first of the ten steps that would get her down off the cursed wall.

That first step was fine.

The second step was not.

The rock cracked and crumbled.

She wobbled, gave a sharp squeak of surprise, then fell. It all happened too fast. She closed her eyes and waited to hit the ground, her mind flashing with the wry thought that she would probably break her neck and die since she had finally found her true heart's desire.

But it wasn't the ground she hit.

She fell right into a pair of strong arms. His arms. She blinked, looking up into his face, knowing she had no time to hide the surprise on her own.

He had caught her so easily. 'Twas as if she weighed no more than a feather.

She took a deep breath, then another, searching for something to say. But her thoughts and words deserted her when his scent filled her nose, her mouth, her head and her heart. He smelled of clean male, rich Spanish leather, and dreams that come true.

"She is looking for a man, is she?" His voice was so very deep, as if it came from his soul or heaven, or perhaps, she thought, after catching the dark glint in his eyes, perhaps that deep voice came straight from hell.

She could think of nothing witty or snide to say. No quip flew from her mind to her lips. No wry thought. No jest to be made.

Sofia Howard was tongue-tied.

She had not thought it possible, she who prided herself on her ability to have the last word. She was not even certain she would be able to find her voice. It was as if her ability to speak flew out with her startled breath and was flying somewhere above her head and clear out of her reach.

He never took his eyes from her as he tightened his hold on her, slid one flat palm up the outside of her thigh, pulling her gown up a little in the process. Then he said softly, "I am a man."

She could not look away. She could not think. She could do nothing but stare up at him for one of those lost moments when time seems to stand still.

Speechless, witless, defenseless, she could only look into those blue, blue eyes of his, because to look at them this close made her heart beat a little faster and her breath speed up. His eyes were the color of his tunic, the same blue as the sky on a summer morn. Then she spotted something there in those eyes, a spark of amusement, then a telling look that said the arrogant devil knew exactly who she had been looking for.

She prayed her face would not give away what she was thinking: how difficult it was for her to face this man, the first one in years whose good opinion meant something to her.

Sofia did not blush. She never had, and she was grateful for that many times over. 'Twas something that allowed her to act brave even when she didn't feel brave inside. Or to hide from the world what she truly felt. Like now, when she had nothing but a mask of iciness to hide the truth: she had met the one man in the world she wanted and the knowledge scared her so terribly that she was shaken clear down to her bones.

"Put me down, sir." She found her lost voice, and fortunately it sounded much cooler than she felt. She waited for him to obey her.

He did nothing.

"Now." Her tone was sharp and she was glad.

His expression changed, as if he wanted to say something, but he did not speak. Instead, one of his arms that held her fell away, the one that was under her knees.

Her legs dropped like rocks. She inhaled sharply, but a moment later his other arm tightened about her back, held her hard against him, breast to chest, while her legs just dangled off the ground.

She looked up at him, trapped against his body. She felt like a cornered animal, penned more by what those eyes of his did to her than the arms that held her against him. He was watching her with that same intense expression, the fiery one she felt go through her earlier, when he was looking at her from all the way across the lists.

She took a breath, a small shallow one, but to her ears it sounded as loud as a scream.

His eyes narrowed slightly as his gaze shifted to her mouth, then he slowly let her slide down his body in mere inches, until her feet were barely touching the ground and her mouth was dry as sea salt.

She stepped back as if she were burned and dusted off her gown. "Sir." She gave him a curt nod of thanks without meeting his eyes, because if he called her bluff she would just die. Right there in the center of the green. She would just melt into the ground and cease to exist.

"You should thank Sir Tobin for saving your neck," Edith told her distractedly, frowning down at her empty bag of sweets.

Sofia froze. Her words came out in nothing but a whisper. "What did you say?"

"This is Sir Tobin de Clare," Edith said as if Sofia should have recognized him. "You have met before."

Sofia's head shot up and she stared at him. His look had not wavered, had not changed.

"I am off to the date seller again, Sofie. You will be fine with Sir Tobin to escort you. I shall meet you at the races, where we will look for your man." Edith took off toward the booths, completely abandoning her with, of all people, Tobin de Clare, the earl of Gloucester's eldest son.

Oh, she had met him before.

But she had never seen his face.

Three years earlier, Camrose Castle

Sofia stood just outside the huge, carved oak doors of the great hall, away from the boisterous crowd of merrymakers that spilled from inside, where all were celebrating the wedding of Lady Clio of Camrose to Lord

Merrick, earl of Glamorgan, a de Beaucourt and her cousin Edward's close friend and vassal.

Well into the wedding feast, the Glamorgan heralds had entered the hall and captured the company's attention with a few long and triumphant notes on their horns, then Lord Merrick had presented his bride with a delicious and rare white-flour cake in the shape of Camrose Castle, complete with spun sugar towers, stone walls made of rose petals over almond cream, and with a working drawbridge over a golden honey moat that had sugar swans swimming atop it, a wedding gift from the earl to his bride, one that made Lady Clio look softly to Lord Merrick just before she began to laugh and cry at the same time.

Sofia had two pieces of that delicious cake, a trick that took some plotting on her part, since some would have accused her of Gluttony—one of the Seven Deadly Sins. But what foolery she thought that was. She was no glutton; she just happened to like cake. How could liking sweet white cake be a sin? Much less a deadly sin?

While she was deviously plotting a way to nab her third piece of cake, she had glanced up and to her surprise found that everyone her age, the youth of the group, squires and ladies, daughters and sons of the noble families, her friends and a few youths who were her cousins, had disappeared completely from the Great Hall.

So she left the hall to search them out and stood outside, looking and wondering where everyone had gone.

"Come, Sofie!"

She turned, recognizing her young cousin's voice.

Princess Eleanor called out to her again. "Come join the game!"

Sofia had to step around a tall and robust acrobat who was shepherding a pack of dancing dogs through the crowd hovering at the doorway. She looked west, and there in the inner bailey, between the stable and the buttery, were most of her friends and all the other young people who had been arriving from every corner of the land just to attend this wedding.

" 'Tis hoodman blind! Come! Quickly!" Her cousin Edward's eldest daughter, Eleanor, was standing in a large circle with the other young people.

In the center of that circle stood a tall youth. He had a black hood covering his head and his arms were out in front of him. He turned slowly, cautiously, reaching outward. He stopped for just a hair's-breadth, ready, taut, then leapt out and snatched for Eleanor.

Her cousin laughed when the hoodman stumbled and grabbed only thin air.

Eleanor kept moving just out of his reach over and over, laughing as the others did, taunting, as was the way of this game, until finally her cousin ducked down and the hoodman's hands hit the buttery wall.

Everyone laughed.

The hoodman turned around, then straightened and laughed, too. He made a mocking bow. "Ha! The Princess Eleanor is too swift for the plodding and lowly son of an earl!"

His jest made some of the those in the circle laugh, the ones who knew who he was. Sofia looked long and hard at him, but she did not think that she had ever met him. The voice was unfamiliar. She would have remembered his height.

'Twas not surprising though, since most of the sons of the King's vassals were fostered out when they were only seven.

While the daughters of nobility were sheltered inside a castle that made them almost prisoners, the sons were sent to serve the warriors of the land and to train as a new generation of warrior and knight, avowed to protect England's future.

While Sofia tried to watch the hoodman, Eleanor laughed again with her distinctive giggle, then covered her mouth with her hand and shifted sideways so he would not catch her.

He turned and moved swiftly toward her again. After a few more failed attempts to trap the King's daughter, the hoodman was on toward someone else, and the princess glanced back up at Sofia and waved frantically for her to come down.

Sofia quickly stuffed that third piece of cake into her mouth until her cheeks bulged with it, then she grabbed her gown and ran down the stone steps. She was still chewing when she joined her hands with Eleanor and watched the tall young man in the center as he chased the others.

After a time of watching the game, watching the hoodman and who he went after, Sofia leaned close to her cousin and whispered, "Do you see, Eleanor, how this hoodman only grabs for the girls with bosoms?"

"Sofia!" Her cousin burst out laughing, a sound that made the hoodman spin around and face them.

"You laugh!" he said, moving toward them.

Sofia did the opposite of everyone else; she took a step toward him, her hands on her hips and her chin held high. "I say that the hoodman is not blind enough!"

The hoodman did not move, but turned a small bit so he was facing her. He cocked his head. "How blind does this new lady wish me to be?"

"Blind enough to not conquer only the pawns who have breasts!"

There was a cheer of raucous laughter.

"De Clare! She challenges you!"

Sofia knew that de Clare was the earl of Gloucester's family name. The hoodman must be his son.

The hoodman gave her a grand bow. "Someone here is not blind, I see."

"Ah! There. He just admitted that he can see." Sofia could not keep the cockiness from her voice. She delighted in twisting his words in her favor.

"See?" He did not move, but stood where he was, his hand rubbing his chin in feigned thought. "Suppose I told you that I have a gift and I can see with my mind."

"Suppose I told you I can fly."

Everyone laughed.

"The lady doubts my powers of perception."

"The lady believes the cloth is not thick enough."

Sofia looked straight at him, knowing instinctively that he could see her.

He laughed again, holding his hands out from his sides as if he were innocent, a performance for everyone. "Perhaps the lady would like to blindfold me herself."

"Do it, Sofia!"

"Aye! Here is a piece of thicker cloth for a blindfold! It shall be dark enough!" One of the young men tossed her a tunic belt made of midnight silk.

Sofia took the hoodman's challenge eagerly and swaggered forward, relishing her victory and this verbal sparring with a tall, young stranger who was a powerful earl's son, particularly one who also needed his ego clipped. "You must kneel before me, hoodman, for I am no thick-headed giant."

He only laughed at her jibe, then knelt down before her.

She stepped closer.

"You questioned my honor." His voice was quiet, for her ears alone.

"How honorable is it to cheat?" Her voice was not quiet. She wanted all to hear. There was no victory in secrecy and whispered threats.

"You claim that I cheat?"

"Aye."

"You sound certain, milady."

"Aye. I am." She gave a sharp nod.

"I see. This is a challenge."

The others began to murmur.

She would not back down from a challenge. She liked this banter between them. "Aye." Her voice was firm and she lifted her chin and looked to her cousin, feeling very fine indeed.

"Then as my challenger, you must pay a forfeit if I prove you wrong."

She whipped her head back around and stared at him. Was he daft? "You claim, hoodman, that you can still catch me with two blindfolds?" She laughed heartily. She would tie the second blindfold so tightly his ears would stick to his big head.

"Aye," he boasted with an assurance that would have been unsettling if it were not so intriguing.

She would never back down from a challenge. Because she was a woman, her pride was almost all she had. She studied him for a long time. She could feel his eyes on her, even though he wore the black hood. She looked down at the silk in her hand. This second blindfold was a double thickness of woven silk and even darker than the hood she wore. She held it up to the sunlight and could see nothing through it. There was no risk here. 'Twas a certain thing.

"The lady hesitates," he goaded.

He was bluffing. The buffoon.

"If you can catch me with both blindfolds, I will pay any forfeit." She raised her chin and looked right at the black hood, right to where his eyes must have been.

"Then tie the second blindfold." He knelt and bent his head for her. As she made the knot, she wondered what possessed him to make a wager he was certain to lose. She stared down at the black hood, wondering for just a flash of an instant what color his hair was underneath. What his face looked like? His eyes? His voice was deep, not like the other lads, whose voices would crack at times and squeak like cart wheels that cried out for oil.

His height was tall enough to hint that he was only a few years away from manhood and probably a squire. There was no doubt he was from a wealthy family, for the cut of his garments was finely done and the fabric heavy with expensive trim and fine needlework. His boots were of glove-soft leather, the kind that came from Spain and cost dearly.

From what he had said she knew he was the son of an earl. He had said as much. But there were many sons of the King's earls she did not know because of fostering.

As she finished tying the knot, she looked down at his hooded head and she cursed herself for not paying more attention during the feast meal, when all the guests were sitting at tables in the hall and she, who sat just below the head table on the dais, was in a position high enough to the salt for her to have seen every guest. Then she would know what he looked like.

If she had only been paying attention, which she had not. She had been intent on stuffing her face with wedding treats and frumenty. She stepped away from him.

"Hoodman! Name your forfeit!" Someone called as he rose to his feet. Gracefully and surprisingly, the way heavily armored knights did.

She cast a quick glance at him. He *was* tall, that one. She retreated a step or two.

"Aye!" All the circle agreed. "Name the forfeit!"

He said nothing, but stood there so tall and straight that it was like looking up at the tower. She felt suddenly small, which annoyed her. She did not want to feel frail and inconsequential.

She waited, and waited.

He was silent.

She wondered what he was waiting for. When he still

said nothing she looked around her, at the others, then shrugged and relaxed her stance. "Perhaps I tied the blindfold so tightly the hoodman can no longer think *or* speak."

Everyone laughed again.

Then his voice cut through their laughter. "I demand three kisses from my challenger."

"*Three* kisses?" she whispered, frozen to the ground like a deer caught in a snowdrift. "What kind of a forfeit is that?"

"The best kind."

There was more laughter and cheering by the others, which annoyed her to no end. Kisses? Who would think of kisses. It certainly had never entered her mind. Think, she told herself. And think she did, quickly, and she spoke just as quickly, "*Three* kisses? Is that not gluttony, hoodman?"

"No more gluttonous than three pieces of cake," he said quietly.

She was stunned to silence—a miracle to those who knew her—and she did little more than stand there in the center of the game circle and gape at him, until she realized what she was doing. She then clamped her mouth closed, an action that rang clear through her teeth and jaw.

She did not stop looking at him, but she could feel her expression change and her eyes narrow to a cold glare. "Fine. Three kisses it is," she agreed in a clipped voice, then spun around and marched over to the outside of the circle, where she faced him with her hands on her cocked hips and her head held high and haughty. "Catch me if you can, hoodman *blind*."

CHAPTER 4

She watched Edith disappear through the crowd. Sofia wanted to disappear, too. Instead she had to stand there in front of Sir Tobin de Clare and act as if her heart wasn't pounding, as if nothing that happened in their past could possibly matter, as if she were as calm as stagnant water.

"There is something between us."

Lud! He felt it, too.

"We have a debt to settle."

Now all she felt was foolish. He was not speaking of the odd attraction she felt, but of the forfeit she owed him.

Face the devil, she thought. *Do it!* She turned back toward him slowly, shook her head and raised her chin so it appeared as if she were looking down at him, even though she was a full foot shorter. "You cheated."

He cocked his head and frowned a little, as if he had expected her to say anything but that. "There was a huge circle of witnesses that day." He gave a wry laugh. "Tell me exactly how I could have cheated before all those pairs of eyes."

"I do not know." She waved a hand in the air. "I am not that devious-minded."

"You? Lady Sofia Howard? Not devious-minded?" He roared with laughter, while Sofia stood there, staring at the half-moon–shaped nails on her right hand.

No one had ever claimed that she did things half-heartedly. Lying therefore should be no different. If she was going to lie, the lie should certainly not be a puny one.

He obviously found her very amusing, for he was still laughing softly. She did not know if she liked that or hated it.

He took a step closer to her. "Tell me, Sweet Sofia, just how did you manage that day to get the Queen to call for you at the exact moment I was about to collect my debt?"

She would never admit to him that she had done nothing, that the Queen's timing had been only pure luck. Let him think she was that mystical and shrewd.

"Come. Confess."

She gave him a smile. "I shall tell you, sir, when you tell me how you managed to chase *only* the girls in that circle who had," she paused, "blossomed."

He shrugged, denying or admitting nothing, a tactic she knew well since she frequently did the same thing.

He pinned her with a penetrating look from those intense and knowing eyes. "I think over the past two years you have cooked up the notion in that cunning little head of yours that I won only because I cheated."

"Three years," she said. "Not two years."

His sudden laugh had a victorious sound that told her she had fallen into a trap of his words. He had known it was three years, but tested her.

He moved so close his hips brushed against her side. "I stand corrected, milady. Over the past *three* years, you have conveniently decided you do not owe me anything because you can claim I cheated."

"There was nothing convenient about my memory. I *know,* not *think.* And I *know* that no one could possibly have moved as quickly as you did, especially in my exact direction." She kept her ground. It was uncomfortable, to have him standing mere inches from her. She could not think as sharply.

But she knew he was trying to intimidate her with his height and size. Men did that, used their physical powers to compensate for the lack of their mental ones. So she tilted her head back to look him straight in the eye, which usually surprised arrogant men because they were used to meeker women. She did not bow her head but would look anyone in the eyes.

However, he did not appear surprised, which annoyed her to no end. The least he could do was be predictable.

"I think what you mean, Sofia, is that you think no one can move as swiftly as you can. Your pride drives you. You believe that you are the only one with a quick mind and even quicker feet." The cad took a step closer. He was almost standing on her feet. She could feel the warmth of his breath when he spoke.

She stepped away. "What I *believe* is that you cheated. Now if you will excuse me, sir, I am off to watch the races." She turned with her nose high in the air, lifted her gown and planned to walk away with a haughtiness that would do Queen Eleanor proud.

She got no more than a few feet.

His hand closed around her upper arm. "I shall be happy to escort you to the races, Lady Sofia," he said so loudly she was stunned, so she looked up. He had almost bellowed it like a herald announcing the King's demands.

People around them turned to stare.

He gave her a slight, courteous bow as he pulled her arm through his, casually, in the manner of courtier doing the bidding of his love. But in truth he was clamping her arm firmly to his side so she could not pull it away, which she had already tried twice.

He began to walk, his strides so long she had to almost run to keep from being dragged along slave-like behind him.

"Would you slow down?"

"Only if you will stop trying to snatch your hand away."

She relaxed her hand on his arm and stopped trying to jerk it back, so he slowed his steps. She would lull him into thinking he had won.

She walked in silence, staring at their arms, at their hands, looking for the perfect moment to pull away and run like the very Devil himself.

But the moment did not come. She did not run. She could not get her hand free. She stared at her hand resting on his forearm, then gritted her teeth and glanced up, eyeing all around them. She realized that they looked as if they were any other knight and lady walking through the crowds. Except the other ladies did not have their escort's big, hammy hand smashed over theirs so they couldn't snatch it away.

"Perhaps, milady, *together* . . ." he squeezed her hand ". . . we can find the man you were seeking."

Die. She wanted to die, but she would never let him know it. With a casual tone that was the exact opposite of what she was feeling, she said, "Perhaps so, sir. You are tall enough to see above the crowd."

Flatter him. Tell him he is tall. It implies he is superior. Most men loved to think they were superior, so while he was preening, she would devise a way to escape him. Somehow. Someway.

They walked along, his hand over hers, her mind racing toward a goal. Neither of them spoke, which was good because she did not want any distraction when thinking was so hard. The sounds of the hawkers and the gaiety were all around them. Normal sounds that broke up her thoughts. Lively sounds. But then she had a dark moment; she had the horrid, sinking feeling that nothing would ever be truly normal again, certainly not whenever Sir Tobin de Clare was this close to her.

His scent. His breaths. His walk. She was stunned to

realize that she was more in tune to the rhythm of his strides and the sounds of his breathing than she was to the loud and boisterous throng around her.

Even worse, her hand almost burned under his touch. She swallowed hard and kept up with him.

"As I remember it. . . ." he said in a thoughtful and lazy tone, "you told Lady Edith this man you sought had raven black hair."

He had heard her describe him to Edith. *Lud! Lud! Lud!* She could feel him looking down at her. She knew if she looked at him she would see that infuriating grin of his, so she fixed her gaze on a juggler who was balancing wooden pins on his ears and nose. She waved her hand at the juggler. "I wish I could do that. Balance pins like he is doing. What amusement that would be." She changed the subject, which usually worked for her. If you had no good answer, just confuse them.

"Interesting."

"Aye. They are interesting the way they can balance so many objects at once. Do you suppose it takes long to learn to juggle? Probably," she answered quickly before he could. "I do find jugglers the best of entertainments."

"I was not speaking of jugglers."

"Oh." She did not ask what he was speaking of. Perhaps he would forget.

"I was talking about this man you were seeking. I find him very interesting."

She looked at him then. "Why? Do you prefer the company of men to women, sir?"

His eyes narrowed slightly and she bit back a small smile of satisfaction.

"What I find interesting is that the man you seek should have black hair."

"There must be a hundred men here today who have black hair."

"True." He paused, then added, "Even *I* have black hair."

She kept walking as if all was well with the world and his comments were no more important to her than the dandelions that floated in the wind.

He took a few more lazy, catlike steps, then added in a pensive tone, "This man was wearing blue, you said. Aye, that was it. You said 'blue.' I heard you clearly."

His sudden grip tightened on her hand before she could move. It was almost as if he could see into her mind before her thoughts were even close to complete. She had been waiting for the perfect moment to catch him off guard. And the devil knew it.

He stopped then. So suddenly it was as if they had run into a wall.

"Why are we stopping? The race is that way."

He was frowning down at his clothing. "How amusing." He looked up, his expression all feigned innocence and devilry. "*I* am wearing blue." He looked at her then, waiting.

She waited longer, letting time work for her instead of against her. She blinked up at him innocently, then gave him her biggest smile. "Beg pardon, Sir Tobin. I did not hear what you were saying," she lied beautifully, sounding as if her mind were in London instead of here.

"I was just making the observation that I am wearing blue." He sounded as if his jaw was just a bit tighter, as if his back teeth were clamped together.

There was hope!

"Are you wearing blue?" She stepped back and gave his attire a long appraisal. "So you are." She paused, then added, "I had not noticed."

He said nothing more, but began to whistle slightly, a jolly and vastly annoying tune as they walked farther along.

She stared straight ahead, her eyes now locked on a scarlet pennant with a lion that flew from a standard near the drawbridge. She tried to think of some way to change the subject.

" 'Tis a small world, is it not?"

She was learning to greatly dislike that casual tone of his. "A small world, sir?" She laughed. "I do not think so. I believe that more than half the court is here and there are many other noblemen who have traveled far, like yourself. I would not call this small," she said brightly. "It seems to me that this is a huge crowd."

He laughed softly and under his breath she could have sworn he muttered the words "stubborn witch."

She refused to look at him. He did not yet know the word "stubborn."

"Sofia." He spoke her name softly and stopped walking so she could not move on. The only choice she had was to look at him.

But she did not. Instead she stood there, looking everywhere but at him.

"Look at me." His voice was quiet, but the tone was still a command.

A command. The perfect thing for her to ignore. Perhaps now she would annoy him the way he annoyed her. She would not obey him, even though some small part of her wanted to look up at him because even though he annoyed her terribly, he was still so very sweet on the eyes.

"Ah!" He snapped his fingers and nodded. "I remember now."

"What?"

"You are afraid if you look at my face you will forget to breathe."

That got her to look at him, just at the same moment she felt the color drain from her face. Those were her exact words, her passionate confession to Edith about the man of her dreams. About him.

She felt her humiliation keenly, down to her toes, and she wanted to close her eyes so she would not have to see the look in his, the action of a coward, so instead she picked up her skirt in her free hand and took a couple of steps.

But he did not move.

She got barely two feet away when he jerked her back. She stumbled. His arm shot around her waist, catching her and pulling her against his chest.

A moment later she was staring up at him, her palms against his chest, her feet off the ground. Again.

He leaned his mouth toward her ear. "Ah, sweet Sofia . . . we must stop meeting like this."

She jerked her head back and away from him. His breath and voice were still chilling her ear and she could not think clearly. "Then stop pulling me around. I am not a handcart!" She tried to wiggle free, but he was too strong. "Put me down, now."

He did put her down, but her toes barely touched the ground before he was moving again, walking so fast with her plastered against his side that for every other step her feet did not touch anything but air. He was half carrying her along with him. She wished to heaven that she were a foot a taller and a few stone heavier.

Through gritted teeth she said, "Stop this! Put . . . me . . . down!"

He glanced down at her with feigned worry. Just a glance. "I would not want you to fall on your face. It is such a famously beautiful face. You might break your lovely little nose." Then he stared straight ahead with a determined look. "Imagine that, Sweet Sofia. No suitors groveling at your feet. What would you do for amusement?"

"I demand that you put me down."

He ignored her and walked even more swiftly.

"Do as I say, sir, or I shall scream so loud the castle walls will crack."

"Try it and you'll find my hand." He looked down at her. "Or better yet, my mouth over yours. Do not forget that you still owe me those three kisses. We could always start here."

"I still say you cheated. Now let me go!" Before she could struggle free, before she could jab a bony elbow into his belly or figure out how to twist so she could kick his shin or some other equally painful place, he turned into an archway that led into one of the guard rooms in the tower near the outside wall.

"Where are you going?" She looked off toward the direction of the lists. The opposite direction. "The races are that way!"

He shifted her under his hard arm so she could not move her body, only pedal her feet uselessly, then he shoved open a door and went inside with her hanging on his hip like a sack of oats.

The air inside was cooler, dark and dank, and a steep and narrow stone stairway led up to the outside crenels of the guard tower. She had no place to run.

He kicked the door shut; it closed with a dull thud, like a warrior dropping from battle or a jouster falling from his mount. It was the sound of defeat.

He set her on her feet and released her so suddenly she had to slap a hand on the stone wall to keep her balance. She shoved the tangled hair out of her face with her free hand and glared at up him.

Her look had no apparent effect on him.

They stood there, staring at each other, locked in a new kind of battle that was not unlike the staring contest they'd had across the lists.

Then he advanced, took a step toward her.

She retreated, just one small step. Her back hit the stone wall, her palms flat against it, pinned there. Suddenly cornered, she raised her chin because she had to look up at him to keep eye contact, to let him think she was not the least bit intimidated.

He planted his hands against the wall, on either side of her shoulders.

He was so close her traitorous breath caught. He

leaned forward until he was but a few inches from her face, close enough that she could feel his warm breath when he said harshly, "Enough games."

She gave him as unyielding a look as he was giving her. Silence stretched out between them, taut as bowstring. Soon her own breath came a little faster, and it was shorter, as if someone were stealing the air she breathed.

She should have ducked down under his arms, grabbed her skirts and run as fast as she could. She knew that, the thought was clear in her head. *Do it!*

But her feet and arms would not obey her mind. She did not move.

Neither of them moved. Neither of them spoke.

Tension spun its threads around them, then something else, something she could not name washed over her, kind of an excitement that was there in both her breath and her blood, a realization, and as the silence stretched onward, something else happened. Something changed. Whatever this thing was between them began to rise higher and higher, like the crescendo at the end of a madrigal, the climax to the tale being sung, the same tense moment when all in the room were on the edge of their seats, not breathing, but waiting.

They were as taut as if someone were twisting them together, forcing them closer and closer. Tighter and tighter. There was almost a sound or feel to what was between them, and it sped like fire through her, made the air between them thrum and sing in her ears, then stole her breath clean away.

It even drowned out the distant sounds of the crowd cheering on the races. It was making everything melt away like small drops of water under a hot, summer sun. The way there is suddenly nothing, just the heat beating down on you.

That was what this feeling was like. That was what

she could not control. The outside world had withered away and there were only the two of them, standing in this dark niche and looking at each other as if they were trapped inside a cocoon of sudden, pounding desire.

She saw the same passion, or something like it, flicker in his eyes, and thought this must be the way of lovers, this thing that clouded her mind and her sense. He felt it, too. And she understood something of love then, of how when you looked at each other, it was as if you were looking into the same reflection. The same need. The same desire. They burned together, he and she.

She knew then and there that she would remember this moment forever, the way you remembered all the important moments that made up your life. This was love, pure and true. A grand desire and passion, things she thought she would never feel. But she felt them now, almost as if she were born with the feelings deep inside of her, where they had been waiting for him alone.

She would not run away. Not that it mattered much, for she could not have done so had she wanted to. Where she gathered the courage to do what she did next would amaze her for years to come.

But then pride was nothing compared to what she was feeling inside of her, between them, around them. Pride did not rush through your blood. Pride did not lift your heart and steal your breath. Oh-God-in-heaven-above but pride did not look like this man.

She was the first to move. She grabbed his head and pulled it down to her mouth, kissing him hard with her lips compressed and her mouth tightly closed.

And she tried to fool herself, to lie and think she was the one who started this, and she would be the one to end it.

I shall give you your kiss. Your forfeit. I shall give it to you now, but on my terms. I will be the one in control.

CHAPTER

5

He knew the moment she lost control. It was in the way she kissed him. She thought it was her idea. It was not.

That single, tight-lipped kiss, the one she thought was paying her debt, changed the instant he ran his tongue slowly along the line of her lips. She opened her mouth and made a small, odd sound, as if all the secrets she had been keeping had just escaped.

She had no knowledge of this kind of desire. He knew that. While only three years older than she, he was years older in experience. But that was not what bothered him for just that one, single moment in time, no longer than it took to stroke her mouth. What bothered him was something different, a strange, niggling feeling that he was losing something in this game he played. He could not name what it was, but he felt as if something were slipping away from him. Warriors were trained to respect their instinct as well as their knowledge and skill. This was pure instinct.

But he ignored it, because he could not define it. Whatever it was, it did not matter to him. It was likely a product of too many tankards of ale and too little sleep the night before.

He moved his hands from the wall and slid them under her, grasping her bottom in his hands and lifting her higher, before he slid one hand up to hold the back of her head, to keep her mouth where he wanted it, to keep in control. His tongue went deep inside her mouth, tasting those sweet secrets she spilled, and he knew the moment she was lost.

He could feel surrender in her whole body. The way she loosened her firm grip on his head and instead, rubbed one hand through his hair as if driven solely by her own desire, as if her active and quick little mind was no longer part of this.

It was in the way she shifted a little and pressed closer to his body, the way her tongue suddenly followed his. This young passionate girl with all her daring, with all her defiance and her bold front was truly burning for him.

It would be so easy to go farther.

Perhaps too easy.

His hand was moving toward her hem, to touch an ankle and move upward. He wanted to touch her legs, the soft backs of her knees, her thighs. He wanted her breasts in his hands, to feel the weight of them, to press his thumbs against the tips and feel them harden because he'd touched them. And he wanted to taste them. He wanted to taste all of her.

He bent slightly, and his palm was around her ankle. The thin leather ties on her slipper were crossed and knotted there. Tangled like confused emotions.

She was not stopping him. She made no move to do so. She was his for the taking.

Sofia Howard, who let no one near her and who chased away anyone who dared to try to even court her, had her tongue in his mouth and one leg almost hooked around his waist.

This was his plan.

But, too, he wanted her badly, and that was not part of what he had planned.

He broke away as swiftly as someone who had been

kept captive, releasing her so abruptly a small, startled cry escaped her lips.

He took two steps back and away. For just one small moment, he did not move. He did not know why, he just did not. His breath was not smooth and even. Neither was his heartbeat. He looked at her then.

She stood there, staring at him from wounded, puzzled eyes, like some small, confused animal that was just kicked or a bird that had fallen from its nest.

"I need to leave." His voice? It sounded deeper than usual, as if it were coming from someone else, like his father.

She looked down as if she were trying to hide the fact that she looked so uncertain. He understood pride, understood his own anyway. But she was a woman, and a young woman, only five and ten. Pride was not important for a woman.

He raised his hand to her face, touched her pale cheek, then stroked her jaw and tilted her chin up with a knuckle.

Her eyes were huge, those eyes that a man could fall into too easily and so many already had, in spite of her need to send them running.

But any cynicism he felt seemed to wither away when he saw there was some moistness there. She was on the verge of crying. Tears seemed to be poised on the rims of her thick black lashes. It surprised him. He did not think Sofia Howard was one to succumb to fits of tears.

Ah, she truly was an innocent to feel a kiss so strongly. But that thought did not stop him. He ran his thumb along her swollen, moist lips. "Meet me in the Queen's garden at the first bell of Vespers, Sweet Sofia. We will finish this."

She shook her head.

He gave her a look meant to spark a challenge and added a laugh of derision. "You will not honor your debt?"

She said nothing, just looked at him for a long moment, the kind of tense and brittle moment when the air hung with something that would not let you turn away. She was gauging him, he knew, and searching for something in his face, but he knew well how to hide what he felt, knew it was most important with her, for she was clever and he did not doubt that she would use any weakness to her own advantage. He knew, too, that she would never find what she was looking for there.

He shrugged, then shook his head. He turned and opened the door, giving the final, parting shot. "I forgot who I was dealing with."

Her head snapped up quicker than a bowstring. "What do you mean by that?"

He faced her. "Only that you are a woman, and women know little of honor." With that he stepped outside and pulled the door closed behind him, then walked a few feet away.

The door flew open and crashed against the stone wall.

He turned, cast a casual look over one shoulder.

She came charging through the open door with her head high and her look fiery. "I know of honor, Tobin de Clare." She almost spat the words. "And I will be in the garden at Vespers." Her hands were in tight, white fists in front of her. She seemed to realize it and relaxed her stance, then placed her hands on her cocked hips and gave him one of her direct looks. "Vespers. After the first bell. Then we shall settle this for good, you and I."

He said nothing. He only turned and walked away.

He loved to win.

Sofia felt lost, almost as lost as she had felt on the day the Queen had brought her mother's things to her. It had been three years since then, almost four, and yet she still stood in her bedchamber staring hopelessly down at the tester bed the same way she had that day.

There on the coverlet lay a long strand of exquisite pearls—her mother's pearls—that were the same, soft color as pale skin under the glow of a full moon. She wondered how something that looked so lovely, so almost magical, could feel so wrong on her. They were her mother's. Was there not some part of her mother in her?

But she did not feel lovely when she tried to wear them. What she felt instead was defeat and frustration. Just like she always felt when she was all alone and faced with the knowledge that she would, at some point in her future, be forced to act female, to behave like a woman.

She took a fragile step closer to the bed, where she dropped a handful of golden beads. They rolled together, pooling in the dip of the coverlet.

Until a few moments before, those beads had been whole—pretty little golden beads that shimmered when she held them up to the candlelight.

Now they were broken, single beads, loose, with no thread to hold them together, like the family she was born into.

She had tried to weave them into her hair. But they had broken, scattered in all directions. She had crawled around the entire room, until she found every last one of them, as if finding them would somehow heal her life.

But it didn't.

The beads, the pearls, both lay on the bed next to a length of fine, embroidered raye, and a deep blue cloak made of the softest wool from Flanders with embroidery so fine the stitches were almost invisible.

These were her mother's most precious things. A legacy passed on from mother to daughter, passed on from one woman to another. Her one link to the family she'd had for only a few years, before time and fate and God took them away so there was no one left but her.

She looked down at the jewels and the clothes, even

placed her hands flat on them, then she closed her eyes
as tightly as she could, wanting and needing at that moment to remember her mother's face.

She could remember when she was small, standing at
the top of the stairs at Torwick Castle. She could remember the cold chill of the floor tiles on her bare feet. She
could remember the size of the great doors at the bottom
of the staircase, doors so big they looked as if they
opened into an enormous new world.

She could remember watching her mother and father
walk down those steps that led toward the great doors of
her family's home, and all the way down, her mother's
long blue cloak would almost float along behind her.

But no matter what she did she could not remember
her mother's face. She opened her eyes and quickly took
her hands away from the items on the bed, as if they had
burned her. She knew the image of her mother was gone
forever and nothing she could do would bring it back.
Even late at night, those times when she lay there with
her eyes closed, half in dreams, trying to see her, she
only saw a blank outline of a woman, like a wall paint-
ing that was never finished.

Once in a while, when she looked into the polished
metal that hung above her laver in her chamber, she
would catch a small glimpse of something vaguely familiar in her own face, an expression, something in the
brow or the chin, or perhaps in the shape of her eyes.

It seemed to her that there should be some kind of law
of nature that would carve a mother's face on the memory forever. She tried repeatedly to figure out how to
wear her mother's things, because she thought perhaps
she could jar her memory if only she could just somehow re-create her mother's look.

But she could not.

The length of silken cloth looked odd, like some
labarum worn by the Archbishop. The cloak looked just

like any one of her own cloaks; it did not make her stand taller or walk down stairs as if she were floating. It only wrapped itself around her and provided some amount of warmth and a bright bit of color.

Whenever she tried to wear the pearls they looked out of place, the same way Sofia felt most of the time.

Frustrated, she sat down on the bed and rested her chin on one fist, swinging her feet in annoyance. Sometimes she wished the Queen had never given her mother's things to her.

But she had, right after Sofia had started her first woman's flow. For two entire days she had hidden in a old storage room in the barbican, frightened, crying, shaking, because she had thought she was dying and was afraid to tell anyone.

Queen Eleanor had found her, coaxed her into confessing all, then explained to her "those things women were supposed to know."

Sofia had understood the importance of that day, what it should have been even before Eleanor told her it was a special time and that was why she was giving Sofia her mother's possessions. She was now becoming a woman. Eleanor explained to her that girls who were betrothed could wed soon after the start of their flow. She explained why they could begin their own lives and their own families. She explained how things were between men and women and where babes came from. That day had been one of those times when mothers were supposed to pass on knowledge to their daughters.

Sofia had gone from girlhood to being a young woman in one single day. She was suddenly marriageable. She was no longer playing at being someone. And she felt the loss of her mother so keenly then, because she knew it was the time when mothers told their daughters about life and birth and love, but the Queen had to do it instead.

Eleanor had handed her the bundle of her mother's possessions, wrapped inside of the blue woolen cloak with its golden threads and intricate embroidery, then left her alone.

She was all alone with her thoughts that night, and with her new body, one that was a woman's body instead the of the old, comfortable one she had always known. It cramped and twinged. Pain rang in her belly like the sound of a snapping bow. It hurt. She had finally cried herself to sleep under that blue cloak, with the pearls and cloth hugged to her chest, because it made her feel as if some part of her mother was there with her.

And now, at this moment, another special day in a woman's life: the first time her heart sang from something she thought might be true love, she stood in the same bed-chamber, waiting for the bells to toll Vespers, looking down at her mother's things, and she felt as lost and stupid and lonely now as she had on that day long ago.

She wanted to ask her mother about what she was feeling. Were her feelings what every girl felt? Did they mean what she thought they meant? Was this wild emotion that ran through her love? It felt like love. If not, it should be love. And somewhere deep down inside of her, she wanted to share the joy of what she felt with some-one who was part of her, share the thrill and the excite-ment she felt with someone important, with her own mother.

Instead she looked at the pearls she did not know how to wear, the cloth that looked wrong when she pinned it to her gown, the broken beads, and Sofia felt that ever-present emptiness come over her again, that desolate feeling that she was living in a different world from everyone else, the same way she felt when she was all alone, and could not fool herself the way she fooled the rest of the world.

She hid from the world her weaknesses and fears with

a wall of false bravado. Her fierce need to strive to be something other than just a woman actually hid her deepest secret, the thing that shamed her and made her fight so hard to be different. That Sofia Howard did not even know what a woman truly was.

Suddenly the bells tolled loudly. The sound made her jump. It was Vespers. She sat there, chewing her lip, staring at her hands and her gown and her slippers. She took a deep breath, then called herself a coward. It took a minute for her to straighten her shoulders, to find the courage to stand up and go after what she wanted.

She started for the door. She could almost feel her blood beginning to warm, to beat like tourney drums through her veins. Anticipation. It was something she had been feeling all day, this wonderful and wildly wicked thrill she felt inside of her just at the mere thought of Tobin de Clare.

She paused at the door to her bedchamber, her hand resting on the thick oak planking. Hope was an odd thing. Even the most cynical person in the world could not completely kill it off. Hope stayed in one's mind, a small spark waiting for a whiff of wind to make it flame.

She glanced back at the bed, then ran over and snatched up the blue cloak. She held it for just one moment, then she threw it over her shoulders and tied the strings tightly under her chin.

A moment later she was running down the steps and heading for the Queen's garden. She opened a door in the Gloriette and went outside into the bailey. She hugged the blue cloak around her shoulders; it was a part of her past.

But the eagerness inside of her, the moistness in her eyes and the tight feeling in her chest and her heart, well, that she was certain was her future.

CHAPTER

6

The sun went down slowly that evening, as if it didn't want to leave but had no choice because the moon was chasing it down. The air grew cool and crisp. It was April, that complicated time of year when the night air hovered between the last, frosty remnants of winter and the warm beginnings of spring. It could be confusing after a day of warm sunshine; it could lull you into thinking you would not be cold again for a long, long time.

But nature always showed signs to remind you of how fickle she could be, like that moment when the winter stars first came out. They blinked and winked high up in a dark night sky, and looked like chips of ice, sparkling up there in the very same way ice winked when it was the coldest day of the year, those times when you had to be careful, to protect yourself because if you didn't, you could lose your fingers and toes.

But as Sofia walked along a gravel-laden path in the garden, she wasn't thinking about the signs of nature or of frostbite. She was listening to the way her shoes crunched on the gravel. To her it sounded like a rabbit munching on a fresh carrot.

Her anticipation was running higher and higher the closer she got to the garden bench. She walked faster, past the plump cabbages and turnips, past the herb plot, where she paused and turned 'round in a circle because the fresh, heady scent of thyme and rosemary drifted into the air and made everything smell hungry.

She slowed her steps when the bench was in sight, suddenly self-conscious of what she was doing.

Imagine what he would think if he saw you running there, you foolish girl?

Sir Tobin de Clare already had plenty of arrogance. If he thought she was even half as excited as she was, he wouldn't be able to get his head through the castle hallways.

So instead of running, she practiced her saunter, counting slowly between steps like one marching into a church during High Mass. When she finally reached the bench, she stood there for a long time before she let herself sit down. She wiggled a moment or two, then tucked her feet under the bench and just sat there. An instant later she crossed them at the ankles instead, then she adjusted her cloak, fluffed out her skirt so it covered the toes of the red slippers she was staring down at.

She sat on her hands, then decided that would look stupid, sitting on her hands like someone who bites her fingernails and is trying to stop, so she folded her hands in her lap, which didn't feel exactly right either. She didn't want to look as if she were praying. She opened her hands and placed them palm down on her lap, then stared down at them for a long, long time because they felt enormous, like they belonged to someone else.

Time seemed to drag like the half-dead. She looked about her, but did not see Tobin de Clare anywhere and certainly didn't want him to come and see her looking for him. Perhaps she should have been late. She drummed her fingers on her thigh, then realized what she was doing and slapped one hand over the other. Finally she just sat there, staring at the tufts of pink heather at the edge of the garden, at the way they half covered the stones. She looked at the newly blooming primroses with bright yellow centers the color of sunshine. Time moved even more slowly, so she picked at the wool of her cloak with two fingers until there was a big, fluffy ball of fuzz between her fingers. She stared at it, then dropped it beside her on the stone bench, shaking her head at her silly nervousness.

An instant later something quick and dark darted down from a nearby tree. She jumped, until she realized it was a small, brown missel thrush with a white breast. The bird had scooped up the ball of fuzz in his beak and flew right past her nose, then headed back toward the tree with the wool in its beak looking as if it had a big blue mustache.

She watched it use the wool to build its new nest, the way birds would every spring. She sat back, locking her hands around her knees as she leaned back farther and watched the bird as it joined its mate in the tree.

This year they were building their nest in an old apple tree, which with each passing year leaned more wearily toward the ground, as if it were getting too old and tired to even try to grow upright. The nest was on a low branch, where it would be vulnerable to the castle cats and the magpies that so often tried to steal the young.

She suddenly wanted to warn the nesting birds away, to tell the them of the risk they were taking. But they would not understand her warning, so instead she sat there, watching the birds build their doomed nest, while she did the one thing she'd promised herself she would never do: wait for a man.

Lady Sofia Howard's dark silhouette was visible from the archway at the upper entrance to the buttery, where a group of young men stood drinking goblets of rich, dark wine from Bordeaux—too many goblets to count.

She was still sitting on the same bench in the garden on which she sat when she first came there, right after the bells tolled for Vespers. Since then, the night air had turned damp and dewy.

Sir Tobin de Clare had watched her pull her cloak tighter around her as time passed, until now, when it looked as if she were huddling there, a March hare among the flowers and herbs, amid the low bushes and trees that now were only black silhouettes.

He turned back toward the others in the room. "She has been sitting in the garden long enough. Two candles have already burnt down to their nubs." He pushed away from the arched wall, tossed back the last vestiges of his wine, and crossed to the other side of the archway. He faced the others. "I have won."

Richard Warwick was leaning against a cask of wine and looking out at the garden. He turned and faced Tobin, spilling his wine, then he laughed. "You did it, de Clare." He shook his head in disbelief, then wobbled slightly from his drunkenness, which did not stop him from lifting his wine cup to his mouth and drinking even more deeply, so deeply it ran down his chin and neck.

The men who were there in that room were all witnesses to the wager. They were the same men who had sought Lady Sofia Howard's hand and been spurned for the effort. All young noblemen, all wealthy men, all proud men. No mere woman, no woman of such pride, even a ward of the King, would play them for the fool, not without some kind of recompense.

Thomas Montgomery raised his cup and staggered forward. "To de Clare!" He swilled back his drink and swiped at his mouth with a sleeve, then refilled his cup and that of Robert de Lacy, who was slumped along a wall like a fallen Punch puppet, his feet propped atop a wooden press, his head back and his eyes closed. "De Clare!" He repeated, lifting his goblet but still not opening his eyes. He sighed tiredly and pulled out his fat purse. He opened one eye to a mere slit, then tossed the whole purse of gold to Tobin, who caught it in midair, his stance and demeanor surprisingly sober, like that of someone who had not a single drop of wine.

One by one the men paid their losses in bags of gold and silver, except for Geoffrey Woodville, who paid in rubies and emeralds because he was an ass and had to feel he was above everyone, even his own peers.

Tobin looked down at his winnings. There was enough money hanging from his hands to buy gold spurs and any number of mounts, as much money as he could have earned in tournaments if he had been like the legend of William the Marshall and had won them all. Even though he did not need the money. His father was one of the wealthiest men in the land. He did not care about the money, but the others did.

They kept giving Tobin toast after loud toast. When their shouting grew more lewd, he stepped away from the wall and turned, facing the garden again, for just a moment, to cast a quick glance back toward the bench where Sofia had been sitting and waiting for him to meet her.

The bench was empty.

He frowned and did not turn back toward the others for a moment, even when Montgomery said something to him and slapped him on the back. He took another full goblet of wine offered him from one of the others, then raised it to his lips and drank, staring at that empty bench and wondering why his drink was not satisfying the emptiness in his belly.

He stared down at the wine; it tasted sour and bitter, which was odd, because they had broken the seal on a cask of Edward's best French import, heavy, sweet wine from Bordeaux.

"To de Clare! Who conquered the Thorn Rose of Torwick!"

"To the best man in the bunch of us! To Sir Tobin de Clare!"

"Aye! To de Clare! I shall wager the Thorn Rose is still sitting on that bench, and that it has turned to ice from her cold and frozen arse! 'Twas worth the loss of my fat purse to see her sitting there all that time!"

They laughed and made more lewd comments about the frost around various private parts of Lady Sofia Howard.

Tobin felt no triumph, certainly no honor, which was the catalyst for this bet, at least what it had started out as—his honor, based on an arrogant comment he'd made in a fool's moment, one from which he could not back down. As he stared into his wine goblet all he saw before him was a pair of violet eyes looking back at him. He listened to the others go on about the frigid and thorny Lady Sofia.

But he knew the truth, what the others did not know. There was no frost in her. Her thorns were there to protect her; it was all an act, one he would have explored further had he not already made the wager and had his honor at stake. He took one more drink of his wine and then for a reason he could never explain, he glanced up.

She stood in the doorway, Sofia Howard, the young woman they called the Thorn Rose. The archway was so massive that she barely filled even a small part of it and she was not small. Yet it dwarfed her, made her look weak and more vulnerable.

She had that same blue cloak wrapped around her, the ends of it clutched in her tight, white-knuckled fists. Her face was colorless as snow, the expression on it nothing but a hard and bitter mask, her eyes narrowed and focused on him alone.

He did not know how long she had been there, but he could see it had been long enough to understand the way of things.

He did not move. He did not speak. He'd done enough humiliating this night. The others need not know she was standing there.

Something sharp and burning stabbed deep inside of him. Something foreign to him, something that felt like it might be shame.

She stood there for a moment longer, as if she were trying to memorize what she was seeing. In that instant, he suddenly understood that this was no ordinary folly, no prank to be forgotten. No jest. No amusement. No battle of pride.

She turned away, slowly, her head high.

For just that one instant he wondered what it took for her to do that. There were no tears. No sobs. No hysterical female crying. All she did was walk away, her head up and the rich, blue cloak dragging heavily behind her.

He stared at that empty doorway for a long time, still seeing her even though he knew she had left. It was as if her image were burned into his eyes. For the longest time he could see nothing else. He shook his head and looked away quickly as he raised his cup to his lips, then drank deeply, over and over, trying to banish the image of what he had seen and even more, what he felt when he saw her face and the look of loathing she gave him.

He said nothing to anyone, but drank until there was nothing left in the cup. Then he drank until there nothing left in any of the ewers.

His mind never dulled, his mood did not change. He couldn't even get drunk. Because all the wine in the world could not wash away the guilt he felt at what he had just done.

TWO YEARS LATER

TWO YEARS LATER

And if any mischief follow, then thou shalt give life for life, eye for eye, tooth for tooth, hand for hand, foot for foot, burning for burning, wound for wound, stripe for stripe.

—Exodus 21:23

CHAPTER 7

It was the perfect day for mischief.

Sofia had spent the entire morning, every single hour of it, in the Queen's solar with Eleanor's ladies, stitching hangings of infamous battles and poking her fingertips with the embroidery needle, until they were bloodier than the battlefield bodies depicted on the tapestry.

Even all her wonderfully inventive gasps of pain, all that sucking on her fingers and frowning did not sway them to let her escape. By the time she did escape, she was convinced that Purgatory was truly a place where all you did for an eternity was sew.

When she finally managed to escape, she went in search of something that would truly amuse her. After all, she had wasted an entire morning. With the exception of one small diversion, Sofia headed for the kitchens and found the perfect thing to keep her busy.

Within a few moments she was scurrying up the steps of the Gloriette at Leeds, heading toward an upper chamber where Lady Edith, who was now betrothed to a nobleman on a diplomatic journey to the north, was sitting by an arched window that opened to rays of warm and precious sunlight. She was bent so her head was lit by the sunshine, which turned her red hair coppery. And she was working intently on a lovely and intricately embroidered wedding tunic for her betrothed, should he ever come back to wed her.

Edith was a saint.

Sofia was not a saint, and she had no desire to be one. She would have never had her friend's patience for sewing and she had learned her lessons on waiting for men many times over, but Edith claimed that her betrothed was a kind man, even though he was almost three times her age.

A kind man. Now that was what the Greeks called an oxymoron. She dashed into the chamber quicker than an arrow from a crossbow. The doors slammed against the plastered walls with a loud bang.

Edith jumped half out of her chair, then looked up startled. After a second she said, "You do know how to make an entrance."

"Always have and always will," Sofia said brightly as she turned to close the doors, her gown whipping around her ankles in a flurry of rich scarlet silk trimmed in threads of finely spun gold. She turned back around, hiding her hands behind her like someone who has a prize to be chosen in one of their hands. She pressed her back to the doors and gave Edith a devious and wicked little smile that, had the King spied that look, might have caused him to lock her in the tower before something dire befell them all.

Edith put down her sewing and stood. She eyed Sofia for a moment, then took a few steps toward her. "I know that look. What do you have? Something up your sleeves?"

Lady Sofia grinned. "Perhaps."

"What?"

"A surprise that will clear all the dullness of this dullest of days."

"I do not find this day dull. I find it peaceful, but I suspect it will not be so much longer." Edith came closer, stretching her neck and trying to see what Sofia was hiding behind her.

"You are a saint and can find the joy in almost anything. I, on the other hand, found this day horridly dull, until a few moments ago."

"Let me see what you have hidden behind you. And it better not be your bow."

Sofia shook her head. " 'Tis not my bow, silly. Fetch that water ewer from the table and then I shall show you."

Edith brought over the water so quickly she was sloshing it all over the floor tiles. She stood before her. "I have the water. Now what?"

Sofia pulled her hands out from behind her and gaily tossed two handfuls of pink, flaccid objects on the Queen's daybed.

Edith squinted her eyes and bent over the tick. "What *are* those things?"

"Pig bladders," Sofia said with a laugh of wicked glee. "I stole them from the kitchen."

Edith made a face. "Why?"

"I spotted them tucked inside a tin the other day when I was looking for that apple to shoot off Lady Juliette's head."

"Poor Juliette." Edith shook her head. "Has she recovered yet?"

"No. She is still having a witch's fit." Sofia's voice was filled with disgust. " 'Twas only one small scratch and she will have to part her hair toward the left for a while. One would think I had skewered her, when in truth, the arrow only sliced through just this much," Sofia held up her fingers, "of her hair. Besides, she was stupid enough to let me try the shot. I was nearly successful, too." Sofia chewed on a nail thoughtfully, wondering what would have happened if her angle had been more to the west.

"What are you going to do with pig bladders? Not shoot them, I hope. And be aware, Sofia," Edith added in a rush. "I will not let you aim your bow at me, nor will I be the stand for any kind of target you wish to take aim at."

"Of course not, Edith." Sofia clasped her friend's hand and patted it reassuringly. "I would never expect that kind of silliness from you. You are much too important to me for that. You are my dearest friend." Sofia turned and picked up a bladder and dangled it in front of Edith's face. "What say you? Would you like to hear my plan?"

Edith crossed her arms and eyed Sofia suspiciously. "I have learned not to commit. You explain first."

Sofia stretched the bladder wide, then she turned to Edith, holding open the bladder. "There. I shall hold it while you fill it with water." She paused thoughtfully, then muttered, "I only wish it was the oldest and strongest vinegar instead of water."

"Why vinegar?" Edith tilted the water pitcher slowly and began to fill the thing.

" 'Tis nothing. Just a thought. Now be careful." Sofia stretched the mouth of the bladder open even more. "Pour slowly."

"Look! It is swelling. And swelling!" Edith paused and tilted the ewer upright.

"Do not stop yet. The thing needs more water."

"I must stop." Edith's eyes grew almost as round as the bladders. "It will surely burst!"

"That is the point, Edith. It must be stretched taut. We should fill it almost to bursting." Sofia held it up and eyed it, then instructed Edith to pour a little more water inside until the bladder had swelled so she could see the water inside.

"Stop."

Edith tilted the pitcher upright.

Sofia lifted the bladder, which was stretched so taut you could almost see clear through it. In fact, she could see Edith's worried face.

"Do not fret so. I promise this will be most amusing. There. 'Tis perfect!" She tied off the bladder and carefully set it on the mattress, then grabbed another one and stretched it open. "Now fill this one, too."

Edith was frowning at the water-filled bladder as if she expected it to explode right there.

"It will be fine. Just help me fill the others."

Soon they had filled and tied twelve bladders into plump and sloshy balls which were stacked in a pile of buoyant lumps on the bed.

Sofia picked up one of the balls and rolled it from one palm to the other, grinning. She looked up and handed it to Edith. "Here. Feel this."

Carefully Edith took the ball and cupped it in her two small hands. She eyed it as if she expected it to pop open any moment.

Sofia picked up another one. "Now follow me." She walked over to the arched window. "Look outside, Edith. Do you see that chalk mark I drew on the stone steps?"

"The circle with the mark in the center?"

"Aye. 'Tis a target, like in archery. The object of this game is for both of us to drop the bladders at the same time, and whoever comes closest to the mark wins." She paused and moved over. "Come now, let us hold out the water balls and start the game."

Edith moved carefully, balancing the bladder, and soon both girls were bent over the arched casement, the balls extended in their outstretched hands.

"When I say drop, we let go at exactly the same moment. Understand?"

"Aye."

"Edith?"

"Hmmm?"

"I believe you stand a better chance to hit the target if you open your eyes. You should take aim at the mark."

"I don't like heights."

Sofia shrugged and said, "Drop!"

They both let go. The water balls fell like missiles from heaven and burst open on the stone step with a loud *splat!*

"Look! Look! Mine was closer!" Edith was jumping up and down, laughing and pointing and apparently forgetting about her fear of heights.

Sofia frowned. Her bladder had bounced just a little before it burst and missed the mark by a good arm's length. "Aye. You did particularly well, for unlike you, I had my eyes open." She paused for a thoughtful moment. "Having my eyes open did not seem to help."

She spun around, eyed the balls for a moment, then grabbed the plumpest one for herself. 'Twould never bounce, she thought as she walked back to the window. "Come, let us do this game again. Whoever has the most target hits by the time we have dropped them all, will win."

"What is the prize?"

Prize? What prize? She had not thought about a prize. She'd had another purpose completely. But, without missing a moment, she said, "My sapphires."

Edith's eyes grew wider, for the sapphires were tear-shaped and a rich blue color, a gift from the King himself. They were the loveliest of anyone's except the Queen's.

"The ones Edward gave me as a reward for finding his favorite scepter."

Edith gave her a wry look. "You mean the one you were using to prop open the trap in the barbican so you could eavesdrop on the guards talking about playing in the hay with the kitchen maids?"

"Aye. The very same one."

"So let me see if I have this straight. If I win, you will give me the sapphires?"

Sofia nodded. "And if I win, you must be the one to accompany the Queen to confession every eve for a fortnight." Sofia looked at Edith. "Agreed?"

"Agreed."

It was not long before plump pig bladders were falling from the tower window like missiles during a siege. They were in a tie; each had an equal number of hits when they finally were ready to drop the last two bladders.

"Whoever is closest wins." Sofia said as she leaned way out of the arch and eyed the target, stalling for a moment, before she adjusted her feet a little to the right. "Now do not drop it until I say to do so."

"I did better with my eyes closed," Edith admitted and squeezed her eyes tightly shut.

"I have an idea, just to make this more interesting, let us both close our eyes."

"Fine," Edith agreed with her eyes still shut.

They both leaned out the window.

"Close your eyes tightly, Edith." Sofia said, leaving her one eye open just a smidgen and looking intently downward. "On your mark . . ."

Sofia waited a little longer, until she heard the squeak of a door hinge.

"Make ready. . . ." Sofia finally closed both eyes when she felt she had the bladder right over the spot she wanted.

The door below creaked open.

"Drop!" Sofia whispered.

They both let go at the exact same moment.

'Twas also the exact same moment that two of Edward's knights walked out the scarcely used western doors and stood directly atop Sofia's chalk target.

In unison, the girls leaned out the window to watch,

each gripping the stone casement in their hands and looking downward.

There came a grunt of male surprise.

Splat! Splat!

The pig bladders hit the two knights square on their heads.

"God's blood!" came the cursing from below.

Edith's mouth fell open and she stood frozen.

But not Sofia. Grinning, she grabbed Edith's hand and jerked her away from the window, then she ran to the doors, dragging her friend with her as she ran down some back stairs and hid in small dark shadowed niche two floors below.

They could still hear the men swearing.

Edith looked at Sofia. An instant later they both began to giggle.

"My Lord in heaven," Edith gasped. "Who was it, do you suppose? No one uses those doors!"

Sofia began to laugh so terribly hard she had trouble catching her breath. "I know the knight in the cloak."

"You do?"

"Aye." She giggled again. " 'Twas Gloucester's eldest son."

"Sir Tobin de Clare?"

Sofia nodded, now laughing so hard she was making snorting noises into her hand.

Edith stopped laughing and studied her for a long time. "Did you know he was in the castle, Sofia?"

"Know he was here? Me? Why Edith! Are you suggesting that I planned this whole game just so I could hit him over the head with a pig bladder full of water?"

"Aye, I am. I have known you for many years, which is why I did not volunteer to put that apple on my head, dare or no. I would not put it past you to do something like this."

Sofia drew herself up into a stance she thought

showed her indignation. "Truly, Edith, what is the likelihood that he would come out those west doors of the
tower? You said yourself that no one ever uses those
doors."

Edith was silent for a pensive moment, then she
searched Sofia's face. She sighed and said, "I suppose
even you could not plan something so intricate and devious."

"Aye." Sofia said clapping her hands. "But what good
fortune it was that he merely happened to choose those
doors at that particular time."

The bell rang announcing None, and the girls left the
tower to meet the Queen in the solar. 'Twas later that
day, though, well after Vespers, that Sofia accompanied
the Queen on her evening visit to the castle priest.

After Queen Eleanor was through, Sofia went inside
the small, dark confessional. Once there, she blithely admitted with no remorse that it was she who had given the
arrogant and cold Sir Tobin de Clare the wrong direction.

So as the Lady Sofia knelt in the chapel, her head bent
in one of the hundred and thirty three prayers she must
say for penance, she smiled, for that one single look on
Sir Tobin's arrogant face—his wet and red face—was
well worth a night of sore knees.

CHAPTER

8

They said revenge was sweet, and it was. Sweeter in reality than it had been in Sofia's dreams for the past two years.

She slept late the next morning, later than was her usual routine. She felt lazy, like a cat that had just finished all of the cream, and she stretched her arms high above her, her hands in fists as she groaned a little, then arched her stiff back and yawned.

She lay quietly under the soft, warm feather coverlet, trying to ignore the coming day. Sounds echoed inside the Gloriette from the bailey below. The watchman's horn. The constant creaking of the carts and wagons which brought supplies into Leeds. A coarse shout here and there. Horses clopping on the stones in the courtyard. Dogs barking. Goats braying. Birds singing on the ledges of the tower.

But those things did not bother her overmuch. She just closed her eyes and the only thing she heard then was the sweet, wonderfully rewarding sound of Sir Tobin de Clare swearing his way into Purgatory.

She sighed, then thought back to the image of his wet and surprised face looking up at her. 'Twas like living one of her dreams all over again and she wished ever so much that she could do it again, with a hundred pig bladders. A thousand! She wiggled underneath the feather covers, then pulled them up under her chin. After a moment of utter satisfaction, she began to laugh, just as she had so often since the day before, and during her penance prayers, and probably even during her sleep.

Finally the hubbub in the bailey grew to such a din that the deaf, or even the extremely satisfied, could not ignore it, so she threw back the covers and rose. She slid her feet into her fur slippers, then padded across the room to the arched window that overlooked the farthest end of the inner bailey. The shutters were open and she rested her chin in one hand and looked yonder toward Canterbury and the world beyond. There was a light breeze in the air, cool and crisp, and it ruffled the hair at her temples and dried out her lips when she moistened them. For a moment she just let that breeze brush against her face.

She heard a sudden shout and the horn blew from the watchtower, then there was the creaking, loud squeal of the portcullis in the barbican slowly rising.

A contingent was coming through. In the distance she could see golden brown dust still billowing in the air over the road. She heard the horses' hooves pounding a hollow, echoing beat across the wooden drawbridge.

It was probably only the King's hunt party returning. They always rose at dawn, an ungodly hour, then went out to kill the animals in the woods. Sport was what they called it.

In Sofia's mind sport had nothing to do with killing animals that were a hundred times smaller than you and everything to do with water-filled pig bladders. She found herself smiling again, then she just giggled, because it was very, very hard not to keep gloating when gloating was so amusing, and she was all alone so no one would see her anyway. It was wicked to laugh so, but that certainly did not stop her.

However, the sounds from below changed in pitch and caught her attention. There was the rattling sound of men dressed in mail and armor. The voices were many and unfamiliar. And there were too many horsemen. Those were not the sounds of a hunting party returning.

Idle curiosity sent her leaning half out of the tower arch, her waist bent against the stone ledge, her long dark hair hanging thickly over her shift so she needed no robe to cover her.

Her hands clasped onto the handles of the iron shutters to better see what was going on below, and she rose up on her bare toes. She could almost make out the first of the horsemen. Almost. His mount was side-stepping in and out of a darkly shadowed archway.

The door to her chamber opened suddenly and Edith rushed in all excited, her voice almost a shriek. "Sofie! You must get up! Quickly!" She spotted her standing at the arch and paused. "Oh. You are up."

Sofia turned back to the window, staying where she was and trying to see who was below. "Aye," she said distractedly. "I am up."

"Hurry. The Queen asked for you. I told her you were still in bed."

Sofia spun around, horrified. "You didn't. I shall get fifty penance prayers for Sloth and have to sew with the Queen's women every morn for a fortnight!"

"Nay. I mean, aye, I did, but you will not be punished because then I lied. God help my poor wretched soul." She made the sign of the cross. "I told her you had a great ache in your head." She crossed herself again and muttered something about lying for friends that Sofia could not make out. "Eleanor said she would send Lady Mavis and Lady Jehane to help with your headache and to help you dress."

Sofia groaned. "Now I do have a great headache. Mavis and Jehane? Lud . . ." She sagged back against the stone wall. The Ladies Mavis and Jehane were fiercely loyal and hell-bent to serve their Queen. The younger women of the court called them the Poleaxes behind their backs, because the two women were rigid as a mace shaft and they could slaughter you with their sharp tongues. Worse yet, they were Eleanor's private friends as well as ladies-in-waiting, the Queen's most trusted. Even the King's men obeyed if either of them gave a command.

Sofia sagged back against the stone wall. "Edith, tell me how can such a great morning turn into such a bad day?"

"I do not think it is bad, Sofie. There will be a feast in less than an hour. You should see the panic belowstairs. The servants and the cook are having fits trying to prepare everything. The Queen herself has been seeing to everything. She says that this day is—" Edith cut off whatever else she was going to say and she looked suddenly ill.

Sofia frowned for a moment, then turned to Edith and asked, "What makes this day special?"

Edith shrugged and wouldn't look Sofia in the eye.

"Why would the Poleaxes need to help me dress? Who has come here?"

"I do not know." Edith turned away swiftly, her hand on the iron door handle as if she were trying to escape.

"Edith! What is going on? What did you start to tell me. The Queen has been what?"

"Nothing," Edith mumbled to the door.

"You are lying to me, your most true and loyal friend in the whole wide world. Turn around."

Edith turned slowly. Her face was bright pink, which meant she was either fevered or lying.

Sofia spun around quickly, hung half out of the arch again and tried desperately to see who was below. The entrance to the Great Hall was to the east, a short distance from the Gloriette, so she had to shield her eyes from the late morning sunlight. But all she could see of the troop of men was one last dusty pair of boots. The men and their colors were hidden from her view by a wooden scaffold built for the varlet who had been lime-washing the castle stone.

The chamber door closed with a telling creak and Sofia spun to face an empty chamber. "Edith!" She ran for the door. "Edith! Come back in here!"

She almost had her hand on the door when it opened and the Poleaxes marched in the way King Edward marched on Wales. Lady Mavis, a tall, gaunt woman with brown hair and a voice as commanding as the Queen herself, clapped her hands. "Inside with you! All of you!"

All of you?

A stream of servants came inside carrying a tub, bucket after bucket of hot water, soaps and perfumes, towels and a huge bucket of chipped ice, which must have come from the King's icehouse in the lower cells of the donjon. Sofia stepped back against the wall, eyeing them unhappily. When she looked at Lady Mavis she was sorely tempted to mimic Edith and make the sign of the cross, or better yet, hold one up in front of her.

But she could do nothing. She was cornered.

Lady Jehane came through the doorway, bringing up the rear, her arms crossed with determination and her look as unyielding as a stone wall. She stopped, scanned the room, then her gaze landed on Sofia. "Her Majesty claims you have a great ache in your head."

Sofia slumped slightly, sliding partially down the wall. She raised one limp hand to her brow. "Aye," she said in a weak, breathy, and withered-sounding voice. Then she wobbled a little so it would look as if she were ready to faint.

Through a small crack she had made in her fingers,

Sofia saw Jehane's eyes narrow slightly before she spun
on her heel like the captain of the King's guard and
marched to the doorway. Jehane cupped her hands over
her big mouth and bellowed, "Hear ye all! Hasten! Bring
the King's barber and his largest pail of leeches to bleed
the poor, suffering Lady Sofia."

Leeches? Sofia's belly tightened. She shuffled sideways to her bed, then collapsed on it, groaning. "I am
too, too weak. Ah. Too weak with . . . with pain to be
bled. 'Twill, oh my. . . ." She took a deep breath.
"Just . . . just make me weaker." Then she let her voice
trail off with a sorrowful hissing sound. Just for good
measure, she whimpered. Twice.

Then Lady Mavis was towering over her, so Sofia
moaned again. And again. Mavis left for a moment and
Sofia took advantage and shifted a bit, then turned her
head just enough to see out of the corner of her eye.
Mavis picked up something, shifted it back and forth in
her hands for a moment, then she turned and came back
toward her.

Sofia closed her eyes quickly. She could feel Mavis
standing over her, pausing, looking down at her. The
urge to open her eyes was great, but she did not do so.

The next thing she felt was a heavy and lumpy towel
landing on her face. It was freezing!

"The ice inside this towel will kill the pain in your
head," Mavis said in a matter-of-fact tone, then she put
another towel full of ice on top of the first one, until
Sofia could hardly breathe and her teeth began to chatter.
Mavis pressed them down with her hands and Sofia
could feel the ice freezing into the hollows on her face:
her nostrils, the sockets of eyes, her lips, her temples. It
was so cold that it burned her skin and hurt like the very
Devil!

"I know all about head pain," Mavis was saying. "Do I
not, Jehane?"

"Aye, Mavis. You always said that ice is better than leeches. But," Jehane paused, then added in a thoughtful tone, "just perhaps, if poor Sofia's pain is truly so very severe, for her we could do both cures."

Both?

"Leeches and ice?"

"Aye. Freeze her and bleed her at the same time."

Aye, and then the two old heartless cats can draw and quarter me.

"Hmmmm." Mavis was thinking.

This is not good.

"I shall fetch the barber immediately," Jehane said. "We wouldn't want the poor child to suffer any longer than necessary."

Sofia could hear Jehane's clipped footsteps heading for the doorway. She shot upright. The towels and ice scattered everywhere. " 'Tis a miracle!" Sofia shouted before Jehane could get very far. "You are truly the best, Lady Mavis. My headache is gone."

Jehane poked her head around the corner of the open door, then exchanged a triumphant look with Mavis that annoyed Sofia, but even she would not have leeches put all over her skin just to continue such a charade. She hated leeches, hated them more than worrying about what was going to happen to her or what these two sly and demanding women would do to her. She also knew that Jehane was not making an idle threat. The stern and dire Lady Jehane would not hesitate to use leeches all over her.

Jehane's shoulders went back and her stance grew so rigid it looked as if she had a lance for a spine. "Well, then, girl! Do not just sit there! We have work to do!" She grabbed Sofia's arm in a steely grip and dragged her across the room.

"But wait—"

"No waiting. There is no time. Lift your arms.

Higher!" Jehane grabbed Sofia's icy hands, lifted them out to her sides, then in less time than it took to blink, had stripped her to her bare skin.

She had no chance for protest, just a gasp here and there and a few whines. She was shoved into a steaming tub that was far too hot and made her yelp, particularly after the icing her skin had taken. She was washed, scrubbed, dunked and dried, perfumed and oiled. Her lips and cheeks were pinched so much that at one point she asked Mavis if she were related to Dickon Warwick.

She was dressed, tied, laced, turned, braided and decorated, then shoved out the door and down the steps toward the Great Hall in spite of her protests, questions, and muttered curses.

With both the Poleaxes on either side of her, she was all but hauled through the halls and archways. She did try to slip her arms free repeatedly but those two women were so strong a dancing bear would not be able to move if they had him in their clutches.

Before Sofia knew it, she was pulled through a small side door and she found herself standing in the front portion of the Great Hall, near the high table, where Edward was already seated.

Eleanor suddenly appeared at her side. "Come, child." She took Sofia's arm. "This is your betrothal feast."

"Betrothal?" Sofia looked at the Queen, who said nothing but guided her through the crowd.

Chatter from the tables and music filled the room, where a high and blazing fire was burning in the huge fireplace at the north end. Musicians nearby played the lute and pipes while a jongleur sang a lyrical song about love and favors and greensleeves.

Alas my love you do me wrong,
To cast me off discourteously.
For I have loved you well and long,

> *Delighting in your company.*
> *Greensleeves was all my joy,*
> *Greensleeves was my delight*
> *Greensleeves was my heart of gold,*
> *And who but my Lady Greensleeves?*

The Queen would not speak, so Sofia walked to those lyrics, feeling like nothing but a ghostly thing in the crowded room. The King was talking quietly to one of his men, then he waved him away, and his gaze lit on her as they wove through the throng.

Sofia cast him a look of complete indifference, and she gave him her most honeyed smile. She would not let him see she was worried and she would not look away from him defeated.

He rubbed one finger pensively over his lip as he returned her stare, then waved an arm in the air. "Here she is!" He looked to Eleanor and said, "Thank you, my dear."

The room grew suddenly quieter at the sound of the King's words. Edward had one of those rich, deep voices that always captured the attention of whomever he was around, and this time was no different. Sofia felt all too many eyes upon her. She did not look at the crowds and at the tables. She was a coward. She did not want to see what was on their faces. She did not want to see an ocean of people from court avidly waiting to watch the willful and infamous Lady Sofia brought to her knees.

The King turned toward a man who sat near and said something.

Sofia's belly sank with dread. She pulled her gaze away from her cousin and looked at the man. He was a tall man, broad in shoulder, but his face was lean, and somewhat familiar. She could not place it exactly. He had a dark beard and hair, which was graying at the hairline. He was dressed almost as richly as Edward himself, but not quite, for no one was foolish enough to outdress the King of England. The stranger was a handsome man, but too old to wed, surely. He was old enough to be her father.

His gaze flicked to hers. His eyes were intense and oddly familiar. She was certain she knew him from somewhere, but she could not place him. She chewed on her lip for a second, thinking frantically. Who was he?

He stood slowly, his gaze fixed on her, acknowledging her in a quiet and gracious manner. From that she decided he would probably not beat her, which she supposed was a plus. Instinct said he was not putting on an air or a mask to hide his deviance. He was certainly no Lord Alfred.

He said nothing, just watched her. He was so very tall, as tall as Edward, who was called Longshanks because of his towering height. Sofia had always thought that was one of the things that made her cousin such an autocratic and arrogant tyrant. He towered over everyone, like God, and therefore assumed he was.

The stranger made a slight bow, then to her surprise, gave her sly and wicked wink before he sat down again with no inkling of a smile anywhere on his features.

Sofia frowned then, for that was a strange thing and she did not know what to think.

Her belly flipped at that thought. Husband, the word echoed in her head. *Husband. Husband. Husband,* like the pounding of the smithy's hammer.

Eleanor grasped her icy hand more tightly and led her away toward the opposite end of the table, where there were steps that led up to the dais and where she would have to take her seat.

They walked slowly and she could feel many eyes on her. Her skin burned from those looks. She stared straight ahead. She was being paraded in front of the whole court. A pig going to slaughter. A slave on the auction block. A woman being given to a man and having nothing to say about it. She had never felt so absolutely helpless in her whole life.

They crossed directly in front of Edward. Sofia turned and looked at him. His expression was far too pleased and satisfied. Sofia knew gloat when she saw it. You don't revel in something as often as she did and then not recognize it when it is right before your very eyes.

She wanted to run.

Eleanor leaned down. "Do not dare. Edward will have your head, child."

"Am I to have nothing to say about this?"

"Be quiet, dear. Edward has made his decision." She patted Sofia's hand. "All will be well. I promise."

Sofia tried again. "I think that you would be better served to lead me toward my execution, not my betrothal, for I find both events to have a similar appeal."

Eleanor laughed under her breath. "Sofie. You will fight this to the very end, but you cannot change it."

"You cannot expect me to rejoice when Edward pays someone to take me off his hands." Sofia could not keep the bitterness from her voice and she did not try. Let Eleanor see how she felt. Perhaps the guilt would haunt her to her grave.

"That is how this is done, as you well know. You have no power without a dowry. It has nothing to do with selling or buying."

"How much gold is that old man getting?"

"Old man?" Eleanor looked at her.

"Aye. He winked at me. While he may not seem old to you, he is very old to me. I know what is happening here. I am not the castle idiot. I do not have to feel the breeze to know which way the wind blows."

Eleanor was quiet, glancing at her as they walked and turned at the end of the table.

Sofia refused to look at her. She walked up the steps

to the dais. She was hurting inside because she could not believe that the Queen, one of her favorite people in the whole world, had betrayed her. She always thought Eleanor loved her in her own way. She had claimed to.

After a moment the Queen said, "Edward wants to see you wed."

"Edward wants. Edward wants. 'Tis not fair. Why should he have a say over my wedding? I had no say over his."

"He had no say either, Sofia. He married me because his father said he must."

"But you are a saint. How could he not love you? He had God on his side. And you were not an old woman."

"He is the King. You are his ward and his subject. No one gets away with all the mischief and mayhem for as long as you have. You are ten and seven and you must wed soon. I could not speak on your behalf any longer. The offer came. It is a fine match. Edward has made his decision."

Sofia wanted to run. She was marrying an old man and they called it a fine match. Certainly he was a handsome old man, but he was still an old man and not a young knight. She would have to sleep with that old man. She would have to bear his babes. He would see her naked and touch her. She would live with him forever and ever.

She could never tell her secrets to an old man. She could not feel the thrill of excitement with him. She would not welcome his kisses. She would not have her blood speed through her veins the way it had once, only once before.

No, she could not. She had no heart left inside of her. It had been destroyed two years before.

Her steps were slower and her feet felt heavier. She could not look at him or anyone else. She stared at the pointed toes of her shoes. *Oh dear Lord in heaven, my life is over. Please, just let me die young. Preferably before the wedding.*

They moved toward the King, where there were empty chairs. All the men at the table rose in unison. Sofia frowned when Eleanor stopped before she arrived at the empty seat near her future husband.

Why was she not sitting next to the old man? It was tradition to share a trencher with your betrothed. She stared at the chair before her, at its carved arms and back. There was a red cushion on the seat.

A sudden chill ran over her.

A tall man stepped up from the side curtains and onto the dais. A second later Sir Tobin de Clare was standing there. He was turned away and saying something to the Archbishop of Canterbury.

She closed her eyes for just one weak instant and felt her knees start to give out. Luckily Eleanor grabbed her shoulder. Sofia steadied herself, her hands gripping the edge of the table and the back of the chair. She felt Eleanor's hand slide up and hold onto her upper arm. Support. She could feel Eleanor's look of concern, but she dared not look for fear she would do something completely humiliating . . . like cry.

She stared at her feet and tried to gather her composure, then exhaled a deep breath she had not known she had been holding. The room stopped spinning and she was suddenly aware again that she was the center of attention.

Sweat broke out on her brow and her belly turned over twice, thrice. She took another breath. Everything inside of her screamed that she should turn and run as fast as she could. Run far, far away to the French or the Germans or the Scots, some enemy of Edward's. 'Twould be easier to do than what she knew was ahead of her.

Eleanor leaned close and whispered, "You will be fine. See? He is not an old man. He is young and handsome. You are strong, Sofia. Look up. Smile. Find your pride and show it to all."

It took everything Sofia had to raise her head higher and higher. But she did, and did it with Eleanor's requested smile pasted onto her tight and dry lips.

"Milady." Sir Tobin took her hand in his. The shock of his touch made Sofia want to scream. He made a slight bow. She stared at his bent head. She felt the sudden urge to grab a pewter wine goblet and bash him with it.

Show him you do not care. Show him what he did to you does not matter. Show him.

Sofia looked up slowly, gathering her pride, and gave him the brightest smile, a smile that she wanted to bring him to his knees. A smile that would slay him and never let him know he had hurt her so badly she could hardly bear to look at him. A smile that would never let him see that she cared or that she even remembered the past.

"Sir Tobin," she said in a sweetest of voices, one that dripped with honey and came from that place where she stored her courage. She sank into a deep and respectful curtsey, quelling the urge to kick his shins while she was down there.

I will not let him see me grow faint of heart. I will not!

"Lady Sofia," he said aloud, then added quietly, "Sweet Sofia." His voice was the same, that deep and unsettling sound that she remembered. It made her breath catch in her throat, and for all of her reserve, for all of her bitter need to hate this man for humiliating her, she could not stop her powerful reaction to him, and it frightened her terribly, to have so little control over something so important. She could feel it down to her very toes.

"Come, meet my father."

He led her past Edward and Eleanor to the older handsome man and now she knew why his face was so familiar. She was looking at Tobin's features, only perhaps twenty some-odd years older.

His father stood and bowed, then straightened to his full height and looked down at her. He smiled; it was a kind and surprisingly less carnivorous smile than his son had. "A pleasure, Lady Sofia, to meet such a lovely and spirited lady. My son is most fortunate." He raised her hand to his lips, bent over it and pressed a soft, lingering kiss there.

She thought she heard Tobin mumble something. His voice had an irritated sound to it, and she cast him a quick glance. He was scowling down at his father's head, still bent and still kissing her hand.

She turned back at looked at the earl of Gloucester, who straightened and gave her another sly and devilish wink that made her frown for just long enough to think clearly.

Why that wicked old devil! He was flirting with me.

She smiled a bright and honest smile, then cast a glance at Tobin, who was glaring at his father.

"My lord. 'Tis an honor to meet you." She dipped into a deep curtsey, looking directly into the earl's eyes. She would not play a game with him, not when he had the most wonderful twinkle in his eye and pure fun in his grin.

"I had heard of your beauty, milady, but mere words cannot capture such a glorious face."

A flirt. Tobin's father was a charming flirt.

Before she could thank him, Tobin made some sound of disgust. "Come," he grumbled. "No one else may eat until we sit down." He all but dragged her back to her seat.

She stood by her chair, then willed herself to calmly sweep her gown away with one hand and sit serenely, observing all as if she were not bothered the least by this day's events. She was succeeding well, when Edward leaned over and ruined everything.

"You are wise to do us proud, Sofia."

She turned and looked at the King. "Your Majesty. Cousin." Then she gave him a smile that should have worried him. It did not work. Edward was not looking any longer because he was leaning close and talking quietly to Eleanor.

Sofia turned back and faced the room. Her eyes caught Edith's at the table just below. Edith looked worried, guilty, and frightened, which was an intelligent thing for her friend to feel because Sofia was going to wring her neck when they were alone.

One of the King's drummers banged on a kettledrum so loudly that the room grew suddenly still; it was as if everyone's voices had been stolen. Even the dogs lying by the huge fire did not move.

Edward stood. He raised his jewel-encrusted wine goblet high in the air, where the rubies and emeralds and pearls caught the light from the fire behind him and seemed to glow and glint and make the moment appear all that much more important. "We have good reason for celebration this day! We feast in honor of two great events. Sir Tobin de Clare has broken through the siege at Brookwood on the northern borders and gained the release of Earl Wynton."

There were loud cheers of *A de Clare!* and toasts in Sir Tobin's name. Shouts came from all over the room and many of the de Clare men stood, raising their cups to him.

Sofia sat there stiff and tense and scared and feeling completely helpless, which she hated.

Edward drank along with the others, then he raised his goblet again. "We have gathered here to celebrate that victory today, along with another reason for celebration." Edward paused meaningfully and looked at Sofia.

She tried to look nonchalant.

"Today, we are proud that two great houses will unite

to form one strong and loyal noble family. We shall witness the betrothal of our ward, the Lady Sofia Howard, daughter of our cousin, the late Baron Rufus Howard, Lord of Torwick, Boden and Runworth." The King stopped for just a hair's-breadth of a moment, then added, *"Finally."*

The room seemed to explode with laughter. Sofia sat straighter, plastered a brittle smile on her face as she tried to look as if she didn't want the stone floor to open and swallow her. She wanted to look emotionless, despite the fact that every emotion she could feel was raging though her. But to the room, to those all about her, she wanted to look as unaffected as the hounds that lay asleep by the great fireplace. She watched a smirk of satisfaction spread across the King's sharp-featured face, which made the slight droop in his eye disappear.

He looked overly pleased with his perfectly vile wit. "As I was saying, Lady Sofia Howard will *finally* be betrothed this day to Sir Tobin de Clare, son of Gilbert de Clare, earl of Gloucester, Lord of Berkeley, Mowbray, Sutton, and Greyfolk, Rudler, and Saltease." He drank a toast to Tobin's father. "May the young couple be as pleased as we are at this moment! For we are pleased . . . and *relieved.*"

The laughter rose again.

Sofia sat with her hands folded tightly in her lap and her eyes straight ahead, staring past the crowd below to a flickering sconce on the south wall, focused, so she would not give away the ache of embarrassment she was feeling.

Queen Eleanor nudged the King in the ribs and whispered, "Enough. You are humiliating her. This is difficult for her. Have some pity for the girl."

The King grumbled something, but heeded his queen and stopped making fun of Sofia and her reputation.

Sofia did not want his pity, or anyone else's. That was

the last thing she ever wanted. Her pride was too wounded, her world crumbling around her so quickly that pitying glances would only make it all the worse. She was afraid to look at Edith, her true friend, afraid of what she would see in her eyes, afraid to look at Eleanor.

"Stand and say something kind about her," Sofia heard Queen Eleanor whisper to the King.

After a moment, Edward stood again and raised his cup. "May our cousin, Sofia," the King nodded toward her and their eyes met for the briefest of moments, enough for them both to acknowledge that he had won this long-standing battle, "be fertile and give de Clare an army of sons!"

A loud cheer went round the room; it seemed to swell on forever. Many men shouted comments about the joy of sons, so no one heard when Sofia swore under her breath, swore the most vicious word she knew. No one heard, that is, except God and Tobin de Clare.

CHAPTER

9

Tobin leaned back and out of the way as a royal servant placed a washbowl studded with sapphires in front of them on the high table. One of his twin squires, Thwack of Camrose, stood nearby, flanking his chair and waiting with a soft towel. From the corner of his eye he could see the lad shifting from one foot to another and could occasionally hear him muttering something to himself; he had yet to learn much about patience.

Another of the King's servants dressed in royal scarlet and gold stepped between Sofia and him, then raised a bronze aquamanile in the shape of a fire-breathing dragon and poured water over her pale hands. He almost laughed at how symbolic the shape of that particular vessel was. When Edward wished them many sons, her resolve slipped and she looked angry enough to spit flames. Instead she had spit a flaming curse.

Tobin had been watching her since then. Once the crowd had quieted, she had quickly regained her control, then made a huge effort to look everywhere but at him. So it did not surprise him when she washed her hands thoroughly, taking her own sweet time with each finger and nail, rubbing the rose petals from the water over her wrists and palms, and never once looking up, acting as if washing her hands were the most important thing in the world. And she well knew he was watching her the whole time.

He leaned closer. She did nothing. He leaned closer still and saw his breath ruffle the small locks of damp black hair near her temple. To her credit she acted numb, which could not have been easy with his mouth a few warm inches from her ear.

So he leaned an inch closer and blew into her ear.

She whipped her head around and faced him, scowling, but not before he caught the sudden shiver that went through her.

Now that he had her undivided attention, he said, "I have to wonder where a lady of noble birth ever learned that particular word."

Her chin went even higher and her eyes grew narrowed and intent. "So you heard."

"My ears are still burning from it."

She shook her head in defiance, raking one hand through the heavy fall of dark hair at her neck. She reminded him of the horses raised and bred by his family, a proud and wild mare that was resisting the rope and the stallion destined to breed with her.

She pretended she did not care, glanced about the room at large, and brushed back some hair that had fallen onto her brow.

He leaned closer. "I asked you a question."

"What question was that?"

"Where you learned such a word."

"Oh." She turned and looked at him then.

From the expression on her face he knew what kind of answer he would get.

"You will be pleased to hear that I learned that word from my cousin, the King. Edward is quite inventive with his verbs. I have learnt all my very best curses from him."

"As king, Edward may say what he wishes." Tobin lowered his voice. "However, had the Archbishop heard what you said you'd be forever damned to hell. He is already not overly fond of females."

"Is any man of the Church?"

He laughed, for she did not know the truth of it. "Some men of God are too fond of women."

She frowned, then started to say something, but he cut her off with a wave of his hand. "That does not matter, here and now. What does matter is that I do not want my betrothed damned to hell."

She sighed with more drama than one of the royal minstrels, then rested her stubborn chin on her fist and stared ahead. "Let me see . . . forever damned to hell or betrothed to you," she paused, tapping a finger against her pursed lips. "What an interesting comparison. I wonder why hell sounds so much more appealing."

He just laughed at her, because if nothing else, he enjoyed the quick bite of her sharp tongue and the overdone gestures that made her anything but meek. She was no sweet maid. No woman to whom love would be a weak and fleeting thing. If Sofia fell in love she would do so with all of her being, for that was how she did everything.

"I would hope you would not teach such words to my sons."

"Fine. I shall teach vile curses only to our worthless daughters." Her sarcasm was not lost on him, but she would not look at him either.

He reached over and gently turned her face toward his. "I would find no daughters of ours worthless, Sofia."

She did not blink. Did not speak, but he could see her thinking and he wondered whether she believed him.

The royal servant stood at his shoulder ready for him to wash. He pulled his hand back and held them both over the jeweled lavabo as the servant poured warm, scented wash water over his hands.

He washed his hands slowly, but unlike Sofia, he never looked away. She could look where she wished, but she would know that now his eyes were for her alone. He wanted her to feel his stare. He wanted her to feel something.

What he truly wanted was for her to feel what he felt whenever she was near. He took in her profile, soaked it up the way one did with a moment made for memory, the small nose she liked to stick up in the air, the firm, square chin and jaw, her large eyes with lashes as long and thick as sable fur, and that mouth, the one that made all the men he knew take one look at her and dream of tasting it, and more. Even he was not immune to that mouth of hers, any more than he was immune to her saucy spirit. "You know what I think?"

"Heaven only knows," she said without a blink.

"I think we should use this water to wash out your mouth."

"Why bother? Your tongue won't be in it again."

God, but she could make him laugh and laugh he did, loudly and genuinely, because he hadn't expected that from her. "Another challenge from you, Sweet Sofia? You still have not paid your last debt. Seems to me it would be foolhardy to acquire new ones."

She faced him then, her eyes a deep and dark purple, and very angry. "Shall I pay that debt here? Now?"

He shrugged.

She leaned over, her mouth just a breath away from his. "Tell me, Tobin de Clare. Tell me. Do you want it now?"

Oh, he wanted it. But she would never know that. He said nothing, just waited to see what she would do, how she would wiggle her way out of this.

But she did no wiggling. Instead, right there in the

Great Hall, before all and sundry, she slid her hands behind his head and pulled his mouth down to hers for a kiss that almost cooked him.

She licked his lips and entered his mouth with her moist tongue, stroked his teeth and played with his tongue, but when he tried to taste her, to take control of the kiss, she pressed her mouth closed as if to prove he could not do anything to her if she did not wish it.

Another challenge.

But he had trained well and knew two could play at any game. He leaned his weight into her, pressed her back against the chair, their mouths still locked together.

"A de Clare!" came the war cry of the de Clare men, cheering him on, and suddenly all around them were the sounds of laughter and bawdy whistles. People were banging on the tabletops and he could hear the King laughing the loudest.

He had her pinned against her chair with his upper body. Her lips were pressed so tightly together that her mouth was hard as stone. He had little choice; he reached between them, hiding his action from the crowd, and slid his hand inside her bodice, then cupped her bare breast.

She gasped and he slid his tongue inside.

He was thinking how sweet victory was, reveling in his success, in the way he could play her the same way the musicians played the lute. She was a cheeky thing, he knew, so quick to battle him at every turn, which made this victory even sweeter because it was harder won. But he knew her well enough to expect her to do something, to retaliate. He expected her to bite him or to pull away.

What he didn't expect was for her to grab him between the legs and squeeze so damned hard that he was the one who winced and pulled back from the kiss, only to find her looking up at him, with deep purple eyes, and victory all over her smug face.

Jesu! She almost squeezed those sons right out of his future. Their future.

He reached under the table and clamped his hand down over her wrist, then jerked it away from him. He did not let go of it, but fixed her with a dark look, then tightened his grip on her wrist and slowly drew her toward him as he leaned down close to her ear and said, "Since you are so eager, perhaps we should consummate things between us this night. We will be betrothed in a matter of moments."

The blood seemed to drain from her face.

"I see no need to wait for a wedding ceremony. You needn't wait any longer. Then, what you just grasped so freely you will find in more places than just your hand."

She glared up at him, mute. There was a small spark of uncertainty in her expression. Or fear.

He did not choose to frighten her—that was her reaction, not his purpose. But there were limits to his patience and she had pushed him too far. She needed to learn that here and now. He liked her pride and spirit, but not when she tried to trample him with it.

The King stood and the room grew still again. The servants had finished filling each and every cup and there were now huge wooden platters piled high with bread placed at every table. Edward took Eleanor's hand and helped her rise to stand beside him.

The music stopped. The minstrel quieted. For just an instant, the only sound in the room was that of the fire crackling.

On Tobin's left sat the Archbishop of Canterbury, who had been speaking with the King, but now he stood, too. The entire room rose on cue.

It was time for the betrothal ceremony.

Tobin cast a quick glance at his father, who was looking at a table below. Probably at some sweet-faced woman who had caught his roving eye again. But his father turned and faced him. He gave his father an unreadable look, one that revealed nothing about what he was thinking.

He moved to his position near his father, still saying nothing, and stood there, shoulder to shoulder, waiting while the Archbishop and King and Queen took their places.

Sofia was but a few feet away, standing with the King and Queen. She was stiff and still, her hands knotted in front of her, her lips tight and her chin up. Her eyes looked out over the room, unseeing, fixed on something on the north wall, but when he followed her gaze he saw nothing. A sconce flickering with oil light. Nothing more.

Her black hair spilled down her back, and when she shifted her weight, it covered the arm and back of the chair she had sat in.

Incredible hair, hair a man could wrap around him when he was inside of her, hair that would keep her where he wanted, on top of him or under him.

All that heavy hair was pulled back from her brow by the thin, golden headpiece—the one he had bought for her and had sent to her room with the Queen's ladies. Did she know it was a gift from him? He did not know, and did not care. All he cared for was that she was wearing it. The band was simple, hammered gold with small pointed teeth to grab even the thickest hair and hold it in place. When he had seen the band at a goldsmith's shop in London, he had thought of Sofia and could think of little else until he had bought it for a pretty sum.

It was enough, that golden band. No jewels threaded through her hair and braids like most ladies of the court. She did not need them. Her beauty was not in decoration. She could wear sackcloth and ashes and still men would want her.

Her beauty was in contrasts. The black of her hair

against the white creaminess of her skin. Her deep violet eyes, their color so vivid, as was the tone of her full, red mouth. Each color was so defined that it made the others appear more vibrant and unforgettable, the way black against white defined the positions on a chessboard.

He wondered what was going through that active mind of hers at this moment. Within a few moments they would be betrothed, an agreement as binding as the wedding itself, if not more so because of the importance of the dower contracts between the King and his own father, one of the most powerful earls in the land.

He would be glad to have this business out of the way; it had damned well been long enough in the making.

He glanced then at the King, who had taken Sofia's hand. Edward was a shrewd man and he knew how to work his vassals so that he gained the most. He wondered what she would think if she knew the truth—if she knew that he had been forced by the King to earn her hand.

Knowing Sofia, she would not think about what he'd had to do for her hand, but instead she would be incensed that she was but a prize to be given to anyone who did the King's bidding.

Lord, but she would make his life miserable if she knew that. With no little cynicism, he revised that thought. She might make him miserable anyway.

"I, Edward, King of England, Wales, Ireland and Scotland, give Lady Sofia Beatrice Rosalynde Anna Theresa Howard. . . ."

Tobin choked, then raised his fist quickly to his mouth and coughed, twice, thrice. He could not bark out a laugh in the middle of this ceremony. All would think him daft. He cleared his throat, then signaled for them to continue, but not before he caught Sofia looking at him strangely. He tried to look serious, but he couldn't help wondering if she knew her middle names spelled out "brat." Sofia BRAT Howard. Someone was a prophet.

". . . daughter of my cousin, Baron Rufus Howard, and a ward of the Crown, in betrothal to Sir Tobin de Clare, son of Gilbert de Clare, earl of Gloucester." The King placed her small and cold hand in Tobin's.

His father spoke next, placing his hand on top of theirs. "I, Gilbert de Clare, earl of Gloucester, give my eldest son, Tobin Gilbert William de Clare, to the King's ward, Lady Sofia Howard, with the understanding that he is to maintain her with the strength of the oak and guard her with the vigilance of the angels."

"In turn," Edward said, "Sofia Howard will abide by him with the virtue of a lady. She will cling to him with the constancy of ivy . . ."

Tobin felt her cringe at that line and glanced down at her. Aye, he thought, Sofia Howard would not cling like ivy to any man.

"She will share fruitfulness with him and stay by his side until death."

The Archbishop blessed them, took the single golden wine goblet, the de Clare betrothal cup, raised it before the room, and blessed it. Next he raised the bread they must share, blessing it in front of all, too, then breaking it into two pieces and handing both to Tobin.

He fed her the piece of torn bread and she almost bit his fingertips. He had to snatch them back quickly. He narrowed his gaze at her as he handed her the other piece of bread, symbolizing that he would be the one to provide for her and their family.

She took the other piece of bread quickly, raising it to his mouth, her eyes daring him to try to nip at her fingers as she had. He could tell she expected to get exactly what she gave. She held the bread there, with a just-try-it look, and he paused, long enough to fluster her. Even though she acted calm he could see the tension in the stiff way she held her shoulders and the slight thinning of her mouth.

He grasped her wrist, holding her hand near his mouth. But he didn't bring the bread to his mouth. He brought the back of her hand to his lips, then, as she blinked at him, he licked her.

If her eyes had been swords, he'd be a skewered dead man.

He couldn't stop his grin and tore into the bread with his teeth, never taking his eyes from her. When he looked at her like this, he wondered how many of these battles the future held. He wondered what the rest of his life would be, with this woman at his side.

The Archbishop handed him the goblet, which Tobin raised to her mouth, his eyes locked on hers as he tilted it so she could drink the wine. He should have drowned her in it, but he would not play her game. Not here. Not now. Even though there was defiance in her eyes as she drank, pure unadulterated defiance, directed at him.

He took the goblet from her mouth, then slowly, deliberately, turned it until he could see the imprint of her mouth on the rim. He raised that part of the cup to his mouth so she could see him drinking from the spot where her lips had been. He took a sip, then licked the rim, watching her eyes narrow at him, then he raised the cup high and drank deeply over and over, until he finished the wine.

His men cheered and yelled as he held the goblet high with a straight arm, like the champion of a tourney holding the winner's pennant. He did not look at Sofia. He did not have to. Instead he turned and faced the room, where all standing raised their cups and drank to them, the betrothed. He had won again.

After the cheers died down, he turned toward Sofia. She looked as if she wanted to hit him with something, so he put the large goblet out of her reach, slid his arm around her shoulders and pulled her against his side, just to annoy her more. With his free hand he refilled the cup from a ewer on the table, then he raised it high again. "To all!" He scanned the room, then shouted, "Drink all to the beauty of *my lady,* Sofia!" He squeezed her shoulder and felt her elbow dig into his ribs. He ignored that small, bony elbow and raised the cup to his lips. She could jab all she wanted but he would drink heartily this day, for he had much to celebrate.

A second later he felt her small heel grind into the top of his foot.

Sofia . . . Sofia . . .

Tobin knew then that he did not need to wonder what the future held, because one thing was certain, his life from this moment forward would never be boring.

Sofia slammed the door to her chamber, then slid the iron bolt. She pressed her back against the door and tried to catch the breath she'd lost from running so swiftly up the steep stone stairs of the tower. It took her a moment, and she closed her eyes and inhaled slow, deep breaths, waiting for her heart to stop pounding. It took a minute to calm down, then she opened her eyes and muttered to herself, "Lud, but I did not think I would *ever* get away."

She exhaled a relieved sigh and shoved away from the door, then crossed the small room with its painted tile floors and gray stone walls. The iron shutters over the narrow window were still open, and next to them, in wall sconces, burned two fat, ivory beeswax candles that cast dim, wavering yellow light over that side of the room. The evening air was not cold, even though the sun had set and it was fast becoming night. The stars were beginning to flicker and the waxing half moon hung in the eastern sky, its corner peeking through the Gloriette window.

Here, near her bed, the air felt warm from a small coal

fire that glowed brightly in the nearby fireplace. She flopped onto her feather-ticked bed with all the grace of a sack of grain. The bed ropes creaked loudly when she landed, but she cared not. She just buried her face in her arms and tried to think.

A futile act. She could not think when her mind was racing over everything that had happened to her this day, reliving it all with numb disbelief. So after a minute or so, she rolled over and flung her arms out from her sides, then stared up at the dark wooden beams on the ceiling as if the answers she needed were engraved there.

But there were no answers. Just huge wooden beams that had been darkened by age and smoke.

"What a fix I'm in!" She lay there, not knowing if she wanted to scream down the walls or cry out for joy.

God-in-heaven-above, she was betrothed to Tobin de Clare. *Betrothed* to him.

But why?

Nothing made sense. Why would Tobin de Clare want to marry her? Arrogant, pigheaded, domineering, over-mighty knight. She flung one arm over her eyes and sighed. Sofia de Clare. She had not thought of such since that night on the garden bench. She wished she had not thought of it now.

But she could not change what she felt inside. When she was with him, the sight of him made her burn with something so strong even her own pigheadedness could not will it away. Even her pride. Even her pain.

Tobin de Clare, who had eyes like heaven and a pro-file that made her think of the marble statues of the avenging angels carved into the cathedral in town. He had treated her so horridly two years before. And she had seen him only in her nightmares until the day before, when their paths had finally crossed again and she had taken advantage of the situation and purposely gave him the wrong direction. One did not ignore such a perfect opportunity for a little vengeance. Those times came so seldom.

In those two years she had thought of him often, usually with some strong tears of anger or humiliation. Over time, she had stopped crying tears over him and over what he had done. But she could never forgive him for making her feel those tears. She prided herself on her strength. Tears were a sign of weakness. She hated to cry. Tobin made her cry, like now, when she realized how very thin her skin was when it came to anything that had to do with him.

She had tried to feel nothing. When word came that he was in the north on some knight's duty, she had prayed that it was a vile one, for even time could not dull the sting of what he had done to her.

He broke her heart.

She had a fierce need to hate him. He deserved nothing but her hatred. However, the longer she lay there, the more she could not hide from the truth. She did not hate him. Well, perhaps she did hate him, but not as much as she loved him, and that was her true dilemma. She loved a man she needed to hate.

There came a loud hammering on her chamber door.

She bolted upright.

"Sofia!"

Tobin's voice. He pounded on the door again.

"Soooo-feeeee-ahhhh!"

That was the loudest whisper she had ever heard. "Go away!"

There was sudden silence. Too much silence. No footsteps retreating, just pure quiet. She watched the door as if she expected him to do something impossible, like walk through it.

She heard a slight thud against it, then it sounded as if he were sliding down the door. She heard something metal, like a chain or belt clink against the tile floor outside.

She waited, then when nothing happened she slowly slid from the bed and placed her feet softly on the floor and walked quietly across the room. She stood in front of the door for a moment, listening.

She heard no sound.

She took two more small and quiet steps and pressed her ear to the oak door, listening for something. The sound of his breath. The shuffle of his boots. A footfall.

There was nothing but utter silence.

She chewed her lip and waited. It seemed like forever. Had he left?

She bent down, then knelt and placed her cheek on the cold tiles so she could see under the door. There was a shadow, a small bit of blue, the color of his tunic. He was sitting on the floor with his back against the door.

A moment later she heard a loud belch.

She sat back on her heels and looked at the door with disgust. He was drunk. She had lost count of the times he had raised his cup to the room to honor some beautiful part of her, as if she were nothing but something to look at, a beauty made of fingers and toes, hands and cheeks, skin and hair. She had never in her life had so much of her person toasted. "Go drink and cavort with your men," she said with disgust. "Leave me be."

"Drink with my men? Why? I have been with my men for months." He paused, then added in a lowered voice, " 'Tis not their company I crave. I want you, sweet. Come, now, open the door. I have wine for us."

As if wine were an enticement. Did he think her a man with nothing better to do than drink and belch and bellow to the world over some woman's skin?

She said nothing.

" 'Twill be just us. You and me, sweet. Come. Let me in."

She could hear the clanking together of pewter cups, as if he were shifting or standing, then there was another short rap on the wooden door. "So-fi-a."

"I will not let you in here. Do you think me that stupid?"

"I promise you will like it if you do."

"I've had the bitter taste of your promises, Tobin de Clare. Now go away!"

"What promise is that?"

Well, now that she thought of it, there had been no promise between them two years ago, only a meeting in the garden, one he never intended to keep, one that was only made to prove he could make a fool of her and amuse the mean spirits of a group of cruel young men, all of her failed suitors.

She heard a slight scratching sound and looked down.

His finger slid under the gap in the door and was wiggling. "Come to me, my Sofia."

She walked over and stood on his finger.

"Ouch! Dammit!" He snatched it back under the door and mumbled something indistinguishable. Then came that same deep voice again. "I shall wait here all night, Sweet Sofia."

"Fine. Do as you wish. Enjoy the cold floor. I am going to bed."

" 'Tis too early for bed . . . alone."

She unfastened the closures on her silk gown, which took her too long. Her fingers were fumbling and clumsy, which made her more frustrated. Finally the gown slid to the floor and she stepped out of it, then hung it on a metal hook near her old clothes chest and the small table with its cushioned stool where she would sit and comb out her hair every morn and night.

She removed the golden headpiece, the one she wanted to rip off her head the moment she found out it had been a gift from him, sent with the wily Poleaxes, those traitorous women who had implied it was from Eleanor when they had dressed her.

She sat down on the stool and grabbed a handful of her hair, then spent the next few tense moments jerking an ivory comb through it and muttering about men and life and love and the unfairness of it all.

It was the dead of night when something woke her. She lay there and listened, then glanced at the door and wondered if he could still be there. She had no idea how much time had passed. One of the two candles had gone out, but the other was too far away for her to see the calibration marks. She lay very still, listening for sounds.

Then she heard it again. A tinny, scraping sound, like iron against stone. Frowning, she turned toward it; the sound was coming from outside.

She threw back the covers and slid her feet into her slippers and crossed the room to the open window. The guards on the castle walls were dark silhouettes moving across the eastern points, torches in hand. In the bailey below there was nothing but black night, no movement, no horses or people that she could see. But her eyes were still becoming accustomed to the darkness.

A second later something flew through the window at her and she jumped backward, thinking it was one of those nasty bats. She waved her hands in front of her face and jumped around for a moment, then realized there was no bat in the room. She rubbed her eyes, then looked again.

There on the floor was a three-pronged metal hook with a rope attached.

My God . . .

The hook suddenly skated across the floor and caught on the stone ledge; the rope went as taut as her nerves.

Sofia moved over to the window. She had to lean outside and hang onto the shutters to see directly below the Gloriette. The rope began to wiggle and pull, then a cloud that had been covering the moon drifted by and misty moonlight shone down on Tobin's upturned face.

"What in the name of God and all the saints are you doing, you drunken fool?"

"Conquering my lady!" He hung there with one arm outstretched, about ten feet off the ground. "Vanquishing the siege! I am in the King's favor, you know. Damsel mine! Did you not hear the toasts to my valor?"

Any moment she expected him to beat his chest like the Irish warriors. "I heard the toasts. But the man I know has no valor or honor."

"Ah, So-fee-ah! I will soon be there to prove you wrong. Then you can squeeze me all night."

"I hate you, Tobin de Clare! Stop this now."

"I cannot. Since you will not let me inside through the door, I am climbing up there to you." He swung out on the rope again, back and forth, and called out, "Oh, fair damsel in yon tower."

"Shhh! Or I shall tower you." She grasped the hook and tried to pull it loose. The thing would not budge, so she used both hands and pressed her foot against the wall for leverage. Still she could not move it. It was embedded securely into the stone of the ledge and with that huge oaf's weight pulling taut on the rope, there was no way she had the strength or the power to loosen it.

She ran to the small table and pulled out the chain belt that held her small eating dagger, then ran back and began to saw on the fibers of the rope. "You had best lower yourself back to the ground or you will break your drunken neck! I am cutting the rope."

"Cutting it?"

She peered over the edge as she sawed away.

He began to move more swiftly, climbing hand over

hand. He had moved a good five feet upward before she had even cut one single thread.

"What are you cutting it with, your sewing clips?" He began to laugh as he hung there.

"A knife," she said through gritted teeth. She dug into the rope and sawed faster. "My dagger!"

"Dagger? The one you use to cut your meat? Ha!" He began to laugh harder, which made her saw furiously.

Sofia glanced down and saw he was only a few feet from the window, scaling the rope all too easily. She sawed faster and faster.

"You can never cut this rope in time. 'Tis oiled and waxed." There was irritating amusement in his voice. "Stand back, my lady, and await your betrothed!" He flung one arm out and dangled there with the rope clutched in one strong arm, his sword arm.

His free hand crawled over the ledge.

She grabbed the dagger and, in frustration, stabbed at his hand, but she missed.

"Jesu!" Tobin's forearm and the top of his head popped up over the rim of the ledge. "Put that puny thing away before you hurt someone with it."

"That's the idea, you fool. Go away!" She slashed at him again, but he reached out and knocked the dagger from her hand with one swipe.

She spun and watched the closest thing she had to a weapon skitter across the floor and slide under her bed.

"Sofia." He grunted and started to pull himself up onto the ledge. "You know you cannot fight me on this. I have won. Accept it and enjoy it." A moment more and the pigheaded oaf would be inside her room.

She glanced at the shutters, leaned out and grabbed the handles, then slammed those iron shutters closed.

"Dammit, Sofia!" The rope went suddenly taut.

She had to use both her feet for leverage against the

wall so she could pull the shutters together tightly enough to slide the iron latch over the bar catch. After she did, she stood there, her breath exerted, her heart beating drumlike in her chest.

"Sofia."

"Go away, Tobin. Climb down, for you will not be coming in here this night! Or any night!" She started to turn away.

"Wait!"

"Why?"

"I cannot climb down." He paused. "My clothes are caught."

She turned back and saw it then, the dark blue strip of his tunic that was wedged between the closed shutters; it was the strip that had the two back closures on it.

He *was* caught, truly caught. In the shutters. Which were locked. And she was not going to unlock them. Ever.

She covered her mouth with one hand and began to laugh.

"Are you laughing?"

"Aye," she said between breaths.

There was a long pause of silence, then came a deep command, "Open the shutters."

"I don't think so."

"Sofia!"

"Pray tell?" She sauntered in a casual circle, waving one hand. "What is wrong, Sir Knight? Are you truly stuck?"

"Open . . . the . . . shutters."

"I thought you knights were supposed to be trained in strategy. Are you not? It seems to me that you should have thought of this possibility before you took siege, oh great warrior." Then she really laughed, bent, placed her palms flat on her knees and howled.

She could hear him swearing over her laughter.

"Was not that the exact same word you said would damn me to eternal hell?"

He repeated it.

"What if the Archbishop heard you? Oh, and please don't teach that word to our daughters, sir. Perhaps our useless sons, but not our daughters."

"I am not jesting with you anymore . . ."

"Who is jesting? I am perfectly serious."

"Open the blasted shutters."

"Farewell, Sir Knight! I shall bid you good night . . . adieu." She yawned loudly.

"Sofia!"

"Ho . . . hum! I'm yawning. All that celebrating just wore me out."

"When I get down from here I shall wear you out."

"Are you threatening me? Your own betrothed? And you, a gallant knight. Wherefore art thy chivalry, sir? Have you not heard of courtly love?"

She heard him mumble something, something that sounded like, "I'll give you courtly love."

"Tell me this," Sofia said. "Was that another threat?"

"Open the shutters."

"I cannot. Besides, there is not time. For you see, I'm off to bed." She turned and danced across the room, humming sweetly because it drowned out his threats and curses and the pounding on the shutters.

He could pound all night.

She drew back the coverlet, kicked off her slippers, and crawled into bed.

After a minute she got up, because of his hissing her name and hammering so loudly even the dead could not sleep through it. At the foot of her bed, she opened the chest and took out her despised sewing box, filled with torturous items like steel pins and sharp needles. For the first time she could ever remember, she was glad to have that sewing box. She rummaged through and pulled out two small balls of silk tapestry yarn, cut some off, then wadded them up and stuck them in her ears.

She cocked her head and listened for a moment. The pounding was muted, not much louder than her own heartbeat.

The perfect solution! Humming, she put the sewing box away and crawled back into her soft and comfy bed. In a matter of moments she was fast asleep with a huge and satisfied smile on her face.

CHAPTER

10

There was an old Spanish proverb that Tobin had heard somewhere; it claimed water was for oxen and wine for kings. 'Twas most fitting when he'd had too much of the King's wine the night before, and now it felt like there was a team of oxen stomping around inside his pounding head.

He sat in the Great Hall, waiting to break fast . . . or to die, whichever came first. His elbows were planted on the table, the heels of his hands pressed against his eye sockets to dull the throbbing pain there.

From the quiet in the room he figured that he was not the only one suffering. They said the King was not coming down. The Archbishop left the night before, teetering in his saddle. His father and most of the men-at-arms were in the same shape as he was, head down, waiting for food and uttering an occasional moan, but mostly, they were blessedly silent.

He was just about asleep, facedown on the table, when his father kicked him hard in the back of the calf. Tobin's head shot up. He winced, then turned and scowled at his father. "What did you that for?"

"Lady Sofia." His father gave a slight nod toward the arched entrance, where she stood, surveying the room with an unreadable look.

Tobin closed his eyes. A mighty effort.

She hummed loudly and out of pitch as she crossed in front of him, a strident sound that was as welcome to his ears as a cat fight.

Custom dictated that he rise as she approached. He tried to, but had to use two hands to push himself up, and then rested one palm down on the table so he wouldn't wobble.

"Good morn!" she said in a tone as bright and intense as the sun, loud as the first bells of Prime. She stood by her heavily carved chair, paused a moment, then grabbed the chair arms and dragged the thing back across the floor tiles; it scraped and scratched and made a horrific sound like a knife on a dry whetstone.

Sharp pain shot through the top of his wine-abused head, rang clear through his teeth, and landed squarely in the backs of his eyes, a twanging, piercing pain that felt as if a broadsword had struck him there. He gritted his teeth, his jaw so tight it went numb, but a groan escaped anyway.

Tobin shielded his eyes, head down.

She plopped into the chair with so much vigor that it scraped again, then she grasped the seat and began to hop forward, still sitting in the chair so its legs clattered and clopped on the floor.

Jesu! He drew back, flinching, then seized the chair, and lifted it straight upward with her in it. He placed the chair softly, ever so softly, before the table.

"Why, thank you, sir." Her voice was all honey. Then she waved a hand in a careless motion and knocked over her pewter goblet; it landed against the rim of a silver platter, and sounded like the hammering of a smithy. She fumbled with it three more times and finally he leaned over and grabbed the thing, turned it upside down, and gently set it down on the table.

Tobin sank lower into his chair, unseeing, but not unfeeling. He felt something all right. Pain.

A servant righted Sofia's goblet and filled it, then moved to Tobin's cup. He slammed his hand over it, shook his head slightly, then moaned under his breath.

She turned to him, fighting a slight smirk. "What? No wine this day, Sir Tobin?"

He grumbled something useless about not being thirsty in a low tone that about killed his ears.

"I am thirsty." She drank some of the wine, then turned and leaned forward. Right into his face, she said, "I am about to die of thirst. See how very much I drank?" She jammed the goblet beneath his nose.

The hair of the dog bit him.

Hard.

His belly lurched. He shoved the wine from his face and turned away, just as a servant placed a platter of pickled eels before him.

His belly tumbled and turned like an acrobat.

"Pickled eels, sir?" Sofia asked all too sweetly. "This batch has been aged . . . months I believe. Smell them." She motioned for the servant to lift the platter. "They are a special delicacy that I ordered *just* for you."

He stood so quickly that his chair flew backward. Its back banged hard against the floor. He heard his men groan in unison. But he couldn't see them, because he saw nothing, only a green blur as he slapped a hand over his mouth and made for the door.

"Did you know, Edith, that the word *bride* comes from an old word used for *cook*." Sofia sat under the huge old apple tree, her back against the trunk and her knees clasped in her threaded hands. She stared dismally at an abandoned bird's nest. "Cook!" She made a snorting sound. "Disgusting, is it not?

"I do not think it disgusting at all."

"That is because you *want* to be wed. I do not."

"I think that day at the Miracle Plays you would have

wanted to be wed to Sir Tobin. You just did not know who he was."

"Perhaps. But that was before I knew his true and vile nature."

"He made a stupid mistake. That bet was cruel. But you have made mistakes, too. Think of how you treated Lord Geoffrey and that Spanish prince. You were not kind, Sofie. Can you not forgive Sir Tobin?"

"He hasn't the wit to ask for forgiveness," Sofia shot back, quickly angered because the oaf had not even tried to apologize. "Why would I want to marry someone who is so cocksure, obnoxious, *and* a drunk?"

"He is not a drunk and you know it."

"You should have seen him hanging from the tower last night."

"He was celebrating your betrothal and drank too much wine." Edith paused and her eyes grew distant and dreamy. "I would love it if a man risked life and limb to climb a tower just for me. How perfectly romantic."

Sofia gave a dry laugh. "Romance had little to do with his motives. I am certain it was not me he was thinking of when he climbed that tower, but himself and what he alone wanted. In fact, I would wager he was not even using his head, but thinking with something else altogether."

"Well, that certainly makes no sense. Why would he climb a tower if there was no one there? Of course he was doing so for you. And what else can one think with? We only have our head with which to think."

Sofia just shook her head and drew a circle in the dirt beneath the tree. "It does not matter."

Edith looked up. "Did you ever find out how he finally got down?"

"According to the castle guard who was watching him, he worked his arms from his tunic, I guess it took a while, and then he shimmied down the rope. When I awoke, the tunic was still caught in the shutters. I dared not open them, just in case he was still there. But after I dressed, I went belowstairs and checked from the outside." Sofia grinned. "The tunic was dangling there; it looked like a blue and white flag of surrender."

She crossed her arms in a pleased way and grinned with wicked glee. " 'Twas certainly one of my better moments, slamming those shutters. That, along with telling the kitchen that Sir Tobin demanded those eels this morn to break his fast."

"You know something?" Edith shook her head. "I do not believe I have ever seen someone truly turn green before. The man's skin was the color of a cabbage."

"Aye."

"I feel rather sorry for Sir Tobin."

"Sorry for him? After what he did to me? You are supposed to be my friend."

"That's why I feel sorry for him. You will keep making him pay for his mistakes."

"Then perhaps he should work harder at not being such an idiot so he does not have so much to pay for."

Edith turned and looked at her for a long time. "You really are in love with him, aren't you?"

Sofia did not answer readily, but closed her eyes. "I do not want to be."

"But you are."

Sofia turned to her friend. "I don't understand him." Her voice had turned quiet, serious.

"What do you not understand?"

She stared down at her clasped hands. "Why he does the things he does."

"He is a proud young man, always has been, perhaps too proud. I have heard stories that he had trouble when he was fostered. My brother says 'twas Earl Merrick who turned him 'round." Edith paused and then added,

"He is much like you, I think, in that he likes things done his way. He is stubborn and full of pride."

"Is that what you think of me? Stubborn and full of pride?"

"Sofie, you are like the sister I never had. I love you. But you have to admit that you are some-times . . . strong-minded."

"Aye. I am proud if it, too. I will never simper. I like having a mind of my own."

"I know you do. And sometimes I wish I could do what you do. I wish I could be like you. But I cannot. I do simper."

"You do not. You are not weak, Edith. Your nature is sweet and kind and gentle and everyone loves you."

"Aye, but I can disappear in a room. You never do, Sofie. Everyone always knows when you come into a room."

"Does Sir Tobin? I am not certain."

"His eyes are always on you. 'Tis just you are so busy trying to look elsewhere that you do not see it."

"I still do not understand why he acts as he does."

"Mostly he is reacting to what you do. You are not easy, Sofie. You know that. You make people work to be close to you, as if they have to prove to you that they truly care. That they are worthy. Look at what you do to the King."

Sofia scowled at her, not liking the way that sounded. "Aren't you the perceptive one today."

"I am your friend. I am just telling you the truth. Would you rather I lie?"

"Like you did about the betrothal feast?"

"I did not lie." Edith chewed her lip. "Not exactly. The Queen made me swear not to tell you anything."

"Even if you had told me, I am not sure it would have mattered." Sofia stood and dusted off her gown and hands. "Which is why I have forgiven you."

There was a moment of thoughtful silence. Sofia grasped a low branch and stood there looking about her and seeing nothing but the questions she still had. She sighed. She would probably never know what his motives for marrying her were.

"What was that huge sigh for?"

"Because I still cannot understand this betrothal. Why me?" She looked at her friend. "Why does he want to marry me?"

"Sofia, almost every young knight in the land has wanted to marry you at one time or another. You have to ask why? You are so beautiful. Look at yourself!"

Look at herself? Look at the outside. Could not one person look to see what was inside? Sofia hung there, her hands grasping that tree branch and her arms stretched taut as she stared at the ground for the longest time. For just a moment she thought she might cry. She could feel the tears rise into her throat and her eyes.

"There is the bell for None. I must meet the Poleaxes."

Sofia groaned. "I am so sorry."

"Oh. Don't be. They are going to teach me all those things I need to know to run my husband's castle. Today I shall learn to card wool."

Sofia wondered if Edith's betrothed would ever return to marry her. But she did not say anything, because she knew it bothered Edith, too, even though she tried to hide it.

Edith turned to leave. She took a few steps and swept back the low branches of the tree, but stopped and turned back to Sofia. "If you want to know why Sir Tobin is marrying you, then why not just ask him?"

CHAPTER

11

The last thing Tobin expected was a message from Sofia. He thought she would go out of her way to avoid him, figuring she had exhausted herself and inflicted enough pain for one day.

Instead she sent a servant with a message to one of his squires, Thud, who came directly from the stables where he had been tending Tobin's favorite mount.

Tobin listened silently, then glanced up from polishing his sword. "She requests that I meet her in the chapel?" He kept polishing.

"Aye, sir."

"When?"

"Before Compline."

"Odd . . ." he murmured, rubbing a cloth over the steel of the blade. He tossed the cloth onto his shoulder, then rubbed a hand pensively over the rough stubble on his chin, wondering what she was about now.

He said nothing, but held up his sword; it caught light from the window and shone bright enough to blind any opponent he faced, with the possible exception of his betrothed. He took his time and checked the blade, running his thumb down the edge while he tried to convolute his mind into thinking like she did.

He gave up and stood, then jammed his sword into its

scabbard. "Tell the Lady Sofia I will meet her now, not at Compline, and not in the chapel, but in the court below the Gloriette tower."

Thud stared at him as if he were mad.

"What is it? Have I grown a second head?"

His squire mumbled something.

"Speak up, lad. I cannot understand you."

"Should you not meet her as she has asked? Lady Clio says a chivalrous knight does his lady's bidding with a free and happy heart."

Tobin laughed in a dry tone. "And Earl Merrick does so with Lady Clio? He follows her everywhere like a lovesick swain, ready to do her every whim? I have seen that is not the case, as have you. Remember what things were like when Merrick first came to Camrose?"

Thud winced. "Aye. 'Twas not a quiet time."

"Understand this." Tobin stood and faced Thud. "Women are as different from each other as are weapons of war. There are maces, picks, swords, axes, lances and crossbows. Merrick's Lady Clio is more of a sword. You can clearly see her coming at you. But my Lady Sofia is more dangerous. You have to watch your back with her. She is like a crossbow fired at you from high in a tree. You never see what's coming until it is too late. Then you are standing there pierced clear through."

Tobin crossed the room to the lavabo and washed the oil from his hands. "The trouble is," he continued, "we men need women as much as we need our weapons, as much as we need our mounts and our armor. But the singular truth is, you are better off to love your sword, your armor *and* your horse before you ever give your heart over to a woman."

He dried his hands and turned back around. "As for my lady, were I to be chivalrous, she would make my life a misery. Just go now, and do as I bid."

Tobin tossed the towel aside and by the time he had turned about, his squire had left.

"In the courtyard?" Sofia whirled around and stared at Tobin's squire. "Now?"

The squire stood in the doorway nervously shifting from one big foot to the other and watching her warily as if he expected her to suddenly draw a weapon and smite him right there.

She paced the room. This was not part of her plan. Why was he doing this? She stopped and crossed her arms over her chest and tapped a foot impatiently. Now what?

She raised her chin and turned. "Tell your master that I cannot come now. I am far too busy." She waved a hand in the air. "Tell him I shall be finished in a while, say two hours. We will meet then. At the well near the eastern wall."

"Aye, my lady." The lad made a slight bow and left.

Sofia plopped down in a chair and rested her chin on one fist. Two full hours. What in the name of heaven above was she going to do for two whole hours?

"The stable after Sext? He actually thinks I will meet him in the stable?" Sofia leaned back in her chair near the glass-paned windows of the solar and stared at the squire.

The Poleaxes had gone down to the storerooms to fetch a basket of freshly shorn and washed wool. Edith was sitting nearby concentrating on carding a clump of knotted fleece with a flat pair of bristled wool carders. Sofia sat in a wide chair, a long thread of yarn swirled in a pile near her red leather slippers and a hand spindle rolled easily between her palms.

The lad swiped a forelock of damp hair from his eyes and stood with his shoulders back, his hands somewhere behind him and his big feet together. "Aye, my lady. He must attend his horse, which became lame and needs care and supervision. He begs . . . nay . . . uh . . . rather, he asks, nay, that is not right either," he mumbled looking down.

The lad stood there, muttering and shaking his head as he searched for his word. Finally he looked up. "Sir Tobin says that you may meet him there."

"Oh, he does, does he?"

"Aye."

"Well I, too, have plans and duties."

"Sofie," Edith warned in a half-whisper.

Sofia whispered back, "I know what I am doing." She turned and faced the boy, whose flat woolen cap was askew and the bright colored pheasant feather decorating its side drooped lower every time he brought a new message. "Tell Sir Tobin I cannot meet him at Sext. I will be busy then. You may tell him I shall be waiting for him before None, say an hour before. We will meet at," she paused, then turned around and chewed on her lip for a moment's thought, while Edith was waving her hands at her in protest. Sofia ignored her and turned back. "We will meet at the entrance to the herb garden near the kitchens."

The lad hung his head a little and his shoulders drooped. "Aye, my lady," he said on a sigh. "I shall tell him." He turned slowly, then shuffled out of the room.

"You are playing with fire. Just go meet him wherever he wants."

"I shall not. He is being stubborn."

"And you are not?"

She waved her hand in the air. "That does not matter. Everyone well knows I am stubborn. Besides which, it was my idea to meet in the first place. I should be the one to dictate where and when." But she set aside the spindle and stood, then stepped over the pile of spun

wool. She crossed the few steps to the window, braced
her hands on the ledge and waited until the squire came
out of the tower entrance. She watched him run across
the bailey and head for the stables, the feather in his cap
bobbing as he ran.

"The stables at Sext," she muttered. "Humph! What
does he think I am . . . a dairy maid?"

"The west wall before Sext?" Tobin shook his head
and stared at his horse's hoof. He took a hoof pick off
the wall and began to clean the area until he could see
that there was no stone there, nothing that would make
his mount lame.

He stood and ran a hand up the horse's leg, over the
fetlock and up along the tendons, checking for swelling
or tightness. There was none.

He straightened. "Outside the smithy's hut, an hour
after Sext."

"But, sir—"

"Just give her the message." Then Tobin turned and
strode from the stall.

Before long, the whole castle knew what was going
on. Some had come out into the bailey to pass Thud, the
poor bedraggled squire, a bit of cheese or a tankard of
ale as he traversed back and forth, up the tower stairs
and down again, then around the castle more times than
most could count.

By nightfall, Squire Thud had collapsed from over-
exertion and was lying facedown in the middle of the
bailey, his tunic sodden with sweat and the feather in his
cap broken and floppy. He was carried to a bedchamber
by some of Sir Tobin's men and given a cool bath and a
fine meal of the King's rich Bordeaux wine and fat, succulent beef pasties.

'Twas not long afterward that King Edward summoned Sir Tobin to the mews, where the King's falcons and hawks were kept fat and happy. At the same time Queen Eleanor requested Lady Sofia's presence in those same mews.

Edward and Eleanor stood at the entrance, waiting when Sir Tobin came in the west side, and Lady Sofia from the east.

They both stopped at the arched entrance, then looked to the King and Queen.

Edward pinned each with a black look and said, "You two are meeting here in the Mews at . . ." He paused and the bell sounded for Vespers. "Ah, there it is. . . . Vespers."

He turned to Eleanor. "Shall we go my dear, and leave the lovebirds to their cooing?"

"Aye, sire," Eleanor said with a smile, taking the King's arm. "Perhaps we should have used the dovecote instead. More cooing and all."

"Do you think so? Hmmm. I do believe this is best. Here they can peck at each other all they want." Edward raised his long arm into the air and made a fist, as he did whenever there was a battle to be fought. Then he shouted for all to hear, "Let the feathers fly!" And the King and Queen walked out the door.

CHAPTER

12

For Tobin, this moment was like facing the enemy on a battlefield. There was the same tension in the air. She stood across from him, unmoving. Her jaw looked as tight as his felt.

The only sounds around them were the ruffling and scratching noises from the cages of the hawks and falcons. A few feathers floated out from a nearby cage and drifted to the dirt floor. There was the shrill, guttural sound of a raven, the piercing shriek of a hawk. But no human sound.

The air grew thick and heavy the way it did when it was ready to rain or snow. She looked frozen, her hand resting against the stone of the entrance, her features stony and sharply defined, like a marble statue. Her only motion was the subtle rise and fall of her chest with every breath she took.

It had been a long day of battles with her, this woman he had chosen to be his wife, the one whose hand he had to earn through service to the King. But when he looked at her like this, somehow those frozen nights in the north, when the rain and snow and ice pounded down on them, when there had been little food, all of it now seemed long ago and well worth the price.

She was a beauty. Incredible on a man's eyes and hell

on his mind and body. Whenever he looked at her, which he was usually compelled to do by some strange need inside of him, he understood why every young nobleman he knew had wanted her to wive. He understood their frustration when she would have nothing to do with them. He understood their desperate need to claim her for their own and their anger and their need to avenge their broken pride when they failed.

But after two long years of Edward's whims, he had succeeded where they had not. She was his. The betrothal was set, signed, and blessed by the Church, and nothing short of death could now break that pact between the King and his father. 'Twould never happen.

She stood there trying so hard to look at ease, but she was not. She tried to look indignant and poorly used. He almost laughed because he was not certain who was using whom today. Finally he decided he had given her enough trouble for one day, so he relented and spoke first. "You wanted to see me."

She did not speak, but stood there, not looking angry or petulant, but a little lost, as if she had just awoke and did not know where she was. This facet of her, this vulnerable side he had not seen before, made him back down.

He closed the distance between them slowly, approaching her the way he approached the wildest of the de Clare horses. He spoke softly, not threateningly. Just said her name on a breath, again and again.

She turned and stared up at him from those wild purple eyes, her lips soft and moist and waiting for him. He wanted nothing more at that moment than to close his arms about her and kiss her until they both needed more than only the touching of their mouths and the foreplay of their tongues.

He reached out with one finger and traced her jaw softly, up to the line of her dark hair, near her shell of an ear, where there were thin and curly pieces of black hair that sprang and coiled around his fingertip when he brushed against them.

He bent his head, moving his mouth toward hers. God, but he wanted her. When his lips were almost touching hers she blinked, as if she were just now seeing him there before her eyes.

She shoved him back. "Do not!"

Her voice was shrill, almost as if she were frightened. But Sofia Howard was not someone he thought was easily frightened, so he ignored that.

She seemed to quickly compose herself. "We must talk." Her voice was even now, calmer.

He gave a sharp laugh. "If we are to talk, then both of us need to speak. I do not know why you summoned me."

She mumbled something under her breath.

"Sofia. I cannot hear you. Look at me."

She did, then her eyes narrowed as if she blamed him because she could not find the words she wanted. "I wanted to ask you a question."

"What?"

She drew her shoulders up and raised her chin as high as a queen. "Why did you ask to wed me?"

So that was what this was about. He wondered what she would do if he told her the truth: that he wanted her because she was a rare beauty, because all the other men he knew wanted her, because she was a challenge and he liked challenges, and for some reason he could not explain, he decided the first time he ever saw her that she would be his.

If he lied and gave her a vow of undying love, if he played the besotted swain, she would use that vow against him and never give him any peace. 'Twould be a weakness exposed. She was not the kind of opponent to whom a smart warrior gave any ground.

Pride was an issue here, as it always was between

them. She already had an overblown sense of herself. He would not add to that. He leaned back against a tall column, crossed his arms and just watched her.

She waited for his answer, while he tried to find the right one.

"I am waiting."

"I can see that."

"Are you cooking up some lie? Is that why you hesitate?"

"Nay. I will tell you. You have plenty of land and wealth, Sofia. Thanks to all your antics during the past few years, the King is desperate to see you wed."

She stood there without a single expression on her face.

"The way I see it, if I don't wed you, no one will."

She sucked in a deep breath; it made a sharp and long hissing sound.

"You have to admit that you have chased away every suitor possible. I am about all that is left. I figure if I do not make the sacrifice, then—"

"*Sacrifice?*" Her face turned pale, then her face and neck began to redden.

"You know what I mean. Someone has to do it, otherwise Edward will be hell to live with. Every time you rejected a suitor, Edward levied scutage on his vassals so he could add more gold to your dowry. The truth of it is, none of us could afford it much longer.

"And besides, why wouldn't I want you? I can put up with almost anything for your rich dower price, even a spoiled woman with too much time on her hands to do much more than make mischief."

She was bright red and barely breathing.

"Such mischief as those pig bladders filled with water or the toads in my bed." He shoved away from the column and held up a hand. "And before you say anything, I know you paid the stable boy to put the toads there."

She looked angry enough to spit toads.

For one moment he wondered if in his need to deflect her rebellion, to take her down a peg, he had gone too far.

"Are you finished?" Her words were clipped. Her shoulders were stiff, and her hands were clasped tightly in front of her, the knuckles red and bloodless.

"I believe that about covers my reasons."

"Fine." She turned and walked away from him. Her head high and her steps measured and even. He watched her go, watched the control with which she made her way across the bailey and into the archway where there was a door that led up to the tower stairs and her chamber high above.

For just a moment, that one moment when his memory was fresh with her controlled and quiet manner, as the moon crept over the eastern wall, a sickle moon in the same shape as the tool the villeins used to cut live stalks of wheat from the ground, he wondered if he had just made a mistake.

She had made a mistake. She had allowed herself to believe that someone could love her. Walking away from him with her head high and her eyes dry was one the hardest things she had ever done.

A fool! A fool! That was what her mind cried out as she took each step.

Her lips began to quiver and she pressed them tightly together. Moisture rose in her eyes and burned in the backs of them. She blinked away the tears and took the stairs slowly, one at a time, until she was finally inside her chamber where the candles had not yet been lit and the room was dark in all its corners. Light from outside made a slight shadow on the floor as she turned and slid the door latch closed.

A moment later she threw herself on her bed, buried

her face on her arms and cried. He did not want her. He wanted a placid monarch and her dowry price.

She sobbed so hard that her breath caught in her chest. She cried for all she never had. She cried for what she had lost. She cried for ever believing that she could have something good and sweet, like love. She cried because she had nothing left inside of her but a thousand tears.

It took a long, long time before she could sit up. By then the moon was just a glowing sliver in the black night sky. She looked down, ashamed, because she knew the truth then: she was not good enough for anyone to love. Her father could not love her. Tobin could not love her.

All those suitors only wanted her because of what she looked like, she knew that. Every one of them failed the test; they could not prove to her that what they wanted was something more than only a beauty to wear on their arm the way warriors wore their swords. She was a possession. A decoration.

She had foolishly forgotten the one single lesson she learned early in her life, the one taught her first by her father.

In her desperate need and desire to have Tobin de Clare love her, she had forgotten that she cannot allow herself to need anything, particularly the things she could not have.

She did not have a father and mother; she could not need them. She did not have love; she could not need love.

She had been abandoned young, learned the lesson then that she needed to control everything. But she had forgotten that. She had forgotten why she distanced herself from those who claimed they would help her. The truth was, there was no one she could trust but herself.

She began to sob again, crying for all those foolish and wasted moments when she dreamed that her life could be different. She could not hope or believe in someone other than herself. She could not, because they would only let her down.

She walked to the table, lit the nearby candle, and took it from the iron holder above the table. Sitting on the table top was a polished metal looking glass, the one she used to check her hair in the morn. She leaned over and looked into it, saw the tears dripping down her face, the swollen lips and red eyes and the blotchy skin that all came from her tears, tears she should never have shed.

She swiped them away and looked at her face, the face they all claimed was so beautiful. The face that was the reason people looked at her.

She stared long and hard in the looking glass, then she threw it across the room. It slammed into the stone wall with a loud clanking sound.

Beauty was a worthless thing. It never got her a mother. It never kept her father at her side. It did not make him love her or value her. Beauty never gave her anything but trouble.

She stood and crossed the room, bent down, and picked up the metal looking glass, then she went to the chest near her bed and took out her sewing kit. She pulled the small scissors from inside, the ones shaped like a swan, and she went back to the table and propped the mirror against the stones of the wall.

For a long time she stared at herself. Then she took the scissors and the small dagger from her belt. She stared at them, wondering which one would do the most damage. She picked up the dagger and raised it to her face.

She looked in the glass, the dagger clutched in her fist. Tears came from her eyes and blurred the image before her. She grasped a handful of hair and she sliced it off. Then she grabbed another; and cut it. And another. Her long black hair fell to the floor in heaps, one section after another.

When she was done, she lay down the dagger and used the clips to cut off more hair, until it stuck out from her head in clumps that looked like the spikes on the side of the western wall.

She stood then and took a leather bag from a hook nearby, and she stuffed all the long black hair into it, then tied the strings into a tight knot. She lay down on the bed and curled into a tight ball, her hands clasping her arms so she was hugging herself. Her eyes were tired and burned from all those tears. She closed them and a moment later she was asleep.

It was well after Sext the next day when Parcin, the captain of Tobin's men-at-arms, came to find him in the stables, where his mount was chewing on hay and had showed no signs of lameness.

"Sir?"

Tobin turned. "Aye?"

His man was holding a brown leather satchel. "I was told this was yours."

"Mine?" Tobin frowned. "Where did you get it?"

"Early this morn, as we were riding out to hunt, a lad came up to me near the gates and told me you had purchased this. He asked if I would deliver it to you."

Tobin had not purchased anything. He took the sack and tested its weight, seeing if it was a trick. He knew of a man who was given a satchel, told it was a gift and there was an adder inside. This did not feel like a snake. It was not bulky. He dropped it on the ground, knelt and untied the strings. He looked inside and saw nothing but black.

Frowning, he turned the sack upside down.

Yards of gleaming black hair, Sofia's black hair, fell into a tangled lump on the yellow straw below.

He stared at it, shocked into silence, then he straightened and swore viciously. A second later he turned and slammed his fist against the wooden wall.

His man flinched.

Tobin spun back around. "What lad? Where?"

"I do not know who he was, sir. He wore a broad-brimmed red hat, like the crofters. His face was filthy and black. He wore a woolen tunic, brown and rough, and braies."

"Where did she go?"

"I do not know. I did not—" He paused. "She?"

"Aye, the lad was my betrothed."

Parcin looked like he wanted to be ill. "I did not know it was her. I . . . I . . ."

Tobin raised his hand. " 'Tis not your fault. But think. What else did you see?"

"I did not see her after she ran out the gatehouse."

Tobin was quiet.

"He, I mean, she left the castle about the same time as the supply wagons."

Tobin shook his head. It was late in the afternoon and she had a full day's start on him. He left the stable muttering about women and hair and stubbornness and fools. His long legs ate up the ground and his hands were in fists as he walked toward the King's rooms to tell Edward what she had done now.

Off in the distance, near Canterbury and a few miles away from Leeds, a young, dark-haired lad in a red hat and rough woolen clothes, his face smudged dark and dirty with candle ash, caught a ride toward London with a small caravan of entertainers.

CHAPTER
13

For Sofia, the next days were truly a lark. She rode with
a small troupe of performers led by a kind young man
who had hair the same color as the copper pennies his
acts earned. He was a juggler and a jongleur, named
Alan of Wisbury, and he could make the crowds laugh
and cry and charm them with his friendly blue eyes and
freckled cheeks. With him was his wife's father,
Bernard, a massive man who was a rope walker and acrobat and who had a huge dancing bear, named Satan.

There was Miranda, Alan's wife and Bernard's daughter, who told fortunes and could also walk the rope no
matter how high it was strung, and their six year-old
twin daughters, Maude and Matilda. The twins liked to
tumble and do somersaults through the air from their father's and grandfather's big arms.

None of them knew Sofia was not the lad she pretended
to be. To them, she was an orphan—which was the truth; a
wanderer, which was the truth; and teller of fanciful
tales . . . well, Sofia figured she had always lied well.

Life in the King's castles had taught her much about
men, because there were so many of them around for her
to observe. She learnt early that men swaggered and spit.
They boasted over even the smallest of incidences and
made jests about privies and garderobes. She had heard

the grooms tell stories about spying on the maids bathing in the river or watching the stablemaster in the hayrick with the cook. Basically, impersonating a man meant being about as arrogant and uncouth as possible.

'Twas not so difficult to mimic, now, when she needed a new identity. One night she managed to quaff a whole tankard of ale with the best of them and belch on the spot, six times in a row, while she sang a bawdy song. She won the first chunk of hot bread. She could even fart if need be, but she had to eat stringy mutton and turnips to do so, which was not too difficult, since that was what they ate almost every night.

The small troupe had moved through the countryside and on to London, but they could not cross the bridge, because the week before four of the arches had given way, worn by time, lack of maintenance, and from the harsh ice from the winter before. Alan had paid their passage tolls with new ha'pennies that her cousin Edward had minted in lieu of the old coins, which were supposed to be cut in halves and quarters. But over the years when his father, King Henry, had reigned, the old coins had been cut, then clipped and shaved and clipped again until their coinage value was half the weight of what it should have been. Sofia had not seen the new coins until Alan had pulled one from his purse and shown her before he paid the tolls.

Quarrymen poled them across the Thames to dark sections of the warrened city, part of London that Sofia had never seen before. There were narrow alleys where it seemed as if no one ever slept. On the houses and taverns there were still thatched roofs that could catch fire and spread with little more than a light breeze. Two buildings had burned down before her very eyes. The streets were a place where dogs moved along with the people, children hawked goods and where you could get your throat cut as easily as you could get your purse snatched.

But for Sofia, sheltered as she had been, it was all a
new adventure and she saw not the danger, only another,
fascinatingly wicked side of living she had never seen
before.

To her delight, Alan had taught her to juggle the first
night she joined them, and she was mastering the task
rather splendidly, at least she thought so, since she could
do it without her tongue sticking out of her mouth.

So she stood on the street corner in the dark side of
the city, before a small crowd, tossing three red wooden
balls in the air as she balanced on a small log.

"Hie, there, Ned!" Alan shouted her lad's name,
cheering her on as he passed his broad-brimmed hat,
gathering coins from the small crowd gathered around
her. She had told Alan and the others that her name was
Edward, a lie that gave her no little amusement, since
she was certain that the King, and her namesake, had
most certainly ordered her found.

She was cavorting rather well. The bells on her shoes
were tingling and her confidence was high enough that
she was just about ready to add the fourth ball.

Then something hit her. Hard. Slammed right into her
legs. She flew sideways, and sprawled facedown on the
cobbled street. She caught her lost breath and inhaled
mud and stink and whatever else was beneath her face
and nose.

Through a daze of stunned pain, she heard laughter
from the small crowd and a curious snorting sound.

Someone was nudging her ear.

She shook her head and pebbles flew every which
way. She spit once, then looked up.

She was staring at a pig, nose to snout; it snorted in
her face, then pressed its cold, damp snout to her muddy
cheek as if it were giving her a kiss. The crowd laughed
even harder.

"Get away from me, you fat swine!" She batted at the

air in front of the pig and pushed herself upright, while the crowd kept on laughing loud and heartily. They began to toss more pennies into Alan's hat than they had with her fine juggling act, a fact that aggravated her to no end.

She was bruised and aching, but her pride was hurt more than her body. She really had wanted to add that fourth ball. She turned, scowling, and watched as the pig trotted innocently down the street where a whole heard of swine milled and poked and grunted along, getting under carts and knocking people sideways.

Alan walked over and held out a hand. "I should have warned you about the wild pigs. A country lad, like yourself, would not know how they plague the streets of London. Damn things are 'round every corner."

She stood, scowling at the pigs and then at her filthy clothes. "I truly wanted to try that fourth ball."

Alan laughed and clamped an arm around her shoulder, then gave it a squeeze. "Stop sulking. We leave tonight for Hereford. You can try your fourth ball there, me muddy lad." Then Alan moved toward the others and began to tell his latest tale.

Sofia swiped at the back of her tunic with a bare hand. She was covered in mud. She gave up and shuffled along, picking up her wooden balls and tucking them into a sack slung on her back, then she made her way along the street to where the wagons were waiting and a crowd of children were gathered around the bear cage, poking and prodding and trying to make him growl.

Satan, a silly name for the dancing bear, who happened to be the most placid animal Sofia had ever seen, made the King's sleeping dogs look ferocious. He would not growl, and most times, would not dance either. Bernard had stolen him when he was only a cub and his mother was killed in a bear baiting ring. But Satan was as much a part of the troupe as were the others.

They left London later that very same night, traveling in a long wagon shaped like a sausage, with wide doors and small curtained windows. Bernard drove a wagon with a tent made of canvas and pulled Satan's wheeled cage along behind him while the bear slept. The long wagon rocked and rolled along the hills and roads outside of London, and Sofia slept easily inside as they headed northeast and far, far away from all that she had left behind.

At Leeds, all hell had broken loose. King Edward was so angry he wanted to put a price on Sofia's head. He claimed that would have most of the country looking for her before she got herself killed. He liked that idea because then she would be back in days, he said, and he could kill her himself.

But the Queen would not allow him to put a price on her and made him see that to do so would truly jeopardize Sofia's safety.

Tobin convinced him that since the betrothal was final, she was now his responsibility. His alone. He swore on his sword that he would find her and bring her home.

But Edward and Eleanor were leaving soon for Camrose Castle, in the Welsh Marches, where they were to attend to the christening of Earl Merrick's newest son and Edward's godchild. This was a welcome relief to Tobin, for he preferred to look for Sofia himself, with only his men and not the added complication of having the King's men along, too. Tobin was certain that only because of the King's trip had Edward agreed to let him do all the searching for Sofia.

And search he did.

Tobin and his men had been looking for her for nigh on half a week. They had scoured the countryside around Leeds. His men had questioned all who passed by and one small clue had sent them off toward Canterbury on a wild goose chase.

Day moved into night, and night into day, and still there was nothing. No sign. No word. No clue. It was as if she had disappeared in a puff of smoke. They were off toward London, where he knew anyone could hide and not be found for years.

It was late afternoon when the skies had darkened, almost nightfall when it began to pour. Pounding and unrelenting rain turned the road sloggy and slowed their progress. He and his men were soaked to the bone when they came over a rise outside Rochester. Tobin knew he had to finally let his men rest. They stopped at an inn, but he did not sleep, could not sleep. He lay there thinking of all the things that could happen to Sofia. She was such a fool, so young and naive. For all her pluck and sauciness, she was still young and ripe for someone, almost anyone, to harm.

He turned onto his side and punched the lumpy mattress a few times to try to get more comfortable.

But he could not.

The truth was, he did not want to be here in this bed. He wanted to find her. He wanted to be on his mount and combing the countryside. He wanted a sign from God or from somewhere so he knew she was alive and safe and just causing trouble, not in trouble.

He closed his eyes and inhaled a deep breath through his nose, then he exhaled slowly. It was a technique he used before battle, something to calm him down. His emotions ran deep and had always caused him the most problems. But he did not know how to change that. He felt what he felt.

Earl Merrick always told him that his pride and his temper were the things that would get him into trouble. He had to learn to control what Merrick said were his youthful emotions.

Tobin hated it when Merrick was right.

So he lay there feeling helpless and angry and scared.

He had not worried this much since the time Sir Roger de Clare had disappeared almost from under his very nose. And he did not particularly like Roger. As it turned out, Roger *had* been harmed. He was hanged in the forest and left to die, until he was found by a wild young woman named Teleri, who was now Sir Roger's wife.

What if Sofia were hanged?

Tobin tossed and turned and muttered a curse. Every time he closed his eyes, he saw her face, saw it the way he had last seen it: the proud lift of her chin and her complete control when he had foolishly told her the trumped-up reasons why he was marrying her.

He had lied. He had lied to her, and he was probably lying to himself. The truth was he did not know what he felt. Except confused. He was always confused when he was around her. And every time she left him he felt as if he had done something wrong . . . again. It was almost a pattern. She was there and he did or said something idiotic. His words to her had come straight from his ego and pride. He could not speak from his heart, because he was certain he did not have one.

But he had pride. Pride was a difficult thing; it could color how you viewed a situation and make something completely stupid seem like the right thing to do. Pride had made him say what he had said to her.

Both his pride and hers.

And when he closed his eyes to finally sleep his last thought was this: he did not know who he was angrier at, her or himself.

"Aye!" Alan shouted to the crowded tavern room, waving his arm and bowing before them. "We will perform for our supper!" He took out his lute and began to play and stroll around the warm room, with its huge fire and the oil torches on the plaster walls. Alan sang a rowdy and amusing tale, one of a fishwife and her poor henpecked husband.

The serving maids stopped serving and just watched, tapping their feet to the melody. Everyone in the room was listening and laughing to the amusing words.

Sofia sat at a table with Miranda and the children. Bernard was outside, seeing to Satan in his cage near the stables behind the inn. Sofia had learned on her first day with the troupe that entertainers performed for everything. For meals, for lodging and for coins, for bear food, whatever the situation called for.

Tonight was no different. The tavern was filled with travelers and local villeins. The place was warm and fairly clean. There was soot on the walls from the huge fireplace and the tables were not greasy, at least the buxom serving maids wiped them off once in a while.

Alan finished his bawdy tale and the patrons laughed. The tavern mistress, who stood behind the bar next to the ale kegs, turned her pink face and looked at Sofia. "So lad. What sort of trick do you do?"

Sofia stood and puffed out her chest the way men did when they boasted. She swung the sack of wooden balls from her shoulders and hopped up on the table top, then she swaggered back and forth, poking her chest with her thumb. "I juggle. *Four* balls!" She took out two balls, then held one up in the air and tossed it high. She tossed the second ball after it, then jauntily caught both.

"Four balls?" the woman scratched her chins and said, "Ain't never seen no one throw four balls. Tell you what. I'll feed you all, everyone in the troupe, plus that huge bear if you can juggle four balls to the count of fifty!"

Alan looked at her and winked.

"Fifty? Hmmph!" Sofia said with a cocky wave of her hand. " 'Tis nothing!"

"Then let us see you perform, laddie!"

"Aye!" Came the shouts. "Perform!"

"Throw yer balls high, laddie!"

Sofia swept a deep bow, then threw one ball up, then the next. She moved up and down the table top, her feet swift and easy. She had become fairly proficient at this. And she liked the challenge of it, the motion and quickness.

She added a third ball and the room cheered. She moved her hands faster and faster. Her feet, too.

"Go, lad! Go!" came the calls.

She grinned, then tossed the balls high, and leapt from the table onto the bar top. The tavern mistress laughed and clapped her hands as Sofia danced up and down the top and tossed her balls higher and higher.

"I only see three balls, laddie!" Someone shouted.

A second later Sofia was juggling all four balls and shouting, "Count! Count!"

And count they did. The whole room was counting.

"Ten . . ."

"Eleven . . ."

"Twelve!"

The balls flew from her hands and in bigger and bigger circles in front of her eyes and over her head, her hands tossing them with a confidence she had never yet had.

"Thirty!" came the call.

She threw the balls higher.

The crowd began to clap with each number. "Forty-two!"

"Forty-three!"

"Forty-four!"

She was almost there. Almost.

"Forty-seven!"

She tossed the balls up and in a flash, grabbed the falling ball and threw it up behind her back . . . a new trick!

"Forty-nine!"

She shifted. One step back, then reached out . . .

The ball should have come down.

She frowned.

Where is the ball?

That was her last conscious thought.

In the distance, Tobin spotted the warm and welcoming lights of an inn on the edge of a small, sleepy village. He had split up his men, each group taking a different road. They had been riding long and hard, searching with little success. He raised his hand high and signaled toward the lights ahead. Before long they rode up to a small, stone tavern with a wooden sign that hung by one hinge and flapped in the gusty wind.

Tobin's man, Captain Parcin, pounded on the door and soon their horses were stabled and Tobin and his men were inside, where a smoky but blessedly warm fire blazed brightly in the huge fireplace. The place was small but clean and soon the alewife who ran the place had her wenches serve them a hearty mutton stew and crusty brown bread, along with foaming tankards of ale.

Tobin sat at a table before the fire with his feet propped on the hearth, trying to think like Sofia. A futile effort.

He was worried, for it made no sense that she could disappear the way she had. She was not that wise in the ways of the outside world. He hoped to God she had not met up with the wrong person. She could be raped and lying dead in some distant woods for all he knew.

He took a long swig of ale, then stared at the golden flames of fire as if there were answers waiting for him there. His anger was almost gone now, he knew, because the truth was he was just plain worried, certain that something dire had befallen Sofia when it had been his duty to protect her.

And he had failed.

He took another drink, then wiped the foam from his mouth with the back of his hand and started to reach for a piece of bread. A buxom wench with a head full of light blond hair had been twitching her bottom in front of him long enough for him to take notice. Now she leaned down near his shoulder and brushed her breasts across his cheek while she refilled his tankard.

He glanced up at her, surprised to see she had a dairy-maid's skin and all of her teeth.

"If there be anything else ye'd like, sir, all ye haf ta do is ask Gunnie, here." She drew her hand slowly over his shoulder.

Three of the other wenches began to giggle and whisper and wink at some of his men, men who had just a while ago been exhausted and cold, now looked willing and ready for a full night of pleasure. The women began to chose men and some sat in their laps and began to giggle and flirt.

Gunnie started to move away but Tobin grabbed her hand and pulled her back. "Tell me who has been in the inn in the last week."

"Lemme see . . ." She rubbed her pointed chin for a moment, then said, "I worked most every day this week. There were the usual lot. A few farmers taking their goods to market in the city. The regular one who always stops here. We had one Italian merchant and his wife, they barely spoke the King's English. There was Tinker John."

"Who is Tinker John?"

"He travels the countryside."

"Anyone with him?"

She shook her head. "That one always travels alone, he does. Odd duck."

"Why?"

She shrugged, "Just is. Doesn't say much. Strange eyes."

He could almost see Sofia spotting a tinker and climbing into his wagon. "Where was he headed this time?"

"Surrey or Gloucester, can't remember which." She turned. "Hey, Bess? Where was Tinker John headed this trip?"

"Surrey!" A plump girl with blond curls and big teeth called out.

"Aye, I was half right."

"Anyone else?"

"Just those pilgrims came through last night, oh, I almost forgot. Friar Francis with his choir boys."

"How many were there?"

"Hmmm, say ten or so. Every last one of 'em had voices like angels, they did. Each sang a solo hymn for their meal. 'Twas like heaven right here in the Old Keg and Boar."

That pretty much ruled out Sofia. Tobin had heard her hum and that had been enough.

Parcin leaned closer and asked quietly, "Are you thinking she was with them?"

Tobin shook his head. "With the voice of an angel? I don't think so. She could easily have been with the tinker or stowed on his wagon. That's what I'm thinking."

"Hey, Gunnie!" Bess called out. "Remember the juggler?"

Gunnie began to laugh in a huge, bellowing laugh, and the other women and even the alewife herself were laughing with her. Gunnie slapped herself in head and said, "How could I forget him?" She turned back to Tobin. "A small band of performers, a jongleur and rope walkers. They had this dancing bear with them. The bear didn't dance for us. All he did was sleep. But what was the best was this tall laddie who kept trying to juggle for his meal. He stood right up there on the bar and tossed them wooden balls high in the air. He was doing real fine, he was, dancing and hopping and then he got cocky, added a fourth wooden ball, then threw 'em too high. Well, he missed. Them's hard balls. Knocked himself out cold." She broke into laughter again. "Dropped like a rock, he did."

Tobin straightened and exchanged a knowing look with Parcin. "Was the lad about this high, slim, with black hair that stuck out from his head?"

"Aye, that be him. And he had these strange colored eyes, he did. Purple they was. Never seen purple eyes before. Was a spunky lad, at least he was until he went down."

Tobin stood and grabbed his cloak. "Did they say where they were going?"

"Northeast. The singer was talking to a messenger who told him about some birthing celebration in the Marches, Glamorgan, I think. A place where performers could pick up a pretty penny for a few days work. When they left, carrying out that poor laddie, I heard 'em say they was headed that way."

Sofia would not go with them to Glamorgan, that he knew. Tobin tossed some coins on the table and turned to Parcin. "Get the men ready. We're riding out now."

Tobin went to the door and opened it. The wind had died down and it was dark but he knew they had to ride quickly, even if they did so by torchlight.

Parcin stood. "Get yourselves up and mounted. We're to north this night."

"Got what I want to mount right here in my lap," one of the men said.

There were quiet moans and groans from the others and the serving wenches were whining among themselves.

Tobin turned in the doorway and looked back at them. He eyed the serving wenches, then looked back at his men. "If you can fuck, you can ride." Then he walked out.

CHAPTER

15

Sofia awoke with a blinding headache. She sat up and blinked, then looked around.

"Ned's finally awake, Mama!" Maude shouted as if her her mother were in Cornwall.

"Wide awake!" Tildie shouted just as loudly.

Sofia winced and slapped her hands over her ears, then moaned and fell back on the seat. The twins were perched on either side of her, as if they had been watching and waiting for the moment she opened her eyes. Their voices were as loud as trumpets, or at least they felt that loud to Sofia. She took a deep breath. "What happened?"

Tildie looked at her with her wide eyes and said, "You knocked yourself out."

"Aye." Maude nodded. "With the wooden balls. *Clunk!*" She slapped her hand on her head. "Right on the noggin."

Sofia groaned, then touched her head. There was a huge egg-shaped knot on her crown.

Miranda was up front, near Alan, who was driving the team that pulled the wagon. She slid open the peep and stuck her head inside. "How are you feeling?"

"Embarrassed."

Miranda laughed. "Are you well enough?"

"Well enough. But my pride is hurt terribly."

"It should not be. You made our year most profitable," Miranda said.

"Profitable?" Sofia frowned. "How?"

Alan looked over his shoulder. "The tavern keeper gave us two golden crowns when you went down, Neddie, me lad. After she stopped laughing, she said she hadn't seen anything so amusing in years."

"Aye," Tildie said, nodding and giving her a child's serious look. "We are the very best entertainers ever. You should knock yourself out all the time."

"No one understands true talent when they see it," Sofia muttered. Then she shifted to her knees and moved forward. She pulled back one of the side curtains. "Where are we off to next?"

"Glamorgan. Camrose Castle."

Sofia felt all the blood drain from her face.

"The earl and his lady are having a huge celebration for their newest son. We should make enough in two days to last us until next winter," Alan said.

Earl Merrick and Lady Clio?

There was no way Sofia could go there. Surely they would recognize her. "Stop the wagon! I cannot go to Wales," she said in a panic.

"Why?" Alan frowned, then slowed the wagon and looked inside. " 'Tis safe. Fairly safe, now that Edward has built so many fortresses along the Marchlands. The Welsh have settled down and they would not harm us. We only have to worry about our own countrymen and the outlaws that plague the roads and forests of England."

Come up with something quickly!

Sofia stood and grabbed the door. She faced them. "My mother made me promise on her deathbed that I would never go to Wales."

Miranda looked at her. "Why?"

Why . . . Why . . . Why?

Sofia put her hand on her chest. "My poor father was killed by a Welsh archer. An arrow. *Phsst!* Right in the chest." Sofia poked herself, then looked at the twins, whose eyes were wide. Sofia glanced up at Alan and Miranda. She felt a sharp stab of guilt in her belly. She had done little but lie to them, these people who were so kind to her. She averted her eyes because she did not like it that they cared when she was telling them the biggest lie she had told yet. She opened the door and hopped outside.

Alan and Miranda stepped down, too.

"You need not worry about me. Just let me off here and I shall trot back to that inn, since I was such a smashing success there."

Alan smiled.

"Perhaps find a ride to London," she told him.

"You need not leave us." Alan slid his arm around her. "We've grown rather fond of you, me lad. You are welcome to stay as long as you want."

"I've traveling in my soul, you know. Being a wanderer and all. I've a strong desire to see more of the city. You will do much better without me. The wagon is cramped and I have been here too long."

Alan nodded and clapped her once on the shoulder, then he went to talk to Bernard.

Sofia looked up and her eyes met Miranda's. "You have been good to me. And I thank you." She reached out and put a few of her own coins into Miranda's hands.

"Nay, you need not—" Miranda said and tried to hand them back.

"Aye. Please. Take them. I have more."

Miranda looked at her. "I do not know who you are or why you are afraid to go farther. I suppose it is the same reason you are trying to be a lad."

"You know."

Miranda nodded.

"Do the others know, too?"

Miranda shook her head. "Nay. Sometimes it takes a woman to know a woman." Miranda smiled. "I wish you well . . . Ned."

Sofia hugged her and whispered. "I am Sofia."

Sofia stepped back and she walked back to the wagon and reached inside to hug the girls. She turned and bid Alan, Bernard, and the sleeping bear farewell.

Soon she was standing alone on the side of the road waving good-bye. Her arm grew tired and her shoulder began to tighten, so she just watched until the wagons were nothing but silhouettes, like small flowers bobbing off in the distance.

She turned away finally. She did not move. She just stood there.

What to do? Where to go?

She crossed her arms and tapped a foot; it helped her think. She could take the road back to toward London as she told them she would and truly explore the city, see its underbelly, but she'd watch out for the wild pigs this time.

Aye, that seemed most likely. She took a few steps and then stopped, because she thought of home—well, not her home exactly, for that would have been Torwick Castle, where she had spent her first four years and which was part of her dower lands. But as far as she knew there was no one there but the steward appointed by the King and whatever servants were needed to keep it from falling into disrepair.

No, the home in her thoughts was Leeds or Windsor. Wherever the King and Queen were was her true home, she supposed, the only home she could remember. She paused then, thinking of home. She wondered what they all thought of her escape, then chewed on her lip for another guilty moment. She had never said good-bye to

Edith, her dearest friend, and she could not have done so to Queen Eleanor either.

But she felt empty when she thought of them, as if she had lost something valuable and precious. She closed her eyes as a pang of homesickness swept over her, and she began to cry. Cry! She couldn't believe she was crying again! Like some blithering fool, she was standing there truly missing all that she had thought she despised.

She would have wagered the world on a silver platter that she would have never, ever felt this way. But she did. She cried for home. She cried because she had lied to good people. She cried because she did not like what she had become.

It was an ugly thing to see herself as selfish. She stood there on the road and realized that she had made some terrible mistakes because of her own strong will to do what she wanted and not what others wanted.

She was not proud of what she had done; it ate at her like a worm that makes the apple rotten. So she took a deep breath and walked, trying to get past what she was feeling. But walking was not enough and soon she was almost trotting down the road, heading back toward the south, her arms moving with her running strides, helping to move her along at a faster pace.

Then she began to run, run as fast as she could, trying to run away from what she had done.

It was quite a while before she began to tire and she was no longer running or trotting but walking, every so often kicking a small gray stone ahead of her, then moving to catch up to kick it again, and again.

She wondered how many kicks of that silly stone it would take to get to the village, how many kicks if she were to walk clear back to London. After a moment she stopped and looked all around her.

She was completely alone.

'Twas an odd feeling and one she did not know if she

liked or not. How very strange that when you did not have something, it seemed like the most valuable thing in the whole wide world and then when finally you have it, you were not changed one bit because of it.

A mayfly buzzed around her face, and she swatted it away. It flew away and lit atop some horse grass growing on the side of the road. There were trees on both sides now and to the west were low bushes and then thick forest and woods. She started to move on, hoping to find the inn soon, but she had no idea how far away it truly was. She was hungry and tired, but as luck would have it she spotted some berries tangled amid the low trees and scrub brush.

She left the road and crawled through the brush, snagging her braies on the thorns, but she found a ripe cache of wild gooseberries. She filled her tunic with them, then sat down in the low brush and ate her fill. They were juicy and sweet and they made her think of the pies at feast time and sweet buns filled with fruit coming warm from the ovens.

She lay down for a moment, just to rest. Only for a short time. She lay her cheek on her hands, swatted away a few flies, and soon she was fast asleep.

"Ye figurin' some pigeon is likely to come along this way?"

Sofia opened her eyes at the sound of that raspy and gruff voice, but she didn't move. The voice that woke her was frighteningly close by.

"Aye." Another more gruff voice answered. "We'll follow the road for a while, mates. There'll be someone wot wants to part with 'is purse for the sake of 'is neck." The man began to laugh and others laughed with him. "Mebbe they'll lose their necks and their purses, too!" The laughter was not amused or kind; it was cruel and evil, and she was scared.

She could hear the subtle shifting of their mounts and the jangle of reins. She did not know how many of them there were. From her position, she could only see the back legs of three mounts. But there were more than three voices. They were in the woods, just this side of the road, and it sounded as if they were barely a few yards away from where she lay.

She was afraid to do much more than take one shallow breath after another for fear they would spot her. If she could see them, even partially, surely they could see her. All they had to do was to look in her direction.

A bee buzzed a nearby weed and lit on the white flower, then moved to buzz her head. It circled and circled her head, then her ear. It lit on her neck. She held her breath and prayed it would fly away.

Go away! Go away!

It stung her and she jerked in pain, but covered her mouth with both her hands so she would not cry out. The sting burned up her ear and head and down her neck, over her shoulder. She could feel the bee struggling to free its stinger, which was still piercing her skin. Tears filled her eyes and she squeezed them tightly closed and lay there unmoving, waiting to hear the sound of the men riding away.

Slowly the bee stopped struggling and was still, still as she had been. The men talked for a moment more, then she heard the sound of their horses riding off down the road.

A sob escaped her lips and she slowly pushed herself up to her knees and elbows. Fear and relief mixed together to make her tears flow again and her breath still short.

She knelt there for a long time, then she brushed the bee from her neck and sat back on her heels, trying to control herself. She was shaking and her belly was tight and she thought she might be ill.

An instant later she heard a horse neigh. The lashing sound of reins. The thunder of hooves beating the ground. So close it was almost as if the rider were on top of her.

In the distance, she heard a male shout.

Oh, God in heaven above, they had seen her!

CHAPTER

16

She turned and ran into the woods as swiftly as her feet would carry her. Her heart pounded with her steps. Leaves and branches brushed her face and arms. Scratched her skin. She kept running.

She jumped over a fallen log and skidded in the slick, damp moss. She fell to one knee, still sliding, but got up. Off she went again. She was not certain if she was hearing the rider come after her or the thunderous beating of her own heart.

She dared not stop and check, so she just ran on, then saw an opening and cut sharply to the west, through a thicket and into a clearing. She pumped her arms and legs as fast as she could and ran and ran because her life depended on it. Outside the clearing she turned to the north, hoping to lose them.

She slid under a fallen tree, then scampered over huge rocks and slid halfway down a slope, past another clearing where there was a brook. She ran through the rocks and the water and up the bank into a copse of thick old trees that hung almost to the ground.

She looked left, then right, and ran for a huge tree in the middle, leapt up and grasped onto a branch, then pulled and swung herself up. Cowering there, she hid in the crook of the tree, her heart pounding and her breath lost. She took short, shallow breaths, quiet breaths, because she was afraid, so afraid.

There was the sharp crack of a twig. The crushing sound of leaves. She heard a horse approach and froze on the tree branch.

She sat so still. Her knees were pressed against her chest. One hand clutched the branch above her. The other rested on the trunk. She barely breathed now, because her life depended upon this.

She could not see down through the thick green leaves and did not dare move to see better. She was afraid of what she might see staring back at her. All that mattered was that she stay hidden and safe.

There was only one rider. One man. She could hear his harsh breath, the snorting of his mount, the heavy stomping of horses hooves, the sound of twigs cracking beneath them.

Time moved by so slowly, stretching out like years. Sweat began to bead on her hairline; it was already soaking her clothes. She gripped the limb above her even tighter. The splinters and knots in the bark and wood cut into her fingers and palms.

For a moment, she almost thought he had discovered her. She held her breath, afraid to make even the motion of inhaling for fear he would know she was there.

But then there came the welcome jangle of reins and the man spurred his mount out and off toward the north.

Sofia exhaled and sagged a little bit. Her heart was thudding in her ears and the sweat dripped down her temples. She waited a long time before she even tried to move. She shifted, pulled herself up and stood on the branch, keeping her balance by clinging like ivy to the upper branch.

An instant later from the corner of her eye she caught a sudden flash of blue. The sound of a horse rearing. Then a huge gleaming broadsword slashed through the leaves by her head and cut downward, clear through the branch she was standing on.

The branch cracked and broke off, fell out from under her and to the ground. She screamed and grabbed onto the upper branch with both hands, holding on as tightly as she could. The weight of her body jerked hard against her arms and she hung there, her feet and body dangling in the air.

She looked down.

A man's face stared up at her.

It was a face she knew all too well.

"Damn you, Tobin de Clare!"

He sheathed his sword and leaned casually on the pommel of his saddle. He watched her hang from the tree, not saying a single word.

"Are you just going to let me hang here?"

"You climbed the tree. I have to believe you wanted to be there."

She cursed again, then stared down at the ground, way, way down there. It looked a lot farther down than when she climbed up here.

Her hands were slipping. The bark was cutting into her palms. She didn't have the strength left to pull herself up. There were no branches lower to stand on.

There was nothing but the ground below her. And Tobin, waiting. A very angry Tobin.

She preferred broken bones to broken pride. She closed her eyes and took a deep breath.

One . . . two . . . three . . .

She let go.

She expected to feel the ground, hard and damp, and the jar of it ringing up through the bones of her legs when she hit.

Instead she hit a mailed chest. She felt the soft whoosh of his breath brush her hair as his big arms clamped around her.

She was sitting on his saddle pommel. Her eyes shot open to find herself staring into his, into those blue eyes. Cold blue eyes. She did not like the flintlike look on his face. Clearly he did not find her adventures amusing, in spite of the laziness of his posture.

He was furious.

"You oaf!" She looked away and began to brush herself off. "You could have killed me with that sword."

"Believe this and do not forget." His words were sharp and tight, like the jaw they were coming from. "It took every bit of patience God gave me *not* to kill you."

"Edward would not allow you to kill me." Her voice was haughty and sure and she gave him a direct look. What she saw in his face made her wish she could take back her words.

"Nay, Sofia. Edward would not allow me to kill you. He would like to do that for himself."

She kept arguing with him.

"Be quiet, woman! Already I am sorely tempted to beat you. Do not push me." He had never in his entire life felt the urge to hit a woman, till now. Sofia had pushed him that far. He gripped the reins in one tight, white-knuckled fist.

She called him something under her breath.

Luck was with her for he did not hear what it was. He clamped his arm hard around her squirming body and kneed his mount forward, pulling her back against his chest so hard she gasped.

Her breathing was fast. He could feel the motion of her chest against his forearm, but wisely she did not speak again. She just sat in front of him in the saddle as stiffly as one of the tree trunks they were riding past.

"How did you find me?"

" 'Twas not easy."

"There were outlaws. Brigands. I heard them talking.

That was why I was running. I thought you were them."
She paused. "I thought I was going to die." Her voice
cracked into a half sob.

"You are fortunate to be alive at all." He did not feel
sorry for her and he would not let her tears affect him.

"You are holding me too tightly. It hurts my ribs."

He shifted and pulled her across his leg. "Put your
arms about my neck, so you don't fall off."

She slid her arms up and locked her hands around his
neck, then wiggled a bit and finally settled her bottom
between his legs on the pommel.

After a moment or two, she leaned her head against
his shoulder and she began to cry.

They rode back into the inn a short time later. Sofia could see some of Tobin's men waiting, and when
they rode into the courtyard, the men saw her and dismounted.

"Go inside and order some food. We'll follow." Tobin
dismounted and reached up and grasped her waist, then
lifted her off the saddle and set her down, his body pinning her between him and the horse.

A stable lad came running and took the reins, then led
his mount away. Tobin grabbed her hand and pulled her
with him and shoved her inside the inn.

A blast of hot air hit her in the face along with the
strong scent of greasy mutton and the sharp yeasty tang
of spilled ale. With his hand firmly on her back, he
guided her across the crowded tavern room to a table
where some of his men sat. They looked at her with
odd looks she could only describe as half-annoyed and
half-pitying.

She did not need to be pitied. She did not want their
pity.

Tobin pulled out a chair and shoved her into it.

She turned and gave him a glare, but it did no good,

for he was not looking at her. His eyes were on a bar-maid, a big blonde with an udder chest and fat hips. Well, not fat, but bigger than hers so she liked to think of them as fat, especially when the woman's eyes were all but eating Tobin up.

She strolled their way, a tray filled with hot food and foamy drink propped on one shoulder. Her free hand was on her hip, which swayed and rolled more than the boats on the Thames.

Sofia glanced back at Tobin, who was still looking at the woman when she bent between them and set the tray down on the table and her pink breasts in Tobin's face.

"You came back." She said in a breathy voice.

"Aye, sweet."

Sweet? What is he doing? He calls me sweet.

For a moment, all Sofia could see was the woman's plump, round bottom, right in her face. So she wedged her way in front of the woman, so the back of her head was between the woman's breasts. Sofia grabbed the rim of the table and she pushed back.

The woman grunted and took a step back.

"Hmmm, stew! I am 'bout starved." Sofia scooted her chair next to Tobin's, then grabbed a dish of stew and a hunk of bread and began to stuff her face.

The barmaid ruffled Sofia's shorn hair. "Game, lad, he is. How is yer head?"

Sofia scowled at her and muttered, "Fine."

But the maid was not paying attention. She only had eyes for Tobin. "Tell me, Sir Tobin. Is he your little brother?"

Sofia choked on her food.

Tobin patted her on the back while she coughed and he handed her a tankard of ale.

She hated ale; it tasted like water and old moldy bread.

"The lad is my . . . groom."

Sofia glanced up and gave him a pointed glare.

Tobin flashed her a white grin. He was enjoying this. *Damn him!*

"Aye, the boy does smell of the stables."

Tobin clamped his big hand on her thigh under the table and kept her seated. "We've taken your rooms for the night. Send up a bath to my room and I'll see that the lad rids himself of the smell . . ." he paused. "And the nits."

She would like to nit him.

"Anything you desire, Sir Tobin. Your room is the one on the end, right? The one with the biggest bed." The barmaid winked, then sauntered away.

"Sit," Tobin said into her ear. "The way you are dressed, and with that hair, you will stay a lad until I return you to Edward."

Sofia looked at him. "Go to the Devil."

He gave her a long stare, then laughed and said, "I think I already have."

CHAPTER

17

"I will not take my clothes off with you in the room."

Tobin was stretched out on the plump feather bed, his feet crossed at the ankles and his arms resting behind his head. He was chewing on a witch hazel twig and watching Sofia pace in front of the steaming tub. "Then I will do it for you."

"You will not."

He started to get up.

She raised her hand. "Stop! Do not." She reached around and undid the closure on the back of her tunic. "At least turn your back."

"I am quite comfortable as I am."

She stopped. "Fine." She dropped her arms. "Then I shall undress in the hall, where all your men can see me."

"Checkmate," he said. His Sofia. She was a worthy opponent when it came to this kind of byplay. "I will close my eyes." Then he did.

"Give me your word. On your honor that you will not look."

"Aye." Was all he said. He would give her no words of a vow he intended to break. He waited, then opened his eyes enough to watch her.

She turned her back to him and grabbed the hem of the tunic, then pulled it over her head. She had bound

her breasts with a piece of linen and she began to untie
the knots and then slowly unwind the cloth. 'Twas one of
the most erotic moments he could ever remember, waiting for her to finish unwinding that cloth.

When she finished, she bent slightly to pull off one
boot. He caught a glimpse of a full pink breast. She tried
the other boot. It was stuck and she had to hobble in a
circle to pull it off. Her breasts jiggled and he could see
the nipples grow hard and pointed.

She glanced up once, her eyes narrowed suspiciously.

He had closed his just enough to fool her.

She waited.

So did he.

Unfortunately for him, she managed to pull off the
boot. A shame, he would have liked to see her hop like
that again.

She spun around almost as if she read his thoughts,
But he had shut his eyes again. He moved the twig to the
other side of his mouth with his tongue, then sucked
on it and began chewing again. He could hear her pad
lightly across the room.

She stood by the bed. He could feel her watching him.
She waved her hand in his face a few times.

"My eyes are closed, sweet."

"Then how can you tell I'm here?"

"I can feel the air from you waving your hand in front
of my face."

"Oh." She paused, sounding disappointed, then she
said in a curt tone, "I do not want you to call me that
anymore."

"What?"

"That name. Sweet. You called that barmaid 'sweet.'"

"Jealous?"

She sniffed. "Hardly that." Then she went back to the
tub. "Humph!" she muttered and tossed a ball of soap
into the water. "Me . . . jealous of some fleshy tavern

wench who walks like a ship under full sail." She
strolled around the tub in a circle, mimicking the maid.

"Anything you deeee-sire, Sir Tobin," she said in a
throaty voice as she swung her hips from side to side and
wiggled her bottom.

He wasn't certain what he wanted to do more, laugh at
her or lie with her.

She peeled off her braies, still circling her hips around
and mumbling about how many men the maid must have
lain with. How a shrewd person would be wise to fear
some rotting disease. Apparently finished, she stopped
wiggling and muttering and stepped into the water.

She eased down into the wooden tub and gave a long
and luscious moan. "This feels so good."

Sweet Mother, but she was a beautiful woman. And a
handful. 'Twas not easy to look at her like this and truly
believe she was his, finally, this spirited young woman
of seven and ten. They were young, the two of them. But
it seemed like years ago when he first saw her.

It *was* years ago. Five long years.

He would be one and twenty at Michaelmas. How many
years would they have together? Fifty or more? A lifetime.
Sweet Mary and Joseph, he hoped it was a long one.

She had her back to him as she washed and scrubbed.
Her skin was soon glistening in the red glow of the coal
brasier, and he watched her slide under the water to dunk
her black hair. When she did, her long white legs came
almost out of the tub and he caught a glimpse of the
shadow between her thighs.

Lord, but his action this night, lying there unmoving
like he was, should keep him out of Purgatory forever. A
true test of strength no tourney could best, for no man
could possibly lie there as he was and do nothing. So he
watched her, drank in his fill of her. He wanted to get up
and pull her from the tub. He wanted to touch her. He
wanted to lick the water from her body. He wanted to

strip off his clothes and join her. God's blood, but he
wanted to join with her.

He waited, then gave up the possibility of going
straight to heaven after he died and stood quietly, covert-
ly, pulled his linen undertunic over his head and began to
untie his chausses. He pulled the points aside and
stripped out of them, then untied his loincloth and let it
fall to the floor.

Before she could turn about, he was kneeling on the
wooden floor behind her.

"Tobin!" she shrieked and crossed her arms over her
breasts! "You have no honor! You gave me your vow."

"Not truly. All I said was 'aye.' I did not say aye to
what."

She frowned at him from over her pale shoulder. After
a moment her eyes widened. "What are you doing?"

"Washing your back." He ran his hands over her damp
back, over the soft, soft skin and he leaned down and
kissed the nape of her neck, then her shoulder and her
spine. He reached lower, until his hands were on her buttocks and he rubbed them, then squeezed them, kneaded
them.

She stiffened for a moment when he first gripped her
there, but soon she moaned a soft and quiet kind of
moan, the kind that was the same as saying "do it more
and more and more."

He gripped her by the bottom and picked her right up
out of the tub and stood, holding her in front of him.

She shrieked, but it was too late, he stepped into the
water and sat down with her in his lap. He released her.
She spun around and almost killed him.

"Careful, brat!"

"Let me up."

He shook his head and grasped her wrists and pulled
her forward so her palms were flat against his chest. He
leaned back and closed his eyes. "Wash me."

"Do I look like your servant?"

"A hundred years ago and it would have been your duty and honor to bathe visiting knights."

"Aye, we women have come a long way."

He laughed and took her left hand. He placed the ball of soap in it, then put her hand and the soap on his chest and began to rub over the coarse, curly black hair there until it was lathered and foamy.

He opened his eyes to find her staring at her hand and watched as she raised the other one and began to rub through the lather, to play with the foam and draw small circles with her fingertips.

"You learn quickly."

She gave him a wicked smile, then grazed her fingers over his nipples.

He grasped her wrists and pulled her forward, so they were breast to chest. He looped her hands around his neck and lowered his, then held her by the waist and slowly moved her upper body so the lather was between both of them and their bodies moved in slick sliding motions.

Soon they were both moving on their own and he moved his hands to her head and clasped it, then pulled her mouth to his. He gave her soft, nipping kisses, on the corners of her mouth, along her lips. Then he flicked his tongue over her lips and she opened her mouth with a deep sigh.

Then they were kissing each other, deep, long and wet kisses, where their tongues played together and taunted and drew the other's into their own mouths. He sucked on her tongue and she did the same to his.

She mimicked his every move, as if she wanted to be taught the ways of loving, all the ways. He took the soap and her hand and moved both lower and made the same foaming lather there as he had done on his chest. He took the soap and lathered the shadowy hair between her legs, kissing her mouth the whole time and swallowing her weak protests when he touched her between her legs, when his fingers drifted over her.

He moved their bodies again, sliding together and up and down so they both could feel every inch of skin, every soft or hard muscle, every rib against rib, every plane of their bodies against the other.

The water was growing colder now and the room was fast chilling. He pulled her away from him and placed a kiss on her nose. "Come, the water is cold." He held her as he stood, then grabbed a towel and ran it quickly over their bodies and scrubbed her hair dry before he did his own.

Small black curls were forming around her face and her eyes looked huge and dark and intense, as if he could step into them and lose himself there and never find his way out again.

He swept her into his arms and carried her to the bed, jerked back the coverlet and placed her on the linen sheet, then he crawled under with her and began all over again. The touching, the kisses, the soft words.

"Touch me . . . Touch me . . ." he said and placed her palm on him. He moved his hand to her body and stroked her from her shoulder to her knee, long soft strokes where he barely touched her soft skin, just drew his fingers over her again and again.

"You are so soft. Your skin is so soft," he murmured, then he moved his mouth to her ear and asked her to stroke him.

Her hand moved tentatively at first.

"Harder," he whispered. "Harder."

And she did. She pressed the palm of her hand against him and began to move.

He groaned, "That's it . . . that's it . . . Don't stop."

Then he kissed her deeply, their mouths locked together until he moved to her neck and her ears, where he tasted her with his tongue and breathed into her ears and waited for her to shiver in reaction.

"Tobin . . ." she said on soft breath.

He lowered his mouth to her breasts, tasted them, sucked on the tips and rolled his tongue around them. He moved downward, his mouth on her ribs and he followed each rib with his tongue slowly, as if he were drawing them on her body.

He pressed his lips to the soft dip under her ribs and kissed the softest and whitest skin he'd ever seen. His head dipped to her navel and he tongued it, then sucked on her soft belly until he made a love mark there, and another—one on each side. He buried his face there, taking in her scent and nuzzling her belly until she gripped his head in her hands and sighed.

His mouth traced the bones of her hips, the line of her hip and thigh. He shoved back the covers and ran his tongue along the inside of one thigh, down, down until he was near her ankles. He moved his shoulders between her legs and he kissed up the other leg, stopping at the knee.

He shifted her legs up so her knees were bent and her feet flat on the bed. Her kissed the backs of her knees, wet them with his mouth and blew on them. He licked upward, slowly, drawing damp lines along the skin on the inside of her thighs.

Until he reached center of her. He blew his warm breath on her there, knowing she was wet and could feel the chill of his breath there.

She gasped and called out his name.

Then he kissed her there, that place for lovers only.

She cried out to heaven and tried to shift away.

He gripped her buttocks and kept on, deepening his kiss from lips and breath to the stroking of his tongue, the sucking of his mouth, until she was crying and moaning and telling him not to stop.

She was so close, her pleasure was but a touch away. He could feel it in the quiver of her legs, in the new taste of her. She was coming. She was coming.

One more flick of his tongue and she cried out and spasmed, pulsing against his mouth and gripping his head tightly in her clenched hands.

She kept swearing to saints, pleading to Mary and saying she was dying. Finally, she was finished, her breath hard, labored just a moment before it began to slow and ease. She just lay there.

He shifted, crawled back up her soft body. She slowly opened her eyes and looked into his.

The wonder he saw there almost broke him, almost pulled him in to a place from which he could never escape. He could not look at that look very long, so he drew her legs up and settled between them and he began to move, slowly at first, just rubbing against her, hard against soft, moving and shifting so he was against her most sensitive spots.

When he was certain she had the rhythm down, he slid his hands upward and cupped her breasts and then drove his fingers into her hair and kissed her, still shifting and moving only against her.

Their kisses grew hotter and more intense. They moved faster and then he shifted his hips, stopped, and changed angles, then just barely entered her, only slid the tip of him inside. "Can you feel me?"

"Aye, Tobin, You feel so good."

"So do you. You taste so good. You smell so good. You are so wet and hot." He slid inside a bit more, then shifted out a little, just small, inching movements. "Wrap your feet around my back."

She did and he lifted her up a little higher, then dipped a little deeper. He moved in and out, still not touching her virgin's wall. He would not breach it, not yet. Not this night.

He shifted positions and sat back on his heels with his legs folded, his knees spread wide. He grasped her hips and pulled her slowly over his legs to his cock. He inched inside again, in and out, a little deeper each time, in and out, a little deeper, in and out, a little deeper.

He set the rhythms. He moved her to their pleasure. She was tight and hot and he wanted to go inside as deeply as he could, but he held back, just the heavy wide tip of him was filled with all that sensation. He tilted her up higher and sank inside some more, until he felt the thin wall that told him no man had ever had her.

He did not go any farther, but pulled slowly back, then dipped inside again, and slowly back, over and over, building the rhythm and feeling her response. She lifted her hips higher, she moaned and twisted her head from side to side. He kept pumping in and out until he thought he would explode.

He pushed once, twice; she quivered and her legs shook in violent little tremors. One more thrust and she came hard, pulsing around the tip of him and crying out his name.

Letting her finish was the hardest thing he'd ever done. But he waited, gritted his teeth together and re-cited the names of the saints in Latin, then again in French.

He pulled out of her and shifted, unfolded his legs and lay atop her, rubbing against her belly and her woman's bone, faster and faster, gripping her hips in his hands as he moved, closer and closer to completion, his release growing and climbing higher and higher.

A shudder ran through him and he came hard, his hands moved to her hair and his mouth was buried in her shoulder and neck. His life flowed in pulses, warm and wet between them, onto their bellies and over their skin.

They lay there for a long time, until his breathing slowed and had joined hers. He brushed a lock of her hair from his nose, then took another deep breath and lifted his head.

She was looking at him from those eyes and he was lost already. Gone. He never had a chance.

She raised her finger to his mouth. "You did not hurt me." She sounded puzzled.

"I did not breach you. Had I done so, you would have felt the pain, but only then. Only once."

She frowned, then said, "Why?"

"Why the pain?"

"Nay, why did you not take me completely?"

"We are not wed. Betrothed, but not wed. I will save that act for our wedding bed. Not for this night. This was for us. For now."

"It was wonderful."

"Aye," he smiled, then shifted from between her, and lay alongside of her, looking at her, watching her expression. She looked down at the moisture on her belly and she touched it with her fingertips, then looked at him.

"That is my life. After we are wed, it will go into you. It will mix with your seed and from us, together, will come our children."

She nodded, then just stared at her belly. After a moment, she shifted and looked down at him, ran her gaze from his head to his chest, his hips and lower. She stared at him for the longest time.

He began to laugh. "Don't fret. It will grow again."

She punched him in the arm and said, "I know that."

"Oh? And how do you know that?"

"Women talk."

"What do women talk about?"

"Things."

"Such as?"

"Men."

"What about men?"

"Their hard heads."

"Only their hard heads?"

"And their privy members. What do men talk about?"

"War and weapons and women, not necessarily in that order."

They grinned at each other.

She moved a little closer and smiled at him, the first truly real smile she had ever given him.

He felt something inside of him stop, like his heart.

There was no malice there, no honeyed sweetness that was feigned. No play-acting.

Just a smile.

He slid his arm under her and pulled her close, tucking her head with its crown of black, saucy curls under his chin.

He rubbed his chin over her head, over the soft hair, and she flinched.

He pulled back and looked at her head, frowning. He raised his hand and ran it over the top of her head. "You have a knot."

"Aye." She was quiet for a long time, then she sighed and said. "I was juggling some wooden balls and missed."

"I heard."

"What?" She sat up and looked down at him. "You wretched thing, you. You knew?"

"Aye. That was how I found you, following the trail of your accidents." He paused for a moment, then said, "I thought the wild pig tossing you into the gutters was particularly vivid, at least according to the tavern owner on the corner where you were performing this great and entertaining feat."

She began to laugh then. "I must have looked so stupid and silly."

He gave a sharp laugh. "You? Never."

She sniffed at him and raised that damn chin up. "At least I *can* juggle."

"Aye, just remind me to be out of the country when you try it again, or at least a good furlong away." He smiled at her indignant expression.

She punched him with her bony little knuckles.

He grabbed her and pulled her back into his arms. "Go to sleep."

She lay her head on his chest and was quiet. After a while she said in a sleepy voice, "I hate you."

"I know." He looked down at her and brushed a lock of hair from her brow, then planted a kiss there. He breathed in the scent of her. He stared down at her features, the nose, the full lips, and the face that could drive him mad with anger or desire.

He lay there, thinking about what she had just said, staring up at nothing. He moved his mouth closer to her and said, "We need strong emotion between us, you and I. Hate or love, we both have to feel something." He closed his eyes and fell asleep to the soft sound of her even breathing.

CHAPTER

18

She awoke to a sharp slap on her bare bottom. She rubbed it and scowled up through sleepy and blurred eyes.

Tobin was standing over her, dressed in mail and looking as if he had single-handedly won a war—a tower of manhood and obnoxiousness.

She buried her head in the pillow. "Go away."

"Get up."

"I can't. I died."

"Get up or I'll take that cold bath water and dump it on you."

"God in heaven above . . . You would do it, too."

"Aye, that I would." He started to turn away.

"Don't move!" She sat up and blinked, then groaned and grabbed her aching head.

He tossed her clothes onto the bed. "We have to leave soon. The men are waiting below. We must go to meet the others."

She was wrapping the linen binding around her chest and looked up and asked, "What others?"

"The rest of my men."

She tied a knot in the linen, then another to be sure it would hold her. She put on her tunic and braies, secretly wishing they were clean.

Tobin strapped on his sword and looked down as he secured the buckle. "My man Parcin took half the troop and went to search to the northeast." He glanced at her then. "I could not be certain which way you went. We are to meet them at the crossroad to the Marches this morn."

It took only a few long strides for him to cross the room. He stood next to the bed as she sat there and pulled on her boots. After watching her for a moment, he reached out his hand and used his knuckle to tilt her chin up.

She had to look at him.

His eyes were clear and awake and serious. "You caused no little trouble running away like that."

She did not respond. She had nothing to say, a rare moment. So instead of defending herself, she stood and went to the water and splashed some on her face. Then she dried it and turned, facing him, her hands on her hips and her chin high. "Quit dawdling, then, and let's be off. I am ready."

He gave a wry look and a bit of a smile played around his mouth. He took a step, reached around her and opened the door, then gave her a gentle shove into the upstairs hallway.

They walked down together. She saw the women whispering among themselves near the bar and caught the odd and disappointed look the blonde barmaid cast in Tobin's direction.

Sofia had to fight back a grin and a giggle.

He grabbed some bread and cheese that was wrapped for the road and tossed some coins onto the bar.

"Thank ye, sir," she said without looking up. "A safe trip to ye and yer . . . boy."

Tobin gave them a casual wave and followed Sofia out the door. She looked around her at the sunny sky and the fresh air. "Ah! What a wonderful morn!"

He frowned at her, then shook his head and crossed to his mount, where his men were waiting.

She walked behind him, a jaunt to her step. She cast one quick glance back over her shoulder, then ran to catch up to him. "Tobin?"

He was adjusting the saddle strap and looked up.

She slid her arms around him and said, "Kiss me."

He did not protest when her mouth covered his. He straightened, his hands went to her bottom and he pulled her close, burying his tongue in her mouth.

She was laughing when they broke apart.

He studied her for a moment. "What was that about?"

She grinned. "Not much, sir."

He picked her up and set her on the saddle. "Why do I have the feeling that I should be worried?"

"I do not know. Perhaps 'tis your ego responding. Look there." She pointed to the small window where all the barmaids were gathered, their expressions odd.

He looked back at her.

" 'Tis disappointment you see in their faces."

He was still frowning.

She began to laugh. "You do not understand? I shall explain. You just kissed me in front of them. All now certainly believe that Sir Tobin de Clare prefers lads over ladies."

Tobin swore, then groaned when his men began to laugh.

He swung up in the saddle and clamped his arm around her. "You are in trouble."

"Not as much as you are if the Church hears of this. I unlocked the door last night."

"You did what?"

"I unlocked the door, after you were asleep. 'Twas a while before that maid came in but what she saw convinced her to tiptoe out and shut the door." Sofia began to laugh.

Tobin just put his spurs to his horse and rode like hell.

* * *

The morn was bright and sunny. The air was crisp, the sky above them blue, the trees and grasses a fresh green from the recent rain. His woman was alive and safe and sitting in front of him, her arms resting casually on his, the one that held her so close to his chest that he could feel each breath she took as they rode.

It seemed as if all was right with the world. Blue skies. Sunshine. Ease in his saddle. His woman's soft breathing. It was one of those of moments that made you think nothing could ever go wrong.

Tobin rode at the head of his troop of men-at-arms. They cantered up the road, over low, green hills and across a small stream, where some trees had fallen and their mounts had to pick their way across. They rode onward, 'round a sharp bend in the road not too far from the turn to the Marches.

Over another hill he spotted a thread of black smoke in the air, just ahead of them. Tobin raised his hand to halt his men.

A rider approached, moving so hard over the road that a cloud of dirt spit up behind him.

Tobin waited, then the rider was close enough that he recognized his own man.

Walter of Banning reined his horse to a stop in front of Tobin. "Sir." His eyes flashed quickly to Sofia.

"As you can see, our trouble is over. I found her."

"There's more trouble ahead. Parcin sent me to warn you."

Tobin caught Walter once again glance uneasily at Sofia, who had perked up and was listening.

"We'll talk in private." Tobin dismounted, as did his man. From the corner of his eye he saw that Sofia watched them. Her eyes were narrowed and curious, and he knew her ears were sharpened. He left her in the saddle and gestured for Walter to follow him. They moved quite a distance. He did not want her to hear until he heard exactly what was ahead.

"Those performers your lady was traveling with. They were attacked." Walter shook his head. " 'Tis not good there, sir."

Tobin turned and looked at Sofia. She was watching him and must have caught something in his look. An instant later she kicked his horse hard and took off toward the smoke.

"Stop her, dammit!" Tobin shouted and his men rode after her, the thunder of their horses drowning out his curses. He ran and swung onto Walter's mount, then spurred it forward. He made it past his men, only a few lengths behind her. The closer they got, the more you could see, even with his men scattered over the area.

He shouted to his other men, "Stop her! Parcin!"

He saw his man turn.

"Stop her!"

Parcin ran and mounted, then rode toward her.

Tobin kicked the horse harder and harder. But Sofia was light for his powerful mount and could ride like the very Devil.

She drew closer; he rode harder.

Tobin could see Parcin closing in on her. She turned and shot his captain a sidelong look, then suddenly cut his horse sharply to the left.

Before Parcin could see what happened she had dismounted and run right past him.

Tobin leapt off of his mount and chased after her.

She was screaming, "Alan! Alan! Miranda! Bernard! Oh God! Nooooo!"

He lunged forward and caught her, his arm slid around her waist. He jerked her back against him and turned her away from sight.

She was kicking the air, battering his arm and face with her fists. "Let me go! Let me go to them!"

"Sofia! Don't. Stop!"

She shook her head, screaming, "God no . . . No! Nooooo! Let me go . . . Please . . . Let me go!"

A large male body lay twisted in the grass. The face was unrecognizable from where he stood for all the blood.

Parcin came to his side and Tobin shoved Sofia into his arms. "Hold her."

Tobin walked over to the site. It was bloody and morbid and smelled of smoke and blood and death.

Another man, younger, tall and slim, lay facedown with a foot-long blade wound in his back. It looked as if he had been running for the wagon, which was overturned and burning.

His men stood by a lump in the grass, near where the woods to the west began. He crossed the grass and his men parted as he looked down.

He had seen the horrors of war, seen victors put the heads of their vanquished on pikes and parade them through the streets, had seen men drawn and quartered. But what was done to this woman was the worst thing he had ever seen.

"Bury her first, then the others."

The men nodded. Their faces were grim and taut and looked as he felt. Sick and disgusted and angry.

Sofia was screaming his name and cursing. Screaming and kicking and fighting Parcin. She was yelling, "Miranda! Dammit, Tobin! Maude and Tildie!"

He frowned. There were only three bodies, the two men and a woman. He turned to his men. "Is there anyone else?"

"Not that we could find, sir."

He moved toward Sofia. Took her from Parcin and clutched her to his chest. "Sweet, be still, be still."

He pressed her head to his shoulder and she sobbed and sobbed. "They are dead. They are all dead. . . ."

"Listen to me, sweetheart. Please listen. There are three dead. Two men and a woman."

"The twins. Girls. Matilda and Maude. Oh God, Tobin, find them, please . . . We have to find them."

He turned to Parcin. "Did you see anything else?"

"There is another wagon with a cage. 'Tis empty."

"Satan," Sofia whispered. "The bear."

Tobin began to shout orders to his men to scour the woods, everywhere.

"I want to go, Tobin. I have to go, too. Please. Please."

He was afraid of what he would find. "I cannot take you. You must stay here."

"No! I will not!"

"She stays," he said, then spun around and walked away.

They drew their swords and combed the woods, each man taking a section. The trees were thick and the brush high. Moss hung from the branches and the crowns of the tall trees blocked out the sun.

As sudden as thunder came a loud, deep roar.

His men called from the east. Tobin and the others ran through a dark trail and over some rocks. Two of his men stood nearby, where lay a body—a man's badly mauled body.

"The bear. He is down there." His man nodded down into a slight ravine with rocks and trees on either side.

Four more bodies were along the bank. These had to be the outlaws; they had been torn apart, limb by limb, by the bear.

The bear roared again and stood on his hind legs and pawed the air. The animal wore a collar and rope hung from it.

Tobin heard something and turned. "God's eyes! What was that?"

A small sob and then a call, "Mama? Mama?" A child's wail and sobs.

The bear shifted and Tobin saw a small, blonde head, then another. There were two children cowering behind the fierce animal.

"That bear will rip us apart if we go near there."

"I know. We might have to kill him. But first, move those bodies someplace. Don't bother burying the bastards. Then bring Sofia, tell her we found the twins and they are alive."

Parcin asked, "What are you thinking?"

"The bear might recognize her. She might be able to help. If she cannot control the bear, we will kill it. Bring six of the archers, have their bows out, the arrows notched and ready."

Tobin watched the bear pace in front of the children, protecting them. He did not want to kill the animal. If it weren't for the bear, those children would be dead and the outlaws alive.

He stood there waiting. Soon his man brought Sofia through the woods and to his side.

"Where are they?"

He pointed toward the rocks.

She looked down and saw the bear. "Satan," she whispered.

"The twins are behind him. There on the rocks." Tobin grasped her shoulders. "Now listen to me carefully. Do not disobey me, or I swear to God I will have the archers kill him now. Do you understand?"

She looked into his eyes and nodded. "I swear. I just want the children safe."

"We all do. Now I'm am going to walk with you. Slowly. I want you to call to the bear. We'll stay on this side of the ravine and see how he reacts. Do you understand? I will be at your side. You will not pull away. You will not leave me."

"I understand. I swear."

Tobin grasped her arm tightly in one hand. His

other was on the hilt of his sword. "Come then, slowly."

They moved cautiously out from the trees.

The bear paced on the rocks, back and forth, back and forth.

A child called out, "Ned!"

"I'm here, Tildie! I am here, Maude! Ned is here for you. I swear. You are safe."

The bear stopped, then drew up on his back haunches and pawed the air. But he did not roar or bare his teeth like before.

"Call him," Tobin said quietly.

"Satan!" she said, then louder, "Satan!"

The bear sat back and put his paws down. He watched them, but did not move.

"Keep talking to him and we'll edge closer."

"Hallo, there Satan. Good laddie! 'Tis I, Ned. See?" She held her hands out to her sides. "That's a good bear. Can you dance? Can you dance for me?"

The bear continued to study her, then lay flat on his stomach like a hound and rested his head on those massive paws.

Sofia kept talking quietly to him and to the little girls, kept asking the bear to dance.

Tobin slowly drew his sword, then checked to see if his archers were still ready. The men stood with their bows between their splayed legs, the arrows notched and pulled back near the archers' ears.

They moved closer and closer.

"Tobin, easy. I swear," she said. "All will be well."

"That bear killed five men, Sofia."

"The outlaws?"

"Aye."

"Good. I hope he ripped them to shreds."

He said nothing. He would not tell her that was exactly what the bear had done.

"He will not harm us. Look. He is asleep already."

Tobin eyed the bear and stopped. 'Twas hard to believe but it looked asleep. Sound asleep. He could not fathom that the bear would suddenly drop to his belly and start snoring, but that was what he was doing.

"He sleeps. Whenever he is supposed to dance, he sleeps." She started to move forward.

Tobin pulled grabbed her arm and her back.

"No. Do not worry. He will not harm me. I must take the girls. If you are with me he might harm you."

Tobin gave her a look meant to make her understand he could handle the bear.

She only said, "I will hand the children to you."

He did not like that, but kept his sword raised, because he knew she was right. This time. And he was certain of his men; the archers could hit the bear before anyone was hurt. "Get the children then."

Sofia reached out to them and called to them softly.

The girls crawled forward, crying.

She handed one to him and he tucked the child to one side, his sword still raised and ready. She grabbed the other little girl and handed her to Parcin, who had come down from the back side and was standing on the rock above the sleeping bear.

Tobin looked up. Behind his captain stood four more of his archers. Ten in all. His men were making certain he and Sofia were safe.

Tobin handed the other little girl to his man and he grasped Sofia's arm. "Come."

She knelt and picked up the rope.

"What are you doing?"

"Taking Satan back."

"God's blood! Woman—"

"We cannot leave him. You will not kill him. We must take him with us."

Tobin looked up at Parcin, who gazed back at him

with sympathy. Tobin gave up and said, "Take the children away. We will bring the bear. Then all will ride for Glamorgan."

Sofia turned. "Glamorgan? Why?"

"The King and Queen are there for the christening of one of Earl Merrick's children."

"I knew of the christening. That is where Alan was headed. To Camrose to perform for the guests. 'Tis why I left them." Sofia said nothing else.

Tobin kept his sword high as she tugged on the rope. The bear opened his eyes and stared up at them.

"Come Satan. Come along. 'Tis time to eat."

"Eat?" Tobin frowned at her.

"Aye. He will come along easily if he thinks he will be fed."

Tobin was not so certain the animal would come along anywhere easily. He had seen the outlaws' bodies.

But Sofia tugged on the rope and the bear stood, then she turned and it lumbered along behind them like a big dog instead of a man-killing beast.

By the time they had come through the woods, all that was left of the horrific site were the charred remains of the wagons. She fed Satan bread and cheese and they locked him back in his cage. The lock was broken, but Parcin managed to make a bar from one of his knives and some rope to keep the door bolted tightly.

They were all soon mounted, the little girls asleep, exhausted from the shock. Walter was holding one little girl and Parcin, the other. Both had the twins hugged tightly in front of them as they rode north and east, toward the Marches

Tobin could feel Sofia's teeth begin to chatter and she was shaking. He body was slack and she sat huddled before him, almost as if she were shrinking.

He tightened his arm. He knew there was nothing he could do, nothing but hold her. He could not make what happened go away. He could not change it or even make the memory of it go away.

He was not calm and unaffected by what happened. He was well aware that had he not found Sofia, she could have ended up like Miranda. And for the next few hours he did not know whose hands were shaking more—Sofia's or his.

CHAPTER

19

Tobin chose to split their journey in half, for the sake of Sofia and the twins. But he sent his squire Thwack and a few of his men on to Camrose with news of what had happened. He did not wish to have the story retold in front of Sofia and the children. They did not need to relive the horrors of this day.

So Tobin and the remainder of his men traveled more slowly because of the children. They rode along the winding road that led toward the Marches, which was not as well-traveled as the roads from London to the south and west. By nightfall they had found only a small tavern with one room to let. For the last two hours the skies had been clouding up and the taste of rain was in the air. Tobin decided not to search out better quarters but instead to stay put.

It did not take long before they were seated at tables with wooden bowls of warm food in front of them. The twins perked up when they saw the food.

"I like beef pie," Maude said when she looked at the food and she picked the pieces of meat out of the crust with her small fingers.

"I like butter," Tildie said and slapped a huge chunk on her dark bread.

"I like beef and butter, too." Tobin said, then he handed

the little girl next to him another chunk of warm bread
and watched as Sofia picked at her food, staring into the
bowl but taking little.

"Mama says butter is too dear for us. We only get butter on special holidays. Huh, Maude."

Maude nodded at her sister, then picked a piece of
beef from Tildie's pie when her sister wasn't looking.

After a moment, Tildie put her bread down and she
looked up at Tobin. "Where's Mama?"

Sofia's head jerked up and she looked at Tobin.

"Those awful men took her away." Maude said.

"Are you finished eating?" he asked the girls, changing the subject.

"Aye."

"But if Satan killed those mean men," Tildie looked at
her sister. "Where's Mama and Papa?"

He stood. "Come with us, girls, and we'll show you
your bed for tonight."

"Sofia." He held out his hand to her.

"Why do you call him Sofia," Maude asked. "That's a
girl's name. He is Ned. Aren't you?"

Sofia looked at the girls. "Come upstairs and I shall
explain."

They took the girls upstairs to the only room and only
bed in the place. The girls ran over and plopped on top
of the bed with its puffy goosefeather tick.

Sofia stopped at the doorway and turned to him. "I
will talk to them. I will try to explain."

"Do you want me to stay?"

She shook her head and started to turn.

"Sofia." He said her name quietly. She turned and
looked up at him with those huge eyes. They looked so
empty. He reached out and stroked her cheek. "Get some
sleep."

She didn't say anything, but just turned and closed the
door. He stood there for a moment, remembering. Wor-

ried. She had spent most of the meal staring off at nothing, as if her mind were hiding from what her eyes had seen.

He turned and walked down the stairs. He knew that feeling. He knew what her look meant and knew that sleep would at least be an escape, one she probably needed.

Once downstairs, after a few more rounds of ale, he and his men bedded down on the heavy oak tables or on the floor. Time passed so slowly, with the sharp crackle of the fire and the soft sounds of his men sleeping. But sleep escaped him.

It seemed as if he'd been lying there awake forever, as if it had been hours since the tavern owner banked the fire and blew out all but the one small stub of a candle that sat in a cracked bowl on the bar counter.

The floor was hard, but he'd slept on hard floors and even harder ground. The single saving grace was that he was near the fire. He lay there with his hands folded behind his head and he stared up at the ceiling, where he could see the woven thatch pattern of the roof. Vermin were rustling around in the straw above him, sending flecks of straw drifting down to land near his head.

He could hear his men snoring, one of them was talking in his sleep, but even when Tobin closed his eyes, sleep completely eluded him. His mind would not stop for some reason, so he lay there thinking of Sofia and those twin little girls, thinking about what they had gone through that day.

He and his men were used to war, used to carnage and blood, at least as used to it as one could become. They had seen before the cruelty man could inflict upon man. Yet what they saw today still made some of the men quiet and pensive, some were short-tempered, while others drank too much. For himself, well, he could not sleep.

He remembered the first time he had seen men killed.

He'd been squire to Earl Merrick when the Welsh had struck and killed, and later, when they had taken over Camrose and captured Merrick's lady wife. Plenty of men were killed during the siege and Tobin had seen bloodshed many times since then, enough to make him accept what he had to do.

But unlike other knights who could kill and never think of it again, never truly see the fear in the man's eyes the instant he knew he had lost, Tobin remembered every look of fear, of resignation, of pleading. They were difficult images to wipe from his mind.

And he never forgot the blood. The first time he saw blood spilling out of a man he turned away and vomited. His hands shook for two days and he could not sleep for a week.

Now he lay here once again, not sleeping.

There was a creaking sound, like that of the a foot on a loose stair. He turned and looked in that direction.

Sofia stood on the narrow steps, gripping the handrail and staring at him.

He shifted and stood carefully, so he wouldn't disturb the men. Then he picked his way across the room, stepping over man after sleeping man. He moved up the stairs, to where she was sitting.

He looked down at her.

She was hugging herself, rubbing her hands up and down her arms as if she could not chase away the cold.

"What are you doing up?"

She averted her eyes and shrugged, which was so unlike Sofia.

Tobin sat down next to her, watching her shiver. He could stand it no more and opened his arms. "Come here."

She leaned into them instantly.

"Are you cold?" He rubbed his hands up and down her back, over the bones of her shoulders and her tail bone.

She shook her head.

"Cannot sleep?"

"Nay," she whispered.

He rested his chin on the top of her shorn head. This was not his Sofia, this vulnerable and quiet young woman with the pain and puzzlement that showed in her eyes. He only wished he could take away the events of this day.

But he knew he could not, so they stayed that way for a while, then she shifted, pulled back, resting in the ring formed by his arms as she looked at him.

Her face held little expression and her eyes were haunted, dazed.

His gaze moved to her mouth, then back to her eyes again. When he looked at her face, he wanted her. Every single time. Whether he was angry or not, he still wanted her.

But that was what he was feeling, not what she was feeling. He knew he could act, she was vulnerable and would succumb to whatever he wanted. Or, he could talk to her. He kept one arm around her and brought the other to rest on his bent knee. "Are the twins asleep?"

"Aye, they fell asleep quickly."

" 'Tis good. Sleep. You do not have to think when you are asleep."

"Aye, but you have to stop thinking long enough to fall asleep."

"True. Did they talk about today at all?"

"Some. They are confused. Lost. They don't quite understand that Alan and Miranda are not coming back." She stared at her hands. He wondered if she even saw that she was wringing them together, over and over.

He slipped his arm lower around her, nearer to her waist and took one of her hands in his free one, then he slowly ran a thumb over her palm. "A child does not understand death. All they know is that their family is gone."

She looked up at him, then shifted her gaze to somewhere past his shoulder, her look miles away. "I remember," she said quietly. "God above, how I remember that feeling."

He looked down at her, for she had spoken with such emotion. She had closed her eyes almost as if by doing so she could close out the past.

"You were about their age when you lost your parents," he said.

"Younger, even. I was four when I lost my mother." She paused, then added, "My father died a little later that same year."

"Yet you can still remember how you felt."

"As if it were yesterday." She paused, then added, "I felt as Maude and Tildie must feel, lost and alone. Confused. Frightened and hurt. All those things at once. It becomes almost too much for anyone to experience. To have your life one way and then in just one single moment, in a single event, have it change and know it will never, ever be the same again."

"You remember feeling that way when you were only four?"

"Aye."

"I am not certain I could remember anything from when I was four." He glanced at her and said honestly, "I think perhaps I believed you had to be older to feel the repercussions of death."

"Just because you are young does not mean you do not feel. You might not know what it is that you are feeling, but you feel it all the same. You just cannot put a name to what it is, because you are too young to even know the words to describe it.

"Perhaps you do have to be older to understand what you are feeling or to think about the consequences of losing someone, but you do not have to be older to do the suffering. You do not have to be older to be scared or to feel as if your life is suddenly gone."

He thought about what she had just said. He supposed she was right. "I was ten when my mother died. It was just after I was fostered to Earl Merrick, but he was Sir Merrick then. Before Edward gave him the title and the lands."

"Do you remember how you felt?"

"Aye, I remember. I wanted to kill my father."

She looked at him and frowned. "Why?"

"Because I was told that while my mother lay dying in her bed, my father was sleeping in his with her successor."

"Is that why you hate your father?"

"I do not hate my father."

"You do not?"

"No. I feel nothing for him. He is not worth hating."

She sat there, but asked no more and he was thankful for that. He did not mean to reveal that to her.

After a pause she said, "You were gone from home when she died."

"Aye."

"Were you close to your mother?"

"She was a good woman. Both my sister Elizabeth and I adored her." He wanted to say nothing more about it, to stop this talk. He sent the conversation in another direction, one that was not close to the things he kept deep inside of him, things for him to know, but no one else. "You talked to the children for a long time earlier, before we put them to bed."

"Aye."

"What did they tell you?"

"Mostly they wanted to know why I was truly a girl when I dressed as a boy and had a boy's name. They say I do not look like a girl."

"I would have liked to have heard the explanation you gave them."

Her voice grew choked. "I lied to those people, Tobin. I lied to those kind good people. All because I wanted to have some freedom. All on a lark."

"You did not know what would happen."

"That does not make what I did right. I liked them. They were kind to me. And I lied to them."

He did not say anything. There was nothing he could say. So he just held her. "Did the children say any more?"

"They talked about what happened. In a child's terms. Children see so much but read so little into what they see. 'Tis just black or white to them, no middle ground."

"I suppose that is a good thing, a way for them to be protected until they are old enough to understand all they see and what it means."

"Perhaps. I truly do not know." Sofia paused, then looked up at him. "Maude said Miranda pulled them down from the wagon and told them to run into the woods, and not to come out until she came for them." She looked away, then added, "They did what Miranda asked. But Tildie told me that Satan had killed those bad men, which they had to have seen from where they were hiding."

Neither he nor Sofia said anything. The two girls had seen men mauled and killed by a bear, a bear they played with, the same bear that was protecting them when it turned killer. He wondered how black and white that would seem to those girls.

He could feel Sofia's shoulders begin to shake. She pressed the heels of her hands into her eyes. "God in heaven above, why? I don't understand why? They were good people."

He pulled her into his arms and held her against his

chest. "You never will understand. 'Tis not possible to know, I think."

"But it is not fair. It is not right. What kind of God takes good people away?" She cried then, just a slip of tears and a slight heave of her chest that showed him how vulnerable she truly was.

"Good people die all the time, sweetheart, which is why death is difficult for those who remain behind."

"I know," she said on a sob. "But 'tis not fair. 'Tis not right."

"The world is seldom fair or right."

She did not say much more and her crying did not last much longer. She quieted soon, then sniffed and took a deep breath; it had an exhausted sound.

She should be asleep, he thought. And before he might have insisted she do so. But for some reason he could not explain, he chose not to try to force her back to bed now. He just sat on those stairs and held her to him, listened to her breath and rubbed his hand slowly over her back and neck, then cupped her head gently as she leaned it against his shoulder, because for some reason it felt as if her head belonged there.

"It all seems so very senseless," she whispered.

"I've seen senseless death over and over, Sofia. Every time it happens, you wonder how there can possibly be a reason for it." He paused, tightening his arms around her as she settled more comfortably against him. Her breathing was slowing and becoming even, the breathing pattern of one who was almost asleep. He rested his chin on the top of her head as he leaned back against the stair railing, stretched out his long legs and closed his eyes. "At some point," he said quietly, almost as if he were speaking to himself. "At some point, you finally understand that perhaps there is no reason at all."

A few moments later they were both asleep.

* * *

By midday they rode inside the massive gates of Camrose, through the outer and inner baileys and near the forebuilding of the keep.

Tobin dismounted. He reached up and lifted Sofia down, steadied her with his hand on her elbow, then he cast a quick glance at Parcin and Walter. His two men had been so good with the small twin girls, treating them as if they might break, talking softly to them, showing them hawks and harts and rabbits as they rode along. While watching the girls talking to his men, Tobin was reminded once again of the strength of children, and the versatility of his men. Having seen these men in war, seen the courage and strength and valor with which they fought; it would seem unbelievable that those two warriors could be as gentle as they were with those little girls.

Each man handed down a twin, and the girls stood there, their small faces too solemn, their eyes darting left and right the way a small animal did when it was cornered.

"Come, Sofia. You and I shall take the children inside." Tobin and Sofia each took the hand of a child and they turned and walked together up the steps of Camrose.

The front door opened with sudden force and Merrick came out. "Tobin!" Merrick grasped him by the shoulders and gave him a quick shake. 'Tis good to see you, my friend." Merrick took a step back and his gaze flicked to Sofia.

"Lady Sofia, welcome." Merrick gave Sofia a long look, but wisely kept quiet as she curtsied to him, still clad in her braies and tunic and her shorn hair. "Come inside. The Queen is in the solar with Clio. She is most anxious to see you, as is the King."

Sofia stiffened.

Merrick must have caught her reaction because he added, "As soon as he hears you are here."

Sofia said nothing, but she gave a small sigh of relief.

Merrick looked at the children, so Tobin said to them, "This is Earl Merrick. He is the lord of this castle and our good friend."

The children stood frozen, staring up at the earl.

Sofia added, "He is kind, girls, and will not harm you. I swear."

Merrick cast Tobin a knowing glance. He looked down at the girls, then immediately squatted down so he was eye level with them. "What have we here, Sir Tobin?" He looked back and forth between them. "They are two small and brave warriors, I'll wager."

The girls looked at each other, then Maude said in a clear voice, "We are not warriors, milord. We are *sisters*."

Merrick feigned surprise, then looked from one to the other, frowning and acting silly and confused.

It seemed to Tobin that fatherhood and his lady wife had done wonders for Merrick de Beaucourt.

Merrick rubbed his chin with one hand. "Sisters?" He frowned and then pretended to look closer and from one to the other. "Aye, I can see the resemblance now. I do not know how I could have missed it."

The girls were not identical but their faces were similar and their coloring was the same.

"You were not paying attention," Maude told him, which made Merrick laugh.

"Aye, little one. I swear to you that I shall pay more attention in the future."

Maude actually smiled at him, the first smile Tobin had seen from either child.

Tildie tapped him gently on the arm, clearly wanting to be included.

He turned to her.

"We are twins," she told him.

"Twins? You are not twins!"

The girls nodded.

"Aye. We are," Maude said.

"Well, Sir Tobin!" Merrick said with a laugh as he looked up. "What say you to that? Camrose is the most fortunate of all castles, for we shall have two sets of twins here this day. Your squire is with his brother as we speak. Surely Old Gladdys would rant and rave and dance around one of her many bonfires chanting that such is a sign of good fortune."

"Most fortunate," Tobin agreed.

Merrick glanced back and forth between the little girls. "Wait till my Lady Clio hears of you two. My wife's two favorite people are twins. Do you know Sir Tobin's squire?"

The girls shook their heads.

"Well, I trust you shall soon. He too is a twin and his brother is here at Camrose." He rested his arms on his bent knees. "Now tell me, who is who?"

"She is Maude." Tildie tapped her thumb on her small bony chest. "And I am Matilda, but do not call me that, for I forget to answer." She gave Merrick the most serious of looks. "I am truly called Tildie."

"Well, Maude and *Tildie*," Merrick said with emphasis on the little girl's name, "Lady Clio will be much pleased to meet both of you." He leaned closer as if he were telling them a secret. "She keeps telling me I am not hearty, you know, because we have only one babe at a time. But then she also complains that I am not eating enough sweets, so I can give her a daughter. She does not wish to be the only woman in the family. All three of our children are lads. Not beautiful little girls like you two." He straightened to his full height.

The little girls looked at each other, exchanged some kind of intimate look, then stood there with their eyes only on Merrick, who had just won their hearts with his attention and charm.

"Let us take them upstairs, then you and I shall speak alone," Merrick said to Tobin.

Tobin nodded, but gestured for them to step aside for a moment. "I should speak to the King before he sees Sofia."

Merrick gave a slight nod, then turned back and held out his hands to the girls. "Come along, my young ladies. We shall go to the solar, where you shall see the Queen." He looked down at the little girls. "Have you ever seen a queen?"

"Aye," Maude nodded. "We saw her pass by in a coach once. I even saw her face, but Tildie missed it."

"I sneezed," Tildie told him, sliding her hand in his.

"Well, come along, you two. I think you should see the Queen up close. I shall introduce you myself." Merrick began walking toward the solar, his steps slow and smaller to accommodate the girls'.

"The Queen." Maude leaned in front of Merrick and looked at her sister as they walked up the stairs to the quarters above the hall. She whispered loudly, *"Tildie! We are going to meet the Queen!"*

"Aye, and I shall not sneeze this time."

Tobin slid his arm around Sofia as they both moved forward, but when they reached the stone stairs, he grasped her elbow and looked down at her for a quick glimpse.

She felt smaller to him, as if the life in her had melted away. Perhaps he felt that way because she was being so much quieter. Perhaps because of what she had said the night before. Or perhaps because of what she had not said.

At the top of the steps they turned and there was Lady Clio. She looked at the children, then at Sofia and Tobin. She rushed to Sofia. "Thank God, you are safe." She hugged her and Sofia murmured Clio's name. Clio released her.

She gave Tobin a kiss of greeting on each cheek. "I

have missed seeing you, Tobin." Then she stepped back and looked at the girls.

"Clio. Look here at who I have brought. This is Maude and this is Tildie," Merrick told her.

Lady Clio bent down and smiled at them. "Hallo, Maude. Hallo, Tildie."

They girls curtsied and murmured shy hallos. Then Maude said, "We are twins."

"I can see that you are," Clio said.

Tildie frowned. "Earl Merrick could not."

"But I see that you are the same age and you have to be sisters. Besides which, I know twins when I see them. Even if they do not look exactly alike."

"See, Tildie? *She* pays attention," Maude said to her sister.

Merrick shook his head and laughed heartily. "I promised I would take them to see the Queen." He gave his wife a wink.

"Oh, what a fine thing for them. I shall wait here and then as soon as they have met the Queen, we shall take them to the kitchens and see if we can find a sweet. I believe the cook is making pies this morn. With plums." She turned to the girls again and bent down. "Would you like plum pies?"

The girls nodded shyly.

"Afterwards we can visit my little boys. They are napping now. Edward is the eldest. He is three and into everything troublesome."

"Like his mother," Merrick said under his breath.

Clio ignored him and continued. "Next is Roger. He is not quite two, and the new babe, little William. He was christened two days ago. Would you two like to meet our sons?"

"Aye." Both girls nodded enthusiastically. Then Tildie took a step toward Clio and bravely said, "When I meet the Queen, I shall not sneeze."

"Good." Clio nodded as if she understood perfectly, then straightened and gave a small puzzled shrug to the adults. She looked to Merrick with a smile. "Eleanor is in the solar, love."

Clio turned to back Sofia. "You should go, too. She has been most anxious to see you." Clio gave a quick nod at the thick doors near the end of a narrow hall lined with yellow beeswax candles in iron sconces that gave off a bright and flickering warm light. "Let Merrick take the girls in first, and then you can be alone with her."

Tobin looked down because Sofia's hand tightened on his as she give Clio a weak nod. Sofia's face was pale and wan. She looked as if she were going to be ill. She took a deep breath, looked up at him and said, "I must see Eleanor."

"I'll walk with you," he told her.

Together they followed Merrick and the twins down the candlelit hallway to the room where the Queen of England was waiting.

CHAPTER

20

Sofia did not know what to expect when she entered the solar after Merrick and Clio took the twins away. She knew Tobin had sent men ahead with news that she was found safe, and with some of the news of what had happened on the road. However, she did not know exactly how much anyone knew.

The Queen stood near a mullioned window, her back to the door and her pale hand resting on the back of a deep scarlet tufted chair with a tapestry covered footstool sitting in front of it. The Poleaxes were sitting on her left, at a nearby tapestry frame, stitching and speaking quietly with their heads pressed together; they looked like a two-headed monster from the Greek myths.

Eleanor turned, then, and looked at Sofia.

There was nothing but a long, drawn out silence. She then shifted her gaze over Sofie's shoulder. "Sir Tobin," she said quietly.

The Poleaxes whipped their heads around and stared at Sofia, the expressions on their faces telling exactly what they thought; they looked at her as if she was a martyr involved in a lost cause.

"You have brought Sofia back safely, Tobin," Eleanor continued. "I thank you."

He gave her a slight bow. "My pleasure."

Sofia knew she was not his pleasure, but his problem.

"I would like to speak to Sofia alone."

Tobin placed his hand on her shoulder and gave it a slight squeeze, then bowed and left.

The Queen turned to her ladies and said, "Leave us."

The Poleaxes stood, gathered their skirts and marched toward the door, where Sofia stood.

They were whispering as they came toward her.

"We should have bled her," Jehane was saying in a harsh whisper. "Then she would not have had the strength to run off like she did."

"Aye, 'tis true, Jehane." Mavis walked past Sofia, muttering, "We have learnt a great lesson. We shall not give in to her whims again."

An instant later the door to the solar closed with a sharp click.

Eleanor just stood there, her eyes on Sofia.

There was a long pause of silence.

The Queen shook her head. "You foolish, foolish girl." Her voice was raspy and emotional, then she opened her arms.

Sofia ran into them and buried her head in Eleanor's soft neck, where there was that old familiar scent of cinnamon and anise, of safety and of home. "I am sorry," she whispered. "I am so very sorry."

Eleanor patted her back. "I would say that you are sorry, child. If what I have been told happened to your companions is true."

"It was horrible, so horrible," Sofia admitted for the Queen's ears alone.

Eleanor waited for a moment, then took a deep breath. Sofia could feel the small shudder of emotion. After a moment, she gripped Sofia's shoulders and took a step away from her. "There. Let me look at you." She stared at Sofia's head for the longest time, then frowned. "Good God . . . That hair is horrid!"

Sofia did not know if she wanted to laugh or cry. All she knew was that she was so very glad to see her Eleanor.

"Turn around, child."

Sofia chewed her lower lip and turned slowly.

The Queen stood there not saying anything, just studying her for what seemed like forever. "I shall pray that your hair will grow quickly."

"Aye," she said quietly.

"Wherever did you get those clothes?"

"From the rag picker's cart."

"It looks like it," the Queen said. "I have some garments you can change into before you see Edward."

Sofia groaned and sagged so that it felt as if she almost folded in half.

"You have gone and truly done it this time, Sofia. Edward is furious. I do not believe I can plead for you and that he will listen to me any longer. I am not certain if I were him that I would listen to me."

Sofia stared at the toes of her leather boots, feeling sorry and guilty. She had not wanted to let Eleanor down, but the Queen could not understand what it was truly like for her. Eleanor was the Queen of England, and as such men would always defer to her, if for no other reason than Edward demanded it. Sofia was not a queen. Sofia was a pawn.

"Truthfully," Eleanor continued. "This latest deed was such folly that I do not know if you deserve my support. You have damaged my faith and my trust in you. I will not even start on how Edward feels and believe me I know, for he has ranted into my ear every single night since you disappeared."

Sofia winced at that comment.

"I have always believed that you are spirited. Spirit is a not a bad thing for a woman to have, Sofia. But until you did this, I never thought you were an idiot."

It hurt Sofia to hear that. It hurt her badly. She did make a mistake. She looked at Eleanor, whom she respected. "I have made some wrong choices."

"Perhaps you should ask yourself why." Eleanor watched her closely.

Why? Perhaps she did not want to know why she did what she did. Silent tears flowed over the rims of her eyes and her vision was blurred. Eleanor's face became nothing but a pale oval in a sea of tears, tears she did not want to shed but could not help it.

Eleanor closed the short distance between them, then cupped Sofia's face on her hands and placed a soft and motherly kiss on Sofia's brow. She swiped back the short fringes of hair and sighed. "I do love you, child."

Then she moved to the door and opened it. "You may come inside, now," she said.

Sofia turned around.

In marched the Poleaxes with a train of servants carrying food and water and a tub. She had the sudden and horrid sense that she was reliving another day all over again. She closed her burning eyes and groaned.

The Queen left and the Poleaxes took over. As her clothing was jerked off her, as she was twisted and turned, poked and prodded, and her skin almost scrubbed off, she knew that between the Queen's women and her audience with the King, the very worst was yet to come.

"Damn Edward!" Merrick slammed closed the door to his bedchamber and stalked into the room.

Clio looked up from where she was combing her hair dry by the fire. Ah, she thought. Here he is . . . the earl of Curses. She watched her husband walk across the room and stand near the window in the tower that faced east, opposite of where the sun was setting. Its glow came through another window, where it spilled through the opening and turned the walls and floor the color of wild heather.

She set down the comb and rose, then crossed to where he stood, tall and stiff and angrier than she had seen him in a long time. She slid her arms around his broad chest and rested her hands on his ribs, her cheek against his back. "What is it?"

He inhaled and then placed his big hands over hers. "The King has sent de Clare on another of his wild missions to the north. I swear I would think he does not want Sofia and Tobin settled."

"Well, that cannot be. I would think the King would deliver Sofia into the hands of the first good man willing to take her, antics and all. And as for Tobin, even now he still clings to that pride of his. He is not an easy young man to twist to one's way of thinking. Although I suppose after time, he did listen to you."

"He was afraid of me."

"Aye, he was. But for Sofia, the fact remains that he is one of the few young men who will not let her walk all over him. It seems to me that they are the perfect couple." She smiled and added quietly, "They fight like you and I did."

Merrick gave one sharp laugh. "As much as that?"

She pinched his skin.

"Ouch! Stop pinching me, woman. You and Sofia are not so much alike. Besides, Sofia is not cooking up ale that makes men lose their wits."

"Nay. I believe Sofia cooks up other schemes. But still they will keep Tobin busy."

"Not if Edward keeps sending him off to the wilds on some fool's mission. Tobin was ready to wed her soon. She is certainly old enough. He was firmly ready to take his vows. We spoke of it just this morn. Then he goes to speak to Edward and the next thing you know he is riding off to the north borders again."

"What is Edward going to do about Sofia?"

"He is speaking with her now. I do not know what he will do, but rest assured he has some plan in mind, otherwise de Clare would still be here." Merrick frowned as he stared outside for a few more moments, then he turned around and linked his arms around Clio. "So tell me, woman, what you did the rest of this day. Lie around and munch on sweets?"

"Aye. I had nothing better to do," she said lightly. "What with a new babe, another barely two and the eldest into every nook of this castle. Maude and Tildie were so amused by the children, Merrick. It was such a joy to watch."

"What do think of those little girls?"

"They are delightful and very bright. They spent the afternoon teaching Edward how to turn a somersault. Even Roger was trying, but he could not seem to get his bottom over his head. You would never know what those sweet little girls have just been through to see them with our sons. 'Tis a terrible thing that happened."

"Aye."

"I am always amazed at the resiliency of children. Thud and Thwack were like that. They were wonderful from the first moment I took them in."

"So you told me before," Merrick's voice trailed off as if he had more to say.

"What is it?"

"I was thinking today."

"There is more troubling you. What is it?"

"I thought perhaps we should keep Maude and Tildie here. They have no family left. No place to live. It looks as if Tobin and Sofia will not be together anytime soon. We would be the perfect choice to take care of them."

Clio stepped back and gaped up at him. "Truly? You would like Maude and Tildie to live here? With us?"

"Aye. 'Twould keep you from nagging at me about

being the lone woman in a castle of men. I told de Clare we would take them. If you gave your consent."

"My consent! Oh, Merrick! You know how badly I have wanted a little girl. Now we shall have two!" She raised up and kissed him, but missed his mouth and hit his scratchy chin instead. "You need to shave, love."

"Aye. But we could still have daughters, Clio. I do not believe Old Gladdys and her dire predictions. She is a crazed old bat."

"I do not care if she was wrong when she told me I would never give birth to a daughter. I do not care if all our future children are girls. I would still want to make a home for Maude and Tildie here."

He smiled. "I thought you might. We do have one problem."

"What?"

"The bear. Satan. What in God's name are we going to do with that bear?"

Clio stood there and thought about it for a moment, then she grinned. "I shall send a message to Teleri."

Merrick winced, then he began to laugh. "I swear Roger will challenge me. That charming little wife of his will have him here in less than a week." He was still laughing under his breath. "Poor Roger. A bear along with all those other animals she keeps." He shook his head.

Clio shrugged. "It could be worse."

"How?"

Clio grinned. "We could send the bear to Teleri with her grandmother, Old Gladdys, as an escort."

Merrick laughed loud and hard. "I do believe that things have been too quiet for Roger of late. I told him at the christening that since he married he has become old and dull. I would love to see his face. A dancing bear and Old Gladdys. That old Druid woman made his life a living hell . . . until he wed her granddaughter."

Clio exchanged a devious look with her husband. "You tell me, husband. Shall I send the message?"

Merrick was rubbing his chin thoughtfully. Then he looked at her, nodded and grinned. "Aye."

Then Merrick was laughing along with Clio. A moment later he swung her up into his arms, lifted her to his mouth and kissed her the same way he had so long ago. He crossed the room with her, never breaking that kiss and fell back on their bed, pulling her on top of him and holding her head with his hand so her mouth was where he wanted it.

Kissing Merrick was still the most wonderful thing Clio could ever imagine, just as she had in that stable yard those years ago, even though they had now been wed for close to six years, even though he kissed her every single day. She still felt that thrill, that excitement, that sense of wonder whenever his mouth touched hers. He was still her earl of Lips.

King Edward was sitting in a huge, ornately carved chair near a trestle table where there were maps and parchments spread all over the table top. He looked up when Sofia entered the room. His face was unreadable, but his eyes pinned her. She moved forward with a defiant shake of her head. She would not cower before him.

"Sire," she said as she curtsied. Then she straightened and met his hard gaze.

He was resting his chin in one hand, which was propped on the arm of his chair. His eyes narrowed dangerously and he did not look away. Without saying a word, he turned and rolled up one of the maps, then took his sweet time retying it. He set it aside and did the same to the next map. And the next. Never speaking. Never saying a word to her.

She knew he liked to make tense moments to watch her squirm. The trouble was, it was working. It seemed

like a lifetime before he finally stood up, staring down at
her from his lanky height.

He locked his hands behind his back and began to
pace the room, his long strides eating up the short distance, his eyes staring at the floor.

He turned and looked up. "Sofia." His voice was quiet
and even, as if he were just barely acknowledging her.
But to those who knew Edward, like Sofia did, he was
his most lethal when his voice was calm.

'Twould have been better for her if he were shouting
at her. He moved back to the table, stopped, and looked
at her. His hard gaze fixed on her scalp and not her eyes.

She felt the aburpt urge to hide her head from him and
she hated that abrupt weakness in her. Her fists tightened
at her sides, but she took even, easy breaths.

He turned away and moved to the chair and table,
then he sat down and leaned back, resting an elbow on
the chair arm as he rubbed his chin thoughtfully and
watched her.

She wondered what he was thinking, what he would
say.

He looked away for a long time and there was nothing
but angry and taut silence between them.

When he turned back to her his expression was no
longer controlled. "God's eyes, Sofia!" He slammed his
fist down on the chair arm.

She jumped.

"I should lock you up in the tower and swallow the
bloody key!"

She said nothing.

"You are my ward. You are betrothed to a powerful
family. You are most fortunate that the de Clares have
not used this act of stupid defiance to break the betrothal."

"I am most fortunate or you are most fortunate, sire?"

"Ah . . . you speak, with your usual bitterness, I see.

Apparently seeing men and women cut to shreds has done nothing to curb your defiance."

She looked down, then, staring at her clasped hands and trying not to shake.

"You seem to believe that your bond to the de Clares is not to your fortune." He gave a sharp bark of laughter. "I had not thought you were stupid, cousin. Foolish, but not stupid. We have no need to bind you to them. Do you truly not see? I already have Gilbert de Clare. He is my vassal and he will not break his vows to me. His son is young and strong. You should be praying to heaven that you are not wed to someone like Alfred de Bain."

She flinched at that name.

Edward paused, then said, "I see your skin pale at that suggestion. It should, for we both know what kind of man he is. Did you not know that he wants you? He made a most generous offer for you when you were but three and ten. I dismissed it, even though he continued to make offers. He has buried another wife since then, I believe."

She could feel her lips thin. Her hands were still clenched at her sides.

"But that matters not. However this does. Hear me, well, Sofia. I swear to you now, that should you do something to destroy your betrothal with de Clare, I will give you to de Bain, and then I will turn my back and let him do with you as he wishes."

Sofia stood there, fighting to keep from showing him that she cared, but she knew she could not hide from that threat. It was terrifying.

"Do you have any understanding of what you have done?"

"Aye."

"I want to hear you tell me what you did. I want to hear it from your lips. I want to know what in the name of God you were thinking."

She stood straighter then. "I ran away. Alone."

"We are aware of that."

"As I am aware, sire, that I am a female. Females have no freedom. We have no choice. Men make the choices for us. So I chose to live as a man. I chose freedom, and even if it had only been for a day, for an hour, 'twas my freedom. If you lock me up and swallow the key, even if you throw the key into the Thames, at least I shall always know that, for a fortnight, I had no man who controlled me." She poked her finger into her chest. "*I* controlled my life for those days. And no one else."

"And from what I hear you almost got yourself killed."

"I was not with them."

"I swear to you, cousin, this is the last time you shall have an opportunity for such folly." He stood. "The *very* last time." He clasped his hands behind his back and he stood with his long legs slightly apart, staring at her, waiting or watching, she did not know which.

She refused to ask what he would do. She just stood there as he was, staring and waiting.

He shook his head finally and said, "You will go to the convent of Grace Dieu, in Leicestershire. There you will spend your days praying for humility, meekness, obedience, and sense. And you will stay there until de Clare returns."

"Returns? Where is he going?"

"He has already gone."

Sofia felt something inside of her die, just wither away as she stood there. He was gone. Gone again.

"He has duties elsewhere," Edward continued. "You will stay at Grace Dieu until he returns to wed you."

He had left her. He did not even say farewell. Nothing. She was feeling as confused and as hurt as she had before she escaped.

"I sincerely hope that you have learned a vital lesson from your scampering all over the countryside."

"Aye, Your Grace," Sofia said.

"Then tell me. I want to hear the words from your mouth."

Sofia took a deep breath, then exhaled and cocked her head when she looked back at him. "I have learned that freedom is truly a wonderful thing."

BOOK

TWO

Sofia closed Eleanor's journal and stared down at it for the longest time, resting her hand on the heavy silver cover. The entries and her memories were fresher and clearer than she'd have ever thought they could be, when so much time had passed.

And people said time made you forget. She did not forget, even though that part of her past seemed now like another lifetime ago. She laughed to herself. Perhaps it was.

Now, when so many years had passed, she no longer had Eleanor, the mother she had but never truly realized until she was much older and much wiser. Sofia missed Eleanor terribly. It had been too many years since the Queen had died. The country had mourned, but no one had mourned her more than Edward. The King brought her body through the countryside, marking the path of her majestic funeral with white crosses, symbols of his love and respect for his wife and queen. The crosses were still there and whenever Sofia saw one, she remembered and she cried.

She glanced at the clock again. There was time before she had to go belowstairs, before all began and she had no more time to sit up in her room and reminisce like some old woman.

Sofia set Eleanor's ornate book aside and picked up

the other one, the one with the plain wooden covers and the simple leather ties.

Like the other book, these pages had illumination, but not as much, and there was no colored pigment to the ink, just a few scrolling lines that made a square design in black on creamy but thinner parchment pages. Here were the words of the other woman who had so influenced her life, a mother too in her own way, for she taught things Eleanor could not. But Judith was no queen, though there was no doubt in Sofia's mind she could have been.

Sofia flipped back the cover and began to read.

She came to me on a dismal and rainy day, the young woman who would brighten my life, and bring joy and no little furor to what I had foolishly thought would be my quieter years, for one does not think there would be anything but peacefulness and passive quiet within the ivy-covered, fieldstone walls of a nunnery in Leicestershire, particularly a convent such as Grace Dieu.

But the sky was black and churning that day, spitting rain angrily down upon the earth, where it pocked the ground and drenched all who traveled, as if the Lord Himself was trying to flood the land clean, as He had once done, in those days long ago when He told Noah to build his ark. I have oft times thought that my Lord God does work in mysterious and amusing ways. Surely He must have a wicked sense of humor to be able to look down upon mankind day after day and not laugh at what we do to ourselves? What other explanation could there possibly be as to why Lady Sofia Howard would come into her exile at Grace Dieu in the middle of the worst storm in two decades?

Nay, God has a sense of humor, and fortunately, so do I. . . .

CHAPTER

21

Sister Judith skimmed through the newest entries of the convent's books, where Sister Katherine of Shrewsbury had meticulously entered not only each birth of the keeping cattle and swine, but also their ages:

> *5 boars, i.e.——two ages three years, two ages two, and one, born on the Fifteenth day of April, and now aged one; ten sows, i.e.——nine at three years, and one aged one; ten porcelli lactantes sub matribus (suckling pigs). . . .*

Sister Judith looked up from the precisely recorded pages and pinched the bridge of her nose, her fingertip rubbing the puckered skin of an old and ugly scar that cut down the side of her face and neck and even slashed downward over one shoulder.

My eyes are getting old and weak. Must be from too many years in that hot desert sun.

She cast a quick glance up at Sister Katherine, who was standing before the small desk, her hands clasped in front of her and her look expectant.

Judith dropped her hand to the books, stared at them for a moment, then closed them before she faced the other nun. "Well, sister. Should the bishop need to check the books you so finely documented, there would be no doubt that pork is the chief food consumed at Grace Dieu—youthful pork, middle-aged pork, and/or elderly pork."

"Aye, sister," Katherine said with vast pride and absolutely no awareness of Judith's cynicism. 'Twas like a wind went whistling right past Katherine's ear. Her kind and innocent mind never understood the nuances of Judith's acerbic wit, not that sweet and pious Sister Katherine of Shrewsbury would have understood such had she heard it. She had a purity of spirit, a sweet kind of simpleness and a dedication to God's work like no other of the fifteen Augustinian nuns who lived at Grace Dieu.

The bell outside the walls of Grace Dieu rang loud and long and frantically. Judith placed her large hands on the table edge and pushed up on her good leg. She leaned down, picked up her crutch and tucked it under one arm. "Come." She hobbled toward the door. "We must meet this visitor."

"Are we expecting someone?" Sister Katherine raced after her, for Judith could hobble on her crutch and one good leg faster than any of the other nuns could run.

"Aye. Were I to venture a guess, I'd say that is the King's escort, with his young cousin, the Lady Sofia Howard, who is to reside here until the King or her betrothed sends for the girl."

"But, sister, we do not take in highborn children any longer. Not since Sir Thomas Hunt's young sons set fire to the altar, then buried the reliquary containing our sacred piece of the True Shroud in the vegetable garden."

From the corner of her eye, Judith saw Sister Katherine churn her arms to keep up, so she slowed her step a tad.

"Beside the turnips, they buried it! Turnips! I still cannot fathom it," Katherine muttered.

"Aye, 'twas a sacrilege to be sure, but Lady Sofia is no

child. No cruel lad. She is seven and ten, betrothed to Gloucester's eldest son, second cousin to the King, who paid enough gold that we could rebuild seven altars, travel to Jerusalem and purchase the rest of the True Shroud were she to take it into her head to destroy Grace Dieu's treasures, which I doubt, since she is not a lad of seven or of nine and spoilt silly, as Hunt's brats were."

Judith open the door that led to the courtyard and moved under the cloistered walkway toward the front gates.

Two of the other sisters were already there. Sister Alice of Avon said, " 'Tis a royal guard, sister."

"Aye, I figured that would be them." Judith balanced on her good leg and pointed her crutch at the iron bar that secured the wooden gates. "Open them, now. Swiftly, sisters, before the poor souls drown out there waiting in this devil of a rain."

The bolt slid open and a troop of armed men, wearing royal colors of scarlet and gold emblazoned with a *lion passant,* rode into the courtyard of the convent, the horses' hooves clopping a dull sound on the flooded stones.

Within a few moments all had taken refuge inside and Judith watched the men part as a tall young woman walked from the center of the troop toward where Judith was standing. The girl's face was partially hidden by the wide hood of her blue cloak, but she walked tall and straight and with the manner of a queen, something Judith could respect and came as a bit of a surprise, since she expected a mealy-mouthed, simpering young girl.

The girl stopped before her and shook her head.

The hood fell away.

Judith gave her credit for that action, especially when the nuns gathered nearby gasped at the sight of the proud young woman who stood before them.

They all stared at pure proof of God's perfect hand. The girl's features were breathtakingly lovely—the small but straight nose, the white skin and fine bones, her full mouth, and the shortly cropped hair that was so deep a black it shone like the onyx candle holders that decorated the altar. But it was her magnificent skin that caught Judith's eye and appreciation, white, white skin that appeared untouched by the harshness of an intense sun.

Even before she had gone to the East, Judith had not the pure creamy skin of this young woman. For the first time in years she felt envy.

She stepped forward. "Lady Sofia. I am Sister Judith of Kempston, prioress of Grace Dieu. We welcome you, and may His Lord bless you and keep you well while you are within our walls."

"My thanks, sister." The girl nodded, quickly averting her eyes, but by the time she raised her head up again she had returned immediately to the straight look she had been giving Judith.

No, Judith thought, this was no simpering lass. She adjusted her crutch and raised her free hand, gesturing toward the hallway beyond. "Come. I shall show you to your room."

"Thank you."

Judith looked at the King's men. "Please bring the lady's belongings."

"That won't be necessary."

Judith turned back to the girl with a questioning glance.

"This is all I have brought." She pointed to a small handled trunk that one of the guards held easily and lightly in his large hands.

"You travel light for a noblewoman, Sofia."

"I have all I need," was all she said.

"Then follow me." Judith walked down the long, dark and cavernous hallway that led to the small cells used by the nuns of Grace Dieu.

*   *   *

Sir Tobin de Clare rode north toward the Scots border, on one of Edward's more useless missions. He was to take papers of some kind of agreement between Edward and his sister's husband, King Alexander of the Scots, to a meeting place near Carlisle.

Tobin was still bent in half about it. 'Twas a puny messenger's mission, not one for a knight and half of his men-at-arms.

Merrick had voiced it best when Tobin had told him of the King's order. Merrick knew Edward better than Tobin. "He has a motive, Tobin," Merrick had said as he paced the guard room in long and angry strides. "He would not send you on this mission unless he has some other plan that is cooking."

Tobin knew what that plan was. For some reason, Edward did not want them wed yet. There was no reason for him to be carrying these papers north. No reason other than Edward wanted to put miles between him and Sofia. This trumped up mission had come on the tail of Tobin's royal request for permission to wed immediately.

Parcin rode up to Tobin's side. " 'Tis getting dark." He pointed ahead of them, in the area he had just reconnoitered. "That ridge up ahead will be a good spot to make camp tonight. It looks out over the entire valley and the roads, both north and south."

"Fine. Tell the men we will stop there for the night."

"Aye."

Tobin shook his head and turned in the saddle, looking back as his captain rode along his troops, relaying the plan. He turned back and faced the road.

'Twas a waste of time. They all knew there had been more trouble from the Welsh lately than from the Scots and there were almost no skirmishes near the Marchlands. He and his men were about as safe here as they would be riding into London. He waited until Parcin was

in place behind him again, then Tobin spurred his horse
toward the ridge.

By sunset, just after the bell for Vespers, Sofia was in
the long, dark windowless room that served as a dining
hall, sitting with the nuns at a huge trestle table while
they ate their food with great fervor, and she stared down
at it with great horror.

The bread was dark bread, not the sweet dark kind
made with honey she'd tasted in London when she was
with Alan and Miranda. But heavy dark bread with hard
flecks of whole grain that hardly looked as if it had ever
been milled into flour. Certainly it was nothing like the
smooth bread made from white flour that was always
served at the King's table.

There were no courses, no fowl to begin the meal, no
rich, dark meats, only tough salted fish, ling cod, with a
dollop of muddy-looking mustard, and as for vegetables,
there were only some pale and sickly colored mashed
turnips, without seasoning. Sofia watched the watery
turnips spread across the trencher of dark bread and con-
geal next to those two dry, weathered-looking strips of
salted cod.

The meal looked about as appetizing as dining on her
oldest pair of shoes.

Sister Katherine looked up from her food. "You are
not eating."

Sofia shook her head and took a long drink of the
water in her goblet so she would not have to answer.
Goblets for water, not for wine, because there was no
wine, no sweet honeyed mead. There was nothing but
plain well water.

Sister Katherine turned to the others. "Lady Sofia is
not eating."

They all looked up, chewing, and stared at her as if
she were mad.

Sister Judith, who was sitting at the opposite end of the table, gazed at Sofia as if she could read her thoughts. "Perhaps Lady Sofia is not used to our simple fare."

Sofia was not fool enough to lie in a room where she was surrounded by nuns. Even she did not have that much pluck, nor did she choose to push her luck with God, so she said nothing.

"Perhaps her journey exhausted her," Sister Katherine suggested, and gave Sofia a gentle pat on the hand before she returned to her meal.

Sister Judith gave Sofia an arched look. "When she is hungry, she will eat." That being said, she went back to finishing her food, too.

The meal was over soon after and Sofia made the mistake of standing to leave, only to find goblets and turnip bowls shoved into her arms. She stared down at them.

"Come along." Katherine glanced back over her shoulder on her way out the door. "We must clean up the table and the pots from the kitchen."

"But you have servants," Sofia said. There was a distinctive whine to her voice that she couldn't have masked had she wanted to, which she did not. She went after Katherine. "But I saw them. They made and served the meal."

"Aye," Katherine turned and stacked another heavy pewter bowl on Sofia's forearm. "But they go home to their own families at sunset. We clean up after the meals." She bustled back and forth, back and forth, like a guard on a castle wall. From the table to the minuscule kitchen that was in truth nothing but a drafty wooden shed built off the dining room. "Since we eat the meals, it seems only right that we should clean up after them, don't you think?"

Sofia did not mention that she had not eaten. She did not think that argument would count a whit here.

"Put those in the wooden tub and scrub them clean with the sand."

"Sand?"

"Aye. There in the jar on the shelf. While you do that, I shall fetch some hot water." Katherine bustled outside the small shed, where there was a fire pit for cooking and a tall stone oven.

Sofia frowned at her work, then she looked up, spotted the fat jar, and scooped out a handful of sand. She rubbed it across the bowl; it mixed with the turnips and became huge sticky clumps that did nothing but spread and smear over the metal bowl. She stared down at the clump of stuff stuck to her hand.

"What did you do?" Katherine was next to her, also staring at the mess in Sofia's hands.

Sofia glanced over one shoulder. "I rubbed the sand on it the way you told me to."

Katherine frowned, then looked up at her with a completely baffled look. "But you did not scrape the food off first."

Scrape off the food? You did not tell me to scrape off the food first.

Before she could speak, Katherine lifted a pot of water and dumped it over Sofia's hands and the bowl and into the washtub.

"Ouch!" Sofia yelped and jumped away, shaking her scalded hands in the air and then fanning them.

"Was the water too hot?" Katherine jammed her bare hand into the tub up to her elbow. "Doesn't feel too hot to me. Feels just about perfect."

Steam wafted up from the tub and turned the air moist from the heat. The nun must have had skin like leather. Scowling, Sofia stared down at her red hands and she rubbed them gently together. They still throbbed.

"Give your hands time, my dear, and they will become accustomed."

What was she going to have to do to have her hands used to being boiled? She had no chance to ask, because the next thing she knew, Sister Katherine stuck a turnip bowl in her hands and told her to "scrub."

The night was clear, a thousand stars were scattered over the sky above the ridge. Off in the distance, over the jagged tops of the trees, rose a line of steep, gaunt hills that were Scotland. It was quiet; nothing stirred in the trees that bordered the ridge, and the peat fires around the camp were burning down to a smolder.

Tobin squatted in front of one, an arm resting on his knee as he chewed on a piece of roasted hare. He finished, then tossed the bone in the fire, where it sizzled and caught flame.

He stood, nodding goodnight to the men there and moved to another fire where they were sharing a fat wineskin. He raised the wineskin in the air and drank, then passed it on to the next man. One of them told a bawdy jest that made them all laugh and then Tobin took the time to speak with each man, saying something personal or commending them.

He had watched Merrick de Beaucourt over the years he'd spent with his mentor, first as page, then squire. He learnt the importance of knowing his men well, for they were the ones who guarded his back at the risk of their own lives, and who swore fealty to him, the same way he had to Earl Merrick, Sir Roger, and then the King.

He spoke to the watch guards, then moved to where he'd dropped his saddle, like the others, and he bedded down, lying under the stars with his hands folded behind his head. An image of Sofia's face was there before him, blocking out the stars, the night sky, those hills and trees, everything that was truly there.

She haunted him. Her face would come into his mind whenever he least expected it. He did not know why and he did not like it, but over time he was used to it, mostly because it had been going on for so many years. It was as if she had seeped into and under his very skin, for there were times when she was almost all he could think of; it was about to drive him mad. He wanted them wed, had brought her back with that in his mind as the next step. In fact, he wanted it so badly that when Edward had told him of this mission, Tobin had left swiftly, for fear he would do something treasonous.

He inhaled deeply, then exhaled.

There came a shout.

Tobin sprang up in one lithe motion, pulling his sword from its sheath.

A second later, a band of Scots stepped out of the woods, almost as if they had come from the tree trunks.

He looked left, then right. They were surrounded.

Two of them held his guards fast, dagger points pressed into their necks.

"Yield, English, else yer men die here and now."

Tobin inhaled sharply, angrily, then dropped his sword.

CHAPTER

22

A short time later Sister Katherine led Sofia back to the tiny room that was to be her new home. She unlocked the door and opened it. Sofia had been told that the women of Grace Dieu were locked into their rooms every night at Compline so they could pray in peace.

Sofia figured they probably prayed for release from a life in a place that seemed to be little more than a prison. They even referred the those rooms as cells. The only thing missing were the bars.

She undressed and washed, then lay down on the small, narrow bed, with its lumpy and thin straw tick and no linen sheeting. She pulled the single, rough woolen blanket over her shoulders and felt a chilly draft skate up her bare legs. She raised up on one arm and looked down.

The bed was so short her feet hung off the end. She flopped over onto her back and folded her hands behind her head. She stared around the dark little room and felt more alone then she had felt in a long, long time.

She closed her eyes so she would fall asleep more quickly. Then she would not have to think. Then she would not have to feel. Then she would just be asleep.

But she could not sleep. Something was eating at her. Tension.

It was the same every night. Her mind would take her back to the places she did not want to go back to: sometimes back to the sight of her friends and their dreadful fate. If she ever fell asleep after that, she would have nightmares of being chased down roads or long dark hallways, of being caught and grabbed by grubby murderous hands and having no way to protect herself. She would awake in a cold sweat, her bedclothes soaked and her body shaking.

Then she would lie awake, trying to think of something, anything, else. It never failed. Sometime before dawn, her thoughts went to Tobin. Back when she had no will of her own, back to those kisses she craved and the moments when his hands roved her body and touched her in places that no one but she had ever touched before.

And she would imagine herself in his arms again; it was the only way she could sleep—to think of him. It was the only thing that would block out her fears.

She would lie there and imagine his kiss. His scent. His touch. Even when she told herself she should forget him. Even after he had hurt her that first time, and again. She could tell herself to forget him, but her heart and her mind would not.

The truth was: she was his. Not because of the betrothal, although that did make it official. She had been his ever since the first time she'd seen him, perhaps even since that first hoodman blind game when she was but twelve.

And he had gone and left her again.

Tobin had not even bid her farewell. He was her betrothed. He had seemed to enjoy her and she him. They had been intimate together in that inn and he had held her all night when she could not sleep.

And yet he had not even bothered to say good-bye. He was just gone again, and no one knew for how long.

She called herself every kind of a fool for ever secretly hoping or even thinking he would be different from any man she had known.

The truth was: men left women.

Oh, they could touch you and kiss you and desire you, they could tell you lies and make you promises. They could talk about your children and your future, but men were fickle. They did as they pleased. They trotted off somewhere in the name of duty or of honor or of war, and left you wondering if they had ever even been with you at all. Or if perhaps you had imagined their touches and words and kisses. Imagined even those promises.

So he was off somewhere and she was here, in a convent. For how long, she did not know. Her cousin told her she was to pray for humility and meekness.

She closed her eyes and sighed. She'd had a taste of convent life this afternoon and evening. And her biggest fear was that she did not know how she would live through the boredom of it all.

After her first week at the convent, Sofia collapsed into that small bed every night at Compline, exhausted, closed her tired eyes, and with her last waking breath she prayed for boredom.

The nuns had a lovely boundary garden at Grace Dieu, for which they felt great pride, since they had made it to resemble Gethsemane. The very next day after her arrival, it had became Sofia's duty to weed that garden. When the weeds were all gone, Sofia was to replant it, then to water it, bringing bucket after bucket of water from the well at the opposite end of the convent.

She learned to mix wood ash, garbage, and chicken manure, which stank of the most foul odor possible, and how to shovel and blend them into the soil. She was to rake the garden clean each and every day, and change the water in the birdbath that sat behind the convent, where the hill was so steep she had to the stop seven times and catch her breath before she could even reach the top of it.

When she was not in the garden, she was helping each of the nuns with their duties. She fed cattle. She counted pigs. She mucked out the stables and carted the muck back to the vegetable garden near the kitchens. She gathered eggs from hens that did not want to part with them, and was pecked until she threatened to cut off their beaks and feed them to the pigs. She washed linen and towels until soon her hands were chapped and dry and she had blisters across her palms.

She pressed and cared for her own clothes. She made her own soap. She lugged firewood from the Charnwood Forest where the nuns themselves would chop it. By the end of that first week, she ate the salted cod and the watery turnips. She even ate the dark bread.

And then Easter week came. Blessed Easter, a day when she had no duties whatsoever. Sofia came into the dining hall and sat down on the hard wooden bench. She bowed her head with the others as Sister Judith gave the Lord thanks for their meager fare. Then she opened her eyes and unfolded her cracked and blistered hands.

It was then that she smelled heaven. She knew it must be heaven because nothing on earth could possibly smell that wonderful.

The nuns were chattering back and forth, until the door between the kitchen and the hall creaked open. There was a sudden lapse of silence and the women turned almost as if they were one, their faces expectant and happy.

Then Sofia saw why.

In came the servants and the cook, carrying platter after platter of the most incredible looking and smelling food Sofia had seen since her arrival. One placed a platter on her right.

"Is that what I think it is?" she asked the man.

" 'Tis stuffed pork roast with gooseberries and almonds." He made a slight bow and left.

She grabbed the serving spoon and piled some on her trencher, just as another platter was placed by her right elbow. She stared at the piles of golden beef pies and decided she had died and gone to heaven.

The food was some of the best she had ever tasted and she ate until she could barely move and hardly had any room left for the strawberry tart with clotted cream flavored with almond paste and raisins.

She leaned toward Sister Katherine and whispered, "Please tell me that you eat such wonderful feasts on every holiday."

Katherine looked at her, then frowned. "Aye."

Sofia sighed happily and smiled. "I can eat the salt fish and turnips day in and day out if I know I shall eat like this one time every month or two."

"One time every month or two?"

"Aye. On the feast days, when we do not have to eat salt fish and turnips."

Sister Katherine looked to be thinking hard about what Sofia was saying, then she began to laugh loud and hearty.

The others turned and looked at her.

"Tell us all what is so amusing, sister," Judith said.

"Lady Sofia thought we ate naught but salt fish and turnips every day!"

All the nuns laughed as if that were the most humorous of jests.

Sister Judith chuckled and said, "It seems that our Lady Sofia needs to check a calendar."

Sofia frowned.

Sister Katherine turned and patted her chapped hand.

" 'Twas Lent, my dear. The salt fish, turnips, and dark bread were all we have for our penitential meals."

"Do you mean I shall not have to eat salt fish again?"

"Not till next year."

Sofia gave a loud whoop of joy and they all laughed.

The de Clare messenger, Squire Thwack, rode wildly up to Windsor Castle and reined in his mount.

"Who goes there?"

"Thwack of Camrose, squire to Sir Tobin de Clare! I have urgent business with the King!"

The drawbridge dropped down and they raised the portcullis. The squire rode through faster than a charging knight. A short time later the doors opened to the King's war room, where Edward was going over maps with his advisers.

The squire came through the doors, bowed deeply, then handed a sealed parchment to one of the King's men, who took it to Edward.

He was sitting in a huge chair before the massive map table. "What is this that has your breath escaping you so, lad?" He glanced down and examined the seal. He looked up. "This is from your master?"

"Aye, sire."

Edward broke the seal and unrolled the message. He looked up a few moments later, his eyes narrowed and his manner stiff and controlled, then tossed the message aside. "It seems some of the clans object to the negotiations between my sister's husband and myself. They confiscated the documents and have de Clare and his men. They demand terms and ransom, from both Alexander and myself."

The room erupted in protests and Edward raised his hand. "Cease." He looked at the Exchequer. "How are the coffers?"

"All of the scutage from this year is promised, sire. We cannot possibly—"

"Fine!" Edward cut him off. "Send word to Glouces-

ter. See if he will ransom his son. We cannot." He looked
at de Clare's squire. "Ride back and tell them we are un-
concerned. They can have de Clare."

"Sire?" Thwack gaped at his king.

"I shall deal with my wife's brother directly," Edward
told the others, then turned to the squire. "You are still
here?"

"Nay, sire." Thwack turned and left the room and the
castle, made haste not for Scotland, but instead for Camrose, to notify Earl Merrick.

It was with renewed strength from such a fine meal
that Sofia rose the next day and went about her duties.
She had finished the laundry and was in a hurry to take a
huge stack of towels down the steep stone stairs of the
convent's east wing. She had promised Sister Katherine
she would help her with the convent's account books,
which was better work since it was raining something
fierce outside.

Sofia came around the curve in the steep stairs at a
half run, and hit someone. Hard. Towels flew everywhere. She shrieked and fell backward, slamming her
back so hard on the edge of a stone stair that she saw
stars for a moment.

She winced as she pushed herself up and blinked. She
looked around and saw Sister Judith lying at the bottom
of the stairs, her crutch a few feet behind her and her
face a mask of pain.

"Sister Judith!" Sofia stood and ran down the stairs. "I
am so sorry. Oh. Please. Are you hurt badly?"

Judith shifted a little and winced. "I think I shall be all
right. Help me up, child."

Sofia slid her arms under her shoulders and helped her
sit upright.

"Fetch my crutch."

Sofia scooted across the stones and grabbed the

crutch, then crawled back and set it against the wall. "Let me help you. Please, sister. I feel just horrid. I swear I did not see you." She grasped the woman under the arms and tried to lift her up, but she did not have the strength, for Judith was a tall and robust woman, in spite of her withered leg.

"Just give me the crutch, girl, and I shall do it alone." Judith's voice was sharp and angry.

Sofia sat back, feeling more wretched. She handed Judith the crutch and began to pick up and refold the towels.

The sister struggled with the crutch, then managed to get it at an angle so she could use it to help her rise. She struggled and shifted and gave a couple of gasps that sounded as if she were in the greatest pain.

Sofia wanted to reach out and help, but she did not. She was afraid Sister Judith would snap at her again. Instead Sofia stood up, feeling useless and uncomfortable, not speaking, just chewing her lip. Then she said quietly, "I am truly sorry."

"I know, I know . . ." Judith muttered impatiently, waving one hand in dismissal as she hobbled off down the hallway toward the cells.

CHAPTER

23

Judith lay on the narrow bed. Cursing her pride, for had she been born with more humility, she would not have fallen down those blasted stairs.

It was not poor Sofia's fault. There was a hand rail on that stair wall. But she was an old fool who was too full of pride and did not use railings because she wanted to prove to all that she was still as good as before she was crippled.

So Judith was good and angry, good and angry at her own stupidity.

As she lay there, the pain in her leg was excruciating; it shot through her bones and her muscles, up her hip. She could feel it clear into the marrow of her back teeth. She gritted her teeth together and continued to lie there, waiting for the pain to subside.

She flung her arm over her moist eyes and waited, until finally she gave into those tears of pain she fought so hard against. Judith hated those blasted tears. They were a tangible sign that she was weak and more human than she would have liked. She despised weakness, because she always felt she was no sniveler and never had she been a weak woman. 'Twas something she took great pride in.

There was a sharp rapping at the door. Judith raised up

on her elbows and stared at the door through the mist of those tears that still remained in her eyes. She took a deep breath and called out, "Aye?"

" 'Tis I, Sofia."

"I am resting." She lay back down and exhaled tiredly.

There was a long moment of silence, but Judith did not hear the girl's retreating footsteps. She listened again, her ears sharp. Then she realized she was listening for something she would never hear and called herself even more foolish to expect it. Sofia was not one to retreat for any reason.

"May I come in?" the girl asked through the wooden door.

Judith shifted again and tried to pull herself up. It hurt like the very Devil, but she shifted and arched her back, then scooted up, dragging the dead weight of her leg until she was sitting with her back resting against the straw and plaster wall behind the bed.

She closed her eyes tightly for a moment, until the sharp repercussions of her motions subsided and there remained only a dull and aching throb.

She took a deep breath and exhaled, then she looked up. "Come in."

The door opened with a loud squeak that almost sounded as if the old iron hinges were crying, too. Sofia's dark head peeked out from around the half-open door. She stared at Judith from those wide and curious purple eyes of hers, then stepped inside and turned to quietly shut the door.

"What do you want?" Judith asked, trying to keep the pain she was feeling from showing in her voice.

Sofia cocked her head slightly and looked at her with a thoughtful and perceptive expression. "I wanted to ask if you were badly hurt when you fell?"

Judith closed her eyes for a moment and admitted, "I have some pain." When she opened them again she found Sofia sitting on the bed staring down at her lame and useless leg.

A second later the girl placed her hands on Judith's calf and she began to knead the muscles. "It must hurt terribly, this leg, I mean. Even under my hands it feels so tight and knotted."

Judith sucked in a deep breath, because it did hurt and the working of the girl's hands was like a gift from heaven above on her tight and cramped muscles.

Sofia stilled her hands. "Am I hurting you even more?"

Judith shook her head. "I was in so much pain you could not have hurt me more." She opened her moist eyes and told Sofia truthfully, "You are making it hurt less." She paused for a moment, then added. "Thank you."

"What happened to your leg and to your face?"

Judith smiled a little. The girl was very forward and outspoken. Like she had been. Judith would not scold her for it, for she had heard scolding words often enough over her lifetime. She gave Sofia a direct look at matched hers. "I fell from a horse."

Sofia looked at her leg, then her look drifted up to Judith's neck and face and the girl frowned. "What did you fall on to cut your face and neck that way?"

Judith sighed. She could not evade with this one. "The scar is the reason I fell off the horse. I was on my mount, fighting to defend Antioch."

Sofia's hands froze on Judith's leg and she gaped at her. "You? You were one of the warrior nuns?"

"Aye."

"The nuns who fought like men. Like the knights did? Oh! I heard about the bravery of those nuns. Once I heard of it, I dreamed of it. I wanted to fight in a war and wield a sword and do all the things men can do and women are not supposed to do."

"If the truth be told, Sofia, there is little glory in war. But that is where I was injured. A Mameluke rider came at me swiping the air with his sword. I missed a block and he caught my face, this whole side, actually. And I fell from the horse. He struck the horse and it fell on top of me and broke my hip. I do not remember much. I lay there, taken for dead. When someone finally found me, well, this was what I was left with."

"I am sorry."

Judith smiled and shook her head slightly. "I am not. I would not change my life for anything. Not one single day of it."

"Neither would I if I could have gone to war. So tell me . . ." Sofia straightened, which made her bounce on the mattress a bit. "Where did you learn to fight?"

"To be a warrior you must have many skills, child. Many. Fighting was only part of the skills demanded. The first of which is to be able to ride. I was fortunate. My father was stablemaster at Warwick Castle. I grew up around horses and he made certain I could ride."

"I can ride," Sofia said with pride.

"Not pillion, child, but astride."

Sofia stiffened and stuck her chin up. "I do not ride pillion. I ride astride." She tapped a thumb against her chest. "I could outride some of Edward's men-at-arms before I was ten."

Judith smiled. "Good girl. Men should not be the only ones given the freedom of riding over the hills and valleys of this land."

"So tell me what weapon you mastered?"

Judith shrugged. "Not only one. Most of them. I had to be able to wield a sword or an axe. I can use a bow and a crossbow, the lance and a staff."

"The lance?" Sofia perked up the way a small dog does when you toss it a meaty bone.

"Aye. Why?"

"Did you work at the quintain?"

Judith nodded.

"Teach me."

Judith began to laugh. "Nay. There is no war for a woman to fight and even if there were, I would not see you go. These are the days of court and manners, not wild wars and battles. The Crusades are over. Besides which, you are the King's cousin. He would never allow you to ride into a skirmish, let alone a war battle."

"Nay, he would not. Which is why 'tis so important for me to have the skill."

"You want to learn only to naysay the King."

"That is not so. When you say it like that it makes me sound like a small child."

"Then give me a good reason."

Sofia thought about it for a moment. "He wished me to learn humility and obedience. Bah! I shall only learn what I wish to learn." She faced Judith. "And I wish to learn to use the lance, and perhaps the bow and I would love to wield a sword."

"Nay." Judith shook her head. "Nay, Sofia. 'Tis not for your kind."

"What kind am I?"

"You are a lady. You will marry your knight and never need such skills. Edward would have my head on a pike."

"I will never tell him. Surely I swear to you that I shall go to my grave with the secret. Truly. Please, Sister Judith. Teach me to be a knight."

"Nay."

"But. . . ."

Judith held up her hand and shook her head. "Do not ask again. I cannot. Now leave me. I need to get some sleep. Morning comes swiftly this time of year, and I am tired and sore and when I am asleep, I do not feel the pain." Judith stopped, then added, "You should do the same."

Sofia stood in front of Judith, her face a mixture of frustration and thought. Then she sighed and turned toward the door. She stopped and turned back. "Please?"

Judith shook her head. "Goodnight to you, Sofia."

The girl started to open her mouth again.

Judith held up her hand. *"Goodnight."*

Sofia closed the door, but Judith knew this was not over. Telling Sofia Howard about her past was like dangling a sweet before a child. She shook her head. "You should have never told her, you old foolish woman," she said to herself. "Never."

Thanks to Sofia's long and mutinous relationship with her cousin, King Edward the Hardheaded, she'd had many years of experience at discovering how to get her own way.

She was accomplished at pestering.

For the next fortnight, pester was what she did to Sister Judith. Sofia had a good motive. She knew that if Judith did not believe she wanted to learn a knight's skills with her whole heart and her whole soul, then she would never give in, and Sofia would lose this opportunity, one surely given her by God.

So late one afternoon, after Sofia had done her chores and taken on a few more for good measure, she tracked down Judith in the accounts room, where she was handling the account books.

Sofia rapped on the door.

"Come in."

She opened the door with an air of confidence and stood there with her shoulders back and her look as direct as possible, to show the prioress her ability to take the initiative. "Sister Judith? I truly want to learn those skills that only you can teach me. I suppose I could attempt to learn on my own. But surely you would not want me to learn in a ragtag manner, now would you? Certainly there is pride in the instruction as well as the learning? We would be a team, rather like knight to squire. Aye, that's it! Think of me as your squire."

Judith was leaning back in her chair, a long counting instrument with wooden beads held thoughtfully in her hands, as she listened with what looked to Sofia as quiet interest . . . a hopeful sign, surely. After a moment during which Judith looked at her rather intently, she put down the beaded stick she had been holding, raised her hand and pointed at the door. "Go."

"But—"

"Now!"

Sofia rose an hour earlier than was her usual, which was when Sisters Katherine or Alice had to pound on her door to get her moving. But not this day. Sister Judith was to be up early and tend the convent's sheep shearing.

Sofia sauntered up to the small, fenced area where the shearing was taking place. She had her hands clasped innocently behind her back as she watched the sheep shearing with rabid interest and acute observation—this of course would show Sister Judith what an attentive and fine student Sofia would be. "I say there, what a fine day this is for shearing sheep, do you not agree?"

Judith did not look at Sofia, but continued to give instructions to the other nuns, who were holding the waiting sheep while the shearman and his holders shaved off the thick woolly coats.

"Why, look at all the wool!" Sofia bent and tried to look closer, a ploy to show off her attentiveness, since every good student must be attentive. "I did not know one single ewe could produce so much wool." She thought her comment to detail, such as showing her awareness that the beast was a ewe and not a ram, was a nice example of sharp sight.

"Tell me, do the shears have to be sharpened regularly? I can see the blades, right there . . ." She reached out and pointed and the shearer stopped, looked up at her and scowled.

Sofia had her hands resting on her knees and her head was turned sideways so she could watch the shearing more closely. She smiled up at the man. "The blades seem sharp. Do you oil them?"

"Aye," he answered in a gruff voice.

"Which oil do you prefer? Linseed oil, the kind one would use to polish a sharpened broadsword, or palm oil from the East, which of course is used for axe blades, knives and such?"

"Sofia!" Judith snapped.

Sofia turned her head. "Aye, sister?"

"Run along and finish your duties."

"I have finished." Sofia straightened.

Judith frowned. "You have watered all the plants in the garden?"

"Aye. And I plucked out every single new weed that was beginning to grow."

"Gathered the eggs?"

Sofia nodded, rocking from the toes to her heels and back to her toes again.

"Filled the birdbath?"

"Aye. After I did the morning dishes so Sister Mary could read to the village children. I cleaned out the stable stalls and put in new hay so Sister Bertrice could help with the shearing, is that not right, sister?" She looked to Bertrice.

"Aye. She did a fine job at it, too."

"I took the grain to the mill so Sister Alice can grind it and I fed the fish in the pond, without anyone even asking me to." Sofia waited.

Sister Judith looked thoughtful. She glanced back at Sofia, gave a sharp nod of her head. "Fine. Here." She handed Sofia a pile of sheep skins. "Go wash these and set them out to dry."

Sofia took the skins. "And then?"

Judith sighed. "And then you can go into the chapel and pray first for Divine guidance and understanding of the meaning of the words . . . nay, nil and naught, and then you may pray that the Good Lord gives me patience so I do not have you chained to the wall with a rag stuck in your mouth. Now off with you!"

But Sofia had more devices up her sleeves. She could argue to a fine point the reason why, from her perspective, that giving in to her wants would be beneficial to all, which she did, for the next three evening meals.

"What would happen if outlaws decided to attack the convent?" Sofia asked. "Who would protect you?"

All the nuns looked at her and said in unison, "The Good Lord."

"Suppose Viking raiders came down from the north and burned the convent, pillaging and raiding?"

"This is the thirteenth century, not the tenth," Judith said in a wry tone. "The likelihood of a Viking raid in Leicestershire is about as probable as the likelihood that you, Sofia, will convince me to make you into a warrior."

The nuns all giggled.

But that did not stop her. The very next day she heard that the prioress was indisposed with a toothache. She burst into the dining room, where Judith lay atop the table while Sister Alice had her knee braced on a bench and was tugging on the bad tooth with a set of iron clamps.

Sofia elbowed her way in front of Sister Alice. "Here. My strength has improved vastly from all my chores, especially carrying those water buckets. Let me try."

"Mmmmmfph!" Judith started to shake her head and tried to sit up.

Sofia shoved her down with one hand. " 'Twill be fine.

You shall see." She gritted her own teeth together, grasped the clamps in both hands and pulled back with all her might.

The tooth came out so swiftly that Sofia flew backward and ended up sprawled on the hard floor. She looked at the clamps, then held them up, smiling. "See there? 'Tis out!"

Sister Judith sat up slowly, her hand on her jaw, then she looked at Alice. "Remove her . . . *now!*"

Alice all but dragged Sofia from the room.

It was late, well after Sofia had heard Sister Katherine's key click the lock on her door that she heard the same click again.

There was a quiet rapping and she sat up in her bed and swiped the hair from her sleepy eyes. "Aye? Come in."

The door opened and Sister Judith stood before her.

They looked at each other in silence for a moment, then Sofia asked, "How is your mouth?"

"Better," Judith said gruffly. "Now that the tooth is out."

"Oh." Sofia stared at her hands.

"Stand up, girl. Look me in the eye."

Sofia threw back the blanket and rose, then stood with her shoulders back.

Judith had hobbled outside of the door, then she came back in dragging one end of a wooden trunk that she dropped with a hard thud. "Open it."

Sofia knelt down and unlatched the trunk lid. She opened it.

Inside the trunk was chain mail.

Sofia looked up at Judith.

" 'Tis my mail inside there."

Her heart was suddenly pounding in her chest. Oh, she had won! She had won!

Judith limped over to the trunk and took out a long

mail coat. She looked at Sofia, then casually tossed it to her.

Sofia reached out to catch it. The mail coat hit her in the torso and she fell back flat on the floor with a grunt, the incredibly heavy mail atop her. "Sweet Mary and Joseph! 'Tis heavy as stone!"

Judith crossed her arms and looked down at her. "Aye. That it is. And inside the trunk are mail leggings, cowl, mittens, boots, and a leather aketon for protection underneath."

"Good Lord . . ." Sofia muttered.

The tall sister looked down at Sofia, lying on the hard wooden floor under the weight of only one piece of chain mail. "I shall leave these with you, Sofia." She moved toward the door and then turned. "When you can wear the mail and move freely, I will gladly teach you what I know."

CHAPTER 24

Sofia began by carrying the water buckets up the steep hill to the birdbath not merely once a day, but twice, morning and afternoon. The first day her face was so hot it felt as if her skin were burning up. Sweat dripped into her line of vision, making her wobble under the weight of the yoke from which hung the buckets filled with water.

Lord, who would have thought that water could be so heavy?

But she kept moving, up and up, the water sloshing back and forth as the yoke across her shoulders sank more deeply into her neck. She collapsed at the top, gasping. Then, when she found some air, she just sat there staring down at the bottom of that hill. She did not smile. She wanted to, but she had no strength left to lift even the corners of her mouth.

But she had begun.

It took three days before she could make the climb without stopping to catch her breath. The sisters had started to gather at the base of the hill to watch her. Just Katherine and Alice at first, then others.

A week later she was traipsing up that hill three times daily. And the nuns were clapping their hands to the timing of her steps. Every night before she went to sleep, she donned the chain mail and walked around her small room, first in the coat, soon with the cowl and the coat.

Her appetite increased and she ate as if she had been starved, sometimes waking in the middle of the night with her belly crying out for food, so she took to filling a cloth bundle with bread and cheese that she kept under her bed.

A fortnight later she was not walking up that hill, but running, four times a day, then six. The nuns took to praying for her. They lit candles and ended every prayer with, "And dear and gracious Lord, please help Sofia make it to the top the hill."

She rose before dawn, when the sky told her it was still night and the stars had not yet disappeared. She could not leave her room, so she put on the mail coat, the leggings and the cowl and just walked, in circle after circle, learning to move her arms, learning to freely move her legs. She lay down on the bed and forced herself to stand smoothly in the mail. When she conquered that, she lay on the floor and did the same.

It was over a fortnight past Michaelmas. The leaves had begun to turn golden and brown. The daisies were blooming and the nights were just beginning to turn frosty. 'Twas then that the nuns of Grace Dieu were busy making cider.

Sister Judith was in the buttery supervising the pressing of apples, when there was a commotion outside—a shout here, another shout there. Judith frowned. "What is going on, now?" she muttered, then wiped her hands on a towel, grabbed her crutch, and took a step just as the door flew open and rattled hard against the wall.

Sofia stood there in Judith's old mail, the afternoon sun glinting off the metal links, her shoulders straight and her breath completely even.

"Good day to you, Sister Judith," the girl said with a

sauciness that almost made her smile. Then Sofia strolled into the room as easily as a swaggering knight, her arms loose and swinging freely at her sides, except when she placed one hand on a low rafter and ducked under it, almost in a one-handed half swing to show off that she could move with such ease.

She moved around the small room, flexing this and moving that, making certain that Judith could see the ease with which she moved. She bent down and placed her mail-mittened hands on her knees and looked underneath the press, eyeing the apple juice, then straightened again.

When Judith said nothing, Sofia looked around the room, planted a hand on her cocked hip, then turned to her and asked, "Do you need that basket of apples?"

"Aye, child, but—"

"I shall fetch it." She crossed over to the corner and gripped the handles, then lifted the tub of apples high, so high she actually could prop it on one shoulder. She turned without a flinch or a wince and asked, "Where would you like me to put them?"

Judith laughed and shook her head. "Put them down, Sofia. You have made your point." Judith leaned on her crutch and held up her hands in the sign of surrender. "You win, child."

Sofia looked at her. "Truly?"

"Aye. You have earned the right," Judith said, then started for the door.

Sofia froze. "But where are you going?"

"Outside." Judith turned back and gave her a long stare. "Are you coming?"

"Aye," Sofia almost ran across the room. "Where are we going?"

"To the stables, where you can show me how well you ride." Judith ducked under the low beam of the door and hobbled outside into the bright fall sunshine, where all of Grace Dieu stood, lined up, watching, waiting, their faces and eyes curious.

Judith looked at them, then turned back as Sofia walked outside in full mail, a tall and striking beauty whose glossy black hair had grown to her chin, whose bearing was grander and taller after her training. She was every ounce the warrior.

Sofia looked at Judith, who nodded, and Sofia raised her fist into the air the way the knights did when they bested a man at a tourney.

But then Sofia let out a loud and raucous whoop of glee. "I did it! I did it!"

And the cheers that filled the air carried almost all the way to London.

"Sweet Mary! This sword weighs as much as my horse!"

Sister Judith smiled. "Aye, 'tis a training sword. It is twice the normal weight of a sword."

Sofia scowled at the sword. "Why?"

"To help you get used to it more quickly and to build strength in your arm and shoulder. Here, now. This is called a pel."

"Looks like a wooden post to me."

"That's because that's exactly what it is. Now you will vanquish it. This is your opponent. Practice!"

Judith stepped back and leaned against a post near the stables, and waited.

Sofia did exactly as Judith thought she would. She raised the sword high, just as Judith had the first time, and sliced a horizontal path right into the pel.

Judith could almost feel the jar of the strike ring through Sofia's arm, to her shoulder and probably right to her teeth. It must have hurt like the Devil.

The girl cursed so foul a word even Judith was dumbfounded.

"Sofia!" Judith crossed herself and gave Sofia a stern look, but the girl did not notice.

She was sitting on the ground, the sword next to her, her hand dangling limply as she gripped her wrist and rocked back and forth.

Judith hobbled over. There were tears in Sofia's eyes. Oh, she remembered that pain well. She bent down and picked up the sword, then turned its hilt toward Sofia. "Again."

A fortnight later they worked on the bow, a month after that, the quarterstaff and then came the day when Judith set up a quintain.

Sofia was on horseback, her mailed feet strong in the stirrups.

"Lower the lance a bit. That's right. Now tuck the shaft more tightly into your armpit. There. So the lance is firmly seated." Judith limped back a bit. "Now all you must do is strike it! Go!"

Sofia kicked her mount and bent low. She hit the quintain squarely, then turned back to grin at Judith.

The quintain spun around, building speed. It hit her hard in the back and knocked her from the horse.

Sofia lay facedown in the dirt. Her shoulders were shaking. Judith watched for a moment, concerned. She thought perhaps she was truly hurt, to be crying so hard. She hobbled over and knelt down at the fallen girl.

"Sofia?" Judith put her hand on her shoulder.

"I forgot to duck," she said, then turned her face to Judith. She was laughing, laughing really, really hard, as if it were the most amusing thing to be knocked clean off her mount and flat on her face.

"I shall do it again and duck this time!" Sofia climbed back onto the horse, trotted some distance away, then set her lance and took off. She made a perfect strike, then ducked and kept riding until she could safely turn her mount.

The girl was an amazing rider, better than Judith and certainly better than most men. She had never seen the like of it. The lance was easily learned; it had to do with technique, angle, and the right strike, but the true power, the truly skilled like William the Marshall had been, were those rare horsemen who could ride, ride like this young woman.

Sofia reined in front of Judith, kneed the mount up rampant, then turned the powerful horse in a tight, dancing circle. The horse's front legs came down with a thud and Sofia leaned forward, stroking him and cooing to him as if he were her pet. She looked at Judith, grinned with cocky assurance. "So . . . what's next?"

Judith wanted to laugh at her audacity, but an intelligent person did not give Sofia that much rein. She looked the girl in the eye. "Now you must do it all again."

"Again! Everything? But it's taken months!"

"Aye, that it has. It takes squires years to learn a knight's skills."

"But they're men!"

"Your humility astounds me," Judith said dryly.

"It should." Sofia shook her head proudly. Her shorn hair had grown past chin length, was tousled and wavy and so black it picked up sunlight. "I have learnt these skills swiftly."

"Aye. Now you have trained, and understand the basic techniques."

"Then why must I do it all over again?"

"Because. . . ." Sister Judith turned and started to leave, but then she stopped and cast a quick glance over her shoulder. "Now you must do it all wearing armor."

Then she crossed the tilting yard, ignoring the sound of that vile curse word as she silently prayed for Sofia's immortal soul.

* * *

Merrick de Beaucourt took the stairs up the old tower at an even pace, his expression schooled, but his hand near the hilt of his sword, a dagger in his boot and belt, and his mind alert. He was a large man, tall enough that he was used to looking down at most men. But the Scotsmen who were ahead, leading the way up the steps of this stone keep, were a good head taller, with massive shoulders and arms that garnered any sane warrior's respect.

Barely two steps behind him was a contingent of his own men-at-arms, a precaution negotiated with the angry Scots who held de Clare ransom. Merrick followed the Scots through the winding, narrow tower of a crusty keep built on an outcropping of a massive granite mountain.

He cast a quick glance out the arrow slit and could see nothing but air and the misty crags of mountains in the distance. The positioning of the place made it impenetrable. It had taken him no more than a few minutes to see he would not be storming the place to release his friend. No one could ever argue that the Scots weren't shrewd.

One of them put a key into a huge iron lock. He opened the door and gave Merrick a quick, dour look and a nod of his head. "Yer man is inside."

Merrick entered the room alone.

De Clare was standing with his back to him, his stance straight and stiff. He suspected this was how he greeted his keepers. Were he in Tobin's boots, he would be mad as hell, too.

"Is that any way to greet the man who taught you to wield a sword?"

Tobin spun around. "God's eyes, Merrick! 'Tis good to see you." He started toward him.

"I thought I taught you to fight better. How the hell did you get yourself locked in a tower?"

"Go straight to the Devil." Tobin said, but there was relief and something else on his face.

Merrick gripped Tobin's shoulders and shook him. " 'Tis good to see you well."

"Aye. They feed us well enough, if you can stomach oats and hare or hart. We are allowed to exercise in the bailey below, even in the godforsaken rain. I think all it does in Scotland is rain."

Merrick walked over to a table and hitched his hip on it. His look was direct. "So tell me what is going on?"

"They think their king has betrayed them."

"Alexander has repeatedly refused to pay homage for his English lands. Even though Edward is his wife's brother. Why do the Scots think he is betraying them?"

Tobin drove a hand through his black hair. "It has something to do with a strip of land, a loch and another one of their ancient castles. Edward wants the place. God only knows why. Alexander is caught in a quandary. If he does not give the place over, Edward will take his lands in England. But the old Scot who owns the place has the support of the nearby clans. He will not give up without enough of English gold to make him forget he ever owned the place. And then there is the fact that the Scots do not trust Edward."

"Aye. They have seen what has happened to the Welsh. I would not trust him if I were a Scot."

"I do not trust him and I am his vassal," Tobin murmured.

Merrick shook his head. "I know that I am his good friend and I do not know what he is about lately."

"So." Tobin looked at him in expectation. "How soon do I get out of here? I assume you have brought the ransom."

Merrick took a deep breath, then exhaled. "Edward has taken all the scutage he dares. Parliament meets in less than three months. He cannot exact any more gold this year or he will have an uprising on his hands."

Tobin just stood there.

"He wants your father to pay it."

De Clare swore viciously, then slammed his hand on a table. He stood there, his fist on the table, his head down, his breathing deep and labored.

"Your father will have the ransom here in less than a fortnight."

"No," Tobin said.

"Dammit, lad. Don't be so pigheaded!"

"I want nothing from my father."

"Listen to me. I can only get together half the sum. And that will take a month, perhaps longer. I will go to FitzAlan and some others and—"

"Sell my horses."

"What?"

Tobin faced him, his face and jaw tight. "I said sell the de Clare stock. The whole goddamn stable of them if you must. They are mine, not my father's."

"It will take time."

"Fine. I do not care how long it takes as long as I do not have to accept anything from my father. Nothing."

"I cannot change your mind."

Tobin shook his head.

Merrick straightened. "Then I'd best be off. The sooner I go the sooner you will be freed." He crossed the room and took de Clare by the shoulders, embraced him, then stepped back. "I shall wait while you pen a note to Sofia."

"Nay."

"That is a mistake. You need to write to her."

"And say what? Your betrothed is locked in a tower?" He gave a sharp laugh. "I think not."

"I gave you this advice long ago and I am saying it again. Learn to control that pride of yours, lad, especially where a woman is concerned."

Tobin stood without speaking.

Merrick could see the stubbornness on his face.

"I cannot. You'd best go now. I want out of this place before my hair turns gray."

Merrick shook his head and gave the pigheaded lad a clap on the shoulder. "You will regret this."

"So be it."

Merrick left the room and the tower. He could just hear now what Clio would say when he told her. God's blood, but he would not want to be that young and stupid again for anything.

CHAPTER

25

A year later

'Twas one of those bright October days when the sun shone down for most of the day and turned the tips of the grass in the meadows the color of wheat. Beehives sat in long rows, looking like brown wimples, and golden honeysuckle spun their vines 'round the rough bark of the sprawling hawthorn trees.

A troop of men rode across the road which cut over the low hills near the sleepy town of Farmington. A tall man who sat high and easy in his saddle spurred his mount forward. A few lengths ahead of him rode another man, who leaned low over his mount's neck and was riding so hard that his dark cloak billowed out behind him like the tail of the blue jays that darted in circles over tall stacks of mown hay.

"God's eyes, de Clare!" Merrick shouted when he was almost abreast of the cloaked rider.

Startled, Tobin looked over at Merrick, who signaled for him to slow down. He eased up on his mount until he and Merrick were moving side by side at an easier canter.

Merrick's brow was creased and he gave him an odd look. "You will be glad to get to Leicester, I wager."

"What makes you say that?"

"The fact that you have been riding like the very Devil for most of the morn."

Tobin cast a glance back over his shoulder, where a cloud of brown dust was whirling above the road from his men thundering along to keep up with his pace.

He was surprised, but not surprised, and he gave a laugh, because he had little choice but admit he was overeager "Aye!" He looked at Merrick. "This is a fine day. We are riding to fetch my bride, I am out of that great piece of rock the Scots call a castle, and the sun is shining. I would say all is well with the world."

"Tell you what, lad. You go on. Ride ahead. Your men and I will follow at a more leisurely pace."

Tobin looked at Merrick, surprised. "You do not care?"

"Why would I care? 'Tis not as if your mind is not there already. You have not said but two words the whole day," Merrick grumbled. " 'Tis like riding with a mute."

Tobin looked ahead, toward the hills in the distance. Just beyond was Leicester, then Charnwood Forest and the convent of Grace Dieu. He grinned. " 'Twill give me time alone with Sofia. And I do find that appeals to me, Merrick. I would like to see how she has fared all this time."

"That is the pigheaded Tobin I know," Merrick's voice dripped with sarcasm. "Tell yourself that is why you need to see her, because you think she has changed."

"Sofia change?" Tobin almost choked on the words. "I do not expect that the Sofia I know would change too much. No doubt she has caused the prioress many gray hairs the way she always did to Edward. It is not in her to be a sweet-tempered lass."

"I do not think you would ever want a wife who was meek and quiet. A woman like that would bore you in a week."

"I am not my father," Tobin snapped without thinking. "My wife will not bore me. Ever."

"I did not mean to imply that you were, lad." Merrick

frowned at him, then reached out and gripped his shoulder in friendship. "That is not what I meant. I think you know that."

Tobin was quiet for a moment, then said, "No wife can keep my father's attention long. He has proven that. I will have one wife and only one. I decided that a long time ago."

"And so you picked Sofia. Does she know you are coming to fetch her?"

"Aye. I sent her a message early this morn."

"Well, then. I suspect your bride is waiting." Merrick slapped Tobin on the arm. "Be off with you. Go!"

Tobin put his spurs to his horse and rode away.

"Sofia!" Sister Agnes came scurrying around the corner of the infirmary, her plain woolen scapular clutched tightly in her fists, grape leaves stuck in her linen wimple from where she forgot to duck under the thick vines of the arbor.

She was still out of breath as she stood before Sofia, who was soaking her sore wrist in a warm bath of herbs and salts.

"Sister Judith wants you to come right away!"

"Why?"

"I do not know. A rider came up to the gates. It matters not. She said to come now. Quickly."

Sofia frowned, took her hand from the water bath and stood, wiping the water on the soft leather of her chausses.

"Hurry!" Agnes turned and scurried off again like the mice that lived in the hole near the chapel's altar, her small feet taking three steps to Sofia's long, lithe strides.

Sofia moved with ease and ducked under the arbor when she saw Agnes's wimple snag on a vine. The little nun slapped a hand over it and never missed a step.

The last time Sofia had been called with such urgency

had been when her skills were needed. Robert the Slater had been accosted by thieves. She wondered what was amiss now, and hoped it would not involve her sword hand, for she had fallen on her wrist the day before and jarred the bone. Her grip on the sword hilt was weak and puny.

Agnes pulled open the oaken doors to Judith's office. "Here she is, sister."

Sofia walked through the doors, frowning. "What is so urgent?"

Judith stood, bracing herself with her one hand flat on the table before her. In her other hand was a rolled up piece of parchment tied with leather strings. "This."

Sofia took it, then shoved the string aside and saw the de Clare falcons stamped into the dark wax seal. Her heart picked up speed and her breath stayed in her chest for a moment.

She glanced at Judith, who stood waiting, then Sofia exhaled and broke the seal.

I am coming for you. Be ready.
Sir Tobin de Clare

She blinked, then stared at the message again. She inhaled five controlled breaths, then had to inhale five more.

"What is it?" Judith asked.

Disgusted, Sofia tossed the message onto the table in front of Judith, who picked it up, squinted for the moment it took to read it, then lay it on the table top. "You are leaving us."

Sofia cast a quick, surprised glance at Judith, the woman who was so close to her. The woman who made her what she was. The woman whose mind was as sharp and ready for battle as was Sofia's. She was a kindred spirit, this great lady with the scarred face and the broken hip. A person who made a mark on Sofia's life in a way that few people ever could or ever would again. That she was leaving her mentor, this wise old nun, had not been Sofia's first thought, and she felt some guilt over that. But she was so angry, truly angry.

"I shall miss you terribly, Judith. Surely you know that?"

"Aye, child." She cleared her throat.

They exchanged the same look, one that would have told anyone how very close these two women had become.

"Now, now," Judith said gruffly, shuffling some things atop the desk. " 'Tis not as if we shall never see each other again."

"Aye. I suppose not." Sofia just stood there for a lost moment, then she looked at the message, scowled and planted her hands on her cocked hips. "I do not believe him. Do you?"

"What, my dear?"

"Not one word from him for all this time and then he sends me this!" Sofia waved her hand at the parchment and stood there, fuming. "Look here." She jabbed her finger into the signature. "He even signed his full name and title. His *title*. As if I wouldn't know who he was!"

Wisely, Judith seemed to have nothing to say.

"I am coming for you," Sofia mimicked. "Be ready. Is he not the greatest of courtiers, the most chivalrous of knights? Pah!"

Judith had to chuckle. "He does not appear to be a man of sugary words."

"Arrogant lout . . ." Sofia muttered.

"Well, you haven't much time, child. The rider who brought it said the arrogant lout was but half a day's ride from here. I suggest you go get your things together."

Sofia was staring off at something . . . thinking. "Aye . . ." she said by rote. After a moment she turned to leave, but walked back and snatched the parchment off the table. "I shall take this with me. If nothing else to remind me of how perfectly romantic my future husband can be."

Judith chuckled.

Sofia turned. " 'Tis not all that amusing, you know. Not to me."

"Nay. I imagine 'tis not." But Judith was still laughing. "To you, dear."

Sofia turned and closed the door on Judith's grinning face, then she stormed down the narrow walkways to her room. She slammed the door almost as hard as she wanted to slam Tobin's head. She pressed her back to the closed door and glared at the room. "Damn him!"

She pulled the message out and stared at the words again, then crumpled it up and threw it across the room. She paced back and forth like a caged animal, then she stopped, crossed her arms and stood there, thinking, tapping her foot.

After a second she turned and looked at the note wadded up in the corner. Her eyes narrowed for the longest time, then she smiled wickedly and said, "I shall be ready all right, Tobin de Clare. But will you?"

Tobin came to the edge of Charnwood Forest, where a small brook washed over smooth gray rocks and ran in a rush down through the high grass where it disappeared into a small rise. He reined in and dismounted, then let his horse drink its fill, while he knelt on one knee and filled a skin with fresh water. He tied it off and strapped it to his saddle, then walked back and squatted down. He bent low over the rocks, cupped his hand and took a long, cool drink.

'Twas hot for October and he could feel the dust of the road clinging in a light crust to his cheeks and chin. He removed his soft woolen cap and tucked it under his arm, then slapped cool water over his face. He blinked a few times to let the water clean his dry eyes and wiped them with his sleeve.

His hair fell sloppily over his damp brow, so he dipped his hands back into the brook and brushed his damp fingers through his hair until it was back from his brow and ears. He dropped some cool water on his hot neck, then stood, stretched and yawned loudly.

He took a few deep breaths and placed his cap back on his head at a cocked angle.

He took two steps.

A whining, whoosh of air snatched his cap right from his head.

Tobin swore under his breath and ducked down behind his horse, using it as a shield before he turned and looked behind him.

His hat was stuck into a tree trunk by an arrow, one which was still shuddering from momentum.

He slowly drew his sword, then shifted so he could look about him.

There was pure silence. No sound at all.

Tobin waited, his ears sharp.

Nothing.

He crouched down, grabbing the reins, and he moved his horse along with him as he went toward the shelter of some nearby trees. Sword in hand, he slipped behind a huge oak, pressing his back to the trunk as he peered around.

He moved with stealth from tree to tree, sword up and ready, his eyes darting this way and that, twisting and turning from spot to spot. It took a while to go over the immediate area, but he did.

There was nothing. Not even a sign that the archer had been there. 'Twas eerie and not too comforting. The next arrow could be in his heart.

Finally after checking every tree and bush and rock in the area, he was certain he was alone. Disgusted, he sheathed his weapon, walked over, braced his boot on the trunk and with both hands and pulled the arrow from the tree. Scowling, he stuck his cap back on his head.

"Damn . . ." He stood there for a moment, knowing he had wasted plenty of time. Too much time. Merrick and his men would be much closer now.

He did not choose to wait for them. He could surely handle one archer. 'Twas probably a lad out to pluck a pheasant and he decided to make some mischief.

So he remounted and rode into the forest, but he was more careful as he rode, using his instincts as well as his eyes to scan for trouble.

'Twas not long till he came to a small clearing, where the forest went up a ridge and the road widened and moved up the hillside.

A sudden and sharp glint of sunlight off metal blinded him for a moment.

He pulled his sword.

At the top of the rise was a lone, mounted knight blocking the road. His mail was darkened, not polished like his unmarked helm. He wore half armor, but no markings on his black tunic, just one black plume that extended from the top of his helm.

The visor was up, but from this distance he could not see the man's eyes. The warhorse beneath him was stomping and blowing, anxious for a charge, but the knight seemed unfazed. He raised one gauntleted hand and snapped down his visor in challenge.

Tobin drew his sword and held it high. "A de Clare!" he shouted into the tense air and kneed his mount forward.

The knight drew and charged.

Their mounts' hooves pounded and pounded over the hard dirt of the road.

Tobin watched the knight, looking for weakness in his seat. There was none.

The horses drew closer. Closer. The leaves on the trees were shaking. His heart pounded in his ears. He readied his sword. He would slice downward. Catch him off guard and early.

Then he saw it—the weakness. The knight was holding his sword lower, the hilt not far from his waist. Too low. Bad form.

Tobin smiled.

The knight came toward him.

They were barely a foot apart.

"Your mistake!" Tobin shouted and swung his weapon downward.

But the knight's arm shot up so fast that Tobin missed it. Their sword hilts locked. Something he had never seen.

It threw him a hair off balance. He clamped his knees tightly on the horse.

But the man shoved him. Hard.

Tobin flew from his saddle. He felt the air, then hit the ground so hard his teeth clamped down on his tongue.

He tasted blood.

But not as much as he wanted blood. He shook his head and leapt into an attack stance, knees bent, sword high. Feet moving. Ready.

But the knight had ridden back to the top of the road. He stopped and faced Tobin. He raised his sword high, then opened his visor and looked down at Tobin, standing there feeling foolish and trying to figure out what the hell was going on.

A second later the knight wheeled his horse around and disappeared over the hill, leaving Tobin standing there, dumbfounded.

CHAPTER 26

Sofia put her horse in a back stall, a precaution so Tobin would not recognize him. "There's a good lad." She stroked him, while he had his muzzle stuck into the grain bin on the wall, munching on oats.

"Together we exacted a fine revenge this day." She chuckled, then drew her hand along his flank and over his rump before she left the stall and locked the gate behind her. She moved behind the eastern wall of the stables, whistling and seeing that image of Tobin sprawled on the ground . . . the perfect place for him to be—a low place. She laughed again.

Then came a loud bark of male laughter from nearby.

She slammed her hand over her mouth.

"Laugh all you want."

'Twas Tobin's deep voice. He sounded annoyed. Nothing unusual there.

"Your day will come, Merrick. You wait."

Earl Merrick, too? She mentally groaned. Sweet Mary and Joseph! How much time had passed while she was gloating? She stood there, listening. She had little choice. They were but a few yards away.

"Unseated by some knight all in black?" Merrick howled again. "What a fine tale that is! Perhaps you fell on your head, de Clare. Blacked out. Black knight. Same thing." He kept laughing. "On your ass in Charnwood Forest. Wait till Roger hears."

Tobin used Sofia's favorite curse word.

"Where's your sense of humor, lad?"

"I don't find this half as amusing as you do. Now leave me be if all you can do is bray at me. I'm going to find Sofia."

"Damn . . ." she whispered, then made a quick run for the back of the cloister. Her gauntlet hit the side of the wall and made a clunking sound.

She ducked down behind a cart.

"What was that?" Tobin paused, his hand on the main door to the convent.

"Probably some sheep. Pigs in the yard. Black knights. Ghosts. Witches. You know . . . the usual."

"Go to the Devil." Tobin pulled the door open, then held it. The two disappeared inside.

Sofia slipped into the kitchen building where Sister Katherine was working. "Sofia! Why are you in your armor?"

"Shhhh. . . ." Sofia did her best to cross the room quietly. She turned back and whispered, "Do me a favor, Sister Katherine, and bang those pots around. Make noise."

Sister Katherine frowned, then shrugged and began to tap together the pots and pans. 'Twas a timid clanking, like distant bells. Not enough racket.

Sofia waved her hand up a few times, gesturing to raise the noise. The nun caught on, nodding vigorously as she crashed those pots and pans around something fierce.

At the door, Sofia paused for only a moment, then slipped through and moved in a half-run through the dining room, down the narrow hall and off to side where her room was.

She jerked open the door and slipped inside. Her heart

was beating madly. She began to pull off her gauntlets, then her plate pieces on her chest and shoulders. The mail cowl joined them on the floor with a slinking sound as did the rest of her mail. She tore off the aketon and threw her gown on over her chausses.

She contorted her arm over her shoulder, wiggling her fingers as she tried to do the ties on her gown.

There was sharp knock at the door. "Sofia?"

Tobin! Damn . . . damn . . . damn!

She turned and dropped to her knees and shoved it all under her small bed. "I am coming!" she shouted loudly to cover the sound. She straightened.

"Sofia? 'Tis I, Tobin."

As if she did not recognize his voice. She rolled her eyes. Or his title.

"Open the door, sweet."

"I'll sweet you . . ." she said under her breath. "Gone all those months and nary a word. Then he rides in and expects me to be waiting. *Be ready.*" She tied one of the gown's ties into a knot, then did up the next one.

She got a tight cramp in her shoulder from bending so awkwardly. She winced, rubbed it, then shook out her gown. She started to move toward the door, but fortunately she looked at her feet.

Shoes!

"Sofia? Is something wrong?"

"Coming." *Is something wrong? I'd say so.* She slipped on a shoe and hopped to the door, tying the ankle ties on one.

"Sofia . . ."

She did the other shoe, still hopping. "Cuh-uh-uh-uh-ming."

She took one deep breath and jerked the door open. She exhaled, and smiled sweetly.

Until she looked into those eyes of his. Her heart had been hammering in her chest ever since she'd heard his voice, but now it was truly skipping. She wanted to feel nothing. But her body betrayed her.

Standing this close to him—the arrogant lout—was still the same as it always had been. He became her whole world, in one single instant. Just a breath and he was the only thing that existed.

He reached out and tilted her face up, then lowered his mouth to hers. Just their lips touched, gently, and the knuckle he had under her chin.

He tasted of freshly mown grass and impossible hope, sunshine and man. And passion, oh, she could not forget the passion, for it was one that she had forced out of her mind for months and months.

One strong arm slid around her, low, under her buttocks, and he lifted her up and walked into the room, kicking the door closed behind him.

He kissed her long and with such intense possession, his tongue deep in her mouth, stroking her teeth and lips and her own tongue. His hand cupped the back of her head and he moaned her name into her mouth.

Her hands gripped his shoulders tightly. She could feel the muscles, the tendons, taut and hard beneath her fingertips. He let her slide down his chest and lower body until her feet hit the . . .

Armor.

Her eyes shot open. His were closed.

She kicked backwards, sending the plates and mail farther under the bed with her heel; they rattled together.

He froze. His eyes opened suddenly, then frowned. He raised his head. "What was that?"

"Rats." She grabbed the sides of his head and pulled his mouth back to hers and stuck her tongue inside.

She loved to kiss him. She might hate him, but she loved to kiss him. She loved what he made her feel. She loved the way he tasted.

She was all over him. Her hands rubbed his chest, upward, and into his hair. She said his name, too, into his mouth, onto his lips, whispered it in his ear. Their passion swelled so swiftly it was like straw on fire.

The next thing she knew they were falling back on the bed, together. His hands were all over her breasts. He kept saying her name again and again.

She felt him grab her gown in his fist and he started to pull it up.

She was wearing her chausses. Oh dear Lord! She gripped his shoulders and shoved him hard. He flew back and looked at her, surprised.

She was stronger than she even realized.

He frowned, then shook his head and muttered something about a Scots rock of a place turning him weak.

She sat upright, anxious to get away from his hands. She stood and straightened her gown, twisted it back into place. She looked down at him, one hand propped on her hip and said in a scolding tone, "This is a convent, Tobin. Not a tavern house."

She was suitably haughty, as if she were not just as involved in this pleasure, too.

"Aye. You are right, sweet." Tobin stood. " 'Tis only one more day."

"One more day?"

"Aye. We ride to London now and tomorrow is our wedding."

"What?"

"Tomorrow is our wedding." This tone was as if he had just said the sun is rising, just like it always did. As if their wedding were an everyday thing.

"One day." Her eyes narrowed. She could feel a rush of anger. "You expect me to wed you with one day's notice?"

He looked at her, frowned a bit like she was the one who was mad. "Aye." He nodded as if it were perfectly normal to not have anything to say about her own wedding, to find out it was happening the day before, when she had been waiting for over a year, perhaps since she were twelve and certainly since the day of the Miracle Plays.

She took a long deep breath, decided that Eve should have thrown that apple at Adam and hit him squarely in the head.

Sofia glanced at him, then at the bed. She grabbed a large pillow, walked over, swung back, and hit him in the head with it.

"What the hell are you doing?" he shouted.

"Hitting you!" She whacked him again.

And again.

He held up his arms. "What's the matter with you?" He tried to grab it.

She side-stepped him. "Nothing!" She pulled back and used both hands, swinging with all her newly earned strength.

"Ouch! Dammit! That hurt!"

Nay. It felt so good!

Whack, whack, whack!

She spun around in a circle, building momentum.

He raised his arm to block.

The pillow hit him in the chest and exploded. Downy feathers went everywhere, as if it were snowing geese.

He stood there, looking at her while feathers lit on his whole person.

She waved the feathers away from her face and mouth and waited until they settled to the floor, then she looked up at him.

He had feathers in his eye sockets, on his eyebrows, in his ears and mouth.

He spit out a mouthful and just looked at her. "You're angry."

"Me? Angry with you? *Sir* Tobin de Clare? Whatever gave you that idea?"

He just shook his head, turned, and left the room. Just before he closed the door she heard him say, "Women . . ."

They arrived at Windsor Castle by torchlight, the de Clare and Earl Merrick's men-at-arms making an impressive escort. Sofia dismounted before Tobin could barely turn around.

He turned. She was standing and murmuring to the horse. She glanced up at him and saw the odd look on his face. "You feel no soreness from being in the saddle."

"Nay." She smiled. "I love to ride. 'Tis a fine horse you gave me. She is spirited but has an easy canter."

" 'Tis a de Clare-bred mount." There was pride in his tone. "I broke her myself." He placed his hand on the horse's neck and gave her a pat.

Sofia cocked her head in surprise. Breaking horses, training them, both tasks took patience and a gentleness of hand and tongue.

Tobin had turned and was giving orders to his men. Sofia stood there, eyeing his broad back and wondering what else there was inside of him that she did not know. 'Twas then that she realized she was marrying a stranger.

He could turn her on fire with a look. Anger her with a word. He had touched her most intimate places with his hands, with his mouth, but she knew little of him, of who he truly was, and she wondered what in her lifetime she would discover inside of this man, who tomorrow would be her husband.

Sofia stood at an arched window, staring up at the moon—a plump pearl of a ball in the dark night sky. Stars were blinking down at her. Her room was just above the castle ale house and she could smell the scent of barley and yeast in the air, could hear voices from all sides and corners of the courtyard below.

There was much to do this night. A huge wedding at the royal castle on the morrow. Most of the castle workers would be up all night, and had probably been up for more nights before this.

Guests were already there. She and Tobin, the bridal couple, were the last to arrive. She had chosen to have bread, cheese and wine in her room. Her belly was wild from the moment she had arrived. She felt anxious and uneasy. As if she were ready to step off a cliff.

There was drinking and gaiety in the Great Hall. She could hear the laughter in the distance, the music. Most were drunk, already celebrating the wedding.

Her wedding.

She paused in her thoughts, chewing on her lower lip, then turned and crossed the room. She knelt at one of her small chests and opened it. Her mother's pearls and the exquisite cloth were sitting inside.

Sofia lifted them out, took a few steps and sat down cross-legged in the middle of the tester bed. She propped her elbow on her bent knee and just stared down at them, trying to remember and only being able to forget.

There was a sharp rap on Sofia's bedchamber door, then it opened with a squeak of the iron hinges. Eleanor came inside.

"Sofia?" She looked to the bed. "There you are, child." She shut the door, turned and gave her a long look. "I would like to talk to you." She moved near the fireplace and gestured toward the chairs. A fire burned and cast shadows over the rich tapestry rug on the floor and the tray with the crumbs that remained of Sofia's light meal.

"Talk to me? Why?" Sofia crossed the room. She flopped into a chair, slumping down. "What have I done now?"

Eleanor gave a soft chuckle. "Nothing like that."

Sofia's robe had split open and she caught a soft whisper of warm air from the fire against her bare legs. She stretched them out and crossed them at the ankles, staring at her toes.

Whose toes did she have? Her father's or her mother's? She would never know.

"Tomorrow is your wedding and I thought we should speak of things. Of a wife's duties. Of the bedding."

"I know all about it."

Eleanor smiled softly. "You are certain?"

"Aye."

"Well." Eleanor sat down. "Do you have any questions?"

Sofia wanted to tell Eleanor how was sorry she was that poor dear Eleanor had to do what went on in the marriage bed with Edward. But she knew that Eleanor loved her husband—how was a question she would never know the answer to . . . like the toes.

And Sofia would not hurt her, even if the thought of them doing what she and Tobin did was enough to make her want to cringe. "I have no questions." Sofia stopped. "Oh, perhaps one." She looked at the Queen. "Does a wife ever truly know her husband?"

"Some wives do. But they have to want to look inside the man they love. They have to care, to search for the true man. 'Tis a fact that most men do not easily show what they feel or think. Sometimes a woman must dig it out of them. Men do not like to feel things deeply. They like to act as if they are above emotion. Too strong or powerful or some such foolishness. When a man lets down his guard and shows a woman his emotions, what he feels and truly thinks, know then that he is in love with her. That she has his heart and his trust. 'Tis the only way they will ever let us inside."

Tobin did not let her inside. They had nothing, nothing but lust and passion and that thing between them that stirred her blood and his. No love.

"Anything else you want to ask me?"

Sofia shook her head.

Eleanor stood. She stepped forward and cupped Sofia's cheek in her hand. "You know you are a daughter to me, do you not?"

Sofia looked up and Eleanor and felt her eyes grow moist. She did love this woman. She nodded. "Thank you."

Eleanor walked to the door and opened it, then paused. "I suspect you will find tomorrow night to your liking, my dear. Tobin is young and a good man, not cruel. I believe his heart will be true . . . unlike his father. Good night." Then she closed the door.

Unlike his father?

Sofia frowned. What was this? She got up and went to the door, then opened it and glanced down the hallway, but the candles had been put out, Eleanor was already gone below, and there was nothing but darkness.

CHAPTER

27

The day of the wedding came in with a chill. A white glaze rimed the grass around Windsor Castle. Sofia crawled from her bed and stood. The floor tiles were cold and sent chills up her bare legs. She hopped backward, then scooted into bed and pulled the covers over her cold feet, rubbing them together and shivering, until a servant came in and put wood and hot coals in the fireplace.

She lay there, bundled under the covers, and tried to make herself believe that today was truly her wedding day. She glanced around the room.

Nothing was different. But to her it should have been. The sun should have risen in the west and the moon should have set in the east; the rivers should run backward and time should stop. The world should be turned upside down, because she knew that after today, nothing in her life would ever be the same again.

There was a scratch at her door.

"Come in!"

Edith poked her head around the door. "Sofie?"

"Edith! You are here! Truly here!" Sofia flew out of bed and ran across the room. They hugged each other. "I have missed you so."

" 'Tis been quiet since you were gone, Sofie." Edith released her. "Too quiet perhaps for even me."

"Come." Sofia took Edith's hand and pulled her over to the carpet near the fire. "Tell me all that has happened."

Edith stood there for a moment, looking as if she wanted to say something.

"What is it?"

Edith averted her eyes, then she looked up, her face bright and her smile soft. "My betrothed has returned."

"Hmph! 'Tis about time. He is fortunate to have you, for no other woman would have been so patient."

"You mean that *you* would not have been so patient."

"Aye. You are a saint."

"Not truly." Edith was pensive, then she spoke again, "I did not tell you something about him, a secret I kept all to myself."

"What secret?"

" 'Twas simple to wait for him, because he sent me missives the whole time he was gone. Every few days another would arrive."

"Edith! Why did you not tell me?"

Edith shrugged. "They were beautiful messages and I wanted to keep them close to me."

"What kind of missives? Do you want to tell me now? What does a man say to someone he truly loves to make her understand him?"

"He praised my eyes and my fiery hair. He tells me how very wonderful I am. He says he thinks of me every night before he goes to sleep. That his heart is full of me and only me."

Sofia looked at her friend and could see the joy in her face. Edith knew she was cherished by the man she was to marry.

For just one moment Sofia felt a pang of envy and emptiness, too, for something she would never know, then she smiled for Edith. "I am so pleased for you. Truly. Have you and Lord Robert had a chance to be alone together since he has returned?"

"Aye." Edith would not look at her. "Almost every day."

"Did he finally kiss you?"

She nodded and smiled a huge smile, one Sofia recognized. Oh, he had kissed her. Edith wore the look of a woman who was well-loved and well-kissed.

"Why, Edith. You love him!"

"Of course I love him. He is to be my husband."

"Oh, not duty love. I mean you truly love him."

"He is a good man, Sofie. We will wed before Lent."

"But that is so long away. How can you stand to wait?"

Edith smiled. "I can wait."

"Aye, I suppose. You have patience."

"I have a man who shows me his heart."

Sofia realized that Edith was right. If you had no doubt you were loved and adored, it would not matter as much if you were apart.

How simple a thing that was. Just knowing you are loved. Was it all so easily done with just that? Was that how love bound you together?

She would never know, for Tobin did not love her. All they had between them was a passionate and elusive thing that neither of them could control, but one that seemed to catch fire and burn even hotter whenever they were together.

But that was not love. That was desire. That was want. That was need. But it was not love.

"You shall meet him, today," Edith was saying to her. "Lord Robert is here."

"I should like to meet him." Sofia stood there, awkwardly, feeling alone because she could not talk to Edith about Tobin. She could not bear to tell her what was so painful to her—that she loved Tobin de Clare but he did not love her back.

"I think all of England is here for your wedding! Have you seen the crowd?"

"Crowd?" Sofia shook her head. "We just arrived last eve." She frowned. "There is a crowd?"

Edith nodded.

How many were here for the wedding? She had not thought of throngs of people watching her wed Tobin de Clare. Her belly tightened and she turned suddenly quiet at the prospect of her wedding.

A moment later the door crashed open. In came the Poleaxes.

"We are here to help you dress, Sofia," Mavis said, then she dropped thick-toothed combs, fillets and ribbons in a heap on Sofia's bed.

Jehane marched past Mavis, grabbed Sofia by the arms and began to pull off her robe and linen shift. "Stop dawdling, girl. You need to be bled, I swear to Saints Peter and Paul. Come. Come. The Queen will be here soon." She tossed Sofia's clothing out the door as if they were rags and called for the hot water and tub.

Sofia sagged and groaned, "Not again . . ."

After being painfully scrubbed, pulled and pinched for what seemed like hours, Sofia looked up to see Eleanor enter her chamber. The Queen smiled. "You are beautiful, child. Though I suppose I should not call you 'child' any longer. Today you will be a wife and chatelaine to de Clare's estate and your dower castle."

She turned to the Poleaxes. "You have done a fine job. Sir Tobin will be the envy of every young knight here this day."

Sofia was wearing a gown of a rich, deep violet silk that made her eyes look dark purple and huge. Snowy ermine trimmed the sleeves, the hem, and her black cloak, which was also embroidered with silver falcons, the same design as in the de Clare seal. Silver ribbons flowed through her hair, which was nearly to her shoulders now, but still had some curl, so the ribbons twined in and out softly, picking up light and making her hair look as if some archangel had tossed a handful of stars over it.

Eleanor came over and looked at Sofia, her head cocked slightly. She frowned. "The emerald collar is wrong." She reached up and unclasped it from Sofia's neck. "Here." She handed it to Mavis and turned back to Sofia. "Where are your mother's pearls?"

"I cannot wear them. They always look wrong."

"Let me see them," the Queen said.

Sofia walked over and took them from a walnut box on a table, then handed them to the Queen.

"Sit here." Eleanor pointed to a small bench. Sofia was taller than Eleanor so she sat, stiffly. She could feel her mouth tighten and it was all she could do to keep her hands on her lap instead of in tight fists.

She knew what would happen. The same thing that always happened. The pearls would not become her.

Eleanor undid the clasp and then slid one end about Sofia's long neck, and she began to wrap them, 'round and 'round in a high collar. "There." The Queen fixed the clasp. She stepped back and studied her.

Sofia did not move. She did not breathe. She sat there, waiting for Eleanor to shake her head, to see what Sofia always saw.

Eleanor handed her the polished glass. "Look. 'Tis perfect."

Perfect? Sofia closed her eyes as she lifted the round glass. She took a deep breath, then opened them.

She could not speak for a moment. Her voice had gone. Her hand drifted up to touch the even and perfect pearls, strung in tight-fitting circles that coiled up her neck. She looked so lovely. For a moment she almost could not comprehend it. She stared at the image in the glass as if she could not pull her eyes away, as if she were seeing herself for the first time, and liked what she saw there.

She turned toward the Queen. "They look perfect."

Eleanor nodded. "That was how Rosalynde always wore them, wrapped around that lovely, long neck of hers. Did you know they called her 'the swan' because of her height and elegance. Her skin, like yours, matched those pearls. Looking at you now, it fairly glows with the same depth of color." The Queen gave a small smile and she looked Sofia in the eyes. "I'll never forget the first time I saw her in those exquisite pearls, with all her black hair. Heads turned and the room grew silent when she came into it." Eleanor lifted Sofia's chin a little and looked at her, then released her.

Sofia looked back at her reflection, trying to see the image of her mother.

"No one would doubt that you are her daughter, Sofia. She would be very proud."

But by then, Sofia could no longer see the image staring back at her. Her eyes swam with tears. She looked away, swallowed, and put down the looking glass, then she stood and crossed over to the window.

She could feel the heaviness of her wedding cloak, the weight of the embroidery that almost all but covered it, dragging behind her. It felt strange, as if she were carrying something heavy or as if something were trying to hold her back.

The others in the room chattered for a moment. But she had nothing to say. She took deep breaths and just stood there for what seemed like forever.

"We should go now, dear one," Eleanor was saying. "Edward is waiting. You know how impatient he can be."

Sofia looked out the window one last time, wiped her eyes with the back of her hand, then left with the Queen and her ladies.

It took the King's provost almost an hour to recite all that was Lady Sofia Howard's dowry. Afterward, the doors to the church were thrown open. From inside, the candles flickered like hundreds of stars, casting light against the stained-glass windows that also picked up the late morning sunlight and gave the church an almost heavenly glow.

The King led Sofia's white palfrey to the church steps. He handed Tobin the silver reins, a gesture symbolizing the gift of this woman to him.

Tobin glanced up at her. For a moment he could not see her, such was the sparkle of the silver in her hair and the embroidery on her cloak. Both caught the flickering of the candlelight from inside.

He had drunk too much the night before, and had little sleep. He was sorry now, for this was not the time or the occasion to be feeling the effects of last night's rowdiness. He put his hands on Sofia's waist and lifted her down from the pillion chair.

As he swung her she planted her hands on his shoulders and looked down at him, her eyes wide and her lips full and moist. Something sharp and tangible shot through him. 'Twas a shock that made his senses come alive.

She was so damned beautiful.

He wondered, then, at that very instant, what she was thinking, what thoughts hid behind those purple eyes. He knew what he was thinking: he wanted her. He wanted her more than he had ever wanted anything in his entire life.

But there was something else there, something he could not name, a fleeting thing like the wind, something that was hard to see, but he felt it go straight through him. It was inside his mind and body. All of it was somehow tied to this woman whom he held in his hands.

He set her on her feet, then clasped her hand. He looked down at it in his own—her white soft skin against his hard and sun-bitten hand. He threaded his fingers through hers, then found himself looking into her eyes.

She tilted her head and stared back at him, her face unreadable.

He gave her a quick wink. He could not have explained why, but he just did. She looked as if she needed a wink, something from him. He was glad he did it, too, for she smiled, a true and bright smile, one that almost brought him to his knees.

Without thought or plan or a single word, he released her hands and went to where the ladies of the court stood holding posies of flowers they would throw when he and Sofia left the church.

He scanned the bouquets, did not see what he wanted, then looked up and took a long silvery-blue rose from a festive garland above the chapel eave. He turned back to her, this woman who would become his wife.

She looked confused, her brow slightly knit.

And here he thought he as the only one who was confused.

A moment later he went down on one knee and held out the rose to her, his eyes never leaving hers.

Her stunned gaze darted from him to the rose he held out to her. She looked like a bird that had suddenly found itself falling from the nest, only to learn it can actually fly. Her look softened.

She reached out and took the flower.

What he saw in her face made him wish the wedding, the merriment and the feasting were over. He wanted be alone with her, just Sofia and him.

A cheer went up from the crowd. All including himself were surprised at this gesture: him on his knees to this woman on the church steps, in front of the world, and before God.

She lifted the rose to breathe in its scent, and gave him the softest of smiles. A true smile, which was worth everything. He rose and took her arm, and together they entered the church.

Tobin seated her next to him on a small bench in the choir. His hand rested on his thigh, which was barely touching hers. The King and Queen came in, as did his father with his current wife. Next was Earl Merrick and his wife, the Lady Clio, and Sister Judith.

When all were seated the Archbishop began the solemn Mass of the Trinity with his blessing over them. "Let this woman be amiable as Rachel, wise as Rebecca, faithful as Sarah."

Tobin reached out and took Sofia's hands.

She cast him a quick glance, then tightened her fingers around his.

"Let her be sober in truth, venerable through modesty, and wise in the teaching of heaven." The Archbishop turned and all inside chanted the *Agnus Dei*.

Tobin rose and advanced to the altar, where he received the kiss of peace. He turned toward Sofia, who would, in one more moment, become his wife in truth and in the eyes of God.

He held out his hand to her.

She rose with grace, this woman who was now his, and moved to join him, her shimmering beauty enough to make him wonder if she were real. And there, right at the foot of the great crucifix, he took her in his arms and transmitted the kiss to her, his wife.

Tobin released her and everything before him suddenly blurred. For just a moment. He blinked, because the only thing he could figure was there must have been something in his eye.

CHAPTER

28

After the tense anticipation of the wedding, after a morning of the Poleaxes, and two hours of almost silent ceremony, Sofia stood by Tobin's side at the reception tent where the bridal gifts were presented and chattered like a magpie with all who came up to kiss and to congratulate them.

Tobin's hand rested possessively on the small of her back as he spoke with some baron, his lady wife and son. For just a moment Sofia looked down at the blue rose in her hand. The image of his face came back to her, the expression in his eyes, the way he was looking up at her as he knelt, like some romantic courtier and not the arrogant man she had thought him to be. She felt a small, fluttering joy as she remembered that moment all over again; it was as if a butterfly were there right inside of her heart.

"Sofie." Edith rushed up to her. "You are wed! Truly wed! 'Twas so lovely!" She gave Sofia a huge hug and whispered, "I could not believe it when he gave you the rose! 'Twas it not the most wonderfully romantic thing? The jongleurs are already singing of it! Who would have thought it of Sir Tobin de Clare!" Edith seemed as nervous as Sofia felt, at least more nervous than was Edith's normal state.

Sofia glanced over her friend's shoulder.

A stocky man with brown hair, graying at the temples, and dark eyes stood behind her. He was richly dressed in golden silk, but not overly so with jewels and furs and too much ornament, as were some of the more wealthy of Edward's noblemen.

Edith looked up at her, then stepped back and shyly reached out to the man, who came instantly to Edith's side.

"Lady Sofia, this is Lord Robert of Gavanshaw, my betrothed."

Sofia looked into a pair of the kindest brown eyes, eyes that seemed to look with nothing but doting love on her dear friend. Lord Henry had chosen wisely for his little sister. Now she better understood Edith and her willing acceptance of this alliance with such an older man.

Sofia held out her hand. "Lord Robert." She smiled genuinely, because Edith was looking at him as if he were her whole heart. 'Twas the sweetest thing. "I am truly happy to finally meet you. Edith has spoken so much of you."

"Has she? She does not speak much whenever I am 'round."

"I do too speak," Edith said quickly, then realized that she had just naysaid him. She grew suddenly silent and stared at her toes.

Lord Robert frowned, as if he wanted her honest reaction, not a feigned meekness that was demanded of women by so many men. He looked at Sofia almost as if to say, "Help me with her."

He was a swift thinker, for he laughed. "I suppose you have not had much chance to speak when I keep your mouth occupied with other things, my fiery one."

Edith's head shot up and her eyes grew wide. She turned so bright a red that Sofia burst out laughing.

Sofia slapped Lord Robert playfully on his arm. "You are terrible to tease her so, milord. She is all that is kind and good and sweet in this world."

"Aye, that she is." He grinned. "But I find I must tease her, milady, for I have found that the scarlet on her cheeks is my favorite color for her to wear."

Sofia and Robert laughed together and talked with ease, until each tried to out-embarrass Edith, just to see who could make her flush the more.

"Enough!" Edith finally raised her hands in mock protection. "Both of you are horrid! My cheeks are so hot I need some mead to cool them down." She grasped Robert's arm and clutched it close to her. "Come along, milord. I find I am famished as well as thirsty. 'Tis your duty as my betrothed to see to all my needs and wants. And remember, you must feed me all the very best morsels."

"I think the very best morsel has my arm clutched to her side."

Sofia laughed and watched as Edith happily dragged a grinning Lord Robert toward the huge blue tent where the wedding feast was just beginning.

As wedding feasts went, Tobin thought this one had all the makings of a disaster. He sat there, stabbing chunks of finely cooked meat onto his dagger, jamming them into his mouth and chewing the bloody hell out of it before he swilled back a full goblet of French wine.

It was not a simple thing to ignore the fact that your own father was actively and publicly wooing your new bride.

He watched them dance to the tunes of the minstrels, watched Sofia innocently smile and laugh at his father, who was at his charming best. His latest stepmother, whoever she was, a pale-haired woman of two and twenty called Arden or Anne or Arkin, one of those "A" names, had left the feast early. The poor woman was probably so used to his father's fickle ways that she did not want to be there for what was surely to be another humiliation with some other woman this night. The thing was, it should not have been with the bride. But it was so like his father. He could make a conquest and humiliate his son at the same time.

His father put his hands on Sofia's waist and lifted her high in the air. Tobin's hand tightened on the thickly carved stem of the gold goblet. He could feel the falcon design cutting into his fingers, he could feel the blood leave the knuckles on his hand, he could feel rage race through him.

A hand on his shoulder startled him enough to tear his angry gaze away from the scene.

Merrick stood behind him. "Go take her from him, lad."

"I will not give the bastard the satisfaction of letting him know he can get to me." Tobin took another drink.

"Then you are a fool, for this is not about you. This is about Sofia. She is the only person you are hurting by trying to act as if what he is doing out there does not matter. She is your wife. She does not know. She is only dancing, as a bride should at her own wedding celebration. Have you ever told her about him?"

"Why? He does not deserve the breath it would take to tell her."

"Clio thought as much and told me to tell you to explain to her. She needs to know, if for no other reason than to protect herself."

Tobin frowned and looked over at Lady Clio. She was looking at him sternly. His gaze flicked back to his wife, and he realized Clio was right.

"Go rescue her, lad. This is not the time to be stubborn." Merrick gripped Tobin's shoulder. "Go."

Tobin took one last drink of wine, then put down the

goblet. Without ever taking his eyes off Sofia and his father, he gave Merrick a slight nod, then he shoved away from the table and stood.

He moved toward them. Stepping around the people seated at tables who leaned back and raised their wine goblets, who called out or who clouted him with their good wishes on the arm and back and shoulders. A minor skirmish broke out, petty nobles who were so far into their cups that their horseplay was ribald, but suddenly escalated to where one hit the other with his drinking cup.

Tobin shoved one of them aside and stood between them. Parcin and Merrick were there in a instant, holding the two men and dragging them outside before they could draw their swords.

Then he was standing at his father's back, listening.

"My son is fortunate, Sofia." His father slid a hand on Sofia's back.

Tobin's fist tightened, but he did not move.

"I have yet to have a bride as lovely as you."

"You have had so many brides, *Father.*" Tobin gripped his father's shoulder and stilled him from moving closer to Sofia. "I believe you have a wife abovestairs now."

His father turned, his expression said he was caught off guard.

Tobin stepped between them, using his size and height as a shield to his bride. He gave Sofia a smile that he knew was false, then leaned toward his father's ear and said with quiet menace, "Get the hell away from mine, old man."

Tobin did not wait to see his father's reaction. Instead he grabbed Sofia's hands and pulled her into a circle of dancers. The circle grew larger now that Tobin and Sofia were dancing together. The dancers stood and clapped their hands and feet, while Tobin held tightly to his bride's soft hands and spun her 'round and 'round, watching her

face. The smile she wore grew. She called his name, but
he spun her faster until she was dizzy and laughing. The
sound of it rippled clear through him, washed away for
just that moment his father's lechery, and everything else
but the thought that this woman was truly his.

He slid his arm behind her back and bent, then swept
her off her feet, turning and spinning with her in his
arms as she locked her hands behind his neck and threw
back her head.

"Stop! Stop! Husband!" But she was still laughing. He
turned and walked outside the ring of dancers, past the
musicians and across the room and out the doors to the
echoes of cheers and bawdy jests.

He carried her up and away, through an archway and
out onto the parapet, where the noise from the celebration below was muted by the castle walls and sounded as
if it were far, far away.

A slight breeze caught the ribbons in Sofia's hair and
ruffled it. A few curls fell into her eyes. She took a hand
from around his neck and brushed the hair back. The ermine on her sleeve tickled her nose and she rubbed it,
then her hand fell to his shoulder. She grinned at him.
"You are stealing the bride away from the celebration."

"Aye," he said in a quiet voice, then he lowered her
onto her feet.

They faced each other. He stared at her, his look intense and serious. No fun there. No twinkle of mischief
like there was in his father's eyes, eyes that were so
much alike it amazed her. She wondered how they could
be so different. One so gay and one so intense.

Sofia did not know why he was looking at her so.
There was something in his eyes, something that almost
looked like pain. For just a fleeting moment she asked
herself if she could be the cause of it. She cocked her
head. "What is wrong?"

His mouth thinned a little and he took a deep breath, then faced away from her. He rested one arm on a crenel, leaned casually against it and stared off into the distance. He picked up a small stone and turned it over in his hand, then tossed it into the air and caught it a few times. "You looked as if you needed rescuing."

"Did I?" She laughed, then moved to his side, standing there and looking off toward the west where the sun was setting in a purple and scarlet sky. "Your father is quite interesting. He makes me laugh."

He said nothing.

"There's a bit of a tease to his look."

" 'Tis a look you would do well to hide from." His tone was sudden, bitter, and sharp.

"Hide from your father?" She laughed. "What a goose you are! That is silly."

Tobin said nothing.

Sofia's laughter faded in the awkwardness of the moment. She looked up at her husband and frowned. He was serious.

He had not moved. He just stared out with an expression that seemed so very far away, as if he were not even there with her, or his mind or memory were not there. His eyes were narrowed with bitterness and anger.

Wherever he was, it was not a pretty place.

She remembered with sudden clarity what Eleanor had said the night before.

His heart is true, unlike his father.

She reached out and touched Tobin's arm. "Why did I need rescuing?"

He was silent.

"I was only with your father. He is kind and amusing," she prodded.

"Amusing? I would call my father many things, but not one of them would be amusing."

"Why do you dislike him so? Only because he was paying attention to me? I'm certain—"

"Why?" He turned so swiftly, pinning her with angry and cold blue eyes. "What? You think I am jealous because he has the power to charm every woman he meets?"

"I don't know what to think. You tell me why I should not be kind to him when he is being so kind to me. I am his daughter by marriage."

"Perhaps you would be better to ask that of his wife. Or just ask one of my eighteen younger brothers."

"Eighteen?"

He nodded. "All have different mothers, except the two sets of twins."

"Twins?" she repeated in a dull tone.

"Aye, and that doesn't include my sisters."

Her mouth dropped.

"There's Elizabeth, who is six years older than I. We do have the same mother, Father's first wife. Next is Jocelyn. Her mother was the castle laundress. There is Catherine, Ada, Maude, Janet, Alice and Isobel."

She was appalled. "My God—"

"I do not know what he called the last three girls. I have not been home for a while."

She stood there, not believing what he was saying, or worse yet, what he was implying. But when she looked at his profile, at the tight jaw and the pain in his face she knew he spoke the truth. His father's dalliances were an embarrassment to him. "I did not know."

"I know that. But now that you are my wife you should be aware if it, for your own well being."

"I am not a servant to dally with. Surely he was only welcoming me to the family. I am the King's cousin, as well as your bride."

"A fact he seems to have easily forgotten. I have thought that perhaps that is exactly why he is so attentive."

She inhaled sharply.

He looked at her as if she were too naive for words. "Just because you are married to his first son does not mean you are not fair game. Do not fool yourself, sweet. My father charms with a purpose in mind, and it is not to welcome you into the family."

She reached out to him then, placed her hand on his chest, where his heart beat strong and true. She wanted to soothe his hurt, to take away what he was telling her as if it had never happened.

He pulled his gaze away from whatever he was staring at and glanced down at her hand on his chest. He looked as if that was the last thing he expected to see.

He seemed to relax. His mouth and jaw were not tight and hard looking, the strain in his neck was gone. He covered her hand with his own, then turned and studied her face as if he were searching for something there, something he needed.

She whispered his name.

A moment later his mouth closed over hers and she was wrapped tightly in his strong arms.

CHAPTER

29

Sofia opened the door to her chamber and peered inside. There was no one there, so she pulled Tobin inside. "Do you think they will miss us?"

"I do not care if they do. 'Tis our wedding, not theirs. Let them drink and eat until they burst. Then maybe they will all go away." He closed the door and slid the lock, then in one swift motion he spun around, slid his arms under her bottom and lifted her right up off the floor. "All I want is you."

She hung onto his shoulders and looked down at his upturned face. "Where are we going, husband?"

"To the bed, wife." He tossed her onto the coverlet and followed her down, pressing his upper body against hers and pinning her to the bed with his weight. He grinned down at her. "This is where you belong, woman."

She laughed. "I belong in bed?"

"Nay, sweet." His lips tasted hers, then he spoke against her mouth, "Under me."

He kissed her, sipping at her lips with his, using teasing, gentle and moist touches.

"I love it when you kiss me. I love the feel of your mouth on mine."

"I love kissing you. Now I can kiss you all day and all

night. All of our lives, sweetheart." He buried his tongue deeply into her mouth.

She gave a quiet moan in response. She opened her eyes.

A lock of his black hair had fallen over his brow. She brushed his hair back and looked up into his face, at the shadowed angles where his beard was already growing in rough and dark, at his straight nose and the small cleft in his chin. She looked at the black lashes on his eyes, the way they framed them so darkly and made his eyes look even more blue. The color of them was true and real and deep. And she decided then and there, from that moment onward, her favorite color in the world was the blue of her husband's eyes.

She drew her finger over his mouth and lips.

He kissed her fingertip.

"Kiss me, Tobin," she spoke on a sigh. "Kiss me all over."

He reached out and twined a silver ribbon and a lock of her hair around his index finger, used it to pull her face up toward his. "I'll kiss you, sweet. Believe me, I shall never stop kissing you. All night long my mouth will be there for you, tasting you and loving you. That is all I want." He gave her a soft kiss on the lips, then on her nose and each of her eyes.

His lips brushed over her brows and onto her forehead. His mouth drifted over her cheeks and moved to her ear. "I shall kiss you inside your ear . . . like this."

His tongue dipped inside and he kissed her ear the same way his thrusting tongue played in her mouth. He sucked in a deep breath that sent chills down her neck, over her shoulders and arms, and seemed to center in her breasts, where she wanted to feel his pulling mouth.

"I shall kiss your neck," he whispered to her. "But first we must remove these pearls."

She reached up with her hand, but he grasped it and pressed a kiss to her palm.

"I shall do it." He unclasped the pearls and slowly began to unwind them, pressing kisses on each part of her neck that was revealed. By the time he held the strand of pearls up before her, her eyes were dreamy and her body lax; she felt as if her bones had melted.

She took the strand of pearls and set them on a small table beside the bed. She turned back to him. She loved the way he looked at her, as if she were the only woman in the world. He was looking at her like that now. "Where were we?"

"I was telling you where I want to kiss you."

"Where else?"

He leaned forward and his arm slid under her back and pulled her close to him. "On your chin." He gave her a soft kiss there.

"And your lips and tongue and teeth."

His mouth came to hers. His arms tightened under her. He rolled over with her so she was sprawled atop him. He pressed his hands all over her back, stroking her from shoulder to bottom.

He moved to the ties on the back of her gown, played with them, then pulled them loose, one at a time. He grasped the shoulders of her gown in his fists and jerked it down, pulling her linen shift down with it.

She heard a ripping sound. She smiled, for she did not care a whit. He could rip her clothes off her forever and a day as long as they were both naked and touching each other.

His hand pressed her breast up and his mouth closed over the tip of it. He teased it with his tongue and sucked it into his mouth again and again. Hard, so she felt the pull in the very core of her.

He kissed her breasts for so long. She loved it and she couldn't stop moving under him; it was as if every suck of his mouth made her hips shift up.

Finally he moved downward, pulling her dress with

him, his tongue and lips kissing her ribs, her belly, her waist. He traced her hip bones with his mouth. He suckled her belly low and hard, and made a small trail of red marks there.

"I want to kiss you everywhere, sweet. Taste you. Love you. Hold you."

She loved it when he talked to her. There was little silence to their loving and she liked that. She buried her hands in his thick dark hair.

His head moved lower, to her thighs. He nudged her legs apart. He pulled off her clothes, tossed them off the bed, then sat up, spread her legs apart and just looked at her.

His eyes studied her from her feet, up her legs and to the center of her. He raised his hand to his mouth and licked his finger, then touched her, the center of her, and rubbed slowly, oh so very slowly, watching her the entire time.

It felt so good, she moaned and raised her legs so her feet were flat on the bed.

He kept on touching her, then slipped his finger inside of her, pressing it in, drawing it out, then sliding over the most sensitive part of her.

Her knees began to quiver and shake.

He pulled his finger out and lifted her foot to his shoulder, then he kissed a path down the inside of her leg and stopped before he got to where his hand had been. He took her other foot and did the same thing, kissed all the way to the hollow in her thigh. Then he slid his hands under her buttocks and pulled her toward him, and up to his open mouth.

He blew on her and slowly pressed his lips to her. She was ready to beg for his tongue. She wanted him to do more and more.

He gave her what she wanted. He gave it to her for so long that she was crying out again and again. Still he did not stop. She pulsed against him.

He drank it all in, then finally he stopped when she

was almost crying from the joy of it, when she was certain she could take that same touch no more. He lowered her hips to the bed and jerked off his tunic and undergarments, pulled off his hose, his loin cloth.

He was as naked as she was.

He took her hand and pulled her up, so she was sitting before him and he was kneeling before her, his legs splayed slightly. He looked into her eyes and grasped her hand, then put it over him, showed her how he wanted to be touched.

"Touch me . . . Feel me . . ."

She picked up the rhythm.

He moved his hand to her breast and lifted one and bent toward it until it was in his mouth. She kept moving her hand over him, feeling him grow.

He kissed her ears again and slid his fingers inside of her, telling her how she felt and what he wanted to do to her and that he wanted to do it all night long.

He told her things they would do that she did not know men and women did. But she did not care, for she loved his touch and the things he did to her, loved the way he made her blood soar, and the way he could make the center of her throb around his fingers, his tongue, or around nothing at all.

She felt so hot and warm and wet it was as if she were melting. She gave a ragged cry when she pulsed around his fingers.

He leaned over her and brushed his mouth against hers and made her cry out again, but he told her it would be all right.

She gripped his shoulders and felt him shift, and he pressed his hips down and in between her legs. Like before, he inched inside of her in small amounts, moving slowly, just the tip of him, in and out, over and over.

She twisted on the bed. She wanted him deeper still.

"Please," she said. "Please."

He cupped her face in his hands. "Look at me, Sofia."

She did.

"I swear to you I am going to go all the way inside of you. Now. Where it's hot and deep and wet. I want to be there. Do you want me there?"

"Aye," she said. "Aye. Come into me."

"I will hurt you. You know that?"

She nodded.

He paused and just looked at her.

"Dammit, Tobin, just do it!"

He gave a small and quiet laugh, then lifted her up. "Look at me. Let me see your eyes when I join with you, my wife."

She fixed her gaze on his.

He shifted his hips back and then sank inside.

Something ripped. 'Twas like he was tearing her apart. She groaned, made a soft and whimpering sound that she wished she could take back.

"Look at me."

She opened her eyes.

"Look at me . . ." His breathing increased.

She tried to catch her own breath.

They breathed together, panting as if they had been running a race. But they were completely still.

He was inside her.

She was surrounding him.

The pain was waning, drifting off to a place that did not matter when they were one like this. There was nothing but him inside of her, filling her in ways that had nothing to do with size, but everything to do with the senses.

She could taste him on her tongue.

She could smell him in the air around them.

She could feel him on every part of her—on her skin, on the fine hairs of her legs, on her belly and deep inside her breasts. She was no longer Sofia, a separate being. The being was the two of them.

She ran her hands over the muscles on his back. They were taut and bulged in a way that reminded her that he was male and so different from her.

But why then did this feel so right, when they were so different? She could feel the curly hairs on his thighs, feel them rubbing just a bit against her soft, bare skin.

She shifted her knees up, put her feet inside his thighs, and ran her feet down along his, rubbing over the backs of his knees and down his calves, before she moved up again.

He pressed down harder against her and rested his weight on his elbows.

"I'm going to love you, now. Feel it, sweetheart, and tell me if I'm hurting you."

She nodded and waited to feel the pain again. But she did not. All she felt was him filling her and moving ever so slowly, pulling back and almost completely out of her. She pressed her palms to his tailbone and pushed down, eager for him to come back inside, where it felt as if he touched her soul and where the only pain was not having him there.

How very strange this all was to her. He was part of her now, moving in her, kissing her and his hands were all over her, shifting, so each time he moved it was different and she felt something more.

He whispered her name again and again, said it in quiet moans and in whispered moments, with a rhythm almost like a monk's chant, there in her ears and on her neck and face, against her lips, all those places, he said her name, as if it was as important to his life as each breath he took.

But part of her was worried she was making too much of this, of him touching her, of what they were doing. She loved him but he did not love her. He was doing what he was supposed to do in the marriage bed, nothing more.

But it did not feel routine or mundane. It felt wonderful. She turned her head slightly. Night had come and she could see through the glass of the windows.

In the distance she saw the moon come from behind a dark cloud. She wondered why it looked the same when everything inside of her had changed so. Why were the stars still there, as they always were? Why did the moon look no bigger? Why did the whole wide world move along as it always had, when her world would never be the same again?

He began to move more quickly and she lost herself to the motion of the moment, the thrust that seem to sweep her away as if she were riding on those stars outside, higher and higher.

She heard his name, and realized it was her voice that had called it out. "Don't stop," she whispered against his mouth. "Please, Tobin. Don't stop."

"I won't . . . I won't . . ." he said to her. A breath of words as he moved more surely and quickened the motions of his hips, then clasped her knee in one hand and shoved it up near her shoulder. He rode upward and thrust harder and faster, until something happened and she caught her breath, sure she would die from within at any moment.

Then she slipped away as if in a dream, to another place and time, where her body took her up to heaven and all the way back down again, over and over.

From someplace far away she heard him shout her name, as if he were calling her back to him. He stilled inside of her, frozen, like he had died too. But she felt something warm inside of her.

It came from him, the seed of his life. She could feel him release it. She lay there, under the weight of his slick and damp body, lay there in wonder and relief and an ecstasy that she would have never thought existed in the world.

Together they lay there in quietude, just the two of

them. He drew back and stared down at her. The look on
his face was one of surprise. He did not have the tension
she always saw there. He looked at her as if she were
someone he did not know.

"What is wrong?"

He gave her a bit of a smile, then shook his head.
"Nothing is wrong." His thumb traced her hairline.

"Why are you looking at me like that?"

"Like what?"

"I don't know. Differently."

"Am I?" He shook his head. "There is no reason. I
think you imagine it, sweet." He slid off of her and onto
his side, his head resting on his hand and his elbow next
to her ear.

They said nothing for the longest time, then he said,
"Your skin is so beautiful. It looks like these pearls." He
reached over her and took the pearls from the table, then
lay them across her breasts and shoulders. His finger
traced her shoulder bone, down her arm and over her ribs.

She laughed. "That tickles. Stop."

" 'Twas only a few moments ago you were making me
swear not to stop. You are a fickle wench."

"Ah, you! I am no wench!"

"No. You are my wife," he told her with sudden seri-
ousness. "My wife," he whispered as if he had to do so
to believe it.

She stilled, her eyes fixed on him.

He reached across her and threaded his hand through
hers, and just held it. She lay there, listening to the even
sound of his breathing. Soon his arm relaxed across her
breasts, his hand still holding hers.

"My husband." She turned and watched as his eyes
drifted closed.

And there was nothing more, for a moment later they
were both asleep.

CHAPTER
30

Sofia woke early.

Her husband's hands were all over her, touching and stroking her. They made love by the dim light of the rising sun, then rose to bathe and dress. It was late by the time they descended the tower stairs and moved along the hallways that led toward the hall, where all would break fast.

They walked into the room, her husband's hand on her back. The King and Queen were not there. As was their custom, they broke fast together in their private quarters. The servants had spent most of the early morning hours cleaning up around the guests, most of whom were either still drunk or suffering the after effects of their revelry, their heads down on the tables.

Sofia had expected a few winks and some ribald humor, 'twas part of the wedding, and a part that most of the guests enjoyed. She was prepared for their attempts to make her blush, which she knew would fail, so that gave her some feeling of security. They would never know she was blushing inside.

She was not prepared, however, for the sight before her.

On the back wall, hanging over one of Eleanor's fine tapestries, was the linen bed sheet from their wedding bed. An ugly brown mark stained the center of it, there for all and sundry to see.

She stood almost rooted to the floor. Her stance was rigid. Tears of humiliation filled her eyes. She bit her lip and tried to tell herself it did not matter.

She tried, but failed.

It was no longer the custom to hang the bedding sheet as proof of the bride's virginity. It had not been custom for her whole lifetime and a good twenty or more years before. To do so nowadays was a slap in the face of the bride, an insinuation that she was impure and had to prove to the world her virginity.

She had stopped so suddenly that she could now feel Tobin's startled look on her. For just one fleeting and horrid moment, she wondered if he had ordered this done.

She turned toward him, afraid of what she might see.

He was looking the wall. His shoulders went rigid as bricks. His hand gripped her arm all the more tightly.

He cursed; it was vicious and angry.

"Come!" he said to her in a half-growl as he pulled her to a seat at the table and forced her into it. "Sit."

He strode up to the wall and jerked down the sheet, then threw it into the great fire below, where it smoldered and burned until smoke billowed out into the room and turned the air gray and murky.

Tobin drew his sword and turned, his feet planted squarely apart as he faced the room. "Who did this?" His voice was dangerously calm.

Guests murmured among themselves. Some shook their heads. Others elbowed the sleepers, who looked up and stared in puzzlement at the bridegroom standing before all.

Tobin's voice grew louder and angrier, *"Who did this?"*

Soon he was bellowing it over and over, his gaze moving from one person to another. He paused suddenly, then scanned the room. His eyes narrowed dangerously. "Where is my father?" He turned and moved to the stairs that led up to the private guest chambers above the hall.

"Where is my father?" he shouted as he took the stairs two at a time.

Sofia stood, grabbed a nearby servant. "Go fetch Earl Merrick. Quickly!"

Tobin stood on the gallery above the hall, his hands on the balustrade, his sword in one of them. He looked all over the room below him. "Where is the bastard? Where?"

He spun around and disappeared in the archway of the floor above, his voice echoing back down. "If you did this, old man, I will kill you here and now!"

Merrick ran down the dark hallway, following the noise of shouting in the upstairs hall. He rounded a corner. A few feet away was an open door.

"You bastard!" came the sound of de Clare's angry voice.

Merrick went inside and stopped.

Tobin de Clare stood menacingly over a great tester bed, one hand gripping the woolen drape, his knee pressed to the mattress and his sword point pressed at his father's throat.

The earl was naked, lying stiffly in the bed and looking up at his son. His eyes darted to Merrick as he stepped into the room. Cowering against the wall with a sheet clutched to her was the young and lush wife of a petty nobleman.

She looked at Merrick, shaking, her eyes frightened. "Save us! I swear he is mad!"

"De Clare!" Merrick said. "Cease!"

The woman began to pray quietly, calling on Mary to save her from the devil before them.

Tobin turned to him. "You go, Merrick. Leave me to settle with him. You do not know what has happened."

"Then tell me." Merrick took a step closer.

"He humiliated my wife."

"Drop the sword. His is still your father. We will settle this without blood."

"Nay, I want his blood."

"You have my blood," the earl said. "You can never rid yourself of it no matter how much you wish to, for it runs through your veins. You are my son. My death even at your hand will not change that."

"But I am not you, old man." Tobin's voice had a high and desperate sound to it, then he repeated it more quietly, "I am not you. I am not . . ."

"Tobin," Merrick said in his calmest voice. "You cannot kill your father."

"He deserves to die."

"For what? For his lechery? Because he is weak and cannot walk away from a woman? That is no reason to kill him. You will damn yourself to eternal hell."

"So be it."

"You hate me enough that much, Tobin? Enough to damn your soul to eternal hell?" The earl watched him from a strained face, one that looked so much like his son's. "Even I think that is a waste."

Tobin did not move. He just glared down at his father.

They were so alike in looks that neither could deny the other. Merrick knew Tobin tried so hard not to be anything like the earl, but when he stood there, looking at father and son, it was like he was looking at hell and heaven, at two angels—one that had fallen and one that had not.

"You paid some servant to hang our stained bedsheet in the Great Hall," Tobin said through gritted teeth.

"I did no such thing, son. What pleasure would I have in that?" The earl waved his hand at the woman in the corner. "My night was spent with more worthwhile pleasures."

The woman whimpered in the corner, still muttering her prayers to Mary, Mother of God.

"Get away, you foolish slut!" Tobin tossed the woman her gown. "Go to your husband. You do not need Mary to save you if you sleep in your own bed!"

The woman grabbed the gown and scurried out of the room, still praying and calling him mad as she ran down the corridor.

Tobin turned back to his father. "Then who, if it was not you?"

"I do not know. But it was not I."

Merrick moved closer. "Drop your weapon."

De Clare did not move, but stood there, almost as if he did not know what he wanted to do.

Merrick took one more step and put his hand on Tobin's taut shoulder. "Come, lad. Let us get away from here. I give you my word I will help you find who did this. But I believe him. Your father does not hide his vices. He is no trickster to do this behind your back. If he was going to humiliate you, he would do so in your face."

Tobin was taking slow deep breaths that went on for a long, long time. Finally he pulled back his weapon with a shaking hand and sheathed it, then wiped his palm on his tunic.

The face he turned to Merrick was so contorted with pain and anger that Merrick himself wanted to run Gloucester through for what he had done to his son's life. Instead he put his arm about his foster son's shoulders and led him out the door.

No one at Windsor remembered what servant hung the sheet. Too much celebrating; too little paying attention. With a wedding party of such a size, servants numbered in the hundreds, many hired or borrowed for the event.

Thus, there was no one to bribe. In spite of this, Tobin

blustered around the castle for most of the day, trying through intimidation to get information from anyone he could. He had no luck.

Sofia did her best to push the image and the embarrassment from her mind. Tobin would not let it drop so easily and he grumbled and groused around until finally Earl Merrick and Lady Clio came to the rescue.

They insisted that Tobin and Sofia come to Camrose for the winter, arguing that Torwick, Sofia's dower castle, was scantily staffed and would not be stocked nor prepared for winter this late in the year.

The argument was a solid one, one Tobin readily agreed to. He did so without even asking Sofia, and she was standing there at the time.

" 'Tis a fine plan, Sofia. You will be comfortable at Camrose. Merrick had license to crenellate from Edward years back and it is now one of the finest castles in the Marchlands, second only to Caernarvon."

"I was there, Tobin."

He looked up, surprised. "Oh. Now, I remember."

He had better remember the hoodman blind game, she thought. They first met at Camrose.

"But you know that was before the work was completed. Now the walls are higher and the structures sound. No one could breach those walls. You should see the millworks and the armory. The crenels are solid as mountains. The moat is huge and a fine example of what a moat should be." He paused and looked up. "Except for those silly swans Clio insisted Merrick add. And he did it, too." Tobin shook his hard head. "None could believe it when he did. Swans in a moat. We were all awaiting the boat and oars to be next, then the enemy could row across at their convenience. Merrick took no little ribbing over those birds. But when it comes to Clio, Merrick is soft and bends to her wishes. He claimed the birds were worth it."

She spoke in the most innocent tone she could muster. "Does Earl Merrick ask her opinion?"

"I suppose he does, for she gives it readily enough."

"Does he ask her opinion on matters that affect both of them?"

"I do not know."

She crossed her arms and tapped her foot. "Decisions like where they will live for the winter?"

He turned and looked at her as if she had grown horns.

There was a long moment of silence.

"You are upset because I did not ask you about Camrose?"

"Tobin. I was right here in the room. You acted as if I did not exist."

"I knew you were here."

She wanted to clout him. "Then why did you not ask me what I wished to do?"

He looked at her for the longest time. "I am the husband."

She shook her head and frowned. "What does that have to do with it?"

"I make the decisions."

"I see," she said through a tight jaw. "I am to have no say in any decision because I am not the husband."

"You are the wife. You have your own duties."

"Such as?"

"It is your duty to obey."

She stood there fuming.

"But that matters not, because I prefer to be with Merrick and Clio. They are close as family to me. I prefer being at Camrose to being anywhere near my father. As for staying here, Edward has been making noises about needing someone he could send off to Perth. I do not want to be that someone, Sofia." He looked at her. "Did you wish to remain here?"

She shook her head.

"Then why are we having this argument?"

"We are not having an argument. If we were having an argument, you would know it, Tobin. I swear you would know it."

"You do not want to go to Camrose?"

"I want to go to Camrose."

Now he really looked confused.

She sighed. "I just would like to have been asked what I wished."

He grunted something, something just indifferent enough to get Sofia thinking.

After that, they each spent most of the afternoon seeing to the loading of drayage wagons that would take their things to Camrose. For the whole afternoon, Sofia kept running back and forth to Tobin, asking him if they needed the goblets from the earl of Chester or the silver server from the Baron Rupert or the tapestries from the nuns at Grace Dieu.

It gave her no little pleasure to interrupt him as much as possible. Once the wedding gift decisions were made, Sofia moved on to her belongings. She had them all stacked outside the chamber door, including the trunk she received from Sister Judith.

Sofia had been busy with something when she heard some men grunting and groaning. She went to the top of the staircase and looked down.

Two of Tobin's men-at-arms were struggling to get the trunk down the circular tower stairs.

"Oh, you should have left that one. I shall get it."

The men stopped and exchanged an odd look, then one of them turned to her and looked up. "Begging your pardon, milady, but you would never be able to lift this trunk. 'Tis heavy enough . . . enough to be filled with armor!"

The men laughed at the jest in that and Sofia stood there, wondering if they would be laughing so hard if they knew what they jested about was the truth.

That chest held *her* armor.

'Twas later when Sofia found Tobin in the stables, getting the horses ready for the trip, checking shoes and equipment.

"I was wondering," she asked as he was bent over and rubbing his hand down the mount's leg. "Which dress should I take with me? The blue or the scarlet?"

Tobin looked up from beneath his mount's flanks. "What?"

"Which dress should I take to wear tomorrow? The blue or the scarlet?"

He frowned. "The blue, I guess."

"Good. And which shifts should I pack? The linen and the silk or just the silk?"

He looked dumbfounded.

"And shoes. I must decide if I need my slippers or my boots or both." She tapped a finger against her lips. "Of course then there is the choice of hair ribbons and jewels." She looked at him. "I prefer the rubies, but then it is not my opinion that is necessary, for I am only the wife. The *husband* makes all the decisions. Husband? Which jewels should I take?" She had to grin, because he had fallen so easily into the amusing trap she'd set.

He straightened, giving the horse a pat on the rear, then walked over to her, shaking his head. He put his hand on the small of her back, then let it drift down over her bottom as he bent his head and kissed her full on the mouth. He gave her a slight pat, too, before he pulled back.

There was true amusement in his eyes when he said, "I should grab you, wife, right here and now, whip up your gown and beat you for being so impertinent."

Sofia arched an eyebrow at him, then turned and sauntered away, "Oh, promises . . . Promises . . ."

And Tobin laughed out loud.

CHAPTER

31

It was cider time, late October, when Camrose smelled like ripe apples and you could taste their sweetness in the air whenever you walked outside.

Sofia was in the brewery with Lady Clio and Old Gladdys, the Druid and Camrose's resident witch and troublemaker. She was a spry old thing, dressed completely in black, with white hair that stuck out like a dandelion puff and a face so ugly that once Earl Merrick claimed if you looked at it too closely you would go blind.

But the old woman was as much a part of Camrose as Clio. And Sofia suspected that the proud old woman liked being so outlandish, basked in her oddities, and did so out of pure amusement and a sharp woman's need to try to dupe the men of the castle.

Tildie and Maude had come with them, for Clio's young sons were napping that afternoon. The twins were like shadows around Clio and Sofia. It was good to be with them, to see how they had grown a goodly few inches. But it was not their growth in height and weight that made Sofia pleased; it was the growth in themselves, for they were happy, sweet little girls, quick to laugh and smile and easy to please, curious and sharp in mind. They looked at Lady Clio as if she were a goddess, emulated her actions and gestures, and Clio treated them like her own treasured children.

A cider press sat in one corner of the room, and all over, even lined up outside, were basket after basket of both ripe and overripe apples stacked and waiting to be pressed together and blended into the best of cider for the winter. Across the room, vats of Lady Clio's newest batch of ale were fermenting, while she checked each one, stirring it with a long stick as she added something to one and something else to another. Then she called out recipe ingredients to the old Druid, who wrote them down in a huge book, when she wasn't telling the little girls and Sofia all the Druid wives' tales and superstitions.

"I have never heard such nonsense," Sofia was saying. "You peel the apple, trying to make one long apple peeling. Then you toss it into the air and before it lands you will see the shape of the first letter of your true love's name. Humph!"

Sofia had tried the trick three times.

"Did it work?" Clio looked up from an ale vat. "What letter did you see?"

"Nothing. I saw nothing." Sofia said, not willing to admit that every time she threw the peeling into the air she saw a "t."

Clio gave her a long look that told Sofia she was not fooling her one bit, and the old Druid laughed and helped Maude with the apple the young girl was so diligently peeling.

"Come, Sofia. Here," Clio said, handing her a jar of some potent herbs. "You can help me with the flavoring of this vat."

Sofia handed Clio the herbs she asked for, but her mind was not on the task. Sofia's mind seemed to be on nothing but her husband of late.

She did not want to admit to them that she was so smitten, that her heart was Tobin's and had been for longer than she could believe. She kept that knowledge so very close to her heart, because she was so very afraid that if anyone knew, it would all just disappear.

Since they had come to Camrose, since the day they had wed, she found herself falling more deeply, more madly, and more desperately in love with him than she had been before. It made what she felt so long ago seem like youthful fancy. The powerful feeling she had for him scared her badly, because she had no control over it. It was just there, the way the sun was there and the moon was there and the wind came down from the Welsh hills, those things you could not control.

She tried to back away from what she felt, had even tried to deny its existence to herself, but she could not. She loved him desperately. He was there inside of her, the man who had stolen her heart as easily as Eve took that apple from the tree. And there were times when Sofia felt that the repercussions of loving someone were just as dire.

"This vat has two handfuls of blue heather," Clio called out to Old Gladdys, who was busily writing down the recipe. "Five ripened apples, cored and seeded, three handfuls of apple peeling, a pinch of cinnamon, one of rosemary and one of thyme, two whole nutmegs and a dash of pepper."

"What? No eye of bat and pinch of dragon's blood?" Earl Merrick was leaning casually against the door, a wide grin on his dark-featured face and his eyes only on his wife.

Old Gladdys cackled wickedly and closed the book with a snap. "Nay, milord." She rose and sauntered across the room, her voluminous black clothes moving with her. "I save those precious ingredients for your friend, my granddaughter's husband."

"Poor Roger." Merrick laughed.

The old Druid walked past him and added, "Dragon's

blood is a perfect ingredient . . . if you want to shrivel a man's privy member."

Old Gladdys walked away and Merrick frowned, then turned back to his wife and said in a tone that was half-certain and half-question, "She *is* jesting."

Clio looked up from her alemaking and frowned at him. "You are supposed to be training your men in the fields."

"We are done." Merrick straightened and looked to Sofia. "Your husband bested eight of my most powerful men with the lançe today. He is feeling quite invincible. I told him we shall have to widen the doorways so his head will fit through them."

"Tobin?" Sofia looked up.

"Did someone call me?" Her husband stepped up beside Merrick.

The twins ran over to the men, who picked them up and told them all about the day's events. This scene had become ritual, for the little girls adored riding on the knights' shoulders or somersaulting from their big, warriors' arms.

As Sofia stood there watching them, she was struck by the similar looks of these two men. Their height was equal, although Earl Merrick was broader in shoulder than Tobin. But both had black hair, muscular builds and strong looks, jaws that were masculine and both were handsome as the very Devil himself.

She looked at Clio, who grinned at her and said quietly, " 'Tis not an easy thing on a woman's heart to see so much hard-headedness and magnificent male handsomeness standing together in one small room."

Sofia laughed.

Maude said something to Earl Merrick and he looked up. "I did not know you could juggle, Sofia."

"Sofia can juggle . . ." Tobin paused. "When she is conscious."

Sofia gave him a sharp look. "Do not start, husband."

But the fool went on. "Did you know, Merrick, there is an inn on the western road where they tell the tales of her juggling to the sounds of giggles and grunts and jests. And in London, the wild pigs are—"

"I shall show you juggling," Sofia interrupted, her head high.

"She can juggle," Tildie said seriously. "Watch her."

Sofia grabbed three firm apples from a basket and began to toss them lightly in the air.

"See!" Maude said in an excited tone and the girls began to clap their hands the way they did when Sofia was learning.

Sofia was having a great time, tossing them perfectly. From the corner of her eye she could see Clio and Merrick watching her in a bit of awe and the silly grin on Tobin's face.

"Hand me a fourth apple!" she called out.

Maude took an apple from a basket and slipped it into Sofia's sleeve.

A snap of Sofia's wrist and an instant later she was juggling four apples and laughing in triumph.

She would show Tobin who could juggle, she thought, and she moved toward him, dancing lightly. Tossing those apples higher and higher, grinning at him and as if to say *See. I win.*

Just when she was before him, she called out, "I will juggle five!"

"I shall fetch it!" Tildie called out and she scampered away from Tobin's side and ran to the nearest apple basket. She slipped it into Sofia's sleeve.

A second later Sofia had five apples whipping circles in the air. She was just about to grab the fifth apple in the circle—the triumphant moment of success.

Tobin reached out and snatched the apple from the air.

She dropped all four.

He grinned at her, tossed her apple once, and took a bite of it, then chewed obnoxiously.

Sofia planted her hands on her hips and said, "Damn you, Tobin!"

He and Merrick began to laugh, obnoxious male laughter.

"That was mean," Clio scolded, but now Merrick was chomping on his own apple and the two men grinned, then turned to walk cockily out the door.

Sofia picked up an apple from the overripe basket, she looked at Clio, winked, and she threw that mushy apple at Tobin's back.

It hit him on the shoulder with a splatter of juice and pulp.

He froze, then slowly turned, his eyes narrowed on Sofia.

Clio hit him on the chest with another one.

The women began to laugh.

No one knew who threw the next one, but within moments both men and women were running outside the brewery, dodging soft apples and scooping up more ammunition.

Clio hit Merrick with five of the mushiest apples she could find, then she ducked behind a hay cart, where Sofia had dragged a basket and was pummeling her husband.

Tobin and Merrick were moving in swiftly, one from the left and another from the right.

"Watch out, Clio! They are closing in!" Sofia shouted.

But Merrick tumbled over the hay and onto his feet, grabbing his laughing wife in his huge arms.

Sofia took off running, as fast as she could, her arms pumping and her feet flying over the bailey. "Damned gown," she muttered, then lifted the thing above her knees, above her hose and garter ties. She cast a quick glance over her shoulder and then with her legs free, she really picked up speed, racing for the gates.

"Go, Sofia! Go!" She heard Clio shout to her.

She could hear her husband's thundering footsteps. Closer and closer. He was close enough so she could hear his breath.

She pushed harder and harder.

They ran the distance of the inner bailey.

She cast a quick eye to her left, where the door to the north tower stood open. Their bedchamber was at the top of the second set of stairs.

I can make it! I can make it!

She aimed for the gates ahead of her to throw him off her true destination. Then she cut sharply to the left and sped through the open doors.

He was not fooled.

She made it up the first flight of stairs and he passed her, his longer legs taking the stairs three at a time. He faced her and stopped so suddenly on the step above her that she ran right into his apple-stained chest.

His arms clamped about her.

She looked up at him.

His breathing was harder than hers and hers was burning through her chest.

He twisted suddenly and pinned her to the tower wall with his body, his hands on either side of her head and his face in hers, his breath panting warm across her eyes and cheeks.

His looked turned intense, sexual. His mouth came down on hers, but there was no force to this embrace. No dominance in the meeting of their lips.

They were equals. Neither ever said a word, but she knew he wanted this as much as she did. Just a kiss, mouth to mouth, but it was one that made her senses soar and her legs and knees go numb.

One of his arms slipped behind her and across her

back, his hand cupping her buttocks, his fingertips nestled just inside her thighs. Their bodies touched from mouth to legs, pressed together.

She felt so soft against his hard body. It made her feel womanly and needed and wanted.

His other hand had moved and was flat against the bare skin of her neck. His thumb stroked her jaw, then downward.

His tongue slid through her softened lips and she tasted him against her own tongue, wet and wicked. His hand moved lower and into the bodice of her gown. She could feel the calluses rub against her bare skin. The tip of her breast tightened as if she were suddenly naked and cold.

He held her by breast and bottom, softly kneading them both as his tongue played thoroughly in her mouth, licking and stroking, running along her teeth and then retreating so he could suck her tongue into his own mouth.

He kissed her, long and slow, shifting and spreading his palms down over her bottom and taking his time, as if the kiss needed to be as thorough and long as a kiss could be. When he finally pulled away, he rested his head against her brow, looking down at her. "You taste like apples, wife."

"So do you." She licked her lips. "I like apples."

"So do I." He kissed her cheeks and her nose, then her lips and her brow.

She cupped his face in her hands, stilled it for a moment. She looked into those blue, blue eyes. "What are we doing?"

"Kissing."

"I know that, you dolt. What I want to know is why are you kissing me?"

"I thought you looked as if you needed kissing."

She laughed and pulled her head back, her look challenging. "You're saying that you thought *I* needed kissing?"

"Aye."

She shook her head. "If you think I would buy that flummery, then you do not know me."

"Then you tell me the reason."

She shook her head, making this into another game, because she knew that spark in his eyes, loved the challenge that passed between them. The power. This was a woman's power, hers alone, and she needed to feel it, so she could try to tell herself that she had some control over this love of hers. "I believe, husband, that the true reason is that *you* needed kissing."

He looked at her for a long moment, then admitted, "Aye." But he said it with a glint in his eye that was pure devilry. He pressed her against him and moved slowly, the same way he moved when he was making love with her, rocking her against him with his hands clasping her backside.

She did not want him to think he could master her so easily, with just a kiss, that she was so weak that all he had to do was kiss her to bend her to his will. So she stared up at him and watched his eyes grow dark with desire.

She slid her hands from his temples through his sleek dark hair, then gripped it in her fists tightly and kissed him with all the passion and want that his kiss created in her.

She drove her tongue into his mouth, swept it through and then pulled her lips away, licked them slightly so that her tongue just barely touched his damp lips, then she traced his mouth, the outside, with the tip of her tongue. Stood on tiptoe so she could wield her lips as her woman's weapon, a weapon to spur his desire, his passion. She wanted to make him as hot and needy as she was.

She slowed suddenly; she needed to tantalize. She had learned fast that foreplay was best if it was soft and slow. The more you wanted it, the more you got from it.

She kissed him all over his face, his eyes, his neck and ears until he picked her up a good foot off the floor so her feet were dangling, then he lifted her even higher and buried his mouth and face in the crease of her breast, grabbed the edge of her bodice with his teeth, jerked it apart, and ripped it in two with his mouth, so he could get to her breasts, where he sucked and played with them, flicked his tongue over her nipples and made them hard.

Long moments passed, sweat began to bead on his forehead, and his hair and scalp grew damp with need. She could tell he was feeling the fire like she was. Her body burned for him. Burned like Purgatory.

He turned swiftly, in one motion, and pinned her against the wall, pulling his mouth away from hers. She moaned and her lips sought his but they weren't there.

She opened her eyes. He was looking at her and she knew she was nothing but a wanton, her arms linked about his shoulders, her hands in his hair, her breasts exposed and tight. "Do it now," she breathed. "Do it, husband."

He shifted and slid his thick thigh up so she was straddling it, then he took both his hands away and grabbed her gown in his powerful fists. In one swift and hotly sensual motion he tore it in two.

Cold air hit her damp skin and she gasped, looked up at him in surprise, then she laughed and the sound of it echoed up the stairwell into the tower, sounding as loud as church bells. She did not care. She wanted him hard and fast and now.

His look was so intense, so filled with want for her that she almost melted there, but before she could say anything, before she could even think, he ripped her shift, still watching her face.

He looked down and she followed his gaze, saw that

he had untied his chausses. Then he looked her straight in the eyes, his gaze showing her nothing but the blue fire of a passion so strong it threatened to send them both up in flames.

He pressed his body against hers, pinning her against the wall again with his sheer strength and muscle, with all the hardness that made him a man. He jerked her legs up and out, wide, then lowered his leg and thrust deeply and hard inside her.

She stared up at him, pinioned against the wall by him. She shook her head, letting him know she was as much a part of this as he was, then she clamped her legs around his hips, locked her feet, grabbed his head and jerked it down, kissing him with everything she had.

A moment later they took each other against the tower wall.

Tobin awoke and reached out to his wife, but the bed was empty. He pushed himself up on one arm and scanned the room. It was dark on the west side of the room; the fire had dwindled, and they'd put out the candles so much earlier. The chairs and chests around the room were little more than huge dark shadows and nowhere was the silhouette of his wife. So he looked eastward.

She was standing by a window, tall and sleek, her face in profile, one hand braced on the stone ledge, and the other on the casement. She rested her head against it and was gazing outside. It looked as if she had donned her robe in a hurry, for it was loosely tied and gaped open slightly.

He turned on his side and just watched her standing there. There were more and more moments like this as the days and weeks went on, moments when he would just look at her, when she did not know she was being watched, so she was at ease.

Each and every time he was overcome with something that almost felt like wonder, but stronger than that, so strong he had no word for it. She was his wife, and whenever he looked at her, like he was now, he remembered that they had a whole lifetime together.

Odd how he had so quickly noticed things like the cadence of her breath, the small mole near her right ear, the way she always rubbed her feet together over and over, slowly, until she finally fell asleep.

Every day with her was like a new day, where you were in a strange land full of things to discover. And with that thought something truly odd happened to him. He was struck with the need to know her in ways he never had needed to know another human being.

He wanted to breathe her. He wanted to hold her, to never let her go. He wanted to fill her with his children and watch them grow up with her by his side, every night, every day, forever and after.

And every night, God . . . every night was something so far beyond just being inside of a woman. It wasn't just the act of loving, the way he joined with her. It wasn't just something to relieve the stress of the day or to make him feel good and sleep more soundly. It was more. So much more that if he thought about it too long it scared the hell out of him.

He stayed that way for a moment, taking slow deep breaths, time moving in whispers of moments where all he did was look at nothing but the sheet under him, because he could not look at her any longer without feeling he was lost.

Finally he raised his head. She had shifted slightly, enough so he could see the outline of a rounded breast as it caught some strange and flickering amber light that came in the window. It amazed him the way her skin, that incredible white skin, drank in the color of the light around her. He looked past her toward that light. It was a faint glow in the night sky, beyond her profile, golden, red. He realized it was probably from Bonfire Night, when the hills would be filled with bonfires, burning in celebration of the last harvest and to cleanse the fields for the spring crops.

He threw back the coverlet and swung his legs over the side of the bed and walked naked to stand behind her.

"I did not mean to wake you." Her voice was soft and weak as if it were difficult for her to speak.

He felt her vulnerability, such a rare thing, for she did not show her vulnerable side often.

He slid his arms around her and pulled her back against him, slid his hand inside her robe to cup her breast, to feel the weight of it in his hand. He leaned into her and took in her scent. She smelled like woman, his woman. He pressed his lips to her neck, then pulled his face back. "What's wrong?"

She shook her head, but he felt her stiffen.

"Tell me what you are thinking."

She looked down as if trying to make a decision, then she sighed and crossed her arms over his hands, resting her hands on his hands, her palms chilled from the cold stones.

"Whenever I see bonfires I think of my mother. I can still remember how the villagers burned mourning bonfires for her every evening for months and months. There were times when I thought the skies would never, ever be blue again." She paused. "Even now, when I smell the smoke from a bonfire I feel myself stiffen. It's almost as if I am the one who died." She rested her head back against his shoulder.

He pressed a kiss to her temple.

"I think the scent of those fires must have awakened me."

"Do you want to come back to bed? To try to get some sleep?"

She shook her head. "I am not tired. Odd, isn't it?"

"Nay. 'Tis not. For I find I do not want to sleep either, at least not without you there. I will stand here, sweet, with you in my arms, until the fires fade and your memories and the pain they cause are gone."

She closed her eyes and sighed, relaxing easily against his body. Her hands moved in circles over his.

They stood there, just the two of them, a man and his wife, watching, being together, holding each other, until the fires in the hillsides were all gone and the skies dawned gray instead of blue.

CHAPTER

32

Winter rode in with a blast of ice and snow that year. The hoarfrost started shortly after Bonfire Night, making mornings white and crisp, and the stone floors so cold that on many days you dressed in bed, under the coverlet where your body warmth still lingered.

Icy winds and the cold snapping air continued until December, which came in all white. It snowed at least three times a week right up until Christmas Day and the boar's head feast attended by many guests and noblemen, including the King and the Queen, who had plans to stay with their friends the earl and his lady for the first five days of Christmas, and then move south to Caernarvon.

The men all rode out of Camrose early that morn, with a hunting party that was gregarious and full of sport, because of the huge numbers that made up a royal hunt. They moved into the woods beyond the road, an enormous Welsh forest filled with wild boar, hart and hare, the kind of hunting grounds that any men of sport would find challenging.

Due to the size, the party split into smaller groups. Some went after boar and others after hart. Tobin was bringing up the rear of Earl Merrick's party, when he heard something behind him. He reined in and turned, then spotted a huge boar with tusks that would make the most handsome of trophies.

The beast disappeared with a snort.

He wheeled his mount around and beat through the brush until he found a trail, paw marks left by some of the hunt dogs that must have caught the boar's scent. He rode down into a ravine, where his mount slipped and skidded and almost threw him from his seat.

He reached the bottom. There was an icy brook that trickled through the snow. He looked around him; it was thick with trees and there was little room for trails or his horse. He dismounted, tied his reins to a low branch and followed the dog tracks in the hard-packed snow.

The bushes and trees grew densely here; it was dark and he moved with his sword drawn and ready. He could hear something ahead, not far, a rustling in the bushes, the crunch of a hoof in the snow. He sidled through the trees and moved with quiet and stealth.

He could see the bushes ahead of him shake. He heard the snort of a boar.

Sweet success! He moved in for the kill. Paused near a tall tree, the he leapt into a small clearing.

A huge dark-skinned boar with tusks over a foot long lay on its side, snorting, downed already.

Tobin saw his mistake.

No dogs here.

Instead, he looked into the reddish gold eyes of a vicious wolfpack. The wolves stood like men-at-arms around the whole clearing, their teeth long and bared from the taste of blood. Their eyes flicked nervously from the boar to Tobin.

He froze. Dared not move.

One of the wolves growled, low and mean.

A second later they turned away from the boar and attacked.

* * *

Sofia and Clio spent the morning hours in the kitchens adjacent to the gardens, where they were molding clay boxes for St. Stephen's Day. 'Twas an important part of the Twelve Days of Christmas, for this was the specific day when the lord and lady gave gifts of money and cloth, white flour and blocks of Cyprus sugar to the villeins and servants of Camrose and all of the surrounding villages.

The work had been going on for days, by Clio, Sofia and some of the other noblewomen, even Eleanor and the Poleaxes were among those who had given a hand, for it would never do that the servants made their own hard boxes, which were meant to be broken open at the perfect moment—the celebration that night, after which they would choose the Lord of Misrule.

Sofia finished with the last clay box and washed and dried her hands on one of the cook's aprons. She left the hall with Clio's blessing and ran through the hallways and out into the bailey on her way to her chamber, so she could bathe and get ready for that evening.

'Twas one of Sofia's favorite times of the year. She found that now, she even liked the snow. She picked up a handful of it and packed it into a snowball, tossing it lightly and trying to decide what she would use for a target.

The huntsmen's horn sounded over and over, loud and shrill at the gates. She turned and frowned, for the men were back early and the horn was still blaring. Suddenly the guards on the walls were running and shouting. Servants came out from buildings and the thunder of horses' hooves clattered over the drawbridge and into the bailey.

Sofia moved back and stood there, trying to see through a hundred or more riders.

Earl Merrick was shouting orders.

Someone was hurt.

Sofia stepped up another step and tried to see, but could see nothing but a sea of riders.

With a clatter Clio burst from the kitchens and stood there talking with a squire. 'Twas one of the twins, Thud or Thwack, she could not tell. Clio turned and looked at Sofia with the oddest expression.

Sofia's belly sank. She turned toward the men.

Merrick broke through the other riders, pulling the reins of another mount, one with a man slumped over the saddle, his back and arm so covered with blood that you could not see the cloth or his skin.

For just the shock of the moment, Sofia was unable to recognize what she was seeing, then she screamed her husband's name.

Sofia stood near the bed, feeling helpless and out of place because there were so many people still inside their bedchamber. She cast a quick glance at the calibrated candle in the stanchion. She'd felt this way for almost two hours, because that was how long ago Merrick, along with Tobin's man, Parcin, had carried him inside, laid him on a trestle table in the hall belowstairs, and began to wash and tend his wounds.

Merrick told her Tobin was attacked by a pack of wolves, hungry from the hard and early winter they were having.

His body looked simply horrid, as if there were nothing on his right side that was not torn and bleeding. Even his face had deep scratches and was streaked with so much dried blood she could not tell for certain if he had wounds there or not.

She knew her hands were shaking, so she clutched them tightly, as if she were praying, her fingers threaded together. But that only served to remind her of how Tobin always threaded his hand with hers, ever since their wedding day. And every time he had her heart had picked up a beat.

So she stood there, wondering if he would ever hold

her hand again, watching and waiting, trying to look, but hating what she saw.

She had to take slow, deep breaths to keep her head from turning light and her eyes from blacking out. Clio handed her some wine and made her drink, then stood with her, her arm around her, consoling her until Sofia was able to move close enough to see his face.

Even then, all Sofia could do was stand beside his dark head, her hand on his brow. She hoped he knew she was there with him. His right arm, his sword arm, was full of puncture wounds and rips in his skin and flesh. At one spot, near the elbow, the bone showed through, until they washed it with witch hazel and vinegar and sewed the wound closed.

Tobin had tossed and turned and she knew he was in deep pain, but finally they had used a sponge soaked in juice from foxglove and poppy, a remedy that was supposed to make him sleep and not feel the pain as terribly. She watched and saw that Tobin had slept after they moistened the sponge and placed it over his nose and mouth.

Now they were all in the bedchamber and her husband lay on the coverlet, bandaged and washed and still sleeping. She sat on the edge of the bed and waited for him to awaken.

Finally Merrick and Edward escorted everyone out of the room, even Eleanor and the Poleaxes, who had stitched Tobin's wounds.

Merrick crossed over to her. He slipped his arm around her. "He will be fine, Sofia. It looks much worse than I think it is."

"Aye, Cousin!" Edward said. "I have seen men on the battlefield lose their arms and half their legs and live."

Sofia winced and stared at her cousin. That was supposed to make her feel better?

"We shall bid you goodnight, Sofia," Merrick said

tactfully. "Tobin will sleep for most of the night. Should he awake or need anything, there will be a servant outside the door. Just let him know."

"Thank you, milord." Sofia turned to her cousin and gave a slight curtsey. "Sire."

"Sofia," Edward said.

Then both men left her alone.

She sat down next to Tobin on the bed, and watched his breathing. He was all bandages and bruises. She wanted to lie next to him, to hold him, but she was afraid to touch him, so she lay down alongside of him, careful not to touch anything but his left hand. She leaned over and whispered, "I love you, my husband. I love you."

Then she lay back down and closed her eyes, but just before she feel asleep, she threaded her fingers with his.

CHAPTER 33

"God save me from you nursemaids!" Tobin bellowed so loudly his voice echoed out of the tower and over the bailey below.

"God save *us* from you pigheaded warriors," Lady Jehane barked just as loud. "I swear you are worse than an infant! Now hold still, young man."

"What are you going to do with that knife, woman?"

Lady Jehane paused, holding the knife over Tobin's lower body. "I am going to cut off your—"

"Jehane!" Mavis warned in a hiss.

"Bandages!" Jehane said, then she sliced through one of the chest bandages and set the knife down and took a rag soaked in vinegar and warm water. With it, she began to soak the cloth to loosen it from the wound.

"Dammit! That stings!"

Sofia glanced outside and saw people gathered in the bailey below the tower, listening. This battle between Tobin and the Poleaxes had been going on for almost an hour. She was not certain who would win.

"Ouch! That hurts," he said more quietly, his voice carrying a distinct whine to it.

Sofia saw Jehane look to Mavis and roll her eyes. " 'Twill not be much longer. I need to check each of these wounds and the stitches."

Tobin grumbled something and looked over at Sofia, a pleading look in his eyes.

She had tried to stand well out of the way and as she watched them, she wasn't certain who she sympathized with more, the Queen's ladies or her husband.

"Well now, that is finished. All cleaned and bandaged." Jehane was washing her hands. "In spite of yourself."

Tobin didn't say anything. He just sat in the bed, scowling.

Mavis picked up all the supplies, and Jehane the wash bowl. They moved toward the door.

Sofia moved swiftly and opened the chamber door. "Thank you, both for all you've done. Truly."

Jehane eyed Sofia from her head to her toes, then said, "Are you increasing yet?"

Sofia almost choked. She shook her head.

Jehane turned and looked at Tobin.

"What are you looking at?" he shouted.

Jehane started out the door and over her shoulder she said, "You know, Mavis, perhaps we should have bled her that time."

"You think?" Mavis said thoughtfully, following her out the door. "I do not know. I am thinking maybe we should bleed him!"

Sofia closed the door and set the lock. She walked over to a table and poured a goblet of wine, then brought it to her husband, who was scowling.

"I am sorry you are still hurting," she said, handing him the wine.

He took it, drank some and handed it back to her. "That's enough."

"I was so very frightened, husband. I am so pleased your wounds are healing so swiftly."

"Swiftly? 'Tis been almost five days!"

"Your wounds were terribly deep."

He said nothing, just sat there looking angry at the world in general.

"Would you like something to eat?"

"Nay."

She sighed. "Well, then I suppose you should get some rest."

"I'm not tired."

"Oh. Would you like me to send for Merrick?"

"I do not want company."

She counted to ten, then she stood. "Then I shall come back later."

His left hand shot out and grabbed hers. "Do not go."

There was such a desperate and needy tone to his voice that she sat back down. "What would you like to do?"

He shrugged, then winced.

"We can play draughts," she suggested, waiting to have him deny that, too.

"Fine."

She smiled and stood to fetch the game board and pieces. She set the heavy board on the bed. "Which color would you like?"

"Black. No, white."

"You're certain?"

"Aye. White."

She lay out the pieces. "You can have the first move."

"Wait. What are the stakes?"

"We shall just play for fun."

"Nay. There must be stakes."

"Fine. What would you like me to wager?"

He grinned. "Your clothes."

"Tobin!" She began to laugh. "You are terrible."

"I am serious."

"And what will you wager?"

"Gold?"

She shook her head.

"Jewels?"

"Nay."

"I have no clothes on. What do you want?"

She chewed on her lip. "A child."

And her husband laughed loud and hard for the first time in days.

By the end of that week, Tobin was up, dressed in mail and was in the icy fields outside Camrose with the other knights, working to regain his strength. Every time he raised his sword, his chest felt as if it were going to explode.

He hid it.

He rode his mount up and down the field. Every hoof-beat jarred his shoulder and the bone in his elbow rang as if it were a church bell.

He dismounted without a flinch.

But when he decided to take a turn at the quintain and tilt, Merrick stepped in and grabbed his lance. "Stop this."

"What?"

"You think I cannot see that you are hurting?"

"I hurt." Tobin shrugged. " 'Tis not the end of the world. I will heal and in the meanwhile I shall not lose any strength if I practice every day."

"You are going to kill yourself, lad."

"The only thing that will kill me is dire boredom. God in heaven, Merrick! If I have to stay in that bloody bed-chamber one more day I will go mad."

"You do not have to practice on the field."

"I want to."

"You are the most hardheaded fool."

"Aye," Tobin grinned. "You trained me well. Just ask your Lady Clio."

Merrick barked something and walked away mumbling.

But for all his jesting and stubbornness, Tobin knew Merrick had a point. He was trying too hard. He hurt like hell and it was all he could do to stay atop his horse.

He sheathed his sword and moved off the training field. He led his horse to the stables and handed him to a groom, then rolled his shoulders and winced. He moved to a water barrel nearby, removed a ladle from a hook and took a drink.

A voice came from a nearby stall around the corner, where two varlets were mucking it out. "Ye know, me Bess, she were the one who told me that he paid 'em gold guineas to shame the lady."

Tobin froze.

"Gold guineas! We be saving for a farm outside Winton."

"Why did he want to shame a lady?"

"She wouldn't have him or some such rot."

"What lady?"

"Lady Sofia. The black-haired beauty what's wed to de Clare. He paid Bess and her sister to hang that sheet in the hall."

Tobin dropped the ladle and rounded the corner in two long strides, his sword up and the point at the throat of the varlet who was talking. "Who?"

"Milord!" the man's eyes bulged and he swallowed hard, gulping down his next words.

"I said, who paid them? Give me the name, man, and I won't slit your scrawny throat!"

The man began to stammer. "I . . . I—"

"Now," Tobin said with deadly calm.

"That blond one."

"What blond one?"

"Baron Robert's son."

"Warwick?"

"Aye, sir. 'Twas him. Richard Warwick."

* * *

'Twas not long afterward that Tobin found Richard Warwick in the Great Hall, sitting at a table with some other knights and young lords, all boasting about their prowess on the field and in bed.

'Twas the talk of young men. He had once been one of them. But he was no more.

He strode into the room with one purpose in mind, ignoring the greetings and comments, his eyes focused on his quarry. As he passed, even more wished him speedy health and good will.

At that moment he did not care for good will. He was so angry he wanted to crush something with his bare hands. Warwick's throat for one thing.

He came up to the table where Richard Warwick and Thomas Moore were sitting. He just stood there.

Warwick cast a glance over his shoulder. "De Clare. Welcome. Sit and have a cup with us." He started to move.

Tobin planted a hand on his shoulder, gripping him as hard as he could with his bad arm. "Do not move, Warwick, or I shall be forced to kill you now."

"Kill me?" Warwick laughed, then he looked at Tobin's face and his laughter grew nervous and higher pitched, then faded. "What jest is this?"

Tobin removed his gauntlet and threw it on the table in front of Warwick.

There was a gasp of surprise and the room grew suddenly quiet.

A challenge was made. A glove was thrown. This was no jesting thing among knights.

"I, Sir Tobin de Clare, challenge you, Richard Warwick. In the honorable name of my lady wife." Then Tobin turned and walked from the room.

Sofia found him in the armory, sitting on a bench and oiling his sword.

She came rushing inside. "There you are. What is this foolishness I hear?"

"What foolishness would that be?"

"You challenged Dickon Warwick?"

"Aye." He was not looking at her, but sat there rubbing the oil up and down the blade, then taking a stone and honing the edge till it was more finely wrought.

"You cannot fight him. Look at you. Your wounds are not yet healed. Just look at your arm!"

"What about it?"

"You can barely move it."

"I can move my arm just fine."

"I will not let you do this. It is stupid."

"You have no say."

"You did this for my name. You think I do not know that?"

"I issued the challenge. Warwick chose the time and place. We will meet tomorrow, in the field outside Camrose."

"Nay." She shook her head. "Please, husband. You cannot do this. Please. He will kill you."

"You have little faith in your own husband's skills."

"I have complete faith in your skills, but not when you are ill. Not when your arms and chest have been torn to shreds. Do not do this for me. I do not care about the sheet. I do not care. A piece of bloodstained cloth is not worth your life."

"But I care. I care, Sofia." He stood and looked at her. "It is honor at stake here. Honor, wife. A man must have his honor."

CHAPTER

34

They lined up ten deep on either side of the field, for this was not a tourney, where the crowd was as much a part of the games and the ritual as the combatants. There were no gaily striped tents flying pennants of like colors. There were no galleries with benches for the ladies to wave their favors. There were no date sellers and sausage hawkers, no jongleurs singing of the great jousts of William the Marshall from so many years before, no cheers from the crowd, for this was a solemn moment.

This was not about prizes of gold and horses and weapons. This was about justice.

His wife rushed into the armory, where Tobin was waiting for his squire to bring the lances.

"Thud cannot find your lances."

Tobin was strapping on his armor and he looked over his shoulder at her, his expression irritated. "They are in the weapons room. I put them there myself."

"Let me help you," Sofia volunteered, as she took the buckle from the back of a piece of plate armor and fastened it to the front piece, then drew it tight. "There." She gave him a pat.

It almost made him laugh, the gesture, to pat his armor. He moved to the next piece of plate, the arm guards, and he slid them over his mail and did the buckle himself.

She looked up into his eyes. "How is your arm?"

"Fine." His voice was sharp, but he was tired of answering that question. He had been answering it all morn.

Since he'd made the challenge, Merrick, Sofia and even the King himself had all talked to him, arguing the possibility that he was not physically ready to meet Warwick.

They were all wrong. He was more than ready to meet him and he did not need full use of his arm. He was so angry he could funnel his rage into the lance and sword.

He had no doubt he would win.

But when he looked at Sofia, he saw that she stood there, wringing her hands the way she did when she was upset. She would not look at him, so he stopped what he was doing and reached out to her.

He tilted her chin up so she had to look him in the eye. " 'Twill be fine, sweet. I know you are worried. My arm is strong."

She looked down at her clasped hands and nodded.

After Tobin strapped on the last piece of plate, he fastened his sword belt and turned. "I suppose I shall have to go fetch those lances myself." He did not understand how Thud could miss those lances. But then he had not been into the weapons room in weeks. Perhaps someone moved them.

"Thud was still there when I left." Sofia followed him out the door and up the stairs. The weapons room was on the west side of the castle, near the upper wall, so men could be armed and easily move back to their posts. The room was small, but packed with swords and daggers, crossbows, arrows, quivers, maces and axes and extra mail and plate, in addition to any kind of missile from stone to oil that could be thrown or poured from the castle walls.

Tobin moved more stiffly than usual. His armor was

weighty and made the climb to the room at the top of the castle a long one. He was still sore and his chest was not all that comfortable in mail and plate. He could feel his torn flesh, feel the scabs and the tightness.

He ignored it.

At one point, he glanced outside through an arrow slit. He saw the crowd below and the strip of field. He was ready. His blood sped through his veins. He had been ready since yesterday and the moment he laid eyes on Warwick and thrown that glove.

He opened the door to the weapons room. "I know those lances are in here, Thud." He stepped inside.

A second later the door slammed closed.

Tobin looked up.

His squire, Thud, was in a corner, tied up and gagged.

He turned.

The lock clicked.

"Sofia!" he bellowed! "Sofia!"

But she was already gone.

Since de Clare had sought justice in this challenge, there was to be a judge, an advocate to choose the winner. 'Twas not a death challenge, only justice for the sake of the name of Tobin's wife.

There was no better judge than King Edward, himself. He and the Queen along with Merrick and Lady Clio sat above the others, waiting. Next to Clio was a chair for Sofia, but when Merrick looked, the girl was not there.

He knew that she did not want Tobin to fight any more than he did, and he wondered if in her own stubbornness, she refused to watch.

'Twould not surprise him. Those two were both hard-headed enough for five couples.

There was a blare of a trumpet and the crowd grew quiet. Warwick rode out from the north end of the field, his horse thundering and his plate rattling. He stopped and raised his visor and saluted the King with his lance. Then he rode to the end of the field and took his place.

All turned to the south side of the field. But there was no rider. De Clare was not there. They waited, and waited. The King frowned to Merrick, who shrugged. The crowd began to talk.

De Clare's mount came into view, the armored knight riding tall and lean in the seat. But it was not de Clare's silver armor and blue tunic that the rider wore, but instead the armor was all black, no markings, not even on the tunic to give clue to the rider.

Merrick frowned. He stood. "What the hell?"

"Sit Merrick. 'Tis de Clare's right to choose a substitute, a champion," Edward said. "I suggested it to him last eve. I'm happy to see he took my advice, although I had thought he would choose you, Merrick, and not some unknown knight. Who do you suppose that is?"

"De Clare would not use a substitute. He would only champion himself. Believe me, I tried, too."

The knight rode over to the King and saluted him, then before Merrick could do a thing, the rider wheeled de Clare's mount around with ease and rode to the south end of the field.

The knights faced each other, then saluted, as was the custom. Warwick dropped his visor, and lowered his lance. A sign of readiness. A trumpet would blow to signal the start, but Warwick, the challenged, had the right to signal the set. The signal was the set of his lance.

They would ride until one was unseated, then the battle would continue on the ground, with sword and skill, until a man was down and raised his hand in forfeit. The winner would have his honor avenged and the loser would have to live with his lost pride, more deeply wounded than any sword could ever cut.

The black knight controlled his mount, which was side-stepping and throwing his head, sensing the tenseness of the moment. He set his lance and waited, leaning forward and signaling his readiness for blood sport.

Merrick did not know who this knight was, but watched him closely. He knew how to set his lance, how to keep his mount ready but controlled and he sensed he knew exactly when the trumpet would sound.

The moments went by slowly. The crowd was silent. The chargers, massively built mounts, snorted and pawed the ground, anxious and ready.

The herald raised the trumpet to his mouth.

The high, loud notes of it carried out into the air.

There was a gasp from the crowd, then the thunder of hoofbeats pounding the ground.

The armored riders moved with ease in the saddle, their lances set into their shoulders, straight, points blunted and not deadly, structured so they would slide off the plate armor, making it difficult to unseat the opponent.

The horses moved swiftly despite all the weight and the metal and cloth trappings, trained in this sport, as much a part of the knight's success as was his skill.

They were closing in, closer and closer with each canter. The lances were close, their points passed each other.

The black knight leaned forward, an advantage, for the lance point hit Warwick square in the chest.

The crowd gasped.

Warwick spit out a loud grunt from the impact and leaned to his right, as if he were losing his balance. But he gained control and righted himself an instant later.

The crowd gave a murmur of disappointment.

The riders took their places again, each at one end of the field. Warwick set his lance. The black knight did the same. They waited, horses stomping.

The trumpet sounded.

They were off again. They rode faster this time, lances aimed for surety, for strike and for besting the other.

Warwick was stiff in his hold. Merrick saw that once again the black knight moved slightly on the approach, changed the angle.

This knight was trained better than most of the knights he'd ever seen. 'Twas a subtle trick, that angle and shift, that few could master even if they knew of it. William the Marshall had known, and he won every tourney he ever fought in. Merrick knew, but he had never given that secret away and never would. So it was something to see the black knight use it.

Their lance points passed again. Warwick leaned awkwardly, trying to get an advantage.

The black knight twisted in the saddle. His lance caught Warwick under the arm and sent him flying.

The crowd roared as Warwick hit the ground, then lay there for a moment during which no one knew if he was out cold or just winded.

He shifted and sat up, then stood and drew his sword, holding it high.

The black knight reined in and dismounted, then slapped the rear of his mount so the horse trotted off. They stood a few feet apart.

Warwick was bigger than the lean knight, taller and more muscular, but the smaller man was lithe, even in his armor, and moved with speed as they circled each other, a speed that could be an advantage to offset Warwick's extra weight and power.

Warwick struck out, their sword hilts locked high over their heads. Warwick shoved hard. The black knight stumbled backward, but kept his balance.

He charged at Warwick, the clanging of their swords piercing the air and ringing through the crowd. They parried and thrust and struck, each blocking the other.

A second later Warwick charged, again locking hilts, but this time he used his foot at the back of the other knight's knee, caught him and sent him to the ground.

Warwick's sword point was at the black knight's throat.

He drew his weapon back suddenly as if he were going to do the unthinkable. To drive it through the opponent. To kill in a challenge that was not to the death.

A roaring battle cry pierced the air.

A de Clare!

The crowd turned toward the sound.

It was Tobin, his sword raised as he moved toward Warwick.

"Kill me you bastard! Kill me!" He shouted over the surprise and noise of the crowd. He struck down with his sword and then stepped between Warwick and the fallen knight, who had not moved, but lay there. Still.

De Clare was like a madman, his sword deadly and fierce, moving swiftly and with power and ear-rending strikes that surprised even Merrick.

It took de Clare barely a few minutes to send Warwick's sword flying, then Tobin dropped his weapon and grabbed Warwick by the mail under his arm plates, dragged him across the field and began to beat his helmet against the low stone wall, shouting he would kill him.

Merrick left his seat, ran to Tobin and pulled him off of Warwick. "Stop! Stop! De Clare! This is not to the death."

"He was going for the kill!" Tobin growled. "I swear I will kill him!"

Warwick's helmet was dented and his head and neck were loose, when Merrick finally pulled Tobin away. Warwick slumped to the ground, unconscious.

De Clare stood there, head down, his breath hard and ragged, his gauntlets in fists at his sides. Then he looked up. He pulled off his helmet and turned and faced the black knight, who was just sitting up on the field, holding his head.

De Clare shook Merrick off of him and crossed to the fallen knight. "You bloody fool!" He bent and pulled the knight to his feet, shook him so hard the armor rattled like pans, then grabbed the helmet and jerked it off.

Sofia's black hair tumbled out and halfway down her back.

There was a universal cry of surprise and the crowd began to talk in hushed whispers and stunned realization.

The King swore viciously and loud enough for all to hear. Merrick stood there, dumbfounded, unable to believe Sofia was the skilled knight he had just seen with his own eyes.

But it mattered not, for Tobin was dragging her off the field, his face enraged.

Sofia thought he was going to hit her. He was that angry. He looked down at her. In his eyes was a fury so strong it could have bored holes in her skin.

"You could have been killed! Do you realize that? How close you were to being run through?" He was still shaking her with each angry word. "I swear he was going to kill you when I came on the field."

" 'Twas you or me. I chose me," she said.

"I would not have been killed." He lowered his face to hers. "And even if I had it was my challenge, woman! My honor!"

She met him nose to nose. "Dammit, Tobin! It was in my name that you challenged him! Does that not give me the right to fight for it?"

"Where the hell did you learn to joust? To wield a sword? To ride like that?"

"At Grace Dieu," she muttered.

Tobin drove a hand through his hair and paced back and forth. "Do you know what you have done?"

"I have fought for you."

"You have dishonored me, shamed me before all and

sundry! A woman! They will think Tobin de Clare asked his wife to fight for him."

Sofia stood there, chewing her lip. He had a point, one she had no argument for.

"Do you not see what they will say behind my back? You have cut my pride and my honor out from under me. I have nothing left."

"You have me."

He turned. His look cut like a sword. A moment later he stormed out of the room.

CHAPTER

35

She heard about her folly from everyone. From the King and Queen, from Merrick and Clio, even from the servants. Tobin's men-at-arms would not look her in the eye. Thud and his brother Thwack, the sweetest people in the world, stopped speaking to her. She might as well have been a leper.

Tobin had not been back to their chamber again. For two long nights she slept there alone. She did not even know where he was and no one would tell her. She cried for herself the first night. She cried for him the second.

The morning of the third day, Eleanor came into her room.

"Sofia."

"Aye?"

"We are leaving for Caernarvon today."

Sofia nodded.

"You will be traveling with us for part of the journey."

"Me? Why?"

"You are to go to Torwick. It is your home."

"Tobin and I are leaving Camrose? He did not tell me."

Eleanor was quiet. She took a deep breath. "You are going to Torwick Castle with a few servants and a contingent of the de Clare men-at-arms."

Sofia stood there, realization hitting her like a slap in the face. "Tobin is not going."

Eleanor shook her head. "He is leaving on a mission for Edward."

Sofia bit her lip and stared at her hands. She had not thought of this. She had not thought of the consequences of her actions, only the need to act.

"It is a devastating thing for a man to lose his honor, Sofia. In their minds it is perhaps the worst thing that can happen to them. Most would prefer death to loss of honor. It is even more devastating to a young man with Tobin's pride."

Sofia began to cry. "I love him, Eleanor. I only wanted to save his life. He could have been killed. I could not just sit there and do nothing. I could not just watch my husband ride out to his death. I could not bear it!"

Eleanor sat down beside Sofia and put her arms around her and just let her cry. "I know, child. I know. Ours is not an easy life, we women who love our men. But sometimes when you love something, you have to understand it, deep inside. You have to understand what matters and sometimes, you have to let go."

They rode over the crest of the hills around Torwick Castle a week later. Sofia had not been home for fifteen years. 'Twas odd how different it looked now. Not as huge and cold as she remembered.

She sat atop her mount and looked down at the lushly wooded valley, over freshly mown grass, and up the next rise, where Torwick stood, a gray stone keep and square walls that overlooked all of the river valley and forest below.

This was home. Her home. She did not know how she felt about that, whether it could ever be home to her. A chill ran down her arms and legs, gooseflesh and a numbness that had nothing to do with the number of hours she had spent in the saddle.

She did not know what awaited her there, at that castle in the distance. Memories or images? Or nothing but loneliness?

It did not matter because that was all she had now, without Tobin. So she took a deep breath and kicked her horse into a canter, heading to the home she did not know.

The main room and two of the old bedchambers, hers and her parents', had been made ready. She moved through the rooms a few hours later, stopping and looking around, searching for something that would tell her this was home. She tried to remember anything she could from the past. She tried to see the faces of her mother, of her father.

But when she stood in the those rooms, all she saw was a strange place where it felt as if she did not belong. Her belly was tight, as it had been for nearly a week, since the day she heard Tobin was sending her away.

She felt ill constantly, her food spent most of the day in her throat. Being at Torwick did not seem to help. Even the tray of soup and fresh bread that a maid brought to her did nothing to make her feel better.

She explored, out of desperation. She needed to find something familiar. Just one single thing. She walked down the stairs and along the dark hallways.

The stones on the floors were rough on her bare feet. She moved slowly because the rushlight would flicker if she walked too swiftly and sparks would fall from the rushes and burn the skin on her arms and hands.

The doors to the chapel were heavy. The hinges cried out like hungry infants when she pulled the doors open.

It smelled old inside. Like wet dirt and cobwebs. The dusty wooden benches were lined up the way she thought she remembered, in rows, one in front of another with room to kneel. Here at last was some kind of memory.

There were small arched windows behind the stone altar and some of the panes were cracked from where birds had flown into them. She let the doors close behind her, hardly heard them squeal and shut. She was looking at the altar, where the torch she carried cast wavering shadows that looked like spirits floating in the air.

She walked down the aisle and swiped back a falling cobweb, then moved onward, like a cipher, toward the raised stones that formed the base of the altar.

Here the rock was cut in huge slabs and lay at the edge of the altar. There were names carved into the stone. William. Matilda. Alice. John. Henry. Anne. Names of other Howards. She moved to the right, to a place where the stone was raised higher than the others, where a small but intricate rose and some other design she could not make out were engraved alongside the names of the two bodies that lay beneath.

ROSALYNDE THERESE HOWARD
&
INFANT SON

Sofia stood there for the longest time, feeling something she could not name. She knelt down and touched the words with her fingertips, brushed off some of the dust and then she saw it: her mother's profile cut into the stone.

With sudden revelation she recognized the nose, the chin and the brow. She could see her mother's face. She could see her straight nose, her high cheeks, the fullness of her lips.

She could almost see the pale color of her skin. It was the color of Sofia's. She could see the thick braid she had always wrapped over her head, and Sofia remembered watching her pin it there, watching the way the long silken sleeves of her gowns would fall when her mother raised her arms to secure the pins.

Sofia followed the lines with her fingertips, almost as if she were tracing her mother's face. And in her mind's eye she could see her mother turn and stare at her. She could see the smile she wore when she looked at her, and she could almost hear her voice.

"My angel. Come here. Sit on Mama's lap and I shall tell you sweet tales of brave knights and lovely ladies. Come and smell my perfume and tell me if you think of roses."

Sofia closed her eyes for a moment, because the memory was fading. "No," she whispered. "No. Don't go. . . . Please do not leave me."

Then it was gone, the image.

She opened her eyes and looked down at the profile on the stone.

"Why did you leave?" she whispered the words, the same ones she carried in her mind for so long. "Why?"

She swallowed hard and looked up at the old cross that stood before the window and she called out, "Why God? Why did you take her from me? I needed her more than you could ever have. I needed her. I still need her." Her voice echoed in the emptiness of the chapel, as if the walls were mocking her.

She slammed the heel of her fist against the stone. "Stop! Stop!" She hit it harder, over and over. "I need her! I need her! Don't you understand! I need her . . ."

Her voice cracked.

Tears fell onto her sore fists as she bowed her head and tried to catch a breath. But she couldn't catch it. The sobs that were rising in her throat were stealing her breath away.

"Mother," she whispered, head bent. "Mother."

Her hair fell around her face, dark strands of it caught

on her wet cheeks and into her mouth. She pushed the hair away and tasted the salt of her tears. "Please. Help me. . . . Please. Please. . . ."

Then she lay down on the burial stone and cried. She cried for all she never had. She cried for all she never knew. She cried for all she had lost, hard, wracking sobs, until she cried with dry eyes and no more tears; and when she buried her burning face in her arms, the wild roses on the castle wall had lost all of their petals and the birds in the tall apple trees had flown far, far away.

CHAPTER

36

It had been four months since Sofia had first arrived at Torwick. Four long months with no word from Tobin. It was April now, and as she looked out on the hills before her, there were bright yellow primroses blooming in the grasses, and from this far away they looked like little bees.

The hedgerows along the river below the castle were beginning to live again, their myrtle leaves turning glossy and deep green. Woodbines and the elder trees had fat buds and the rabbits and harts were out in the dewy mornings, nibbling on periwinkles and dandelions.

She stood at the window that looked over the valley. The same window where she watched for her father to come home. The same window where she now watched, secretly hoping for something she knew she would not see—Tobin riding over the hill.

She left the window and went down the stairs, heading outside, because she needed the air in the mornings. She was carrying their child. She knew that, and also knew that she probably had been carrying on the day of the challenge. She could imagine what Tobin would have done had he known that. But she would not tell him of the babe. She would not. If he came back to her, she wanted him to come back for her, not because he felt he must.

The longer she was there at Torwick, the more she remembered. It was almost as if a door to her past had been unlocked the night she cried on the floor in the chapel, the night she found the etching of her mother's profile.

Now that the weather was warmer, she would sit in the castle garden, which she had weeded and planted and worked on incessantly during those first few months at Torwick, those months when the loneliness was almost too much to bear, those months when the nights were cold and empty.

Now it was different when she went into the gardens. She took long walks in the new sunshine, because it made her feel less alone and more alive. But the babe did that, too. For she had just begun to feel flutters in the morning, just once or twice, like a small butterfly was deep inside her belly.

She sat on the garden bench and remembered. Here she had played in the mud as her mother sat on a stone bench, that very bench she was sitting on now, her hands clasped across her distended belly as if she had to protect the babe inside before it was even born. It was here that at barely four years, Sofia had felt the babe in her mother's belly move, her hand under her mother's and her mother's soft look of love and wonder. She hadn't even cared that Sofia's fingers were muddy or that she left small handprints on her favorite silk gown.

It seemed somehow right, in order with the world, that she should feel her own babe as she sat on that bench in the sunshine. She turned her face toward the sun and leaned back. Her belly cramped sharply and she gasped, then clutched herself, waiting for it to pass.

It didn't. The pain grew sharper and she began to cry. "No. . . . No. . . . Please no . . ."

Then she looked down to see blood soaking through her gown and a moment later she fainted.

* * *

Merrick rode over the low hills of Dover, heading for a castle on the edge of a chalky cliff, where de Clare was waiting for a message to cross the channel by ship, a decision between Edward and the King of France.

Merrick arrived with a blast of cooler wind from the channel. He dismounted and wrapped his cape more tightly around him as he crossed the courtyard and followed the servant who took him to Tobin.

Merrick burst into the room.

Tobin turned. "Merrick! You are a sight." He crossed over and clasped him by the shoulders, shaking him in greeting.

From the expression on his face, Merrick would believe that Tobin was not doing well alone, sitting here, waiting for something that could take forever.

"I have news," Merrick said, getting directly to the point.

"Good, good. I have heard little stuck away like this. So tell me. What is this news?"

"You are going to be a father."

Tobin stared at him for a long, long time, before it hit him. He cursed under his breath and stood, then walked away for a moment, his back to Merrick.

"There is more."

"What?"

"Sofia has been bleeding."

Tobin spun around. "What?"

Merrick raised his hand. "She is fine and so is the babe, but she is in bed and must stay there. Whenever she rises she bleeds. Clio and the Queen have seen her. She has been examined by midwives and the royal physicians. They believe she can carry the babe, but she must stay in bed."

Tobin said nothing. His back was still to Merrick.

"You need to go home, lad. You need to toss your damaged pride into that bloody wind outside and ride to your wife."

Tobin still did not turn around. He stood there, his back straight, silent. After a long moment he said, "I will go. Now."

"Good." Merrick nodded, but he still watched his friend, the young man who was like a younger brother to him. "Shall I wait?"

Tobin nodded. He took a few deep breaths, then he said, "Give me a moment. Will you? I think I have something in my eye."

Sofia lay in the silvery dark, her hands clasped over her belly. A half moon cast shadows and light into the room, enough for Sofia to see.

The cramping was not as often now, just small twinges. She took deep, long breaths, because she could almost feel inside her body when she did so.

Her hands suddenly moved, jumped, from a tap hard against her belly. She stared at it, moved her hands and watched for what seemed like forever.

It happened again. Then again.

She laughed out loud. Watching it, she placed her hand over the spot. "Was that a foot or a hand?"

It bulged again.

She smiled. "A foot, I think." She took another deep breath and sighed. "Oh, child of mine, I want you more than God could even know."

Merrick and Tobin had stopped at a tavern to feed and water their mounts. They were inside, finishing off a leg of mutton and tankards of dark, frothy ale.

Merrick lifted his tankard to his mouth and took a long drink. He swallowed, then stared into the ale. " 'Tis not the same as Clio's brew."

"Aye," Tobin agreed. " 'Twill not make you laugh for no reason or spout words in rhyme."

Merrick laughed.

They both sat like that, each lost in thought, neither saying a word.

Finally Tobin looked at him. The younger man seemed nervous and edgy.

"What?" Merrick asked, knowing that with de Clare sometimes you had to pry things from him.

"You love your lady wife."

Merrick smiled softly. "Aye."

"My father thinks he loves women. I do not understand the difference."

"That is because you are trying so hard not to be like him that you cannot see what I think you already know inside." Merrick gave him a honest and direct look. "You won't let yourself feel anything. But you do. You cannot stop feeling."

Tobin stared into his empty tankard. "How do you know if you love a woman?"

Merrick thought long and hard about how he could put what he felt for Clio into words.

"You cannot tell me." Tobin sounded miserable.

"That is not it. I am thinking. Give me a moment." Finally Merrick looked up at him. "This is not an easy thing to admit."

Tobin nodded.

Merrick took a deep breath. "I know because I want to hold her. I want to love her. Because I can't stop thinking about her, even now, years after we've been married. I cannot imagine what my life would be without her in it. When I make love to her, it's still the most wonderful feeling in the world. It's something I cannot describe." He paused, then added, "And when I look at her, when I stare into those wide eyes of hers, I see my children there. The children we have and the children of our future."

Merrick looked at Tobin, whose expression was deeply pensive. "Do you understand?"

"Aye." Tobin nodded. "I understand all too well."

CHAPTER 37

Sofia looked at her husband, at the face she dreamed about every night, and she lay there feeling as if her heart had been ripped from her chest.

"You came back because of the babe." Her voice was flat, which she was grateful for, then he would not know how very much that hurt her.

He stood by her bed. "Aye." Then he frowned and shook his head. "That is not true. I did, but I did not."

She gave a sharp and bitter laugh. "You had better make up your mind."

"I know my mind."

"Well now, that is a first. Coming from the man who has left me . . ." She tapped a finger against her lips. "Two, no three times. Or is it four?"

"Sofia."

"Oh, good. You remember my name. That will be helpful in case our child asks."

He swore and began to pace the way he always did, driving a hand through his dark hair when he turned. Watching him walk the room again almost made her start to cry. She could not help her bitter words. She could not help making him pay a little now for the hurt his abandonment had caused her.

She had made a mistake. To fight his challenge was a

mistake. Prideful and silly and not worth the pain it
caused. She knew that now. But to not have him with
her, to have him run away from her or send her away like
he had was a severe punishment. The pain of it ran deep.

"I am not back for the child alone."

She looked at him, at the true look in his eyes and she
was frightened. She glanced at the window, the one she
waited at for so long and for two men. The truth was:
men left you.

"I came back for you, Sofia." There were the words
she wanted.

Too late.

She could not take the chance again. She was afraid.
She could not let him back into her life just so he could
leave when things did not go as he liked.

She looked at him and felt the tears she knew so well
burn the backs of her eyes. Her throat grew tight and her
chest heavy. She turned away and stared at the wall. "Go
away, Tobin. Just go away."

It only took Tobin two days to figure out her tactic.
She used the servants against him.

He was not allowed in her room.

She refused to see him. She refused to talk to him.

He had even stood there and shouted through the door.
It did no good.

So he took action. He sent everyone away. He paid the
servants double a year's wages and told them not to
come back until Michaelmas, when the babe was due.
He paid off the cook, kept only one kitchen helper who
could bake as well as put together a decent, but light
fare. He sent some of his men-at-arms home, and kept
only the men he needed to guard the gates and the castle
walls. He removed every obstacle except her bedchamber door, and now he even had the key to that.

He came up the long flight of stairs, balancing a tray

on his arm. It was filled with soup and bread and milk, which she was supposed to have according to what he'd been told. He had memorized her diet and meals, the same way he would memorize a map or battle plan. Her schedule was the same as the changing of his guards. He had learnt Sofia's routine.

He almost tripped on a stair and had to grab the tray with both hands. "Damn," he muttered, then switched the tray and gave the door a sharp rap.

He took out the key and unlocked it, then juggled the tray and stepped inside.

She stared at him. "What are you doing here?"

"I brought your supper."

"Where is Adela?"

"I sent her home."

"Is she ill?"

"Nay." He set the tray down on the bed.

She shifted away, as if she could not possibly touch him, she who carried his child in her belly. They had touched each other in too many intimate ways to count, but she was scooting over in the bed as if he had the plague.

"I shall be feeding you from now on."

Her lips thinned and she shook her head. "I do not want you here. Send me my maid."

"I told you she is gone."

"Then send in Peg."

"I cannot."

"Why?"

"I sent her home, too."

Her eyes narrowed. "You sent home Adela and Peg?"

He nodded and lifted the soup spoon toward her. "Open and I shall feed you."

She clamped her lips shut.

He sighed. "We can do this the easy way or the hard way. You decide."

She eyed him for a long time, then sighed and opened her mouth.

He spilled half the spoonful on her.

She held out her hand. "Give me the spoon. I can feed myself."

He handed her the spoon.

"I suppose that you have sent all my maids away."

"Aye." He sat back against the bed post and crossed his arms and watched her eat. "I sent everyone away."

She choked on her milk. "You did what?"

"I sent everyone except John the baker—I don't do bread well—and the guards, because I will not jeopardize our safety."

"So there is no one except you and me?"

He shook his head. "Nary a soul. I will see to your every need, wife. If you are hungry, I will cook and feed you. If you need to be bathed, I will wash you. If you need to be held, I will hold you." He paused, then added, "The same way I have held you in my heart every day for as long as I can remember, at least back to that game of hoodman blind."

She looked at him as if he were lying.

" 'Tis the truth. I just could not admit it to you before." He gave a short laugh that was bitter. "In the same way I could not tell you the truth about why I married you when you asked me. I was a fool, sweet, such a bloody fool. I married you because you were the only woman I have ever wanted. It had nothing to do with the King and everything to do with the fact that I loved you from the first."

He looked away for a moment, then turned back to her. "This is not an easy thing for me to admit, but I think that was why I made the wager. Why I left you sitting in that garden. I was too proud and too vain to admit that I was already in love with you. I hurt you because I could not understand why you haunted me all the time. I am sorry. I vow I will never hurt you again. I know now why I did not admit how much I loved you."

"Why?" She whispered as if she were afraid to believe him.

He took her hand in his and stared down at it, rubbed his thumb over her knuckles and her palm. "Because of my father."

She frowned.

He tried to explain, but it was all still new to him, too. He was afraid he would say the wrong thing, but he learnt from his mistakes that he must not be afraid anymore. "I was afraid of what I feel for you, Sofia. I was always afraid to feel, because I did not want to be like him. Like my father. He loves every woman he meets, then he leaves them and loves another. That was all I knew of love between a man and a woman. So I decided long ago not to ever feel that particular emotion." He gave a sharp laugh. "Then you came along, a wee thing of barely twelve, with no bosom and—"

"I had a bosom!"

"Aye." He grinned. "A small bosom."

"How did you see through that blindfold?"

He grinned. "I will never tell."

She was trying not to smile. He could see it.

"As I was saying . . . here you come along and my life has never been the same since."

"What is it you think you feel?"

"Oh, I know, not think, my love."

"What?"

"That I love you with all my heart. That you are the other half of me. That a day or night does not go by that I don't think of you. There is not another woman in the world who could ever replace you in my heart. You are there as surely as the blood is in my body. If I have to wait on you hand and foot, if I have to send away every servant or grovel on my knees to prove it to you, I will. I will spend the rest of our lives trying to prove how very much I love you."

She was crying, tears were pouring down her cheeks and spilling onto her shift.

He leaned forward and kissed her, lightly, tenderly on the lips. No passion in the touch, just love. Pure and perfect love. "I love you, Sofia. I love you."

He was like a storm that blows in and sweeps you away. Tobin was relentless. He told her how he felt at every moment. He told her things she did not know men told women.

He set out in every way to prove to her that he was true. That his love was hers. One night he brought her a plate of mutton, spelled out in the stringy meat were the words, "I love you."

Each night he sat by her bed until she fell asleep. Just that day she had taken his hand and placed it on her distended belly the way her mother had done with her so long ago and she saw the awe on his face and wondered if she had worn that same look.

That night she had fallen to sleep, then awakened in the night. She did not know why, until she opened her eyes.

Her husband's head was near her belly, his hands softly on top of it as he felt their child kick and turn.

Tobin was crying, great long sobs that ripped through her. She began to cry, too. And she whispered his name.

He looked at her through red and moist eyes, eyes that carried all the hurt they had ever given each other. The pride and the arrogance, the need to win, the defiance, the banter, the battles and even the leaving.

She reached out with her hand and touched his cheek.
" 'Twill be fine. Trust me, love."

"I do not want to lose you, Sofia."

"You are not going to lose me, or the babe. 'Tis our

child inside of me. Do you truly think that a child that is yours and mine would ever not be born into this world kicking and screaming for all it was worth?"

That made him laugh. And she laughed with him.

It was a month later that a royal messenger rode through the gates of Torwick Castle. Tobin sat on the bed with Sofia. They were playing draughts, for they had discovered that her belly made the perfect table for the draught board. Instead of money or jewels or clothing, they were wagering with honeyed figs and sweet dates, two of the many things Sofia seemed to crave constantly.

She wanted pickled eels and eggs for breakfast, and hot beef pies and turnips for lunch, and strawberries and clotted cream made her sick.

When the messenger arrived, the guards sent him straight to the chamber. The poor lad came rushing inside, not expecting to see Sir Tobin de Clare lying on his wife's bed and playing games.

The boy looked at him as if he had grown horns. Then he held out a roll of parchment with the royal seal.

Tobin stared at it with a blank look.

Sofia could feel her hands tighten into fists. She watched him rise slowly and take the missive. He untied the red ribbon and broke the seal. He read the message, then walked over and handed it to her.

It was a royal order for Tobin to come to Parliament immediately. There was a rumor of trouble with the Scots and Edward wanted all his nobles there, as a show of force.

This was not a request. It was a royal command.

Sofia closed her eyes and felt the tears come. Every time the King wanted Tobin he had gone. She looked up at him, knowing her pain and fears were in her eyes but she could not help it. They did not hide what they felt from each other anymore.

Tobin picked up the parchment and handed it back to the King's boy. "Tell Edward I cannot leave my wife."

The boy gaped at him. "But sir . . ."

"You have my answer," Tobin said in a stern voice, but he tossed the boy a gold guinea. "Ride swiftly lad, for Edward will need to find his support from somewhere else. I have none for him."

The boy left and there was an awkward and silent moment; it just hung there in the room.

"Tobin," Sofia said quietly. "He is the King. You must go."

"I will not go. I have run off every single time he has asked. I have served him enough, Sofia. He can behead me, he can throw me in the Tower or he can draw and quarter me if he wishes, but I will not go," Tobin said stubbornly. "I will not leave you again."

He sat next to her, her hands in his strong ones. He raised them to his lips. "I will not leave you."

Sofia looked over at the window and she knew she would never stand there waiting again.

Rosalynde Eleanor Judith Clio de Clare was born the same day that the Michaelmas daisies bloomed in the garden at Torwick Castle. At the first light of dawn, she came into this world, into her father's hands, kicking and screaming, just as her mother had predicted.

'Twas a month later, when all were at Torwick for Rosalynde's christening. The skies were as blue as her infant eyes and the clouds as white as her skin. In the chapel, near where her grandmother and namesake was buried, stood the godparents: Earl Merrick and Lady Clio, and the King and Queen of England.

When the bishop poured a small handful of holy water on Rosalynde's dark head, she squealed in protest, kicked furiously and made her tiny hands into fists that

splattered the water all over the bishop's vestments and
her cousin, the King of England.

And just behind the bishop stood another godparent,
who laughed at Rosalynde. Sister Judith, prioress of
Grace Dieu, leaned upon her crutch and adjusted her
robes, so they hid her gift, a small bow and a quiver of
tiny arrows. She looked heavenward, made the sign of
the cross, and said, "Thank you, dear Lord in heaven
above, for giving the world another warrior."

THE

WEDDING

Sofia closed the heavy book and set it back in the box with the other one. She did so just in time, for a second later the door to her chambers burst open and her daughter, Rosalynde, came running inside.

"Mother, look! Look at my bridal gift!"

Sofia stood and walked over to the bed, where her daughter had plopped down a lovely pearl circlet with a huge amethyst in the middle that perfectly matched her bright purple eyes.

Rosalynde placed the circlet on her head and then grabbed her mother's looking glass from the table. " 'Tis from Edward. Oh, Mother, is it not the most beautiful thing you have ever seen?"

Sofia smiled. "Aye, sweetheart. 'Tis perfect. Your future husband has his mother's tastes."

"Clio? Aye. I suppose he does. Everyone is here. Edward's parents, Clio and Merrick, the King and Margaret, Maude and Sir Paul, Tildie and Sir Peter. I still cannot believe they were called Thud and Thwack, Mother. Why such silly names for two of the bravest knights in the land?"

"Bravest and most noble?" Sofia laughed. "So they tell you."

"Can you believe it is almost time? My wedding day is finally here. I did not think it would ever come!"

"Come, sweetheart. I have something for you." Sofia took her daughter's hand and led her to the small dressing table. "Sit. Here." Sofia laughed and placed her hands on Rosalynde's shoulders. "And try to hold still."

Sofia opened a box and took out a long strand of perfect pearls.

"Oh, Mother. Grandmother's pearls."

Sofia smiled and began to wrap them around her eldest daughter's long and elegant neck. She fastened them just as Eleanor had done for her so long ago. "There. What do you think?"

Rosalynde was crying. "I think this is the happiest day of my whole, entire life!"

"Your whole, entire life? All seventeen years of it?" Tobin stood in the doorway, giving them a smile that still made Sofia weak.

"Papa!" Rosalynde was out of the chair and into her father's outstretched arms.

"Let me look at you." Tobin stepped back and eyed his daughter, who preened this way and that just for him. Her Papa.

Sofia laughed and shook her head. There was such love between those two.

"You are beautiful. Almost as beautiful as your mother."

"Truly, Papa?"

"Truly." Tobin placed a kiss on her forehead.

"I must run now and show my sisters all this finery. Judith will be simply green!" Rosalynde barreled out the door and off to torment Judith, Elizabeth and Alinor, her younger sisters. Her two brothers would not care, for Merrick was only five and John was eight.

He stood there looking at her for the longest time.

"Why are you staring at me?"

"Because you are still so incredibly beautiful." He shook his head. "I don't think you look any different now than the day I fell in love with you."

"Me?" she sighed. "Today I feel old."

Tobin drew her into his arms and said, "You could never be old, sweet. This is where you belong. Lying beside you is the perfect place. I see you and know there is nothing more beautiful in my world." He stepped back and looked down at her, then he took her hand and threaded their fingers together. "Are those tears I see in your eyes, wife?"

Sofia shook her head. "No, dear. I think I just have something in my eye."

JILL BARNETT

New York Times
bestselling author
of *Carried Away*
and *Imagine*

WONDERFUL

After too many years on the battlefield,
Merrick de Beaucourt is looking forward
to a simple life of peace and quiet with a
docile wife at his side. But when he finally fetches his bride-to-be from a secluded
English convent, he finds he needs more
than his knight's spurs to bring order to
his life....

Now available from Pocket Books

POCKET
BOOKS

1406